IN AT
THE KILL

IN AT
THE KILL

Alexander Fullerton

LITTLE, BROWN AND COMPANY

A *Little, Brown* Book

First published in Great Britain in 1999
by Little, Brown and Company

Copyright © 1999 by Alexander Fullerton

The moral right of the author has been asserted.

*All characters in this publication are fictitious
and any resemblance to real persons, living or dead,
is purely coincidental.*

A CIP catalogue record for this book
is available from the British Library.

ISBN 0 316 64862 0

Typeset in Palatino by
Palimpsest Book Production Limited,
Polmont, Stirlingshire
Printed and bound in Great Britain by
Creative Print and Design (Wales), Ebbw Vale

Little, Brown and Company (UK)
Brettenham House
Lancaster Place
London WC2E 7EN

The Rosie Saga

In At The Kill is the third of Rosie Ewing's adventures, each of the three novels standing on its own as a separate story, the first two being *Into the Fire* and *Return to the Field*. In fact a fourth book, *Band of Brothers*, comes between these two. It is a sea story, an account of motor-gunboat action in the Channel as seen through the eyes of Rosie's lover Ben Quarry. In intervals between bouts of savage close-range action Ben is at least as concerned about Rosie's determination to 'return to the field' as with his own chances of returning alive to Newhaven. To this extent, the Rosie Saga may be seen as a quartet.

Chapter 1

Rosie running . . .

She'd stumbled as she launched herself out of the group of prisoners and their guards, *damn* near gone down, stayed up only by a miracle – with virtually no strength left in her but still mustering some – all she'd ever need, a few seconds of it and then the ghost *could* be given up, meanwhile the breaths pumping louder in her ears than the other women's screams, guards' shouts, bedlam of alarm behind her. Shooting should have begun by now, it was a surprise it hadn't; a blessing too since every second counted, not for her own sake but for Lise's chances. Rosie sprinting – in intention anyway, as near to a sprint as she could make it, manacled wrists up high against her chest, head up, eyes on the distant tilting line of trees that she wouldn't ever reach, had no hope at all of reaching but had to be seen to be making for, the dark unattainable funereal edging to the colours of this dying day, the fields' deepening green under a ripening sunset glow. Been running for – what, five or ten seconds? Scream like a siren behind her, and a woman's shriek of 'God, no-o-o!' There'd be rifles levelled, one at least having shifted to get a clear field of fire, and the range still short. *Now* – first whiplash crack – but – astonishingly – still pounding on, lungs and heart near bursting but hope still alive simply because the longer *she* was alive and distracting them, the better Lise's

chance of getting away should be. At least – *some* chance,
might—

More shots – and still – dizzy, arms flailing, she'd staggered again but—

Oh, *Christ* . . .

Her back, left side somewhere. Crack of the discharge and
the hammer-blow, instantaneous stabbing impact throwing
her forward as if she'd tripped, legs in a tangle under her.
Falling: this was where it ended. *All* of it. Another crack like
splitting bone as she went down, blood spraying in a scarlet
shower, the right side of her head. She was down on her face
then, chained forearms folded under her in the warm, lush
grass, and the sergeant – SS sergeant, second in command
of the escort – there already, crouched beside her. Hysteria
from a distance behind him: he'd yelled at the others to get
the women moving again, but one was on her knees and
the others clustered round her. He was leaving them to it,
for the moment: grasping this dead one's upper arm to roll
her over. Right hand immediately coated and sticky with
blood: he wiped it on her blouse before selecting the right
key and fitting it to the wide iron clasps on her wrists.

All blood, and spreading. Rag-doll, blood-soaked, on her
back: mouth partly open but no breath. Dark blood flowing,
thickening, over the region of the heart and the doll's left
breast: she'd been hit in the head too on this other side, *that*
was all bloody. Eyes shut, their lids transparent-looking.
Staring down at her for another moment, muttering, 'Stupid. What fucking hope . . .' He'd shaken his head: shifting
the smeary manacles to his left hand, using the other to pull
her over on to her face again.

Probably couldn't have said why; or if he could have, no one
would guess what reason he'd have given. Except for her open
lips, the brutalized femininity of the exposed, upturned face.
Down-turned now, hidden – *hiding* – in the grass again.

*   *   *

Rosie waking . . .

Lise wouldn't have had time, she guessed. Hadn't given her enough time – or *had* time oneself to think it out, should have dodged and jinked instead of struggling only to put distance between herself and the rifles that had been bound to get her anyway. Some of the shooting must have been at Lise, she thought. She had no recollection of how many shots there'd been. Remembered being hit – in the back – shoulder – and the sense of disconnection as she fell – at least, *began* to fall, didn't remember actually hitting the ground.

Fading greenish half-light. Wet, blood-sticky grass. Pulsing build-up of pain, and shock in the certainty that Lise could not have made it. Otherwise all that shooting—

No more of it now. Only Germans shouting to and fro: and a whistle shrilling – somewhere further up the train.

The pain was in front too, the same shoulder: but right through it, and in her back, that was the worst. Poor wretched back – this on top of lacerations from the whipping she'd endured a week ago, in Gestapo headquarters in Paris. Back and right-side ribs where the lash had curled and ripped, tearing skin and flesh. But the shoulder, the presumably more lasting damage – hurting like this through having moved, tried to ease it?

Better not. Better look dead.

As you will be, anyway. Be sure of it. Glad, too – that you'll never make Ravensbrück. Isn't that a blessing?

Pray for the same for Lise?

No. Pray she'd get away. Very important she should get away: what this effort had been *for*, for Christ's sake.

Dizzy again. Waiting for it to pass. Or – take over, if that was how—

Raucous German – jerky, as from a man running, coming this way. Rosie lying still, obedient to instinct, although logic would have told her it was better to be dead so why not move, show life, draw the shot to finish it? Blood all over one side of her head and face and that shoulder, she realized: could feel – *taste* it . . . That Boche had shouted again – drawing what sounded like an affirmative reply from a nearer one. The guard who'd shot her, maybe. Or the SS sergeant. She could guess which guard would have fired the shot that had hit her, where he'd have started from and roughly where he'd be now, putting his rifle up again – to make sure of it. Which logically one might welcome – to have it done with. Her uncle's voice in memory, reminiscing about '14–'18 in which he'd lost most of his friends, telling her, 'Dying isn't much, Rosie. It's *how*.' More loud German: another answering, then a single, bewilderingly loud shot.

She'd tensed: spasm of pain, then fear of having visibly moved . . .

Nothing else – for the moment. A man hawked and spat: another muttered incomprehensibly.

Lise – *coup de grâce*?

But surely that would have been further away, not nearer.

Silence from the women. They'd seen the ultimate – for the time being, the ultimate at least until they were herded into the death camp. Being herded away now, she guessed, driven by the stocks and barrels of guards' rifles. Maybe hadn't seen whatever had transpired then, that single shot. Rosie with her face in the grass, eyes shut, blood draining into the lush meadowland of Alsace-Lorraine. Hardly have had the strength to move even if she'd wanted to: but still trying to understand what was happening. Pain coming in throbs, weakness a positive thing like lead in her limbs. Pain in her head too: a knife twisting. Also, heart-breaking awareness of the others there, the merciless truth that they were still on the conveyor-belt to Ravensbrück. Rosie lying corpse-like, recalling her recent

travelling-companions' names – Daphne, Edna, Maureen.
And that Belgian woman and her daughter – names not
known. And of course, Lise . . .

Who *might* have made it?

She'd got Lise's attention – when they'd all been out
of the train, being marched – shuffling – towards the
front of it, flanked by the guards and with manacles and
leg-irons clanking. The Belgian pair had been leading, then
Edna, who before the war had been a school-mistress, then
Maureen – the youngest – and the red-haired Daphne; Rosie
and Lise last, with a guard close behind them.

'Lise.'

The dark head had turned. 'Huh?'

'Don't faint or scream, but – I'm going to make a break
for it.'

'You'd be crazy!'

'– going to run for those trees –'

'Two hundred metres –' a startled glance that way, then
back at her: 'at *least*—'

'Going to try it, though. So listen. No – hush . . . When
they start after me – shooting, obviously – the one behind
us now'll dash out to the left – there. Only way he *can* go
– to get a clear field of fire. That'll leave you on your own,
and they'll all be looking that way, Lise—'

'You won't get ten metres – not a *chance*—'

'It'll make a chance for *you*. Only way it can be – they
took my chains off, not yours!'

Leg-irons, she'd meant. They'd left the manacles on her
wrists but removed the leg-irons, to put them on the Belgian
woman. So Rosie had to be the runner – no option, no
argument!

'When I start running, Lise dear – under the train – crawl
under – and into the river. Stay till it's dark and they've
gone. They'll have to go on – *have* to. God knows what then
– get to a house, farm, offer them money . . . Lise, this is a

chance, and Ravensbrück's *no* chance, you know it. And if you can make it, tell Baker Street all that stuff – you *must* – OK? Good luck, God bless . . .'

'Rosie—'

There'd been no time for argument. A guard might have separated them – or chained them together – anything . . . There'd been this chance – or had seemed to be – and in another minute there might not have been. She'd ducked away, started running.

They'd almost surely killed Lise, she thought. It had been – a hope, was all, and in the course of the attempt, the swift passage of what might have been altogether three, four minutes, she'd felt the full weight of the odds against success – although there'd also been mitigation in the thought that at least it would end here, not at Ravensbrück. Another thought now was that that last, single shot might not have been a rifle-shot, might have been from a hand-gun. Picturing it: the SS captain commanding the guard-detail of obviously rear-échelon troops – him or his dog-faced sergeant, it could have been either of those two she'd heard trotting back from the front end of the train, his boots loud on the scattering of cinders, and shouting – although in her visual imagination the officer filled the role better, and if one accepted this it would have been the sergeant she'd heard running back this way, the captain posing dramatically against the sunset glow, pistol at arm's length pointing downward at Lise's head.

Or at her own. And missing – albeit from remarkably short range. Then his posturing arrogance deterring him (and others) from any closer check, from admitting even the possibility of his having missed a virtually point-blank shot?

Something like that, she guessed. In which case Lise *might* have got away. If she'd dived under the train quickly enough, rolling herself over the rails and down the bank to the river's edge, and into it: and if then in all the excitement they hadn't counted heads, only seen one run for it and killed *her*, left it at that – at least until some later stage . . . This was how Rosie had envisaged it – Lise moving instantly and swiftly, while all the guards' attention had been on *her* making her hopeless, suicidal break in the opposite direction. And if Lise had then survived the river . . . Thoughts swam – as with Lise, in that dark, slow water – Lise with chains on her legs and arms to weigh her down. Rosie's head *really* swimming, in the thought of it, imagining . . . Loss of blood might have its own dizzying effect, she supposed; she'd been out, away, unconscious, brain like a bulb loose in its socket flickering on and off, she guessed more off than on . . . Right from the start she hadn't been exactly in prime condition: there'd been some dizzy spells even before the whipping, she remembered . . . And the thought that she'd never said goodbye to Ben. Deliberately avoided saying it, the aim being simply to have *gone*, although they'd had plans for those few days together. Ben coming up to Town from Portsmouth, her flatmate away for the weekend so they'd have had that heaven to themselves – a heaven in the event unavoidably postponed but no thought in mind – *allowed* into mind – of postponement becoming permanent, that one should – oh, Christ, *should* have said goodbye . . .

Must have been here for hours, she thought. Hadn't seen the light go, the actual extinction of it, but it was certainly dark now and seemed to have been so for – well, a long time . . . The train's departure – backwards, probably empty except for its engine's crew, might have been part of a dream she'd had at some time or other. She'd dreamt of Ben, she remembered: Ben in uniform, and bearded – although he'd shaved that beard off, ages ago – with his battered naval cap typically aslant, pointing at her accusingly: 'Said you'd be back for good – after this one last trip?' And her own dumb anxiety to explain – couldn't speak, articulate . . . But also – awake again then, presumably – flashes of light, she remembered. Before or after the train went? An hour or more after the light had gone, in any case. Soldiers with torches sent out to search for Lise, maybe? Although if they'd left by that time, herding the little troop of SOE prisoners forward along the track – there'd been something about transferring to another train, the line ahead of this one being blocked or cut – another train blown up, bombed, or the line sabotaged, whatever?

Could have been the train's crew, she supposed. Some sort of pre-departure check. Or – a Boche patrol, from the local garrison – which surely there *would* be – obviously, sooner or later—

If one was thinking straight – and working on memory, not brainstorm . . .

Sorry, Ben . . .

Dazzling light now, suddenly: and a spasm of agony in her shoulder. A growl – male, French – from close above her – some person stooping over her – 'Jesus, it *is* a woman!'

A more distant voice: 'Is, or was?'

'Hang on.'

Dreaming *this* – surely. French voices – and the familiar odour of Gauloise cigarettes . . .

Inspired by recent thinking – with which it *did* seem more or less to connect? Doubting the reality, trying to open her eyes into blinding light: but hands closed on her shoulders, turning her, pain swept through her spine into her skull. She'd gasped, or cried out, and – mercifully – switched off again; having had just enough time and agony to be fairly sure it was *not* a dream. She came round again – came *back*, became aware of her surroundings again

– still the same night, she guessed, although there was no certainty of it, at any rate in the first few minutes – still in pain and aware also of pain-inducing motion, some kind of motor vehicle under her, lurching pretty well at that moment from rough ground to a smoother surface. Smell of oil, metal and unwashed clothing. Definitely a male smell – smells, an amalgam of them, the Gauloise flavour also an ingredient. Which told her – somehow – this *was* the same night . . . She was curled on her right side, the pain still pulsing but in a numbed fashion somehow, on what felt like sacking in the back of a truck of some kind. A *gazo*, at that – charcoal burner – which was a good sign, in that the *Herrenvolk* and their French minions such as the Milice drove petrol-powered motors, not *gazos*. It wasn't moving at any great speed: *gazos* didn't. Thumping and rattling: and on a hill, she thought, climbing – which a noisy shift of gear seemed to confirm.

'*Patron*?'

A man's shout – from the driver's seat, and pitched up over the engine noise.

'Hunh?'

'Thought you'd dropped off. Listen – been thinking – for all the Boches know, locals could've hauled her off for burial. Sods don't *have* to suspect intervention by anyone like us – uh?'

'Why would they want to bury her?'

Voice of an older man, she guessed. Well – the other had called him *patron* – boss . . . Straining her ears so as not to miss that one's answer – which came after another savage gear-shift.

'Bodies cluttering up their fields. Crows getting at her, maybe – foxes, so forth . . .'

'Within just hours?'

'Who knows when they'll get out there and find no body?

Tomorrow, next day, day after, even – wouldn't be any rush – seeing as they must reckon she's dead?'

'You sure she isn't?'

'No. And since I'm piloting this contraption—'

'Save us trouble if she *is*, mind you . . .'

Chapter 2

'*Is* a heartbeat.' Voice close above her, and a hand inside her blouse, on the ribs under her left breast. The voice of the so-called '*patron*' she thought. 'Definitely . . . Not strong, but – Luc, go find Thérèse. No – *I* will . . .'

'Bloody dog's already letting her know we're here!'

'Only doing its job, poor brute . . .'

Barking, and rattling its chain. By the sound of it, flinging itself against it, its ambition being to get at the intruders. Rosie wondered how they'd got *her* chain off – the locked iron cuffs off her wrists, with no key. She'd become aware of their having been removed – hadn't realized it earlier – when she'd cautiously moved her right hand up to that side of her head above the ear, to feel the already crusting groove made by a rifle-bullet, which if it had been as much as a couple of centimetres to the left would surely have killed her. By the feel of it you could have laid a pencil in it. She'd only probed it with a fingertip – very *very* lightly: lying on her back, having tried other postures but found that any bodily movement provoked bloody agony – as indeed had the lurching and bumping of the van.

Left shoulder must have a bullet still in it – she guessed. Grating against bone, probably against (or in) bone it had smashed. On the other hand, the throbbing pain in front – the front of the shoulder, so to speak, not far above that breast – suggested an exit wound. And a bullet *would* have gone right through, surely – fired from such close range.

Taken smashed bone with it, maybe?

A woman's voice then, shouting at the dog to shut up. And the older man's as he came across the yard with her. 'Like to get the van in under cover right away, Thérèse. Into your barn there? Be light soon, and if they had a spotter plane – which as you'd know they tend to do—'

'All right. *Then* get the girl out. You'll be staying a while – right?'

'A few hours, only. If we may stay that long?'

'Leaving her with me, then?'

'Please. And bless you . . . God knows what, otherwise. She's going to need – as I said, a bit of looking after. Could still be a bullet in her, incidentally.'

'I suppose she's – you're sure of her, who and what—'

'All we know is the Boches had her on a train heading east, when it stopped she made a run for it, and they shot her. Good enough credentials, wouldn't you say?'

'You'd better get the van inside.'

'Yeah.' Voice raised, calling across the yard: 'Luc – van goes in the barn. Back it in, leave room behind the doors for getting her out, uh?'

'*Bien sûr.*' Rosie heard him repeat as if to himself as he got back in, '*Bien sûr, mon commandant . . .*' The van swayed under his weight, and a door was pulled shut. Rosie thinking *commandant* – major. French military – presumably. Unless that had been sarcasm. One knew nothing, except that one was in the hands of total strangers. This one's voice quietly again: 'Not awake back there, are you, by any chance?'

'Yes. As it happens . . .'

'Ah. Great.' Then – leaning out, she imagined – 'She's conscious, *spoke* to me!'

'Straight back now . . .'

Reversing . . . Telling her, 'You'll be all right now – whoever you are. Madame Michon'll look after you, you can count on that.' Heavy bump – over some kind of step or sill, perhaps a drop from brickwork on to dirt. Invading waft of manure, horsepiss, chicken-shit. Perfume – compared to the reek in the cells at Fresnes. The bump had jarred her shoulder, she'd let out a squeaky gasp. Head wound didn't seem so – noticeable. Her head hurt internally, and the shoulder – whole left side of her torso – throbbed with pain, but she felt the week-old whip-cuts in her back more than she did that bullet-graze.

Thirsty . . .

He'd switched off. Pitch-dark in here: still was outside, as far as she knew. Seeing nothing, living through one's ears. But the other one had said daylight was coming. Well – on the floor of a closed van . . .

Rear doors opening. The woman's voice: 'All right, you inside there?'

All right?

She reminded herself: *Yes – compared to Edna. Maureen. Daphne . . .*

Lise?

Vision of her body in that river. Lise's short, dark hair just awash, like weed floating . . .

The woman had waited for an answer, hadn't had one, tried again now, asking in rather gutturally accented French, 'Ready for these two to bring you in?'

German accent?

'Yes. Please. At least—'

'Michel?'

'Here we are.' A hand by way of warning on her foot as he leant into the back: and the Gauloise smell. A cigarette mightn't be so bad: but you'd need a drink first. The man was saying – addressing *her*, she realized – 'My colleague here will do most of this, mam'selle. He has two arms:

regrettably I mislaid one of mine. One question, though
– forgive me, but we're – curious, you know . . . Who are
you – and from where? *Résistante*, no doubt?'
    'I'm an agent of SOE in London, "F" Section.' Whispering.
'If that means anything.'
    'Means plenty. But – you're French?'
    'Yes.'
    'And the train you were on?'
    'I *think* we were going to Ravensbrück. I and others. We'd
been in the prison at Fresnes.' She paused. 'And you?'
    'We are from the Third French Parachute Battalion,
detached to work under the command of Etat-Major of
Forces Françaises de l'Intérieur. Liaison with Maquis groups
– in preparation for when this area becomes a battlefield.
Which can't be long delayed now – please God. We wrecked
the train ahead of yours – an exercise, mostly to show
them how it's done – and some who were in the woods
to observe what might happen when your train arrived
reported there'd been shots fired. So – when the coast was
clear, as you might say—'
    'I owe you my life, anyway.'
    'To pure chance – and our curiosity . . .'
    'There was another girl trying to escape – the other side,
the river. I was creating a diversion for her, nothing else.
I suppose your friends didn't see any – shooting in that
direction, or—'
    'No such thing was reported.'
    'How did you get the chains off my wrists?'
    'Chains?' In the dark, vaguely the movement of a shrug.
'There were no chains. I suppose – I'd assume the Boches
– if you were unconscious, as you were when we found
you—'
    'Then they'd have seen I was alive.'
    'Obviously did not. Now – Luc will be as gentle as he
can.' In a lower tone then, aside: 'We gave her a shot

of morphine when we picked her up. She was mewling like a cat.'

'Poor creature.' The woman . . . 'Listen – I'll go up, see to her bed – in the attic, Michel.'

He'd grunted: 'Luc – you come here, I'll go the other side . . .'

Faint light overhead – she thought. The pain was – bearable. Except at certain moments . . . The dog whining now instead of barking: the rattling of its chain reminded her of similar sound-effects when she and the others had been clanking under close guard through the Gare d'Est in Paris. About – twenty hours ago? Hours, or years?

She was being carried through a low doorway into a farmhouse kitchen. Yellowish glow of an oil-lamp, the stooped and burdened Luc throwing a hunched shadow as he edged in sideways. Doing his best: she knew he was. There was an odour not only of lamp-oil but also – she thought – bacon. Having had nothing to eat for a day and a night, and not having been fed anything like adequately for about three weeks before that, she found herself acutely sensitive to that aroma, had her thoughts on it almost exclusively while they were first clumping up a narrow staircase and then manoeuvring her up a ladder – near-vertical, awkward ascent via a small trap-door into roof-space lit by another lamp – hurricane lantern – on an old chest of drawers near the head of an iron bedstead. The woman had been waiting for them, was helping Luc. Mutters of 'Easy does it', 'Careful, now', 'Oh, mind that beam' . . . Feather mattress, Rosie discovered, as they eased her down on to it. And cool. Shoulder burning hot and pulsing. The cold smoothness of a rubber sheet or mattress-cover, and for a few seconds then a view of the older man's strong, darkly unshaven face. Big nose, and as the light was striking across his face, wide-set dark pits for eyes. Stiff crewcut hairstyle.

Burlier than Luc. One-armed? She hadn't seen, or thought of it, and he wasn't in her field of view now, but that was what he'd said, or implied. A paratrooper with only one arm? She supposed it was possible. Well, he'd *said* it. In any case that was only one surprising detail in all that was happening around her, *to* her.

If it *was* happening . . .

Maybe it was going to be OK, not having said goodbye? One day, a chance to say hello?

Luc's voice through a wave of dizziness: 'I'm sorry – I was clumsy—'

'No. Weren't at all. I thought it *would* be bad, but—'

'You're very kind, but—'

'And now you can kindly leave her to me.' The woman, cutting in. Rosie had barely seen her at all yet, she was no more than a rather bulky, womanly presence. Strong, thick arms and a smell of farmyard. 'Both of you. Except – Luc, bring me a jug of warm water, please? From the stove, you'll see a big enamel jug – under the tap, probably.'

'OK . . .'

'If I could have a drink – anything, water or—'

'Of *course!*'

'Were you cooking, when we arrived? That smell of bacon? Is there any possibility—'

'Sounds like famished as well as thirsty!'

'Yes.' Thérèse – head down close to Rosie's, and a hand on her undamaged arm – 'How long since you had anything to eat?'

'Oh – days. Prison food *then*, so—'

'Luc, wait.' He was on the ladder, halfway down it. She told him, 'There's a pot of soup on the back of the stove – she's right, bacon in it – and bread in the corner cupboard. And we'll need a spoon for the soup. Fill a bowl from the iron pot – bowls are on the shelf.'

'Don't want your hot water yet, then?'

'Put it on so it'll be heating, yes. But the soup up here first – please.'

'*D'accord* . . .'

'Better not fill up with water. If soup's what you want anyway. Unless you really *want* water first?'

'Soup – lovely . . .'

Moving shadows, scrape of boots on plank floors, soft spread of lamplight – too soft for her to have seen more than Luc's general outline, when he'd been on the ladder there – at no distance at all, and facing this way, towards her, but still no more than a dark shape. Civilian clothes, she thought – rough, working clothes. All right – working with the Maquis, dressed as labourers – *cultivateurs*, whatever. She was exerting herself to ward off recurrent spells of dizziness and keep her mind from blurring. There'd been a square of pinkish dawn light, a small window in that end wall, but the woman had just gone to it and hung something over it. Returning, telling Rosie that she'd provide a more substantial meal after she'd bathed and dressed her wounds; she only felt it was important to get sustenance of some kind into her, and the broth happened to be available right away. Should have thought of it before. Rosie's thought was that she might well have had a glass of water by this time: she could imagine it, the cold, clean taste and the trickle of it down her throat. Things seemed to be happening very slowly: she warned herself, *Seem to be, but maybe aren't* . . . Acceptance was the order of the day: compliance and gratitude for huge mercies. Michel joining in then – behind her somewhere, she'd thought he'd gone down but he hadn't – expressing agreement with the idea of food as the priority, and adding that he had a first-aid kit in the *gazo*, its contents including morphine – 'If it should be needed.'

'Probably will. There's a large exit wound, at least no bullet to dig out.'

'Can you handle whatever does need doing?'

'Yes. That's to say, some, but I'll have help—'

'A doctor?'

'Too far – and not safely. No – our *sage-femme*—'

'That's good. Fine. But we also have a powder I'll leave you, what they call a sulphur drug. It's a new thing – miraculous for healing wounds, really magical. When you have the wounds cleaned, Thérèse, you just sprinkle it on – or in – and it forms a crust, under which—'

'Lend us a syringe – hypodermic – can you, as well as the morphine? Michel, listen – you and Luc must be hungry too. Help yourselves down there, if you want. Otherwise – when I've got this done . . . If you're still here by then, of course. D'you have far to go?'

'Well—'

'You said – what, a few hours—'

'Two hours, say. Then we'll arrange for ourselves an alibi with the Destiniers, I thought. We'll have fixed that old tractor that's always giving up the ghost, and be heading back north. If we'd been spotted as we *were* going – at this hour especially – we'd have been coming *from* the scene of the night's action, d'you see.'

'Sooner not know *or* see . . . Can you bear to remain upright as you are, child – for a little while?'

She could – with her right hand grasping the bedhead railing. In fact it was a less uncomfortable position than any other. Whatever she did, her shoulder wasn't going to stop hurting: shoulder, also her front here above her left breast. Exit wound: and like a pulsing spear right through . . . What she *couldn't* do was keep her thoughts off the other women prisoners: visualizing them in some stinking cattle-truck, hour upon hour of utter misery before the halt at Fürstenberg and from there – cattle on the hoof, then, *driven* . . .

To the abattoir.

Lise among them? If the guards hadn't killed her, only recaptured her?

'Listen – would it be easier lying flat? On your face, I mean?'

'I don't think so.' She must have groaned, or something – muttered to herself . . . She explained, 'Thinking about friends who—'

'Lean against me. Here. That's it.' A snuffle of humour: 'Plenty of me to lean on – huh? But my dear, listen – try not to dwell on – whatever, *any* of it – or them. Thinking about them now won't do them any good – only weaken you . . . Save it for when you're stronger. I'll tell you – here's what we'll do now. You hearing me? Fine. Soup first – to warm you, warm your heart. It's good, I promise. We don't do badly here for food, we're very fortunate and there are tricks to play, of course. Have to, or they'd swipe the lot, we'd starve. Mind you, we'd be lined up and shot if—'

'Where is this place?'

'East side of the Vosges Mountains. A place called Thanville isn't far – and further south a larger centre, Sélestat. And to the northeast, Strasbourg.'

'Right on the Boche border.'

'Close enough to it. But to them, Alsace is part of the bloody Reich now, they'd tell you that's the *former* border.'

'Southwest of Strasbourg . . . Close to the Natzweiler camp, are we? Struthof-Natzweiler?'

'It's not far.' She wasn't looking at her.

'Extermination camp.'

A sigh . . . 'So one is told.'

Shaking her head. Rosie thinking, *the only extermination camp on French soil – and I hole up in spitting distance of it* . . . Thérèse was telling her, 'Alsace-Lorraine was Boche territory, for – oh, about forty years – as you would know, I'm sure. In 1871 they seized it and a lot of our folk of French origin moved west. As I said, they don't think of it

here as France now, to them it's land they've re-occupied.
The French language is *verboten* – it's Alsatian only – or
German, of course. In public, anyway – the village street
or shops, for instance, if you did speak French the bastards'd
hear about it quick enough. They conscript our boys as
if they were Germans – into the SS, even. Parents who've
tried to prevent it – you know, hide them – have been sent to
the camps. Imagine – decent, decently brought-up Alsatian
boys forced into *that* . . . But – what I was saying – soup first,
then I'll get these bloodstained rags off you, clean you up –
we'll try some of Michel's magic stuff, eh? Then I must give
them a hand downstairs, I suppose. Porridge might be best
for you, the next stage . . . One thing I should mention – if
there should come unwanted visitors, we take the ladder
away and shut the trap. It wouldn't be the first time. But
another thing is I'll send my nephew – Charles, he's only
thirteen but he helps me out on the farm, and he'll be here
as soon as it's light – he'll take a message to a friend of
mine and my late husband's, she's the *sage-femme* of this
district.' Boots clumping on the ladder: Thérèse murmuring
and whispering on, babying her, 'Lotte knows as much as
any doctor. Her husband was a German, she was born
Alsacienne – like me – but – oh, Luc, that's good, thank
you.' The bacon smell suddenly, overwhelmingly enticing.
At *last* . . .
    'When the water's hot, Luc—'
    'Won't be long. Bon appetit . . .'
    She still hadn't had more than a vague impression of him
– even though he'd carried her up here. And Thérèse was
now between them – getting the bowl and the bread, which
he'd put on the chest. The impression she had was that he
was tallish, thin, and had light-coloured eyes – or that could
have been just a reflection of lamplight in them. Who cared,
anyway – it was the soup she was *really* eyeing, dying for
. . . But Luc pausing now, a few rungs down on the ladder,

in that shadowed area: 'Is there a name we could call you by, mam'selle?'

Names, plural. Code-names, field-names, one had got through a lot of them pretty fast. Suzanne, Zoé, Béa, Angel; Jeanne-Marie, at one time . . .

'Rosalie do?'

'Rosalie. Now that *is* a name!'

Slight juddering of the ladder as he went on down. Rosie already wondering what had persuaded her to give them her real name – the one she'd been christened with in Nice nearly twenty-six years ago. It was an unheard-of thing to have done, on service in the field: but too late now, she'd done it . . . Thérèse was back beside her with the soup, bread in the same hand, spoon in the other. 'Now then – Rosalie. He's right, it *is* a pretty name. Here, now—'

Heaven. The most marvellous thing ever. Swallowing, with her eyes shut, thinking *I'll remember this all my life* . . .

However long or short that might be. The expression 'borrowed time' came to mind, but *stolen* seemed closer to the mark. And a sense of unreality: as if it wasn't hers, she had no right to it. Wouldn't last, therefore? At least one daren't count on it. Another thought was that if she'd been granted one wish, it would be nothing at all to do with her own living or dying, only that Lise should be alive and on her way. Pray for that. If necessary, die here praying for it. Dying at least in a degree of peace and comfort – which was a hell of a lot more than those others – or poor darling Lise—

The water Luc brought was much too hot, almost boiling, would have to be left to cool a little. Thérèse shaking her head: 'Being silly, trying to do everything at once. And Lotte'll say I should have seen to your wounds before anything else . . . It *has* done you good, though – hasn't it?'

'Definitely. I feel much stronger. Fell asleep, I think . . .
Who's Lotte?'

'Our *sage-femme*. I told you about her.'

Sage-femme meaning midwife. But they often tended to
act like district nurses, especially in remote communities.
In ancient times, witchcraft and black magic had been
attributed to them: doctors who'd seen them as competition
had conspired to have them denounced as witches, burnt or
drowned. Thérèse was saying, 'If you can bear it, Rosalie,
I'm going to leave you for a few minutes – show them where
things are, then they can look after themselves. After all –
grown men, soldiers at that . . .'

'The older one – Michel – only one arm, and he's a
parachutist?'

'Believe it or not, he is.'

The man himself, coming up the ladder. 'Am I intrud-
ing here?'

'At the moment, no, but—'

'I've brought the Sulphanilamide. Just sprinkle it on. Also
morphine, and a syringe. But yes, Rosalie – a one-armed
para, you see before you. I'm not the only one. I may say –
we have a very senior commander – a general, no less—'

'Generals surely don't jump out of aeroplanes?'

'Ah, this one does!'

Thérèse cut in: 'I'm going down to show Luc where things
are, so you and he can feed yourselves while I'm attending
to this one's wounds. You can keep her company now, but
after that—'

'Keeping Rosalie company will be a pleasure.'

He stood aside, Thérèse squeezed herself down through
the hatch, and he turned back to Rosie.

'Well . . . In your SOE career, did *you* ever have to
parachute?'

'Oh, yes. Part of our training. And I went in by parachute
on my first deployment – dropped near Cahors, to join

a network in Toulouse. Didn't last long, I may say, that
réseau had been infiltrated even before I arrived. I got out
over the Pyrenees. You know, I can hardly believe I'm not
dreaming this?'
　'Dreaming what?'
　'Being here – alive – looked after!'
　'Well, it's how it is. Obviously you have a strong con-
stitution. Over the Pyrenees, God's sake . . . But other
deployments since then too?'
　'Second one was Rouen – went in by sea. And then this one.
In by Lysander, to do a job in Brittany. Had to run for it yet
again, and there was a car smash –' she touched her forehead
and her left cheekbone – 'which is what caused these scars –
and I woke up in hospital at Morlaix, under Gestapo supervision. From there – Fresnes, the prison. *And* a visit – a week ago
exactly – to Gestapo headquarters in Rue des Saussaies.'
　'They hurt you?'
　'Whipped me. Luckily I fainted – but my back's all cut up.
In fact, if there's enough of that magic powder of yours—'
　'There will be. What better use . . .' He ran a large hand
over his jaw: wide jaw, and a grim, straight mouth. Grim
at this moment, anyway. Shaking his head: 'They've plenty
to answer for. And please God they *will* – damn soon,
at that!'
　'Please God . . .'
　She remembered a similar comment just a few weeks
ago – a man by name of Lannuzel, a Resistance leader in
Châteauneuf-du-Faou in Brittany. He'd said, '*Christ, they've
a bill to settle, when the time comes!*', and she'd agreed: '*On
ropes from lamp-posts – and not too quickly . . .*'
　In the immediate sense it might be a far-fetched hope, but
it was deeply satisfying as a daydream – to those who were
terrorized, imprisoned, humiliated, tortured. And in the
long run – please God – might be attainable . . . Visualizing
one individual in particular: swollen-faced, kicking on a

rope. Young – about her own age – dark-haired, swarthy. A Frenchman, not a German: in fact half French, half British.

Michel had sat down – carefully, at the bed's other end. A big man, shabbily clothed. The musty odour of old working clothes, she realized, that she'd noticed in the van. Cigarette odour too. It was a long time since *she*'d smoked. Michel cleared his throat: 'Listen now, Rosalie. We'll be off soon, but I'll be back – I expect – in two or three days' time. After that – well, no matter, here and now let's agree a plan of action – namely to get you (a) fit, (b) on your way back to London. OK, so this *could* be overtaken by events; but assuming Thérèse can get you on your feet in reasonably short order – well, we have our own base – I don't mean militarily a base, it's the home of one individual, ostensibly a business associate. We're supposed to be mechanics, d'you see, we repair and maintain farm machinery, especially tractors – and this fellow's in that line of business, we do the field work for him. Well – through him, we'd have no problem contacting your people, to arrange a pick-up. Or for that matter you could set it up yourself – once you're fit and mobile, he'd put you in direct touch with his own SOE contact. That's for sure – at the moment it's our own communications link, you see – courtesy of this SOE person's radio-operator. "Pianists" d'you call them?'

'I'm one myself.'

'Are you indeed. What a shame you didn't think of bringing a transceiver with you!'

'*Wasn't* it thoughtless.'

Smile fading. Shake of the head then; looking into her eyes. 'We'll make them pay for the things they've done, Rosalie.'

'Yes. I hope—'

'We *will*. But listen – do you agree that should be the programme?'

'Certainly – and gratefully. Owe you so much already—'

'Owe me nothing. Another question, though – you're French, how come you landed in SOE?'

'My mother's English. Father died – in 1930 – and she dragged me back – to England.'

'Dragged – against your will?'

'France was my home since birth, England a place I'd been taken to only once or twice for visits. Fact is I don't get on with Mama too well. Although I have an English uncle – her brother – whom I adore. Cousins too – one Army, one RAF. Have you and Luc been on the Maquis-liaison job long?'

'About six weeks, here in the field.'

'How did you come to know Thérèse – Madame Michon – as well as you do?'

'Through the person I just mentioned. He's a king pin in the Resistance, with links to Maquis groups and so forth. He arranged for our reception, when we parachuted in, and then of course put us in touch with – well, such people as Thérèse. You can have complete faith in her, incidentally. Seems a little scatty sometimes, but – heart of a lioness. Now – on the subject of getting you back to England – obviously it must depend on the speed of your recovery. So I'd advise you should lie low, recover your strength, and – as I say – when the time comes we'll put you in touch with local SOE. OK?'

'OK.'

'At least, *someone* will. It's unlikely I'll be remaining in this area much longer, so probably someone else – Luc, maybe – but don't worry, it *will* be set up for you . . . And meanwhile, you aren't desperate to put your London people's minds at rest on your own account—'

'Not – desperate, no. But—'

'We *could* get a message sent to London for you – if you wanted. Snag is that until you can handle things yourself – well, my man wouldn't be too pleased if it resulted in a stream of stuff to and fro. Which it might – uh? Communications between him and ourselves already present us with certain problems. SOE's help has made a lot of difference, but frankly it would suit *us* best to wait until you can handle it.'

'What we'd better do, then.' She paused for a couple of long, slow breaths. Dizzy again: letting it pass over. Then: 'I think I did tell you – unless I was dreaming – that when I ran from the train it was so that another girl—'

'You did tell me.'

'Ah. Well . . . The guards had taken off my leg-irons – put them on someone else who'd tried to escape, earlier. So it was up to me – do the running, the diversion. This other girl and I had – *have* – information London *must* get. A traitor – SOE – and certain *réseaux* in which the pianists aren't to be trusted – because of him. Ones he used – he never had his own pianist, used these others. Am I making sense?'

'Enough. Go on.'

'He's now working with the Gestapo, so odds are those radios are being operated by Boches.'

'Perhaps even the link *we* have access to?'

'Doubt it. He was based in Paris, he'd have used networks around that area. But you see – if my friend made it – gets *clear* away—'

'London will get to know about the traitor without your further help . . . Is it hard for you, this talking?'

'It's all right. Is *now*, anyway. But – talking about this other person – her name's Lise – I'd hardly dare hope—'

'Is she – resourceful?'

'Very. But that's another thing – *if* she's survived, she'll have to hide out somewhere – find some kind of a Thérèse of her own, then make contacts like you're offering me just on a plate . . . She'd look for *résistants* for a start, I suppose.'

'She could be lucky. On the other hand—'

'What I'm asking is that if you hear any rumours of such a person—'

'Of course. Of *course*.'

'Thank you. I told her – before I started running – find a farm or something, offer money from London. Now people can see the Boches aren't going to win, there might be *some* chance she'd get help?'

'You're right, that's how they're thinking. Why they're flocking to join the Maquis too. But another question, Rosalie – about this traitor – have your people in London had no suspicions at all of him?'

'They have had. He was being brought back to answer charges made against him. Then – on the face of it – got himself arrested – which of course was phoney, and which they'll be aware *might* have been phoney.'

'So won't they be taking adequate precautions now?'

'Yes. You're right . . .'

'Which might reduce your own anxiety a little?'

'Yes. I suppose—'

'Another aspect of it, Rosalie, is that with any luck we're looking at a very short-term situation here. Although the Allied armies' break-out from Normandy is regrettably overdue – by the way, are you aware of the war situation generally? How the invasion's been stalled in recent weeks?'

'No. In Fresnes – only rumours and propaganda. The landings began June 6th, didn't they – that was the day before they took me out of the Morlaix hospital. And today is—'

'July 1st. Saturday. But in a nutshell – a couple of weeks ago the weather broke. Very bad for a while – nothing could be landed, and the two artificial harbours were pretty near wrecked. The Boches meanwhile – their 7th Army, mostly – have stood firm, and in the process sustained huge losses. In contrast to which the Allies have consolidated on the ground and achieved almost total mastery of the air. So – any minute now, the breakthrough. Break-*outs* – the most crucial being to drive through at Caen, where the fighting's been especially hard, by the sound of it. *Then* we'll have them on the run – any day now, we'll hear of it.'

'What about flying bombs on England?'

'Oh. Well – as much or little as I know – they're firing them off mostly from the Pas-de-Calais and thereabouts – a long way out of reach of the present battle-lines. Air forces will have been doing their utmost, obviously—'

'England's not devastated, on the point of surrender?'

'*Surrender?*'

'The traitor I was telling you about – SOE code-name "Hector" – *he* told me so, in Rue des Saussaies, before the whipping started. He wanted to persuade me – no hope – tell them whatever they wanted. He said the invasion was bogged down and we were about to be driven back into the sea!'

'He was actually present, in the Gestapo headquarters? When they had *you*—'

'Came into the room where I was awaiting interrogation. The whip they were going to use on me was lying on the table. We – discussed it . . . Imagine. SOE agent – me – about to be whipped, and this SOE – *supposedly* SOE, he was our Air Movements Officer – *imagine*, he's there, free, *working* for them!'

'Almost – unbelievable.'

'But a traitor's a traitor: steps over that line, he's *over* it, he's—'

'Garbage.'

'He'd turned up before too – at the Morlaix hospital. Gestapo expected him to identify me – but he couldn't, we'd never met. I only guessed who he was. They did identify me, though – from my earlier deployment, when I'd had to kill an SS officer—'

'You had to kill—'

'– result of which I was already under sentence of death. Soon as they realized that's who I was – well . . .'

Dark eyes on hers. The silence extending until she wondered if he was only waiting for more from her: but he'd grimaced slightly, gesturing with his one and only hand . . . 'Should be a death sentence on this "Hector", I'd say.'

'Yes. There should. My own thought, a minute ago. Been in my head in any case. Speaking of hangings from lamp-posts—'

'What?'

'We weren't, were we.' Off-beam again . . . 'That was – another time.' Another time, another place, another man. 'But – Michel, you're right.'

'But how you'd get to him . . .'

He'd put his hand up again, to his stubbled jaw. Right hand, the nearer one. Rosie watching him in some degree of surprise at that last conjectural mutter, *how you'd get to him* – seemingly instant acceptance of that concept, 'getting to him' as a practical proposition, course of action – by *her* . . . Another gesture with that raised hand: 'You can bet that when our lads march into Paris he won't be there. Or many others of that stamp, I dare say. Your people would issue a warrant for him, I suppose, but –' an eyebrow cocked – 'Does one know anything of his background?'

'Yes.' Her voice was scratchy, mostly whispering. Barely her own voice at all: but the memory behind it unimpaired – surprising even to herself. 'Name's André Marchéval. He was a pilot, damaged his back in a plane crash – before he joined SOE. It meant he could never parachute, but he was – bilingual. University in England – father French, mother British – Scottish I think, living in Scotland now, and the father – engineering business, south of Paris.'

'You know a *lot* about him.'

She'd nodded slightly.

'How come? He tell you?'

'No. He was – I said, coming back to London. Being picked up, so it happened, by the Lysander taking me in. This last deployment. And – at my departure briefing, the – presiding officer, might call him – a man who's known "Hector" a long time, expressed certainty that he could *not* be a traitor. He said they were bringing him back only to scotch rumours – allegations by other agents in the field. Oh, and he had a story to account for all that – malice arising from "Hector" having pinched someone else's girl. Then – big surprise, the bastard wasn't there, at the Lysander rendezvous, and a day or two later I heard he'd been arrested – very publicly, wool over London's eyes, it's obvious . . .'

'This presiding officer as you call him – any doubts of *him*?'

Of Bob Hallowell: who'd been so certain of Marchéval's probity . . . Rosie picturing him in her mind. She remembered having thought he looked ill. In his forties, grey-haired, grey-faced . . . Staring at Michel: her own one good hand up, fingertips on the scarred cheekbone: thinking, *Christ* . . .

Feet scraped on the ladder. Thérèse. A lot of blondish hair, Rosie saw, as she came up through the hatchway – having to twist around to squeeze her wide hips through. The blanket or whatever it was she'd hung over the window at the end must have slipped off, daylight of sorts was seeping in. Thérèse had thrown down a towel and some other things; telling Michel in her Alsatian-accented French, 'You're making her talk too much. We want her rested, not drained. And I'm going to see to her injuries now. If this water's still warm enough. Yes, it is. So she's going to undress. And *you*, Michel – incidentally, Luc's making a very large omelet with cheese. That ought to tempt you down. And my nephew Charles was here, Rosalie, I've sent him off to ask Lotte Frager to come when she can. It's me that's supposed to be unwell, of course. Anyway – Michel—'

'The omelet calls.'

On his feet, stooped under the low roof, reaching as if to take Rosie's hand but then thinking better of it. For fear of hurting her, she guessed. But he'd ducked his head, kissed Thérèse; telling her, 'We'll leave without bothering you again. I'll just call up, let you know . . . *Many* thanks. As always, you come up trumps. But take care, eh? There'll be a search, conceivably it *could* extend this far.'

'Even though they must have believed they'd killed her?'

'So where's her body? Who'd have made off with a corpse? But there was another, too – at least, another *attempted* escape. Rosalie'll tell you. When she's stronger. And if that one did get away—'

'You'll be back in a few days, you think?'

'Think – yes. After that – no idea . . . Rosalie—'

'Goodbye, Michel, good luck. And thank you.'

'For nothing. A thing happens, one reacts to it, that's all . . . But listen. If you've no objection, I'll have enquiries made. Marchéval – engineering business, south of Paris. Wouldn't be more than one with that name, I'd guess. Might not go under the family name either, of course. But even then, proprietor by that name – and our man's in the engineering business, he can put his ear to the ground. Worth a shot, eh?'

'Could be – I suppose—'

'You don't see it?'

'Well – yes, *anything* one knows about him—'

'But *think*, girl. When it all hits the fan, isn't his father's place where he's likely to show up?'

Chapter 3

Killing 'Hector' wouldn't conflict with any SOE principles.
Might even call it standard practice, in dealing with double
agents. Necessary and justifiable even as self-protection.
One traitor dead, how many good lives saved? Or leave
an informer alive, *you're* dead. A precedent she knew of
for sure was when a *réseau* (network) organizer had asked
London for cyanide capsules for precisely such a purpose
and Baker Street had promptly had them delivered by a
courier from London *en route* to his own *réseau*.

She'd woken thinking about it. After a night in which
she'd heard cars or trucks passing on the mountain road;
it had sounded like a small convoy, and during curfew
hours would almost surely have been German. Heading
for Natzweiler, perhaps: one had heard that prisoners from
camps in Germany were shipped there in batches from time
to time, to be finished off. Her waking thought though
had been what attitude would Baker Street take, whether
if/when she did find herself back in working order, they'd
sanction her remaining in the field long enough to eliminate
'Hector' or to arrange for his elimination. Their first reaction
on hearing that she was alive would be to recall her, get
her out of it; it was standard procedure anyway with an
agent who'd been in Gestapo hands and might have been
turned.

And the prospect of getting back – to Ben, who'd have

had no news of her at all since the end of April, the weekend they'd planned to spend together, instead of which he'd have had a telephone call from Rosie's flatmate saying, 'Rosie sends her love and says please not to worry but she can't make it' – which would have told him she'd gone back into the field: by the time he'd have known it, she'd *been* there, pedalling through foul weather towards Rennes. No one at 62–4 Baker Street would have told him anything about her disappearance from Châteauneuf-du-Faou, for instance: he'd have been waiting, hoping, having no idea at all – no more than *she* did – whether the wait would be weeks, months, a year; having only to trust that one day, *some* day . . . Not so different in her own mind, either: the thought of return, *final* return, the war approaching its last stages so you'd have in clear sight the dreamworld she and Lise had envisaged: Lise and her man Alain Noally, and Rosie and Ben Quarry: a foursome in paradise – that had been the vision to which Noally's death had put a full and final stop. He'd been shot in an ambush by the SD – security branch of the SS – in or near Rennes not long after Rosie had spent a night there with the two of them and then pushed on westward to Châteauneuf; Lise had told her about it just the other day when they'd met in a Fresnes prison cell. Noally had been attending a Resistance meeting and an informer had tipped off the SD – an informer whose activities were almost certainly a derivative of 'Hector''s treachery. Rosie and Lise had gone over and over it, in the train between Paris and Alsace, ensuring that each knew everything the other knew in case one survived and the other didn't, and the link to 'Hector' was based on what another *résistant* had told Lise when he'd telephoned, devastating her with the news of Noally's killing and warning her to run for it – which she had done, into the trap in which she'd been caught. A domino-effect though – one SOE circuit blown, some of its members arrested and maybe tortured, and one who talks has links to Noally's contacts in or around Rennes. To which they might have been pointed by Rosie's own arrival, destination Rennes, of which 'Hector' definitely had known. But Noally had been a highly unusual man, and the loss to Lise had been shattering. Her voice in memory, whispering into Rosie's ear in that filthy cell at Fresnes: *If you get back and I don't, tell them what happened to Alain? And that I didn't tell them anything and I have no fingernails on this hand? I fainted: before that I shut my eyes, screamed blue murder, also I thought about being in Pont Aven with Alain, and you and your Ben – Rosie, that would have been such bliss!*

Memory wandered. From some parts, shied away. Underlying the whole thing had been Lise's crushing sadness, and now the doubt as to whether she could possibly have survived – let alone got clean away. Also the problem of coming to terms with her own ambivalence, which seemed like disloyalty to Ben – recognizing that if she'd been fit and able to move now and Baker Street recalled her, she'd be reluctant to go, leaving the 'Hector' mess unresolved – unfinished business and in more ways than one *personal* business: the Lise/Noally disaster, and the train, the girls who'd been with her and had not escaped; and before that herself in that chair on the top floor of 11, Rue des Saussaies, wrists strapped to the chair's arms, dog-whip handy on the interrogator's desk and 'Hector''s eyes and tone of voice pleading, urging her to answer the Gestapo's questions, save herself by sending others to their Calvaries.

In full awareness – his as well as hers – that she could have told them every damn thing she knew and still have been shipped east to Ravensbrück.

How about *him*? When they'd finished with him – what?

Scrape of Thérèse's wood-soled shoes on the ladder. She'd been up here a little while ago – woken her patient, checked she was OK, then gone down to let the dog off its chain and prepare breakfast. Rosie with her eyes open again now, squirming into a position from which she'd be able to sit up. Another pink dawn, she saw, in that little window: Thérèse had pulled the blanket off it when she'd been up before. In daylight there was a view of the mountains framed in it: smoothly rounded, peculiarly balloon-like tops and dark forests that were home to some Maquis groups, she'd told Rosie. In the other direction – which one couldn't see, there being no window at that end – you'd be looking down a twisting, wooded valley at a distant view of steep, grey roofs. A couple of kilometres away, and only partially visible because of the twists in this cleft in the foothills. To the south were vineyards; Thérèse's late husband had begun to experiment with vines on his own land here, but after he'd been killed, and the so-called 'Armistice' – meaning surrender, 1940 – facing economic necessity she'd grubbed them out and switched to a few cows – had only one now – for milk, and numerous pigs, chickens, and a few ewes – produce for which there was a steady and certain local market.

This was Monday. On Saturday, she'd had to soak Rosie's blouse off, where it had stuck to wounds and lacerations. She'd been very gentle and patient, spent about two hours bathing her, sponging the blood off, washing and disinfecting. It had still hurt: the iodine had stung like fire, in the recent, major wounds and also in the festering whip-cuts. She'd reserved the sulphur powder for use after the *sage-femme*'s visit, as there'd only be enough for one application and if it formed a crust once it was on, one could assume the technique would be to leave it on, undisturbed, until the healing process was complete. In fact the *sage-femme*, who'd arrived in the afternoon by bicycle, hadn't wanted anything to do with it at first. She was a small, wiry, determined woman, grey-haired, fiftyish, with small slits of eyes and thin lips that seemed barely to move when she spoke. The name 'Lotte' had been an alternative to her given name of 'Lorette', apparently, the preference of her late husband – who'd been a master wine-maker in Colmar, about forty kilometres south, on the plain between the mountains and the Rhine.

'He was German, Thérèse mentioned.'

'Was indeed.' A challenging gleam in the little eyes. 'And as fine a man as ever walked the soil of France. He despised the Nazis. Oh yes, they'd have murdered him – certainly they would, he'd have been dead by now in any case!'

'What did he die of?'

'Pneumonia. He wasn't a young man, by then. Now – we'll have you in the window there. Bring up a kitchen stool, Thérèse. No – two stools, one for me. Where's that syringe?' Adding presently as she loaded it with morphine, 'You're lucky, to have this. Unobtainable here – except by stealing from the Fridolins.' Fridolins apparently meant Boches; Rosie had never heard the term before. She'd been standing then, to receive the injection – surprisingly, in her left buttock. After it had taken effect they'd put her on the stool, lolling slightly and supported by Thérèse while Lotte used wads of antiseptic-soaked material in forceps to poke around, probing and sterilizing the wounds, also feeling the bones inside the damaged shoulder. By her assessment – and jerky commentary, which Rosie heard only vaguely through waves of sleepiness, hardly any bodily sensation at all – the bullet had scraped under the left clavicle with a glancing impact which had fractured but very fortunately not shattered it, the bullet however being deflected downward, emerging through torn muscle and cartilage ten centimetres lower than it had entered at the back. A little lower still, it would have found the heart – and/or, as Lotte had grimly pointed out, exited through the left breast.

'Christ . . .'

'Yes – plenty to thank Him for . . . Mind you, it'll hurt for some while. You don't get away scot-free from damage of this kind. Morphine or no morphine. She'll have to keep this arm in a sling for a few weeks at least. But she was lucky other ways too: a centimetre or two *this* way – or lower – could have smashed the scapula. The shoulder joint, even. Not to mention the arteries here.' Addressing Thérèse, by this time . . . 'Not surprising they took her for dead. Would have looked to them like a bullet through the heart. And with the blood all over . . . *And* this head-wound. Which again – a few centimetres to the left, say . . . See the way it slants? When it hit her she must have been already falling, she'd had this one in the shoulder first – uh?'

She'd viewed the white sulphur powder with distrust, told Thérèse *she* could risk it, if she insisted, but she, Lotte Frager, wouldn't be responsible for administering some unknown cure-all. Fair-ground medicines, she called such things. Rosie had no recollection of these stages, had been in dreamland by that time. In retrospect had a feeling that they'd been *happy* dreams: which seemed odd. A morphine side-effect, maybe. But her recollections even of the start of it were hazy, a lot of gaps being filled in by Thérèse when she'd woken in the late evening, in racking pain. That night had been fairly hellish.

Thirty-six hours ago, though, and the powder *had* crusted. Through the bandage surrounding her head, touching it very lightly with her fingertips, she could feel the slant of a hard ridge of it above that ear.

Using her good arm to push herself up now: the damaged one was in a sling made of green velvet, perhaps curtain material, with another strip holding it close across her body, while inside the chemise which Thérèse had provided her entire torso was bandaged, dressings front and back.

Bandages were strips of old sheets or shirts.

'Did you sleep all right?'

'Amazingly, yes. Although Bruno's barking had me awake for a while.'

And her heart had been beating unevenly. She'd never experienced any such thing before. It was OK now, quite normal . . . Thérèse saying, 'Fox, probably. Human intrusions, it's a different bark altogether.'

'Clever dog . . . Have you had many human intrusions?'

'Plenty. But mostly friends bringing others in transit. I doubt we'll have any while you're here.'

'D'you mean you've put the word out?'

A shrug: 'I mean it's taken care of. Don't worry.'

'So what happens if other escapers—'

'There are other safe houses, Rosalie.'

'But when they arrived with me, for instance, you'd had no warning—'

'Don't worry, we'd cope all right. How's the shoulder?'

'Hurts. As she said it would. But less than it did yesterday. Back's still sore – same again though, nothing like it was. And my head doesn't hurt at all. Thanks, Thérèse.' Her breakfast porridge – a large bowl of it, on a tray; she'd wriggled around so it could rest across her knees. 'Giving you a lot of work, aren't I? I *could* come down to the kitchen – d'you think?'

'No. The ladder – if you slipped—'

'Michel was up and down it easily enough, with only one arm.'

'He's used to being one-armed. You aren't. He lost his in 1940.'

'Oh. I'd meant to ask, but—'

'He and other survivors of his division left from Dunkirk – in a British destroyer, but he was on a stretcher, and the arm was amputated after he got to England. But – speaking of *you*, Rosalie – if you slipped, and grabbed for a better hold with that one . . .' Nodding towards the strapped arm: '– which you might do, just instinctively

. . .' She put the spoon in Rosie's right hand. 'Manage all right?'

'Easily. Thank you . . . Michel might come today, I suppose.'

'Or tomorrow, or the next day. Who knows? But my nephew – Charles – will be here this evening. On weekdays he comes after school, you see. Rosalie, I don't think I'll tell him you're here. He'd never breathe a word – knowingly – but – anyway, when he's here – well, we'll keep you hidden, and that window covered. Get into trouble if we show lights anyway. And I may have to leave you alone a lot while he's here. He does come into the house sometimes, of course, but there's no reason he'd go upstairs.'

Rosie nodded. Enjoying her porridge. 'OK.'

'Better that children shouldn't be burdened with secrets, when they don't have to be.'

'Better *nobody* should. Lovely porridge, Thérèse.'

'He's more than once had to know about such things before, when I've had escapers here for a night or two. Comings and goings . . . But with you here probably a month or more—'

'*Month!*'

'Lotte said at least that long.'

'Never heard of sulphur drugs though, had she . . . Thanks to Michel, therefore – touch wood. I agree, anyway, about Charles . . . Thérèse – two things to ask you now: I was ready with one, but first about Charles – what sort of nephew is he, a brother or a sister's son?'

'Sister's. Lisette. She was widowed too, and re-married, Charles isn't *his* son – and he and I don't get on. Consequently I only see Lisette very occasionally – meet in the village sometimes. Charles is a very nice lad, though, he adores the animals and the country life, I've left him this place in my will.'

'Does Lisette know you're an active *résistante*?'

'She wouldn't want to know. She won't speak French, even in private, although it's our own natural language, our birthright . . . She doesn't like the boy coming up here, either. Nor does her precious husband. The fact they permit it has a lot to do with what I just told you – his inheritance. They wouldn't risk missing out on that. Huh?'

'You didn't have any children of your own?'

'No. We were not so blessed. Was that the other question?'

'Sorry – no, an extra one. I was going to ask you about Michel, and Dunkirk – summer of 1940. I was thinking – must have been during that retreat you lost your husband?'

'Yes. That time.' Coming from the window, with the light brightening behind her. 'Our First Army. End of May, first days of June. That *dreadful* time. You're right, to connect the two events. About half of them got away through Dunkirk, but the rest were trapped around Lille. Jacques was one of them. Five divisions, and they held off seven Boche divisions for four days. People say this was to some extent what made the Dunkirk evacuation possible. By the end, poor things, they had no food or ammunition left, the survivors could do nothing but surrender. But my husband had been killed before that.'

'I'm sorry.'

'Yes. Me too.' She'd crossed herself. 'But life goes on. At least, life of some sort. Have to – try, don't we? God gives us strength, it's up to us to use it, eh? Survive, then start again – when it's over. Listen now – with a supreme effort, you could manage another helping, couldn't you?'

'Well—'

'Good. Lotte said you had a survivor's strength. "Nothing of her, but she'll come through all right," she told me. *Inner* strength, she calls it. What she admires – the old devil. OK – back in a minute . . .'

The regular intake of real, solid food was already having an effect almost as miraculous as the sulphur powder's. Not only physically but mentally, just these two days had made a huge difference. Thérèse had groused once, 'My God, if I ate like that I'd be the size of the barn out there!' But rest, as well as food, was doing the trick. The one craving she was conscious of from time to time was a desire to smoke. She always had smoked, until the car crash and hospitalization in Morlaix, but since then the only chance she'd had had been a stub-end she'd picked up in a stone-floored passageway in the Fresnes prison and persuaded a comparatively humane wardress to light for her. She'd smoked it because she'd been starving, and it had sickened her. Now, she had no money – had literally *nothing* – and Thérèse who didn't smoke, would have had to buy cigarettes on her forays to the village market, if she'd asked for them; they weren't cheap, and were also rationed, the ration itself minute but saleable. 'F' Section in Baker Street would eventually be compensating her for all the expenses she'd occurred – standard procedure, and more than just compensation, there'd be a reward element in it as well – but providing cigarettes now would have meant immediate outlays of hard cash, of which it was obvious there wasn't much about.

July 10th: another Monday.

Thérèse sat down, on a kitchen stool she'd left up here a week ago. Half an hour past noon: lunch, which she'd just brought upstairs, was a ragout of pork and beans – Rosie having hers in a soup-plate, and a spoon to eat it with. The plentiful food, she'd gathered, was due largely to an illegal system of bartering, run discreetly by local farmers. But at noon, the news had come in a Swiss radio broadcast that yesterday Caen had been taken by British and Canadian troops – the news triggering recollection of

Michel's exposition of the military situation – nine days ago, now, and he'd said he'd be back in two or three.

He'd also said – on the subject of Caen – '*Then* we'll have them on the run . . .'

So there might be rapid progress now?

Another thing he'd said, though, in reference to her own plans, had been that they might be 'overtaken by events'.

Meaning she might still be stuck here, an invalid, while Paris was being liberated and André Marchéval contrived to disappear. In which circumstances – Paris overrun, and the occupiers of 11, Rue des Saussaies either arrested or in flight – *would* he show up at the parental home or business, knowing it was the one place where SOE or anyone else with a score to settle would be likely to look first?

So you'd lose him. SOE would lose him. That bastard out from under: new identity, sound cover story and forged papers. He'd know enough from his training and experience in SOE to manage all of that.

Unless they shipped him off to Struthof-Natzweiler – having bled him dry?

She'd started on the stew. Delicious . . . 'Thérèse, you've surpassed yourself!'

'Lots of it, eat all you can.'

'Doesn't it worry you that Michel hasn't come?'

A wag of the straw-coloured head. 'I'll be glad when I see his *gazo* drive into the yard, certainly. As long as he steps out of it – he *and* Luc, preferably. But they don't run to a time-table, you know. Big area – I don't know exactly from where to where, but it's a lot of territory and there must be hordes of Maquis in it. Their numbers have been greatly swollen lately – did you know?'

'Yes.' A nod. 'Same all over France.'

'What Michel's coping with is the problem of so many groups widely separated, all wanting this, that and the other – and straining at the leash, he said, he and his colleagues having to restrain them from poking their heads up too soon.'

'I suppose if the big breakthrough *is* coming now—'

'They'll still have to lie low, and wait. Paris will be a primary objective, obviously, but he anticipates an encircling movement to the south of it, north across the Seine then and east to the Rhine – and through *these* parts, therefore. That's how *he* sees it.' She'd picked up her glass of wine. (Rosie drinking milk. Being good. Diet prescribed by Lotte.) Thérèse's blue eyes on her thoughtfully. Light-blue eyes and full, round cheeks, rounded chin, skin roughened by wind and weather but with no lines or creases in it yet. With her pink-and-white colouring and the mop of blonde hair she could easily have passed as German.

She'd put her glass down. 'You're on edge, Rosalie.'

'Am I?'

'Yes, you are. And – well, good heavens . . . After all you've been through . . . Rosalie – no matter *what* news Michel brings you – put your health first, don't try – think of doing *anything*. It'll be over soon – and you've done your share already, God knows. Even from the little *I* know—'

'I'm sure it's good advice—'

'But you're going to ignore it.'

'No. Thérèse, I appreciate your concern—'

'I'm *concerned* that you should simply relax, accept the fact you've been badly injured and you're now a convalescent!'

'Well – exactly. I *am* – thanks to you. The other business – it'll be London's decision, not mine. They'll recall me, I might be able to set something moving first, that's all. There are things I know – an individual I know – and recent experience makes it – in my opinion rather clearly my *personal* business.'

'To do with whatever Michel was finding out for you, I suppose.'

'Yes. His own idea.' She'd nodded. 'You were with us, you heard him.'

'Yes. I did.' Glancing away – distracted . . . 'Just a minute.' Moving to the window: Rosie hearing it then too – aircraft of some kind, low and already close. 'It's a Storch.' She had it in sight. 'Spotter plane.' She'd drawn back a bit. 'Coming right over us. The sort Michel was looking out for. They use them a lot round here.'

Her words were lost as the hammering racket peaked, then fell away; the machine could only have been a hundred metres or so up. Rosie wasn't getting any view of the outside world meanwhile – or much light either – with Thérèse's bulk across the window.

The plane had passed out of her sight too now. Turning back . . . 'Flying northwest – Lunéville, Nancy direction.'

The sound was nearly gone: a fading summer sound, as innocuous as a mower on a distant cricket-field. Thérèse sat down to finish her lunch. 'But listen – whatever this is you're contemplating or Michel's suggested – *when* you're fit, you'd be stupid to show yourself in public – anywhere, in the open. You're known to them, identifiable – they may still actively be searching for you. Not to mention that here in Alsace the language would give you away. And – surely, with the war on its last legs now—'

'But it *isn't*, is it? We aren't out of Normandy yet – let alone anywhere near Paris. People like me and the others I was with are *still* being shipped east to the camps. They want to brush us under the carpet – last thing they want around is us, to tell our stories!'

'Surely all the more reason to lie low?'

'Are *you* lying low?'

'Yes – I am—'

'By sheltering me, Thérèse?'

A spread hand on her chest: '*I* haven't been imprisoned, tortured, darn near killed. And like as not they're looking to

have another go at you! Rosalie – I know you're not married,
I remember Lotte asked you – but isn't there anyone special
in your life – worth staying alive for?'

She'd put her spoon down in the empty plate. Acknowledging to herself that it was a good question, really *the*
question, and maybe not a bad thing to be reminded of
it. She nodded: 'There is, yes. Man called Ben. Australian,
as it happens. And you see, Michel isn't only looking into
this other thing for me, when I'm fit and he's back he'll be
putting me in touch with London – my bosses – via some
person I think you know, or know of—'

'So?'

'So I'll get picked up, flown out.'

July 18th: Tuesday. Evening. Not in the attic, but on the first
floor, in Thérèse's bedroom. She'd been down in the kitchen
earlier, but Thérèse had left her when she'd heard the clatter
of her nephew's bicycle, gone out quickly to forestall his
bursting into the house; she'd pulled on an old jacket that
might once have been her husband's and blundered out,
muttering, 'See you later.' Rosie had come up here, as
they'd agreed she would, to be out of the way in case
they came back in together or the boy did on his own.

She leant back in the shiny horsehair-stuffed armchair,
closed her eyes. She'd been sewing, for about the past
hour and a half, needed to rest them for a minute. Oil
lamps weren't the best things for needlework. Relaxing,
listening to the silence of the house and night. *Last* night
there'd been a lot of bombers over – heading into Germany,
evidently on a different flight-path from their usual route or
routes. It was the first time she'd heard air activity here on
anything like that scale: there must have been hundreds of
them streaming over, squadron after squadron, a drone of
engines that had gone on seemingly for ages before the tail
end of it faded eastward; she'd lain there picturing the night

sky full of them, visualizing as she fell asleep the helmeted and masked crews in individual aircraft, thundering on into the Boche heartland.

And some Boche city in flames. As English cities had been often enough, in recent years.

Hadn't heard them returning. Either she'd slept through it or they'd taken a different route homeward. Direct route, one might guess, shortest distance between two points; but fewer returning than had gone out eastward, you could be sure.

She'd made her recent transition from attic to the lower floors in two stages. First, four or five days ago she'd decided there was no longer any reason to stay in bed, and with this Thérèse hadn't argued, in fact had found some old clothes that more or less fitted. Rosie had then spent two days just sitting around or prowling up and down under that low ceiling, or squatting at the window watching the slow drift of high cloud from the west and listening for the arrival of a *gazo* – which still hadn't come. By the end of the second day she'd rebelled again: despite a day and a night of drizzle and lower temperatures, the attic felt increasingly hot and airless, altogether too confining: and she'd had enough confinement. Thérèse had commented sarcastically, 'Next thing, you'll be trotting down to the village, calling on the mayor!'

'Would he be glad to see me?'

'Oh, charmed, I'd guess. Offer you a glass of Gewürztraminer, probably. Especially as there are Boche officers billeted in his house!'

'Might give *him* a miss, then. But seriously, Thérèse . . .'

Finally they'd settled for her coming down in the evenings only, after curfew, when at least there wouldn't be any neighbours dropping in. And for any other less welcome visitors, Bruno would give tongue and she'd take cover.

Negotiating the ladder hadn't been difficult at all; although

Thérèse had then to climb up it to shut the trap-door, then lift the ladder down. Any searcher who meant business would of course have seen it lying there, gone on up and perhaps found clues to the fact that the attic had been occupied, but a perfunctory look round such as Thérèse said was the usual thing in a routine police check-up wasn't much to be scared of – as long as they weren't looking for a particular individual, i.e. hadn't been tipped off. The local police, when not under German supervision, tended not to be looking very hard for people to arrest. If they had Boches with them, of course, it could be a different matter.

Thérèse must have found it a relief not to be clambering up and down with a chamber-pot two or three times a day. Although the deal was only to *stay* downstairs in the evenings, having found she could use the ladder safely she could also make briefer visits at other times as well. And for meals: she was only too glad to lend a hand at the stove – one hand, in theory, but on her own she'd been furtively using the other one too – with care, naturally, and still having the sling's support. Jobs like roasting and grinding wheat at night for the morning's porridge. For sewing too – mending and altering, fixing up old clothes which Thérèse routed out from somewhere or other; none of them could ever have fitted *her*. But – had to start *somewhere*, getting back to normal.

She fully intended getting herself out for air and exercise before much longer, too. Nights, she thought, would be safe enough – around the farm, at least, at weekends, when Charles came during the day and not at night. She was thinking about this – how and when to broach the subject – when she heard the outside door open and then slam shut, and Thérèse call, 'All clear, Rosalie!' So she'd have finished the evening chores and sent the boy home. Rosie went down, found her in the kitchen discarding the rather foul old jacket; chicken feathers drifting around, in a strengthening of the now familiar farmyard fragrance.

'Sorry – such a long time. Lot to do though, and I can't leave it *all* to the kid . . . Now, however – what we were talking about –' kicking off wooden-soled canvas shoes – 'heavens, *hours* ago . . . Oh, I'll get us some coffee, in a minute—'

'I'll do that—'

'No – sit down . . . Please. Much easier with two hands. Besides, Rosalie – what I was saying – what we were talking about when Charles came – you'd mentioned – unless I misheard completely – you're a war widow, too?'

Rosie frowning: 'Didn't I mention it before?'

'No – you did *not*. You've been here – what, eighteen days – and kept such a thing to yourself?'

She smiled, shrugged. Right shoulder, movement of the right hand . . .

'Subject just never came up, then. But – if you're interested – he was a fighter pilot. Royal Air Force. Battle of Britain, all that. In fact he was in the RAF before the war – we married in '39, a few months before it started, and he was killed – shot down – in February '42.'

Thérèse gazing at her. Slight shaking of the fair head. 'My turn to commiserate. But really – so *secretive*!'

'Well – not consciously—'

'I mean – when we've talked about *my* man being killed—'

'What I meant was, not secretive deliberately. To be frank, it wasn't what you'd call a marriage made in heaven. Could be why I don't talk about it. *Think* about it much, even.'

'That's sad, Rosalie.'

'Yes. Started happily – *terrifically* – but—'

'Not a good husband, uh?'

She shook her head. '*Not*.'

Johnny Ewing: Squadron Leader. Who'd thought he was

God's gift to women, and believed in spreading it around.
In retrospect all she felt for him was a mild contempt. And
to talk about it – about a man with whom she'd once been
passionately in love, and who'd died a war hero, of sorts –
it was easier *not* to.
'You must have been very young.'
'I was twenty, when we married.'
'And you haven't been tempted to re-marry?'
'I have, as it happens. Have been tempted, I mean. The
man I told you about, when you asked me?'
'A short name, I remember. Bim, Bam—'
'Ben.' She smiled. 'Short for Benjamin.'
'Ah, yes. But – not for marriage, huh?'
'It's this job of mine. That's – really all . . .'
'Ah. I understand.'
'His job too, really. He's in what they call Coastal Forces
– motor gunboats and torpedo-boats. He's been wounded
twice, quite badly. Any luck, they'll keep him ashore now.
But primarily it's *this*. He hates me doing it.'
'Could one blame him?'
'No. In fact I promised him this would be the last time.'
'So in terms of what we were discussing the other day—'
'I'm *longing* to be back with him.'
'Would he have any way of knowing you were arrested?'
'Nobody would. Probably not even my SOE bosses.
Beyond the fact I've disappeared from where I was.'
'They'd know *something* bad happened.'
'But as for marrying – I hope – when the war's over,
if we're both still around, and feel the same . . . Or even
before that – *if* they recall me – and if I can get to look a
bit more like a human being than I do now—'
'Rosalie, such nonsense!'
'I don't know. I do know I'm an appalling sight *now*. But
– until the time comes—'
'If you love each other—'

'I love him, and he loved me as I *was* – so yes, maybe, with luck—'

'Apart from your hair, Rosalie, which has to grow a little—'

'Looks as if goats have been at it, doesn't it? It wasn't a prison haircut, although you might think so, they hacked it off in a hospital at Morlaix. Shaved *this* part. With the best of intentions, obviously . . . But that's the least of it – what about being scarred from head to foot? All right, head to waist – and knees, Gestapo did *that* too – but –' touching her forehead, and that cheekbone – 'these mostly. OK, my hair'll cover *this*, eventually—'

'You're still a most attractive—'

'Like something the cat brought in!'

'No – you really *are*. And those scars will disappear quite soon, you'll see. With your hair grown – it's lovely hair, and that colour, the coppery lights in it – incidentally the scars aren't so disfiguring, you know. You think they are, when you look in the mirror that's what you focus on – uh?'

'You're very kind, Thérèse. But I try *not* to look in the mirror, frankly.' Glancing across the room at a yellowish one in a dark, heavy frame. 'I've been giving that a wide berth.' She added, touching the pad of dressing on the inside hollow of her left shoulder, 'One thing I really do thank God for is that this wasn't any lower. Not talking about being plugged through the heart, either—'

'Your breast. Yes. Lotte said that too.'

'Very, *very* lucky.'

'Bim-Bam can thank God too, I think!'

Both laughing: Rosie thinking that the name might stick . . . Thérèse shaking her head: 'Actually – no joke, is it? Definitely would not have been. But it's truly amazing, such luck – effectively, no *lasting* damage. And you have *lovely* eyes—'

She'd checked abruptly. Her eyes on the door. Quick

glance at Rosie then, but Rosie already moving, on her way. Hearing from halfway up the stairs a double rap on the door – and a metallic clash as the dog's weight came up hard against its chain. Not barking, though – whining: at someone it was glad to see? Thérèse then – in Alsatian, but the obvious question: 'Who's there?'

'*Me*, Aunt. Down, Bruno . . .' A boy's voice, switching into French that was accented exactly like Thérèse's: 'Bike's got a puncture – wondered could I borrow yours – since it's late, and curfew—'

Friday, July 21st. There'd been rumbles of bombing and/or gunfire the night before last – half asleep she'd wondered, the war couldn't be this close so soon, could it? – and this last night one single, very loud explosion that had woken her. She hadn't known what time it was – having no watch she only knew the time of day when Thérèse was with her or she was downstairs within sight and sound of the clock in the kitchen; its ticking was audible all over the little house. But the explosion had woken Thérèse as well, at about three o'clock, she said, and she thought it might have been a plane crashing. If so, it would have been a bomber, presumably, and couldn't have been far away; in these mountains somewhere, she guessed. There had been aircraft passing over earlier, apparently – which Rosie hadn't heard. Another item of breakfast-time interest had been a statement in a Swiss news bulletin an hour ago to the effect that there'd been an attempt by senior German staff officers to kill Hitler. He'd been hurt only slightly, had spoken bitterly and defiantly on German radio last night; it seemed a bomb had exploded under the table at some military conference at which he'd been presiding.

Thérèse's comment was, 'The devil looks after his own. But they can see the writing on the wall. Some of them wanting to get their coals out of the fire before they're caught in it themselves.'

Not unlike all the French who were rushing to join the Resistance, Rosie thought. She didn't say it – having no wish to hurt Thérèse's feelings. It would be a comment for *her* to make: she and her like, who'd been *résistants* since 1940 or thereabouts, and knew the truth of it. *Les résistants de '44*, old hands like her were calling the new converts, former fence-sitters or even collaborationists. It would still hurt, though, to have it commented on by an outsider; and in the past few days there'd been a certain wariness in their relationship, due to Rosie's insistence on 'going walkabout' in the dark – starting tomorrow, Saturday, when nephew Charles wouldn't be around in the evening, or even possibly tonight after he'd gone home. This would be the last night of the old moon, easier therefore for Thérèse to show her the layout of the farm than it would be tomorrow.

'Thérèse – just thinking – when I push off, leave you in peace—'

'God. She's off again . . .'

'Well – it's three weeks now, I've been cluttering up your house. And I *am* pretty well fit. Of course, if Michel *doesn't* come—'

'When you push off, you were saying – what?'

'To be ready to, really. Thinking of disguise, of sorts.' She touched her short, dark hair. 'OK, I can wear your scarf over this, but some of it may still show, and I was thinking – if I could dye it grey, d'you think?'

'Could.' A nod. 'We'd bleach it first, then dye it.' Snort of humour: 'What else – two sticks to hobble along on?'

'Uh-huh. But seriously – must *not* look as if I'd been injured. Look old, different, but—'

'I suppose . . .'

'Have to do without a sling too. Could you help with the hair?'

'Want more bread?'

'Well—'

'Go on, help yourself. Yes, I'll bleach and dye it for you. You'd be silly to stop wearing a sling, though.'

'Well – I'll try not to use the arm more than I have to, and – look, hook the thumb into my blouse or jacket – like this? A sling would really mark me – wouldn't it?'

'If they know where and how you were hit. Maybe you should assume they would. Yes, I suppose . . . Want more of this?'

Chicory mixture. She shook her head. 'No – thanks. But if we could do my hair rather soon now – so that when Michel does turn up—'

'Oh, Lord, what's this . . .'

Gazo engine: and the dog barking its head off . . .

A *gazo* truck: a load of horse manure, courtesy of a neighbour. Thérèse had been expecting it – for her vegetables, apparently, but it would be left to rot for at least half a year before application, she'd said. There was plenty of it about, as most farms hereabouts used horses for ploughing and carting; and she didn't like using the pig variety so close to the house. She went out to assist in the unloading, and Rosie took the breakfast things to the sink.

She couldn't help being on edge: *needed* to be ready to make a move. First and foremost, to get into a position from which to contact London. Having been here three whole weeks – long, slow weeks, at that – and thinking a great deal off and on about Ben still not knowing she was alive. Not knowing anything at all, please God: but it was conceivable that if SOE finally decided she must have come to grief, they might start breaking it to him gently.

For 'they' read Marilyn Stuart, who'd been Rosie's 'Conducting Officer' or guiding light when she'd been a trainee, and was still her closest chum and sometime colleague on the staff in Baker Street; Rosie had introduced Ben to her, the three of them had had a meal together, and it was bound to be Marilyn he'd call on when the silence became unbearable.

Marilyn would *try* to play it by the book – not tell him anything at all.

Another source of anxiety, though – stashing cups and saucers in the drying rack now, Thérèse still out there unloading horse-shit – a major cause of the restlessness that worried Thérèse so much was 'Hector' and what might be happening in the Allied drive on Paris, or around it. If an advance was in progress, which from BBC broadcasts it seemed to be. In particular there'd been mention of a new offensive and extremely hard fighting east of Caen, which might match up with what Thérèse had said, quoting Michel, about an encircling movement to the south of Paris and in this direction. Although there again – in terms of her own needs and priorities – with Michel's non-appearance, and the fact that he was the only way she knew of to contact London, via some local SOE *réseau*, in his continuing absence it was beginning to look like pie in the sky. Thérèse hadn't any solution to offer, either; one had to assume that her own Resistance connections were solely with the escape-line to which this farm was available as a safe-house. It was frustrating, especially as Rosie was beginning to feel she *could* think about making a move now – that physically she'd be up to it. The sulphur powder was crumbling off her various wounds in brownish scabs and flakes, and seemed to have done the job. Her back was to all intents and purposes healed, only striped in two shades of white. The head wound was no more than a recessed roughness with new hair thickening around and through it, and the shoulder wounds, front and back, were bruise-coloured, still slightly crusted, indentations. Effectively they *were* bruises, the shoulder felt bruised and nothing more; she thought – hoped –

that by now the fractured bone might have joined itself up again.

Her heart hadn't played any tricks, since that one night. It had alarmed her at the time, but she'd more or less convinced herself she could forget it.

Thérèse pushed the door shut behind her, slid the bolt across. 'That's that. Oh, you've cleared up.' She sat down – buttocks overflowing the stool – leant with her forearms on the table. She was distinctly odorous. 'What were we talking about?'

'My hair – dyeing it?'

'Oh, yes.' A sigh, wag of the head. 'So we were.'

'But if it's difficult—'

'No.' Tired smile. 'I was just telling myself – no peace for the wicked . . . But – not difficult, no. I could do the bleaching right away – I've got that – and get grey dye in the village. I've a friend there who's used it in similar circumstances, as it happens. Have to go into the village anyway. Stay upstairs, will you, while I'm out?'

'Of course, but – Thérèse, I *am* taking such advantage of your kindness. I'm sorry—'

'You needn't be. If you weren't here there'd be other things keeping me just as busy. Maybe more so. And I'm enjoying your company – that's the truth . . . Anyway, I'll do the bleaching when I've milked Clotilde.'

'Thank you. You're – *extremely* kind . . . Going to the market, are you?'

A nod. 'Taking the chicks I killed last evening.'

'And tonight – here I go again – will you show me round out there – after Charles has gone?'

'Because of the damn moon, eh?'

Silence, looking at each other. Rosie anxiously – aware that she *was* being a bloody nuisance, also, in Thérèse's view, pig-headed, but in the circumstances hardly knowing how not to be. And Thérèse simply *looking* at her: a

look saying something like *All right, if you're so keen to
piss off* . . .

She was lonely. Would have been unnatural if she hadn't
been. Heart of a lioness or not. Even a lioness would get
lonely, sometimes.

'Thérèse – I admit, I'm a cat on hot bricks. But you can
understand it, can't you? I mean – I'd hate you to think I
was ungrateful, didn't appreciate—'

'– like to slow you down, that's all. To start with the odds
as heavily against you as they *must* be—'

'I doubt the Boches would be looking for me now. Even
if they were three weeks ago, by now with any luck they'll
think I'm dead.'

'You'll take Michel's advice, when he turns up?'

'Of course. I *want* his advice – help . . . He's an excep-
tional man, isn't he?'

'You noticed.'

'Must be a worry for you too now – that he might not
turn up?'

'Oh. So many if *this*, if *thats*. But –' movement of the
heavy shoulders, shake of the blonde head. 'How often
that sort of doubt's in one's mind. In the air we breathe,
isn't it?' She pushed herself up. 'Keep saying our prayers,
Rosalie. For the time being there's nothing else.'

Chapter 4

She was near the top end of the smaller cornfield, the northern apex of Thérèse's land, when she heard a *gazo* grinding up the hill, from the direction of the village. Hardly the time for traffic on the mountain road – getting near 10 p.m., curfew hour.

Coming *here*?

Suppressing the hope: at least, trying to. For three weeks now every time she'd heard one – this *same* hope, that this might be Michel, at last – had been closely followed by the same let-down. Deepening the frustration of being stuck here while elsewhere things were moving fast.

Humiliating, really. Man saves your life, you find yourself relying on him totally, and he disappears. In fact she'd more or less decided that if he hadn't turned up by the end of this week she'd take off on her own. Find a *résistant* somewhere, somehow, play it off the cuff. What she'd suggested to Lise, in fact: both of them well aware of the danger involved in approaching *résistants* or for that matter SOE agents or escape-line people without introduction or quickly provable identification, to convince them you were not an infiltrator. Anyway – no option, no more than Lise would have had. You couldn't wait for ever: irrespective of what else was going on. In fact a *lot* was – as one might have hoped – and not so very far away, quite possibly involving Michel and his team. On Sunday Thérèse had attended Mass in the village, and had come back with the rumour – credible enough – that the Boche 15th Army was currently being moved west to reinforce the 7th, moving by road and rail but over the Seine only by a limited number of small ferries, since every single bridge had been destroyed either by sabotage or bombing. Definitely good news – that the reinforcement had become necessary, as well as the bit about the bridges – but also might explain Michel's continuing absence.

There was about a hectare of corn at this top end of the farm, in two fields separated by a stream which rose somewhere up there among the balloon-like summits but at present didn't have much water in it. It was bridged in three places, bridges of tree-trunks overlaid with planks, and she'd just come over the westernmost of them. No problem: the new moon was only a sliver, but it was a lot better than none at all; this was Tuesday, and since Thérèse had shown her around the farm on Friday, last night of the old moon, Rosie had done the circuit on her own on each of the three nights in near-total darkness.

Marvellous to get out. Cool night air, and space, starlight . . .

That *gazo* had changed gear pretty well exactly where it would have to if it was going to turn into the yard.

A mesh wire fence divided the cornfield from a long strip of cow and sheep pasture. No sheep in it at present, only Clotilde; the ewes and a couple of half-grown lambs which Thérèse was keeping were down at the bottom. Rosie steadied herself with a hand on the top wire and swung her right leg over it: then the other one. She was wearing a culotte cotton skirt, provided by Thérèse and altered by herself, and over her blouse a loose-fitting ex-army sweater that had seen much better days. Vintage '14–'18, probably. She'd patched the worn-through elbows and re-knitted the neck, and rather liked its loose, floppy comfort. Standing close to the fence, watching downhill – towards the back of the house and the cowshed. Vegetable beds surrounded the house on three sides, and the cowshed was to the right – open on this side, to this pasture, and with a small door and ventilation slots in the side facing on to the yard. On the other side of the house – the left, looking down at it from this direction – between it and the straggle of roadside hedge and trees was a gap through which, if the *gazo* did turn in, she'd expect to see it on its way into the yard. If it had its lights on, anyway. The house faced on to the yard, of course, with the barn opposite it and sundry other outbuildings off to the right – including a long stone building, now used for storage of farm equipment, which in the days when they'd made wine here had been the *chais* – bottling, storage, et cetera.

There were no lights on the *gazo*, but she did see it – briefly – emerging from the shadow of a clump of firs, then passing out of sight behind the house.

She started down along the line of the fence. Legs stinging from encounters with nettles: and not letting herself believe in this being Michel, or Luc. The most likely thing was neighbours from up the road – Destiniers or a family by name of Roesch, for instance, which were the names one heard most. Destinier was an old man, with a haggard unmarried daughter who looked after him, must have done most of the work if not all of it, and was a close friend of Thérèse. They'd been mentioned by Michel, she remembered, as people he'd planned to use if he'd had to explain his visit here that night. Marie Destinier must be a *résistante*, she guessed, probably involved in the escape line with Thérèse, but that didn't apply to the Roesch lot, as far as one knew. This could be one or more of either lot dropping by – within only a few minutes of home, therefore safe enough in regard to the curfew.

She'd stopped again: it wouldn't have been a good idea to burst in, especially if the visitors happened to be the Roesch family – or more distant neighbours, for that matter. Squatting on her heels, breathing the cool, earth-smelling night air, hearing Bruno barking his head off down there. His sole purpose in life, poor thing. Oddly, she remembered Michel saying that or something like it to Luc on the night they'd brought her here. Waiting, listening, exerting patience: it still *could* be Michel but she wasn't taking chances, i.e. rushing in: thinking of which – that line *Fools rush in* – title of a song to which countless times she and Ben had danced. His voice in memory crooning in her ear, *So open up your heart and let/This fool rush in* . . . If this *was* Michel, and everything worked out the way he'd said it might, that self-styled 'fool' might soon receive news that would put a song back in *his* heart. Please God. And please God let him still be receptive to it. Well, damn it, he *would*. Scars or no scars. Otherwise – Christ, scar *him* . . .

The barking had ceased but the *gazo*'s engine was still running. Only Thérèse could have silenced Bruno, so she must have come outside. Rosie got up and moved on again, down the slope of field; envisaging Michel and Luc down there backing the *gazo* into the barn as they'd done that other night when she'd been in it, not knowing where she was or in whose hands or effectively whether it was Christmas or Easter. She could see Thérèse's cow – Clotilde – lying out in the middle of the pasture – which was about the width and twice the length of a football field, with an even slope down towards the house and yard. The farm as a whole sloped down eastward, with the house and outbuildings, and farther – farther from the road – the chicken-sheds and runs and then the pig area, on that more or less level central part. And below, from there right down to the bottom, were hayfields, one of which had been cut and currently had the sheep in it.

Gazo's engine *still* pounding. Would have switched off by now, she thought, if they'd been staying. Thérèse's voice then, for the first time: words indistinguishable but pitched high as if calling to someone at a distance – or over the noise of that engine's sudden revving – which it *was*.

Moving out. Like a shadow across that gap again.

She heard it thump over the rise: then down into the road. Then a shift of gear, and turning uphill, the way it *had* been going. Marie Destinier on her way home from some visit was as likely as anything. Goodbye to wishful thinking about Michel and Luc, anyway. Coming up close now: second gear-shift. The road abreast of where she was now crouching again – natural caution, not wanting to attract neighbourly gossip, such as who the hell's wandering around Thérèse Michon's fields at night – the roadside was only about fifty metres away. And whoever that was, they weren't showing lights.

Odd. If it *was* Marie. Unless her lights weren't working. Smelling it now – charcoal fumes, on the westerly breeze. For the moment the moon-sliver was covered. Owls hooting: there were a lot of them around here. If it had been the Destinier woman she'd be taking the left fork a few hundred metres up the road; if a Roesch, a right-hand turn just after it. Rosie continued on down, now and again in contact with the fence and on smooth, well-grazed turf. Cowpats were the only hazard. Old, sun-baked ones were no problem, but she wanted to avoid stepping in the other kind, having only the wooden-soled, cloth-uppered pair of shoes she'd been wearing on the night of the car smash. She'd managed to hang on to them in Fresnes, even: maybe because the thieving, butch wardresses hadn't thought them worth stealing.

Car? *Another?*

Stopping, listening again. Confirming to herself that it was not only a car, but petrol-engined, not *gazo*.

Squatting down. Right shoulder against the wire. Pale

wash of moonlight, Clotilde a black hump in it, as motion-less as a rock in sand. Petrol-powered vehicles usually meant Boches: especially after curfew. It was on its way up from the village, so if the *gazo* had dropped someone off here . . . She caught her breath: *it* wasn't on *its* way up, *they* – more than one car – were on *their* way up. Which would mean some kind of raid. Thérèse wouldn't be hearing them yet either – if she was inside the house with the door shut: which by now she would be. Rosie up again and running – diagonally across, aiming for the west side of the house, the way through the vegetable garden into the entrance track where it dipped into the yard. But – bloody hell, the cars were coming too damn fast for this, she'd about meet them head-on, at that point – if they *were* coming here. She swerved right, aiming now for the milking shed: straight through it and please God be banging on the kitchen door – or better, inside it – before the cars' lights lit the place up. Even a few seconds' warning – get the ladder down, tonight of all nights Thérèse having left it up. Would you *believe* it . . . The moon was almost behind her now; and Clotilde was lumbering to her feet – disturbed by Rosie, not by the cars, although they were now quite close and – coming too fast to be intending to turn in? *Go on by, please* . . . Running clumsily, out of practice and unfit, and having one arm pinned upset one's balance. First time she'd run since—

Scream of engines crashing into high gear: then the first one's tyres showering dirt and stones as it swerved into the entrance track. Second one then – same skidding turn, thumping over the rise and into the dip, on the leader's tail.

She'd stopped. Hearing Bruno barking his head off. Crouching, to reduce her silhouette – right out in the open here. Not that they – Boches, or anyone else – had any view this way at this moment. But – God, the cowshed looked like a trap now, too. Open, easy access and easy reach, pitch-dark inside: but a trap for sure. They'd search outhouses as well as the house itself – unless they were stupid, which regrettably they seldom were – and the milking-shed being bang-up against the house might be the first one they'd look in. Michel *might* be in the house with Thérèse: or someone else might be. Another mental picture – irrespective of whether Thérèse was alone or not – was of the attic ladder still in place under the open trap-door: they'd left it up, this evening. Thérèse for the first time not bothering; partly because she'd had an old hen boiling in a cast-iron tureen, with onions and turnip.

Car doors slamming: a German shout, and a crash as one of them kicked at the door, shouted again in that brutal language.

Thérèse upstairs getting the ladder down, Rosie hoped.

Get over to the hedgerow.

Thinking about it for about a second: then moving. More German shouting, and Bruno sounding frantic. To get to that undergrowth along the roadside made sense: from where she was – where she'd so stupidly put herself. Well – what alternative, for God's sake . . . From those windows for instance, one of which was Thérèse's – once they got up there, with a grandstand view of everything out here . . .

Thérèse had screamed: Alsatian-German, high-pitched protest. Then a shot: pistol or rifle. Pistol-shot, she guessed. She was running, her breath coming in short gasps. Bruno had stopped barking. Thérèse's wail again, starting in German and ending in what sounded like French but wasn't comprehensible; a *real* scream then, and German fury responding, drowning her out; one of them might have hit her, and the door into the kitchen either crashed shut or flung back against the front wall of the house. Shut, Rosie guessed: there were still German voices and other movements in the yard but nothing of Thérèse in it now, the others must have taken her inside with them. Those still outside would be checking the barn and other outhouses, of course. Lights moved here and there, a torch-beam flickered along the roof-line, paused to spotlight the attic window in that end wall. Down at ground level then: the vegetable area and the pathway through it. And if the sod was coming through *there*—

'All right, Clotilde, all *right* . . .'

She'd slithered to a stop: there was no hope of making it to the roadside hedge. She had her arm round the cow's neck – up close, leaning against the animal's smelly hide – using *her* for cover – of sorts, and as long as the animal allowed it. Clotilde restive, swinging her big head round, shifting her feet . . . Rosie sure some Boches would soon be looking out of the windows. Should have stayed at the top of this field; could have got to the roadside cover up there easily. OK – easy hindsight too: the priority had been to warn Thérèse. As it was she'd been taken completely by surprise; they'd search the whole place, and whether or not there was anyone else here now, once they looked in the attic they'd know damn well there *had* been.

Thérèse alone in there meanwhile, facing questions, threats, fists. They'd shot the dog – had come meaning business, were in their own view on a certainty, not just enquiring. Shoot anything, any *one*. But on business connected with that *gazo*?

But if so, wouldn't one car have gone on after it, once they'd seen it wasn't here?

Alternatively, therefore – might be looking for one escaped female prisoner? No connection with the *gazo*, the timing of tonight's two visits just coincidental? If there'd been a tip-off, for instance?

'Stand *still*, Clotilde!'

Having to move with her, though – sidling along. Imagination turning cartwheels: and thinking ahead just a little way – if the beast decided to turn round – simply duck under her belly to the other side. Ridiculous: she could see that on the face of it it might even be comic. But in reality – since the result of being spotted might be a bullet— Even less comical for Thérèse in there.

Flare of light – inside the cowshed. She'd glanced that way because she'd heard something – the door in the back wall opening, probably – and seen a torch beam probing around inside. It was shining out into the field now, sweeping the smooth slope of grass dotted blackly with Clotilde's muck. Sweeping *this* way – she ducked her head, blinded, the beam holding steadily right on *her.*

No. On the cow. Or he'd have reacted by this time. He'd seen a cow – not Rosie close up against her, stooping, heart drumming . . . The light flicked away, was illuminating the inside of the shed again, allowing glimpses of a thickset man in plain clothes turning his back this way, poking that beam around and some of it reflecting back at him. She'd seen white shirt-front: guessed there'd be a pistol in his other hand. Plain clothes and general appearance indicative of Gestapo.

'Clotilde – *damn* you . . .'

Turning. Suddenly, and not slowly either. Rosie edged back, keeping the animal's swivelling bulk between herself and the man in the shed: at the same time sharply aware that it was *not* now between herself and the first-floor windows. That bastard still inside the milking-shed, torch-beam wavering around, despite there being nothing in there except a fixed feeding-trough and Thérèse's milking stool – as far as she remembered, from the conducted tour on Friday. Clotilde had got all the way round and for some reason best known to herself was starting towards that Boche – towards her shelter. Slow, lumbering progress, Rosie up close again, side-stepping, abreast of the animal's fore-quarters in the hope that any visible leg-movements might coincide. But why the Boche should be hanging around in there—

Examining the shed's back wall, it seemed. His stocky figure showing up blackly this side of the light. She realized suddenly – having a pee. Had been – was now bouncing on his toes, shaking the drips off, then buttoning himself up – torch still in hand, one-handed therefore for the rest of it; pistol holstered, presumably. And all finished – torch shining downward as he stepped out into the yard and pulled the door shut behind him. Clotilde had heard that closure, and stopped, stood gazing that way as if the man's departure had perplexed her.

No way to get her moving again if she didn't want to. You'd have needed a stick. But – OK, distance to the shed now only about twelve or fifteen metres: one quick dash . . .

German voices: the kitchen door no doubt open. Gruff-toned exchanges, what sounded like orders and acknowledgement; then a car door opened, and shut. Second door, ditto. Starter whirring: the engine fired. One car and two men leaving, was her analysis. Another of them went back into the house. Rosie deciding, *now*: good a moment as any. Clotilde still immobile, staying put behind her out there in hazy moonlight as she darted across this almost grassless patch of open ground, into the shed's darkness.

Reek of urine . . .

They wouldn't check in here again, she thought. *That* one wouldn't, anyway. But the car that was on the move wasn't going out to the road, it was heading slowly along the track leading to the poultry and pig areas. Engine-sound diminishing, already barely audible. Those two on their way to inspect the sheds and styes, no doubt. It did seem fairly evident that they'd come looking for some person or persons who'd have been in the *gazo* and who for some reason had been assumed to have dropped off here, but in fact had not been made welcome by Thérèse. Forget about Michel, therefore, he didn't fit into any such scenario. But guessing at what *might* be happening – for the sake of understanding this and anticipating future moves: Thérèse, she imagined, in there protesting, 'No, not a soul, *nobody*'; and maybe 'That's where my nephew sleeps when he spends the night – because of curfew, sometimes . . .' Then he – the Boche in charge – telling his minions, 'Check the rest of the place. Outhouses . . .'

Then curious about the clothes she'd been fixing up? Smaller than could possibly fit Thérèse – *and most of them in the attic*?

Thérèse: 'Of *course* they're not for me. Helping out young friends in the village – old clothes don't need ration coupons, do they . . . Yes, up there's where I do most of my sewing.'

Because the kitchen and her bedroom were cluttered enough already and there was nothing to sit on in the other rooms. Which was the truth – two other rooms on the bedroom floor were bare, nothing in them except Thérèse's winter garments in an ancient wardrobe in the larger one, no other furniture either there or in the little box-room, which was big enough for a baby's cot but no more than that – and empty anyway. And the ground floor mostly kitchen – the big room one virtually lived in – a whole family would have – and a larder, and the WC in what must have been the farmhouse scullery, a largish stone-floored space which now also had a bathtub in it – only a cold tap, hot water obtainable by bucket from the kitchen. Two thoughts out of all this: one, whatever line of evasion Thérèse dreamt up there was really nothing she could have said that the Boche would easily believe: and he didn't have to disprove anything. They never had to: were cleared to kill or torture merely on suspicion. Effectively, on whim . . . But point two, how could it take several men more than a few minutes to search just a few small rooms, two of them empty?

That car was coming back – faster, bouncing over wheel-ruts. Rosie had heard the hens kicking up a row, heard the car now instead. She was in the shed's rear right-hand corner, where she'd be out of sight if one of them decided to take another quick look inside: final check before departure . . .

Which might be imminent.

Leaving Thérèse here, unharmed – please God?

Car braking to a halt. Doors opening: muttered exchanges between the two men as they disembarked. There'd have to be at least four altogether, two to each car. Could indeed be more: half a dozen, say. By the sound of it, at least that number outside now: as if those inside had been waiting for the others and had now gone out to join them.

Thérèse's voice, high and thin – and in French again, surprisingly, the forbidden language: '– *told* you over and over, why can't you *believe*—'

Loud, brutal-sounding German, Thérèse pleading in Alsatian. More shouting. Some of them might have got into the other car: its engine starting now. Turning it round, she guessed. That Boche bawling at Thérèse: and what sounded like a scuffle. A guffaw of laughter was startlingly incongruous: actually, foul, in terms of how one was envisaging the scene . . . Rosie stiff and still in her corner, hardly breathing. Knowing that once they took you . . . Thérèse would know it too, of course: she'd know it all. One car had gone: by now she'd have been forced into the other. Yes – second engine starting: spurt of tyres in farmyard dirt as its driver gunned it forward.

The clock's noisy ticking seemed like betrayal of Thérèse: as if the house and everything in it should be lifeless – with her, its heart, torn out of it. Surveying the mess in the kitchen, Rosie hearing her in memory: *Survive, then start again, God gives us strength – up to us how we use it* . . .

She'd be needing *all* her strength.

The suddenness of such events was shocking in itself. One minute safe – you *thought* – as safe as caution and your experience could ensure it – then *wham*, no safety anywhere, no such thing existed.

Hadn't for poor Bruno, either. Shot in the head, a dark heap in the yard.

They'd gnawed chicken-bones and dropped them here and there. Taken other food as well. Cupboards and shelves had been emptied, pots and pans and everything else pulled out, strewn around.

Looking for what, among saucepans and suchlike?

Well – what *might* be stored among such items, that was relevant to the present situation . . . Guns, maybe, plastic explosive, ammunition? Or other Maquis stores – tins of food of British or US origin, which might have been parachuted in. Or radio equipment. With Maquis up there in the forests, if the Boches thought they had reason to believe Thérèse was involved with them?

The ladder was still in place, and the attic had been ransacked, bedding pulled off and the clothes she'd mended tossed around. There'd have been nothing else for them to find, but it would still have been obvious that Thérèse had had someone living here. She'd have denied it, of course – for Rosie's sake, to give *her* a chance to get away – and the denial would be enough to convict her. They'd most likely have troops here in the morning, turn the whole farm over. And since Thérèse almost certainly *did* have links to the Maquis, there might well be an arms-cache somewhere on her land.

Sooner one got clear of the place, the better. They didn't *have* to wait until morning, quite likely wouldn't. She was sorting out the stuff she'd take with her – not all of it, because some of tonight's team might return and remember there'd been female clothing lying around. Wouldn't have counted or memorized items, one might hope . . . Anyway – be *quick*: there was no way hanging around could help Thérèse. Just cross your fingers for her, count your own blessings and bloody scarper . . . Although the prospect of setting off largely directionless and severely handicapped in various ways didn't have all that much going for it either. No papers, was the crucial thing. Papers – identity, residence, work, travel, food and clothing ration cards et cetera – were all that entitled you to exist. Compared to that really crippling lack, having no money – literally not a *sou* – was only a minor drawback. Especially considering that by daylight the surrounding countryside might be lousy with road-blocks and patrols. You'd only need to be stopped once – just one routine check, you wouldn't get any further. Especially with the language complication. No papers *and* wrong language, for Christ's sake . . . Sweating, panic flaring: deep-breathing to counter physical reactions, slow the pulse-rate, pounding heart. Telling herself that nothing as far as *she* was concerned was new, or any worse. She'd stick to the same programme – somehow establish contact with a local SOE *réseau*, then perhaps with their help stay out of sight and circulation until either a pick-up was arranged or papers covering a new identity could be provided. Either locally, or from London, but preferably the latter. Because one couldn't trust *all* local sources all that far . . . But one had only to survive for that length of time: then you'd either be out or – well, *comparatively* secure. And for a start – *now* – find Marie Destinier, who'd surely provide temporary refuge – until whatever had stirred this up blew over – and she might have practical suggestions for the next stage, a move westward towards Nancy, for instance. Although – all right, any such move, *without papers* . . . Despite recalling only too vividly that road-blocks had been

frightening enough, sometimes, even *with* bloody papers –
and where it was OK to talk French . . .

Sitting, for a moment. Heart going at about twice normal
speed. Telling herself well, it *would*, give the poor thing a
chance . . . And get help from or through this Marie person.
No papers or Alsatian, so make the journey – to Nancy,
or wherever – in some way hidden. In a farm-cart under
farm produce, or in a *gazo*'s boot, say. If she – Marie – was
associated with Thérèse in running part of an escape line,
she'd have ways and means, or links to those who did have.
Then in any place the size of Nancy there should be some
representative of SOE, and some way of making contact –
doing so *without* getting one's throat cut in the process.

Water was still hot in Thérèse's battered kettle; the Master
Race having enjoyed her hospitality and left dregs in several
tin mugs. There was also a wine bottle smashed in the sink.
Angry at finding it empty or near-empty, perhaps: it was
how those thugs *were*, that was all. She rinsed out a mug,
and found the chicory mixture. Also milk, bread, and a few
salvageable scraps of chicken. It was worth a few minutes'
delay, made sense to eat while one had the chance – sooner
than spend the night lying in some ditch wishing one *had*.
She was ignoring her heart: when it was ready to slow up,
it would. *Soon*, please. One felt – shaky, weak . . . Moving
around in search of a container for her gear, while taking
the edge off her hunger. Settling for a basket – deep, with
two flap-up lids and a central carrying-handle – in which
Thérèse had on occasion carried poultry on her visits to the
market. Didn't seem to be a suitcase anywhere, and this
would do just as well. Better, in fact, in some circumstances.
She took it up to the attic, packed into it one skirt, one shirt,
two blouses, a spare pair of knickers, a nightdress which
only today she'd washed and ironed, some stockings and
a pullover. Her bra she'd have to wash and dry overnight,
when necessary. But also – importantly – a scarf which

Thérèse had said she could have – cotton, blue with white stripes and a white edging. She tied it on, covering the scar on the side of her head and most of her grey-dyed hair, in front of the yellowed mirror.

Like a waif or stray, she thought. Desperate-looking waif or stray. No chicken, either. Leaving the mirror abruptly, cramming in a last mouthful of food and trying to put that image of herself out of mind.

The sling?

Yes. For the time being, and while still in this locality, i.e. quite a few hours by *gazo* from where she and Lise had left the train. It seemed unlikely the Boches would be looking for her here, not only because of the distance, but they might also see it logically as being in the wrong direction, from an escaping British agent's point of view. Why head for the German border, for Christ's sake? Clever old Michel – to have brought her over to this side of the mountains. Even if his decision had been dictated by Thérèse being here and his knowing she'd cope. From where they'd picked her up they'd come about eighty kilometres as a crow might fly, and probably half as much again, Thérèse had estimated, when you took account of the winding mountain road. But – on the subject of this sling – be sensible, continue wearing it this side of the Vosges, then anywhere towards Nancy, ditch it – so as *not* to look like walking wounded. And with that in mind, a coat of some sort might be worth having – useful anyway, but to wear half-buttoned and rest the arm in if it still needed that.

Thérèse's rain-jacket, as she'd called it? If she hadn't been wearing it?

She hadn't: it was in her bedroom. A sort of golf-jacket; quite old, with buttons, not a zip-fastener. Nondescript brown, and distinctly loose-fitting – which was fine, it flapped around her and reached below her hips, hid her shape. She could have been a woman of – hell, forty.

At least. With unkempt grey hair in view, bloody *fifty*.

At the top of the field she climbed over the fence, out of Thérèse's land into the roadside scrub, and plodded on uphill. Feeling it, by this time. Tired, and muscles aching. Even the basket with so little in it was a weight. She'd done more in the last few hours than she had in nearly two months.

Humiliating. Considering how fit she'd been before that – cycling all over France . . .

Wednesday now: getting towards 3 a.m. A quarter to, maybe. And the moon getting close to setting – no great worry, with a clear sky and about forty million stars. Plenty of cover – this stuff she was plodding through; if she heard anything coming she'd just drop down and wait until it passed. But nothing else was moving: not a sound, except the wind's, no bombers overhead tonight. Stumbling on: wretched shoes weren't meant for country trekking, either. In the course of her rummaging she'd tried on a pair of Thérèse's, old leather ones, but they'd been far too big.

Thinking of Thérèse again. Then of Lise – whether she'd drowned in the river, or been shot, or recaptured, or—

Crossed fingers for that highly improbable 'or': and switching to thoughts of Ben. Old Bim-Bam: fast asleep in the Coastal Forces base at Portsmouth, she hoped – and managing to keep hope alive, please God. *See you. Ben* . . .

She'd found it: the fork off to the left first, best part of a kilometre uphill, then the entrance to the Destinier place after another – well, half-kilometre, maybe. It had felt like about ten. The farm track she was on now was lined on one side with firs; there were fields on both sides and a herd of cows in the one to the right. All lying down – lucky buggers. Thérèse had told her the Destiniers had this milking herd, a very large flock of sheep and a small acreage of vines. The old man had been a *vigneron* in a much bigger way in his younger days, she'd said, but this was little more than a hobby now, a superb wine but only enough for his own and family friends' consumption, and she'd thought maybe a few special customers. It was the wine Thérèse had had – her only real luxury, for which she'd traded eggs. Although having adequate supplies of food was a luxury in itself. Some system of withholding marketable produce, worked presumably between fellow operators of an escape line, to ensure escapees could be fed – and the Maquis supplied, she guessed. They hadn't discussed it because there'd been no need for her to know anything about it.

Stone in a shoe: and not the first. She crouched to fix it. Warm, hard-baked earth with wheel-ruts in it. *Bloody* shoes, though . . . She'd have liked to have rested here for a while, but she was up again, hefting the basket, pushing on, keeping close to the trees where it was darkest. Only starlight now, the young moon had dipped behind the mountains.

The Boches wouldn't have found *much* food in Thérèse's house tonight. There'd been times when they would have, but—

Those were roofs, buildings, discernible ahead. Against starry sky, straight edges. For a moment she hardly believed it: from Thérèse's description she'd expected about a kilo-metre of this track, not just a few hundred metres. Unless she'd been literally sleep-walking – which wasn't impos-sible. At least, walking in a daze . . . She'd stopped again. Making out the house to the left – identifiable by a chimney on it – and a lower but similarly sloped roof to the right. Barn or barns, she guessed: other outbuildings, a winery maybe. A bird of some kind swept past her at about head-height: swoosh of wings, movement of air as proof of how closely it had passed. Probably an owl. Well, what else . . .

A dog began barking – somewhere ahead, amongst the buildings. Inside, maybe. She kept going. The Destiniers were going to be woken in any case, and the animal was probably on a chain: seemed to be customary, around here, although you'd have thought they'd let the poor brutes run free at night.

Let *them* run free was right. Dogs, plural, barking like mad now: and a glimmer of light showing suddenly in an upstairs window of the house. Rosie aware of dizziness now and then: from glancing up quickly like that?

She hoped to God these people wouldn't turn her away. If they did – *what*?

Sufficient unto the day. *More* than bloody sufficient . . . Shuffling on. Sharp eye out for dogs . . . Pausing then as an iron latch rattled – and a door jerked open. Ahead and to the right, she thought, not at the house. Light there too now – an oil-lamp, yellowish radiance on an ancient timber door in the stone wall of a barn: then dogs visible for a moment bursting out. They hadn't let themselves out . . . She'd stopped, prepared to defend herself with the basket, called, 'Hello!' The dogs approaching more slowly, crouched and snarling, with that light behind them. She called again, 'Hello? Please – I've come from Thérèse—'

'Tobie! Théo! *Stay!*'

Female: but harsh, commanding. Rosie standing stock still, and the dogs crouching, motionless . . . The voice – Marie Destinier's presumably – called in French, 'Who are you, what d'you want? You say from Thérèse?'

'I've come from her house, yes. Been living there. Are you Marie Destinier? I'm sorry to disturb you—'

'What's happened?'

'Gestapo – taken Thérèse. I was outside, walking around, I—'

'*Taken* her . . .'

'Two car-loads of them, they—'

'Come where I can see you. Into the light. When did this happen?'

'In the last few hours.' Approaching the shifting lamp-light and the tall figure behind it. Exceptionally tall: like someone on stilts, almost. Trick of the light, perhaps. She explained, 'A *gazo* came first and went off again. I don't know who, or why, I wasn't close enough. Then a few minutes later these two Gestapo cars – I heard them coming up the hill, petrol engines, coming fast – I tried to get down to the house to warn Thérèse, in case, but—'

'Stop where you are. What's that you're carrying?'

'This?' It occurred to her to put it down. Rubbing that hand and arm with the one in the sling then. 'Clothes, that's all. Anyway – they left, taking her with them. Whatever they were looking for, they'll have seen *I* was living there – that *someone* was – and Thérèse would have denied it, so –' shaking her head '– that reason alone, I suppose . . .'

The lamp-light was on her: Marie holding the lantern up high, lighting herself up too. Tall, and as straight as a hop-pole. Facially – well, Thérèse's adjective 'haggard' hadn't been any exaggeration. Of course the lighting didn't help: but black hair swept straight back, fixed somehow behind her head; pale, hawkish face, deepset eyes.

Wearing work-stained dungarees – at three thirty or four in the morning, for God's sake. She'd lowered the lantern, having completed her own inspection. 'What's your name?'

A window was pushed open, on the first floor of the house: a man's voice, questioning shakily in Alsatian.

'Excuse me. My father.' Raising her voice then, but surprisingly answering him in French: 'Thérèse Michon's in trouble, Papa. And we may have an overnight guest. *Another* one – but I'll handle it, don't worry.'

'What kind of trouble – Thérèse, you say—'

'I don't know – yet. Tell you later – or in the morning. Leave it to me – eh?' Back to Rosie: 'Well—'

'My name's Rosalie.' The window had banged shut, and one of the dogs had shifted in closer to her, flopped down again, watching. Wolfish: long-legged and scrawny – like its mistress. Marie turning away, the lamp swinging, shadows even of the crouched dogs elongating . . . 'Come in here. Théo – quiet . . . *Stay*, both of you. Come on . . .'

Inside a van was standing with its *gazo* motor dismantled. Partial explanation of the dungarees? Marie was hanging the lantern on a bracket: turning back to her now: a gaunt, strange-looking woman, frowning at her: 'Are you ill? Better sit down.' Reaching to flip down the lid of a tool-chest. 'There. How did you know of us – this farm's whereabouts, and my name?'

'Thérèse spoke of you quite often. And she told me where you lived.' Rosie sat down on the box very, very thankfully. 'No, I'm not ill, just – rather exhausted . . . But you, and people called Roesch she talked about – over *that* way? I've been with her almost a month – you wouldn't have known, I suppose.'

'We knew there was someone, that she had her hands full. It was necessary to know that much. Do you think it might have been you they were looking for tonight?'

'Might have, but I'd think more likely whoever was in the *gazogène* that came first. At least – how I've been thinking of it.' She shrugged. 'I was going to say – another reason for inflicting myself on you is a man by name of Michel – only one arm? He mentioned you when he brought me to Thérèse.'

'*He* brought you to her . . .'

'He was coming on to you, then. To fix a tractor – as a reason for being here? He and Luc?'

A nod. 'The last time I saw either of them. Yes – all right . . . How did you come to be with them?'

'I was a Gestapo prisoner, with some others, in a train taking us to Ravensbrück. We *thought* Ravensbrück . . . Well – the train stopped because of another which Michel had wrecked – blown the line the other side of it, I think – I made a break for it, and I was shot. Killed, they thought. But I wasn't, and – even *more* luck, later in the night Michel and Luc came along and found me.'

'And this was – yes, nearly a month ago . . . You're – recovered?'

'Pretty well. Thanks to Thérèse. And – Lotte.'

'Ah –' a nod – 'Lotte – of course . . .'

'I'm a bit weak still, not really fit, but—'

'You want to shelter here?'

'If you'd allow it. Not for long, I promise, but – maybe more than just one night – as you said to your father then—'

'Only to give him a quick answer. No – of course . . .'

'Well, thank you. But – Marie, if I may call you that – d'you think something may have happened to Michel?'

'*You* think it might have?'

'He said he'd be back in a few days – twenty-five days ago. He was going to put me in touch with certain people. And since I'm well enough to get moving now – I'd rather counted on his help, but—'

'I could find out. We'll talk later, anyway. After you've slept.' A grimace: 'Doubt *I'll* get any. You'll be wondering why I'm up all night, messing with *this* – eh?'

The van. The back of it hinged upwards, when lowered would serve as a ramp – for livestock, obviously. Rosie looked back at her, waited for the explanation.

'It's an emergency. You're a second stage of it. You heard me tell my father – *another* guest. We already have two – aviators, English. Royal Air Force. This explains the *gazo* you saw – they came in it. The person driving was a stranger to us, he'd come from the direction of Strasbourg, must have diverted to pick them up at some other place, and all he had then to guide him were the names of Thérèse Michon and of this village. He'd stopped twice to ask the way, he told me. An educated, intelligent person – doctor, I *guess* – but really, with no *idea* . . . Obviously it's whoever persuaded him to bring these two who should have known better.'

'You mean when he stopped to ask the way he somehow alerted the Gestapo?'

'No. Couldn't possibly. Couldn't have reacted that fast. Either *he'd* let it be known where he was going, or whoever gave him his instructions – God knows who, since because of you Thérèse was for the time being – off-bounds, you might say. Anyone working with us would have known it.'

'He left them here, and went on, then?'

'He shouldn't have gone near Thérèse. Some emergency, panic – someone arrested perhaps, another brought in to help but doesn't know enough, and – there you are. Could have been you or I, but in fact – Thérèse. She'd have sent him on to us here, of course.'

'I imagine you won't keep those two here any longer than you can help.'

'No. But we can't move them on immediately. Much as – yes, you're right . . . But I should have said – the *gazo*'s driver was *en route* to Colmar, I suspect to the hospital. If he's a doctor, as I've assumed – a certain manner, a certain smell, even – you know? – if I'm right about that he'd have an *Ausweis* permitting him to be out after curfew. Why they'd have thought to make use of him, you see.'

'And the Gestapo team couldn't have known how close they were behind him. Or that he'd have come on *this* way.'

'If they'd known there were aviators on the run, perhaps they had a tip-off – Thérèse's name, and where her farm was

. . . Maybe from whatever kind of mess it was at the other end. As you say, couldn't have known when he'd be there, let alone come on this way. So it was almost, but not quite, the worst of bad luck. Bad enough if they found Thérèse had been sheltering *someone.'*

'Me, though, not airmen, which they'd have been looking for, and with clothes around in the attic, where I was living. So they'll be looking for me now – some woman, anyway – *and* for your aviators?'

'Perhaps.' Narrow shoulders shrugging . . . 'Thérèse may have given an explanation for the clothes. Some child she'd looked after – something . . . She's no fool – won't tell them anything, either. That doctor, though – if they'd known his destination would be the Colmar hospital . . . That's what – worries . . . You see – they'd think, the main road to Colmar. Not this way. I mean they'd guess he'd go that way, and take that route themselves after Thérèse's place. One car anyway. Christ! Wouldn't want *him* caught. He was *here*, I accepted these two from him – and we know nothing of him!'

How he'd stand up to interrogation, for instance. Rosie nodding, understanding. Her heart had steadied somewhat, but this affected her too: that unidentified amateur arrested, spilling the beans, sending Gestapo *here* . . . Marie resuming – on a different tack now – 'What I was about to explain – why I need this vehicle back on the road at once now. Fact is, there's work for it to do before we can move those boys out . . . Oh, you're dead tired. I'll take you in, tell you as we go . . .'

The two airmen were in some outhouse, apparently. It would have been used for similar purposes before, Rosie guessed. Leading the way over to the house, Marie was explaining that she wouldn't be trying to move them on immediately; with the Gestapo alerted there might well be searches, road-blocks and so forth, but meanwhile she needed to have the van back on the road in any case. 'Moving lambs. We have a big crop of them, this year, I've set up some deals and they're about ready. Well, now instead of next week, that's all. It'll fit in well. Two or three trips – and then one more, and that time I'll have the two English on board and nobody'll spare us a glance.' She'd crossed herself: shifting the lamp to her other hand then as they reached the house, jerking a door open and leading the way into a stone-floored hallway: big kitchen off it to the right, two other rooms on the left, stairs rising at the back. It was more spacious than Thérèse's house. Marie stalking up the stairs, carrying the lantern, and Rosie following with her basket. Dark staircase leading to an equally dark passage, the lantern throwing shadows, Marie's positively gargantuan . . . Gloomy as well as spacious: she wouldn't have wanted to live here. Although for the present it was a refuge: safety, you might call it – until you heard those Citroëns come roaring into the yard, Gestapo spilling out – so damn sudden: out of nowhere. Well – out of other people's blunders. Nothing one could have influenced oneself or known anything about until disaster struck. The same, effectively, as being fingered by 'Hector': you'd have no chance, no more than a rabbit has when the noose jerks taut.

She felt the dizziness again. Heartbeat still wasn't right. Effort of climbing stairs, on top of earlier exertions. Rest, she told herself, was all she needed. Be fine, by morning. Bloody *have* to be . . . Left at the top, and Marie pointing: 'Bathroom, with *toilette*.' Then along the passage: 'This is where you can sleep. If I get time for any I'll use the couch downstairs, not to disturb you. Rosalie –' glancing round as she led the way in – 'May I ask where are you from, what did you do to be sent to Ravensbrück?'

Quite a large room. Two iron beds, one smaller than the other: hers, of course. She dumped her basket on it: feeling too exhausted to decide – faced with that question – how much or how little to divulge. Whether to explain herself at all . . .

'Could it wait until tomorrow?'

'Well – Michel knows your background, I imagine?'

'Oh, *yes*—'

'But you could be some person who was *not* with Thérèse – uh?'

'With a scarred face, to back up the deception? I've scars on my back too – a Gestapo whipping.'

Frowning, shaking her head . . . 'Says it all, doesn't it? In any case it's not that I disbelieve you. But – sit, just a minute? In case you sleep late . . . The thing is – Rosalie – I *could* send a message that would get to Michel – or to Luc – via their associate. If that's what you'd like?'

'Please. I'd like nothing better.'

'I have to warn them about Thérèse in any case. So at the same time I'll tell them you're here.'

Tell *them* . . . Struggling to think straight . . . The only person she wanted to know anything about her was Michel himself. On the other hand – thoughts of that unknown *gazo* driver in Gestapo hands: hence – potentially – extreme urgency. And Luc must know the contact whom Michel had mentioned – 'king pin in the Resistance', he'd called him – who had access to an SOE *réseau*. Might well be this so-called 'associate'. In any case, contacting Michel – or Luc – was her only good way out of this. She nodded to Marie – who'd perched herself on the edge of the other bed – upright, gauntly dark, white-faced, long muscular-looking neck, straight nose jutting: posed there like a cormorant on a rock – who might take off, alternatively might spread her wings to dry . . . Smiling – Rosie was – not only at the imagery, but *liking* her, for being – well, frankly unprepossessing, not getting much out of life but still putting it – her life – on the line, for those airmen for instance, and now for *her*. She nodded, to that question about telling Michel and Luc and whoever else it was – 'Yes, tell them, please. But – incidentally – Thérèse was worried for Michel too. Couldn't she have got news of him the same way?'

'No. *I* am the communications link with that person.'

'Then she could have, through you?'

'Perhaps. But one tries to minimize—'

'Of course.' Lines of communication were potentially insecure: the less you used them, the less that applied. Thérèse probably hadn't liked to ask. OK, it made sense . . . 'Marie – I *will* tell you. Better you should know, anyway. I'm an agent of SOE – Special Operations Executive. I was on the run and the Boches caught me, now I'm on the run again.'

'But they think you're dead?'

'I hope they do.'

'And you're English?'

'My mother is. Father was French – so *I* am. He died, she took me to live in England. But that's – who, and what.'

Slow nodding. 'One understands – Ravensbrück . . . But I wonder also – is your aim now to return to England?'

'Oh.' Shutting her eyes for a moment. Still not entirely sure. She temporized: 'A lot depends on Michel.'

'The two airmen we have here, you see – I can't say how long it may take, once I send them on, but—'

'I could go that way too, you mean.'

Thinking about it: concentrating . . . Imagining herself in that situation: what one might call the line of least resistance. A parcel – to be passed from hand to hand, shipped out, no longer functional . . . Looking up again, meeting Marie's questioning, perhaps slightly impatient gaze. She shook her head. 'Only if we *can't* contact Michel. All right?'

Chapter 5

July 31st: just post-dawn, with the sun coming up out of Germany and gilding the round-topped mountains. It looked clear up there, those balloon-tops already hard-edged, although at this level mist still hung like smoke. Rosie adding her own small quota to it – smoke from a Caporal: all right, Occupation-type Caporal, naturally, with probably as much sawdust in it as tobacco, but still a smoke – courtesy of Marie, who'd be reimbursed eventually by 'F' Section SOE for all of this, and not least for the risk of her own and her father's life.

Rosie had told her ten minutes ago, when leaving the kitchen to get herself ready for departure, 'I'll never forget you *or* Thérèse, Marie. Or cease to be grateful to Michel . . .'

'Give him my regards, when you see him?'

She wasn't sure she *would* be seeing Michel. Or even that he was still alive. Marie was simply assuming that he was, that he *must* be. So OK, share that faith . . . But Marie's telephone call had come from Luc and had said nothing except that this priest, Father Gervais, would be coming to fetch her. Hadn't even said that – only that he'd be passing, fetching some woman who'd been staying with cousins in Colmar but whose ancient mother was dying and asking for her, and Luc had told him the Destiniers were good friends and very hospitable, would surely give him/them a meal and a bed for the night. It hadn't been necessary to say more – there was only one way it made any sense. Father Gervais had duly arrived – last evening, and stayed overnight; it was for him that Rosie was waiting now in the yard. He'd been out here before breakfast, to flash up the charcoal burner on his *gazo*: she could see the red glow of it over there, beside the barn. The *gazo* belonged to some well-heeled parishioner who often allowed him the use of it, he'd told them. Parish of Dieuze, forty kilometres east of Nancy, on the road from here to Metz. That was how he'd put it: whether it meant they'd be taking her on to Metz she didn't know, but it had sounded like it. Made no odds, she was in their hands – for the time being, in this padre's – and she didn't *have* to know – beyond the fact that she was now Justine Quérier, and had papers to prove it. She'd memorized the details – date of birth, home address – her mother's – mother's name Hortense – et cetera. The scars on her forehead were attributable to her having been injured in Rouen in an air-raid: she'd had a teaching job in Rouen at that time, but since sustaining the injury to her head that night she hadn't been able to concentrate too well.

The real Justine was deceased, a former resident of Sarrebourg, where she'd been a teacher in kindergarten. (Ostensibly – fictionally – before moving to Rouen, of course.) Height and weight were all right – roughly – but for the date of birth, which also matched Rosie's approximately, grey hair was definitely wrong. Her scarf would cover it, as long as she was careful, but if she was going to have to rely on these papers for any length of time she'd have to bleach and dye herself back to normal. A bit of a toss-up either way: she felt she needed the grey hair. While the photo on the identity document was a bigger and more immediate problem: would have been fairly miraculous if it *had* resembled her at all: and it did not. The most fundamental difference was that Justine's face had been fat, with virtually no bone-structure visible, and the only solution or partial solution – arrived at in discussion last night between Rosie and Marie – had been to put padding in her cheeks, strips cut from an old shirt and folded over and over into wads.

She still didn't look like Justine. Different, certainly: not much like Rosie Ewing either.

A voice behind her: hand on her shoulder: 'Keeping you waiting, is he?'

Otto Destinier – Marie's father. Jerking his head back towards the kitchen, referring to the priest: Rosie moving out of the doorway, not only making way for him but having learnt to keep a certain distance. He was in his sixties, tall and stooped: clearly it was from him that Marie had inherited her hop-pole figure. Rosie had made friends with him during her few days here by taking an interest in his vines and wine-making equipment and techniques: old oak barrels which he'd said his grandfather had used, for instance.

'Early to work, M'sieur?'

'No earlier than usual.' He had a pipe going, with tobacco in it that he'd grown himself. A lot of tobacco was grown around here, apparently. 'But it's high time you and Monsieur l'Abbé were on the road.' Thin smile, then: thin face, sparse grey hair, blue eyes – which his daughter had *not* inherited. Poking at Rosie's arm with a gnarled forefinger: 'Be sure he keeps his eyes on the road and his hands on the wheel, eh?'

Imagination stemming from his own inclinations, no doubt. And for 'smile', read 'leer'. Like an old goat – truly not unlike one, and regarded locally as pro-German. Marie had surprised her with this information when discussing arrangements for getting the two RAF men away – Bob, who'd been the Halifax's flight engineer, and Arnold its mid-upper gunner. They'd left on Saturday in the van, sharing the back of it with a dozen twelve-week-old lambs – Marie's third delivery trip in the course of the weekend. In reference to the chances of being stopped and searched she'd told Rosie that, thanks to some well-publicized remarks attributed to her father in the early thirties, both he and she were regarded by the Boches as '*V-männer*' – *Vertrauensmänner* – meaning trusted people, French pro-Nazis. Otto Destinier's mother had been German – hence the name he'd been christened with – and a decade ago he'd gone on record as saying that Adolph Hitler was the sort of man they needed in France, the country being stiff with Jews and bolshies, and so forth. He'd changed his views since then – Marie had added, if they'd ever been his views, not just ill-judged self-advertising when he'd been standing for the office of president of some wine-growers' association in which the Germanic element had been numerous – but some of the local people of French origin, the Destinier family's natural friends and associates, were still wary of him.

'In some ways it's advantageous. For instance, this business now – if they're searching—'

'Won't come here?'

A shrug. 'Can't guarantee they wouldn't, but on the other hand we aren't automatically regarded as suspect – despite our French blood. So as far as other French-origin *Alsaciens* are concerned – you can imagine—'

'When the Boches are kicked out, will you have problems?'

'No. Or anyway not for long.' She'd pointed to the blue-hazed mountains. 'Plenty up there, who'll put the record straight. And plenty down here who've done damn-all, who'll have *that* to answer for. Resistance friends elsewhere too – in particular, I might say, the man I telephoned, who passed my message on to Luc. He carries weight, that one.'

Michel's 'associate', no doubt.

Old Destinier had stooped, giraffe-like, kissed her cheek. Stubbled face, rank tobacco smell. 'Leave you now. I've already taken my leave of Monsieur l'Abbé. I wish you a safe journey and a long and happy life, Mam'selle Rosalie.'

'I can't thank you enough – you and—'

'Thank *her*, not me. Adieu . . .'

Shuffling away, as the others came out. Marie was carrying the priest's small bag of personal effects, since he was laden with bottles of the previous year's Destinier Riesling. Marie told Rosie, 'Half of that's for Luc – or Michel, or both.'

Rosie smilea at the priest: '*Isn't* she kind?'

'One of her virtues, surely.' He was about Rosie's age: anyway not more than thirty. Slim, of average height, with a rather long, pale face, humorous mouth and eyes. Taking his bag from Marie, carrying it and the wine over to his *gazo*; the dogs were snuffling around. Rosie picked up her basket – right-handed, still wearing the sling, although the time might have come to discard it now. 'You're very efficient as well as kind, Marie. To have arranged this so quickly—'

'Luc's doing, not mine.'

'Those others weren't. The aviators. And you did set this up.' She shook her head. 'The one really *awful* thing is Thérèse; if you do get word of her—'

'I'll pass it along.'

The priest had conducted a Mass for Thérèse, last night. Since the Gestapo had taken her there'd been no news at all. Marie had paid a neighbourly call down there on the Friday evening, had found nephew Charles coping all right but knowing nothing beyond the fact that the place had been ransacked and his aunt had been arrested.

'Well – *first* thing he found was the dog's corpse in the yard.'

'Oh, God, I should've buried it, or—'

'How could you, you had to clear out quick.'

'But *poor* Charles!'

'Don't worry. He's no softie. Got his head screwed on, that kid.'

He'd found the place deserted except for hungry animals and an unmilked cow – on the Thursday evening – and next morning his mother had called at the police station, where they'd only confirmed that her sister had been taken into custody by 'the military authorities'. Marie had let the boy believe this was the first she'd known of it. But she'd be going back down there this evening to see if there was anything she could do – might for instance bring the cow up here so at least he wouldn't have the milking chore. He'd have more time soon anyway, with school holidays starting in about a week.

She said quietly – about Thérèse – while Father Gervais was busy with the *gazo*, 'If they decide they've reason to keep her – or send her away—'

'Please God they won't.'

'– *if* they do, they're liable also to burn her place down. It's happened before – teach the rest of us a lesson . . . But her best hope may be that they'll soon be racing to put the Rhine between themselves and us. Unless they try to hold the mountains. My father thinks they wiil. They're thick enough on the ground in the valley here, God knows, he *may* be right . . .'

There'd been good news, over Swiss radio. The Americans had smashed their way through at St Lô – on the Tuesday, and the day after – Wednesday 26th, the day Rosie had arrived here, limping into this yard at about three in the morning – they'd taken Coutances, which according to the commentator was a major strategic gain.

Crossing her fingers. Still a hell of a long way from *here*. Something to be said for that, too: Boches still in Paris, Gestapo presumably still in Rue des Saussaies, 'Hector' – touch wood – not yet gone to ground.

A shout from the priest: 'Are you ready, Mam'selle?' He had the engine running: then the *gazo* rolling out. Father Gervais braking, then leaning over to push the passenger door open. 'All aboard!'

They came up the winding mountain road into a sudden blaze of sunshine – then plunged back into forest. Sun breaking through again intermittently as the road cut to and fro. Roller-coaster country, with impressive views occasionally where the trees thinned or drew back briefly from the unpaved, winding road. More a track, in fact, than a road. Father Gervais had a pencil sketch of his route, with notes and names of villages: one called Villé, they'd just passed through.

'Pretty, eh?'

'Yes. But – so different . . .'

'You mean Germanic?'

'I suppose. I was thinking Austrian – even Swiss.'

'You could be right. The carved sign on that inn, for instance . . . Life's hard up here in winter, I'm told. Did you notice how the houses have their backs to the road, open into their own small courtyards?'

'Yes – I suppose so . . . But you've been over these mountains before, have you, Father?'

'Not for years. And not this part, even then. No –' touching his crumpled map – 'without our mutual friend Luc's guidance, we'd be nowhere.'

'D'you know him well?'

'No. Not well. You?'

'I'm not sure I'll even recognize him when I see him. *If* I'm going to. Even Michel – whom you don't know well either, I heard you tell Marie.'

'Getting round to the question you really want to ask, how come I'm involved with these people at all – eh?'

'Well.' She shrugged. 'One's curious, naturally.'

'And the answer's simple. If a blacksmith can be a *résistant*: if a baker or a bank-clerk can be – and if priests can serve in armies, in uniforms of sorts?'

'Of course . . . But do your superiors know about it?'

'Would the bank-clerk's branch manager know?'

She shrugged. 'Only if he was involved too, I suppose. Obviously you've been asked such questions before.'

'May I ask some of you?'

'Why not? Long drive ahead of us, after all.'

He'd taken a right turn on to an even narrower, rougher track. They were up high, by this time. Glancing at her . . . 'I think first I'll yield to temptation, and accept the smoke you offered me. Mine are in my case behind us – as I don't usually smoke before midday, I thought I wouldn't—'

'No excuses are necessary, Father. I'm dying for one.' She fingered two of Marie's Caporals out of the packet, and gave him one. For the past hour or so *she'd* been resisting the temptation, under the impression that he was a non-smoker and might prefer it if she didn't. But a box of matches had materialized in his nearer hand. 'If you wouldn't mind—'

'Of course.'

He explained, 'Going this way – from that last turn, if you noticed – not much of a road, but –' leaning over to the match, then back again – 'thanks. If we'd held straight on, the way I came yesterday, we'd end up passing through a village called Rothau – just south of Schirmeck – where in the first place they were stopping everyone – all right, may not be doing so now, and nothing so *very* alarming about it even if they were—'

'And in the second place?'

He glanced at her, looked away again. Expelling smoke . . . 'Going this way instead – avoid Rothau, that's all.'

'But *what* in the second place, Father?'

'Well.' Shift of gear. 'If you insist . . .'

'I don't, if it bothers you so much.' The explanation hit her, then: she nodded. 'Natzweiler's somewhere around here, of course.'

He'd grimaced. 'Sooner not have mentioned it *or* gone near it. Rothau's the station for that place, though, and it's – very picturesque.'

'Christ.'

'Well – I should take you to task—'

'Yes – I'm sorry—'

'– but in the face of *that* . . .' He'd paused. Shaking his head. 'There's also a stone quarry – right beside the road – in which they work their prisoners to death . . . But listen, now – by way of changing the subject. Dress-rehearsal – imagine they've stopped us, I'm a German quizzing you. I've taken your papers, I want the answers off pat – OK?'

'Go ahead.'

'Name?'

'Justine Quérier.'

'Address?'

'Sarrebourg. Well – Souillac, Rue Celeste.'

'Place and date of birth?'

'Sarrebourg, 1917 – November 13th. About a year older than I really am, therefore.'

'Father's name and occupation?'

'Joseph Quérier, post-office clerk. Mother Hortense Quérier, née Lebarque. She's dying, she sent you to fetch me.'

'Didn't *send* me. As your *curé* and your mother's, I came, that's all. What were you doing in Colmar?'

'Oh – staying with a cousin. For – a rest . . . In fact *near* Colmar, not right in it. At home I've been looking after old Mama, you see – since a house fell on me, in Rouen . . .'

'House fell on you: I like that. Not trying to amuse, either.' A nod . . . 'You're an actress – as well as whatever else . . .

So – a question you would *not* answer, if a German asked it. Are you a very *experienced* agent?'

'Agent?'

'You said I could ask questions.'

'There are questions *and* questions, Father.'

'Well.' The cigarette – what was left of it – waggling between his thin lips, ash scattering over one lapel. 'I'll try a different approach. What drives you?'

'Drives me?'

A nod. 'Question perhaps more to your liking. I thought – less technical, more personal.'

She drew on her cigaarette. 'Still not an easy one to answer.'

'I'd have thought you'd have had it settled it in your mind from the outset. You'd have volunteered – effectively to live and work under constant threat, extreme personal danger, twenty-four hours a day?'

'You make it sound –' She checked herself: 'I mean, it's not *always*—'

'Is the driving force simply patriotism?'

'I love France – certainly.' She shrugged. 'And I hate Germans. And they have to be defeated, so—'

'Hate them for what they're doing to France?'

'Yes – and to *us*. Well – we *are* France.'

'You don't hate them simply for being German – like not liking cats . . .'

'It does come down to that, though. What they do becomes what they *are*.'

'Except some might only be doing what they're forced to do, they'd be shot if they didn't?'

'Would *you* do disgusting things to people if you were told you'd be shot if you didn't?'

'I *hope* not. But if I came from an entirely different background – if I hadn't been imbued from an early age with certain ethical standards, moral precepts—'

'They're supposed to have those standards too, surely. It's one of the things that sicken me. They actually go to church, call themselves Christians!'

'They've had other ideas drilled into them more recently. What *they'd* call patriotism and don't see as conflicting with their religion. Well, of course, they've accepted the doctrine of violence and their own superiority far too readily – a defect that *is* in their blood, maybe – in your own view, what they *are*, therefore . . . Have you seen – you personally, Rosalie, at first hand – examples of the sort of brutality – what you called disgusting things—'

'Very *much* at first hand.'

'Really.' He was following her example, squeezing his cigarette stub into the dashboard ashtray. This had been a very luxurious automobile, in its day. Dashboard of bird's-eye maple, for instance. Glancing at her again: 'You've faced torture, you mean?'

'Yes.'

'And not given way?'

'Actually, not. But on one occasion – to tell you the absolute truth, if it had gone on a minute longer—'

'But it didn't, and you did *not* give way.' Looking at her: she'd shaken her head. He was watching the road again: 'You can thank God for your strength then. Be proud of it, too – and my admiration is unlimited, Rosalie – but as I say—'

'I *would* have given way. Another few seconds.'

'What was at stake? It was an interrogation, obviously—'

'They wanted names and addresses, mainly.'

'Which you did have?' He saw her nod. 'Of *résistants*?'

'Yes.'

'Who'd then have been arrested, I suppose.'

'Shot, or sent to the camps. Tortured first – for *other* names.'

'I wonder if you would have given in.'

'Yes, I would have. I'm not going to tell you what they were doing—'

'My guess is you might not have.' Looking at her again: several quick glances between her and the twisting road ahead. 'I think it's conceivable that you wouldn't. With those other lives at stake – don't you think – when the moment came you might have found you *couldn't* – however much you *wanted* to?'

'No. Much as I'd like to say "yes" to that. There's a point at which pain – and terror of even worse pain – and mutilation – unless one's lucky enough to faint, of course—'

'Ah . . .'

'Answer *me* a question, Father?'

'Go on.'

'If a German – say Gestapo, but any of them – came to confession and told you of unspeakable things he'd done—'

'It would depend on the genuineness or otherwise of his contrition. Of course you realize that fewer than half of them are Catholics – besides which, they have their own military padres—'

'If this one said he was very sorry and he'd never do it again, tra-la, you'd give him absolution?'

Tight-faced, staring at the road ahead. Working his jaw-muscles, she saw, like pulses. Glancing round at her then: 'Give me another cigarette?'

Over a crest, a few kilometres after passing through another village. Then a left. The sun was high and hot: downhill now, the narrow road cut like a furrow into wide-open slopes curving down to blueish woodland. Cattle were grazing: further back there'd been sheep daubed with paint. In forest again then, the heavy green meeting overhead, shutting out the sky. The road was even more twisting than it had been, with several especially sharp bends. Near the bottom of this bit, Father Gervais told her, they'd be joining a road coming from the village that he'd avoided and bringing them to Schirmeck.

'Where we turn west, to the Col de Donon. Steep drop then.'

He hadn't been talking much, in the last few kilometres. Might still have been grappling with her question about the granting of absolution to torturers: pondering either the question itself or perhaps her brashness in challenging him with it. He had – or was supposed to have – his cast-iron certainties, and she had her – all right, prejudices. Even if, to her, they amounted to certainties. And right now, he was helping to save her life. Which wasn't a *small* thing. As she'd pointed out to the two airmen, Bob and Arnold, when they'd been grousing about being cooped up for so long, complaining that they might almost as well have just hoofed it, travelling by night and hiding by day in ditches, making towards Normandy and the Allied lines – she'd pointed out to them that if they were caught by the Boches, they'd only need to show their service identity discs and they'd suffer no worse fate than being shipped off to a POW camp, whereas any French man or woman caught helping them would be put against a wall and shot, or beaten to death in the course of interrogation, or consigned to some resort such as Buchenwald or Natzweiler. Also the fact that for every escapee who made it back to England via an escape line, an average of twelve to twenty French people would knowingly have accepted that risk.

She hadn't told the boys in blue who or what she was. To them she was only a French woman who happened to speak perfect English.

Father Gervais was crushing the stub of his second cigarette. He'd just shifted up another gear: they were

climbing again, after that long sweep down through forest.
He glanced her way, found her eyes on him and cocked an
eyebrow: 'All right?'

'Yes. But one thing I'd like to say – while it's in my
mind—'

'Go on, then.'

'Only that I'm very conscious of the risk you're running
– for a total stranger, at that. One tends to take such things
for granted, I'm afraid.'

'*Should* be able to. We're on the same side, after all. Now
I've got something to say too. We have Marie's bread and
cheese in the back there, but at the present rate of progress
we'll be in Dieuze by about midday. So we'd better eat
lunch quite early. All right with you?'

'Perfectly all right. We did start early, didn't we? But do
you and I separate at Dieuze?'

'Yes. That's the plan.'

In Schirmeck there was a road-block, at the junction. Striped
poles blocked off the right-hand half of the road from each
direction, with two French *gendarmes* at each barrier and
a *Wehrmacht* truck with helmeted soldiers in it parked
opposite the turn-off.

'Don't be anxious now, Justine.'

'Well, of course not . . .'

Except for a familiar hollow in the gut, damp palms,
accelerated pulse-rate. Just *normally* accelerated, not going
crazy. Despite the fact she'd been through about a hundred
checkpoints before this, but never with papers as flawed as
Justine Quérier's. Also, desperate to adjust the headscarf,
restraining herself only with difficulty from what might
seem a display of nervousness. She had discarded her
sling, thank God, pushed it under the seat soon after
they'd started out. Father Gervais bringing the *gazo* to
a halt – both front windows were already wound right

down – and one of the pair of *gendarmes* from the barrier in front of them approaching the driver's side. Checking the registration plate on his way.

Stooping at that open window.

'Your papers, Father?'

'Of course. I should mention this vehicle is borrowed, not my own.' Extracting his and presumably the *gazo*'s documentation from a wallet. A smile at Rosie: 'He'll want to see yours too, Justine.'

'That's a fact. I will.' A small, polite smile revealed a gap in his front teeth. He also had a little moustache that might have been pencilled on, sticking-out ears and close-cropped hair greying at the temples. There was no traffic anywhere within sight or sound, no pedestrians either. This *gendarme*'s partner was leaning against the wall at the corner, picking his teeth or nose, and the other pair were chatting to the Boches in the truck.

'What's the purpose of your journey, Father?'

'Collecting this young lady from relations near Colmar, bringing her home to Sarrebourg. Her mother's very ill.' He dropped his voice. 'In fact, dying. And this one isn't – well – isn't *entirely*—'

Facing this way, she could only guess at his expression, but the *gendarme* was looking sympathetic. Father Gervais accepting his papers back. 'Now *your* papers, Justine.'

The tone you might use to a child; but the *gendarme* cut in with 'We won't bother with those.' Quick shake of the head, and Father Gervais looking at him in surprise; Rosie with her papers already held out in that direction, not having heard what he'd said but suspecting the scarf *had* shifted, might have uncovered the scar over her ear – so obviously from a bullet – might also have revealed grey hair, while Justine Quérier's age was shown in her papers as – what, twenty-seven. Father Gervais had put his hand on hers, pushing it and the papers back on to her lap: 'He doesn't want to see them.' Nodding to the *gendarme* then: 'Thank you.'

Straightening, touching the peak of his *képi*. 'Drive on, Father.'

From Schirmeck to the Col du Donon was about ten kilo-metres, all of it at that high level: the village of Donon itself then, before the nose-dive to the plain, a drop of maybe a thousand metres in what seemed like no time at all. Several more sharp turns at the bottom put them on the road to the next village on Luc's list – Abreschviller.

'Sounds German.'

'Not unusual, in these parts. But long before that, there's a bridge over a river—'

'The Meurthe?'

'No. The Meurthe is – back *that* way. About twenty-five kilometres, I'd guess, to its nearest point. This is quite a small river – where the bridge is, anyway. May I think be a tributary of the Sarre. As in Sarrebourg?'

'Right.'

'Does the Meurthe mean something to you?'

'I knew it was – hereabouts, that's all.'

Where the train had stopped and she'd made her short dash, where Lise might or might not have gone into the river. Somewhere – Rosie had worked it out with Thérèse – on the Nancy side of Baccarat, probably. But that question about Lise: she'd lived with it for a month, almost dreaded having an answer before much longer.

Because it wouldn't be a *good* answer.

Father Gervais continuing, 'Anyway – near that bridge might be a good place to stop and have our snack. And I can replenish with charcoal.'

There was a sack of it, he'd mentioned, in the boot. Into which, incidentally, the *gendarme* hadn't even glanced. Might have been full of Sten-guns – anything. Zeal fading, maybe, with Allied armies breaking out of Normandy? She touched bird's-eye maple, asked, 'How far to Dieuze?'

'From Abreschviller –' consulting his notes – 'on the small roads we'll be using – about forty kilometres. From here – say fifty. Hour and a half, maybe.'

'And you remain there, do you – in Dieuze?'

'No. *You* do.' Quick smile: 'Only as a staging-point, don't worry.'

Heading near enough due north now, she guessed. They'd stopped at the bridge, got the bread and farmhouse cheese out and made manageable sandwiches of it, he'd topped up the charcoal burner, they'd each made a short promenade – in opposite directions – through the wood. Then got started again, eating as they drove.

Abreschviller – after about twenty kilometres. Then Lorquin: and over a canal, taking a back road into Sarrebourg – which wasn't as large a place as she'd expected – turning left in the centre of it, over the river Sarre and then out northwestward, another winding lane that seemed to go on for ever. Only farm traffic on it. He was staying clear of main roads of course, where checkpoints were more likely: was well aware – admitted it *now*, hadn't earlier – that Justine Quérier's papers wouldn't have stood up to very close inspection.

'But I keep them when you leave me in Dieuze?'

'Might as well. Luc'll get them back to me. By the way, I should apologise for giving that *gendarme* the impression that you might be brain-damaged?'

'Perfectly all right. Might adopt the idea myself, in fact. As long as I'm looking as I am, anyway.'

'As you are?' Glancing at her curiously. 'What d'you mean?'

'All scars. And tufty grey hair. Sort of – demented.'

'But that's nonsense. And I assure you, the scars aren't as

noticeable as you may imagine. And since your hair's covered by the scarf – you dyed it grey, Marie mentioned . . .'

He was looking at her mouth: and quickly away then, at the road ahead. Men did tend to focus on her mouth; Ben had referred to it once as her I'll-eat-you-alive mouth. But in her present state – and from a priest?

Marie might have told him that she was sensitive about her changed appearance. Morale-building exercise? Imagining that strange-looking woman murmuring to him, *Look, Father, if you get a chance* . . .

Wouldn't put it past either of them.

Crossroads, finally, at a place called Espérance; they were turning left, westward, having been on that road from Sarrebourg for about twenty kilometres; it would be another ten from this point to Dieuze, he said. She put her head back, closed her eyes, thinking about Michel and Luc and the next stage, getting in touch at last with 'F' Section. Which would lead to Ben hearing she was alive – probably. *If* he'd been given reason to believe she might be dead . . . In any case a huge improvement would be that one way or another she'd be on the move, at last. A month had been far too long to be helpless, making virtually no decisions for herself. Not given to self-analysis, she hadn't appreciated until now how much she *needed* to have the reins in her own hands – how she always *had*, until just recently.

Well – for quite some time. Since Johnny had been killed, and meeting Ben, and joining SOE . . .

'Rosalie?'

Michel's voice . . .

'Uh?'

Stirring: as a front wheel thumped jarringly through a pot-hole. Not Michel's voice, nothing like it. Father Gervais's – telling her, 'Dieuze. We're here. Wake up, Rosalie!'

'I was dreaming . . .'

'I know you were.'

But how could this be Dieuze already, when only a few minutes ago – or so it seemed—

'River down there is the Seille. Rises near here, flows right up through Metz, in fact it joins in with the Moselle there . . . But I've turned off the road we were on, d'you see – that one continues west to Nancy. And here now, around this corner – oh, hold on . . .'

Two *Feldgendarmes*, Boche military police, watched the *gazo* as it swung around the bend. Field uniforms, boots, caps not helmets, slung Schmeisser submachine guns. Watching all and any passing traffic, she supposed: or just sunning themselves, browning their pink-pig faces. Or even – for heaven's sake – just waiting to cross the road. Out of sight now; Father Gervais muttering something to himself, perhaps a prayer of thanks. There was a church on a rise, rather isolated on this edge of the village – southern edge, the position of the sun told her – and below the road on the other side, the left, a view of the continuance of the river winding through pasture where cattle grazed. It looked cool down there.

She hadn't realized the church was their destination until they were pulling up at the gate in the iron railings.

'You have that basket, haven't you? I'll bring it: you can have it in the pew beside you. All right?'

'If that fits into the programme . . .'

'We're a little early, that's all.'

'This is your church, is it?'

'No.' He'd got out: she did the same; he took her basket out of the boot and joined her on the pavement. Glancing back towards that corner, but the *Feldgendarmes* hadn't come this way. Answering her question: 'No – I'm based in Sarrebourg. The priest here – he knows what we're doing, there's no problem – is Father Matthieu. Listen: you'll be picked up either by Luc or one of his colleagues, who'll know you as Justine Quérier. You're to be in the seventh pew from the back, in the right-hand section. Your mother, as you know, is very seriously ill; it would be appropriate if you were kneeling. I – Father Gervais, from Sarrebourg – have arranged for you to be met here and taken to her. In Metz, by the way.'

Walking up the gravelled path towards the church's carved oak doors. Sun like a furnace blazing down. 'So Mama's in Metz, now.'

'Yes. In hospital. Whoever comes for you—'

'Luc, or—'

'Some parishioner of mine, helping out. It's been arranged for you, that's all, you *can* be a little – well, disorientated.'

'Brain-damaged.'

'If you like.' He stopped, just short of the doors. 'I'll see you into your pew now, but first –' putting the basket down, and taking her hands in his – 'Rosalie – God bless you, and keep you safe.'

'And you. Bless *you*, for all you've done.'

Half that parcel of wine was for Luc, she remembered. But she didn't want the weight of it in her basket, so didn't remind him. He took her arm: 'Seventh pew from the back, on the right. Come on.'

A priest passed through, once, burly in his soutane, pausing halfway up the aisle to look back at her before continuing and vanishing through a door leading, she supposed, into the sacristy. Her knees ached. Having no watch she had no clear idea of how long she'd been here, but it couldn't have been less than an hour.

Tempting to push herself up, and sit: but safer to endure the ache. Why *would* a scruffily dressed, battered-looking female spend hours in a church just sitting?

Enjoying the cool, perhaps . . .

And allowing the mind to wander.

See you quite soon, Ben darling . . .

Forget about 'Hector'? Signal them only that you're here, more or less mended, would be glad of a Lysander pick-up?

No – not Lysander. A Lysander didn't have the range. Hudson, probably.

But ask, *Did Lise make it?*

Knowing damn well she wouldn't have. It had to be at least ten to one against her having survived at all, maybe a hundred to one against her having got right away. Therefore, in whatever signal one sent, tell 'F' section about 'Hector' – confirmation that he *was* a traitor, working for the Gestapo. If Lise had got through, they'd know it already; but she wouldn't have, she'd have gone as surely as Alain Noally had gone – devastating the last weeks of her life. During that time the harsh fact of his death would have been a lot harder to bear than anything the bastards had done to her.

Even the business of the fingernails. One hand entirely nail-less.

'Hector' certainly deserved to hang. Die anyway: but preferably on a rope.

Christian thoughts, these, from the seventh pew from the back of this very old, very beautiful small church. Thoughts – or a fixation, aberration? What Father Gervais had sensed, perhaps? But what *about* an eye for an eye, a tooth for a tooth? Not that one was contemplating striking bargains or fair exchanges: she whispered in her mind, *I confess it, God. Mary Mother of Jesus, I'll tell you too, I want the bastard dead.* Her face in her hands, head bowed, knees aching – partly because in Rouen a year ago a sod of a Gestapo interrogator had made her kneel on the edge of a shovel's blade, the blade then being angled upward by the weight of another thug, a heavyweight, standing on the shovel's handle. That had been just one of the preliminaries, a warm-up to the main event – courtesy of the people 'Hector' worked for. Her eyes moving while she thought about it – peering out between her fingers, appreciating the church's cool, shadowed depths and remembering how when Ben had first seen those scars he'd hugged her knees and kissed them, tears glistening in his eyes.

Smiling to herself; thinking, *Some tough old salt, my Bim-Bam* . . .

'Rosalie?'

She'd jumped . . .

'Sorry. Woke you, uh?'

A long, angular figure in a workman's overalls slid into the pew beside her – into a forward-leaning position with his behind pushed right back on the bench and elbows on his knees, having then to twist half sideways to allow for his length of leg. 'Congratulations – such a quick recovery.' Glancing round, light-eyed in the gloom: he'd brought with him an aroma of machine oil. Attention back on her then: gleam of teeth as well as eyes. She'd replaced the padding that fattened her face, having had a rest from it for a while.

'Sorry if I've kept you waiting.'

'Great to see you, Luc.'

'Same here.' His grin might have been described as wolfish, but it was also shy. All right, a *shy* wolf . . . 'I'm taking you to our dump in Metz – OK?'

Chapter 6

He'd parked his *gazo* on the other side of the road, further along, where there was a gate into the slope of field above that river view. An observer wouldn't have reckoned on its driver being in the church: truck with open-topped load-space containing a set of tractor tyres, some fence-posts and coils of wire, and the inscription on its tail-gate reading DP AGRICULTURAL ENGINEERS, and in smaller print below RAOUL DE PLESSE, METZ.

So Michel's 'associate' had a name, now.

Luc took her basket from her, gave her a hand up into the passenger seat then pushed it in beside her feet. Wordless, pushing the door shut then: Rosie with the impression that he was still thinking of her as an invalid. Watching him go round the front to his own side: he had a strangely dipping, long-strided walk – a lope, that went well with the working clothes, his disguise as a mechanic, but you'd never have taken him for a captain or lieutenant – whichever he was. The light-coloured eyes, she remembered, and the voice, but nothing else, not for instance the narrowish, fine-boned face. He'd been in the sun a bit: made his eyes look even lighter.

He'd climbed in, pulled that door shut. 'On our way, then.'

'How far, roughly?'

'The slow way, maybe seventy-five kilometres. Slow way because your papers aren't all they might be, uh?'

'Getting papers at all, at such short notice—'

'Thanks to the bishop . . .' He had the truck moving. 'Listen – cover-story is I'm taking you to the hospital – in Metz, being on my way back there anyway, the Father asked would I drop you off? Sick mother there – right?'

'Which hospital?'

'Let's be vague. I'd need to ask where it was, anyway. But – Thérèse was arrested, is that right?'

She told him about it, while he circled back towards the centre of the village and then turned off to the left, on to a country road leading out northwestward.

'No word since, eh?'

'Nothing. Marie Destinier – well, if she hears anything I imagine she'd let you know.'

'We're not likely to be down that way again. At least, I'm not, and Michel won't be around anyway . . . Invasion forces on the move at last – you hear about it?'

'Yes – now and then—'

'Once it gets going, it'll be an avalanche. A few weeks, no more, we'll be back to real soldiering. Please God . . .'

'Don't like what you're doing now?'

'This undercover stuff . . . No, not so much. We're not one of what they're calling the Jedburgh groups, you understand.'

'No, I don't.'

'Inter-allied groups, dropped to work with Maquis forces. They're in uniform. All over France now. At this end – well, when the fighting comes closer *we* can put on uniform, stop pussy-footing around . . . Meanwhile I can tell you we've been busy enough – so have the Maquis.'

'I believe you. We heard – at Thérèse's – that a lot of bridges had been blown?'

'Delaying the transfer of a Boche armoured division from Strasbourg to the Normandy front by more than three weeks.'

'*That's* something!'

Nodding, hunched over the wheel: 'It's not all, either.'

'You say Michel won't be around?'

'He'll tell you himself. You'll see him quite soon, don't worry; but – it's not strictly my business, what he's up to. Only to the extent that I'm taking over his job here. Well, he's set it all up now, to that extent it's *done* – only a matter of – you know, keeping tabs, and waiting for the serious stuff to start – eh?'

'So he's – what, going back to your regiment?'

'No. New assignment. Nothing I can talk about – well, obviously . . .'

'How did you come to be in this sort of undercover work, Luc?'

'Michel, is how.' Tight corner: dragging the wheel over . . . 'He was a natural for it because of his missing arm – who'd imagine he'd have *dropped* in? Or be any threat to them? Well, *that's* a laugh, believe me. But mostly they're surprised he can manage a few nuts and bolts . . . Anyway, he was allowed to pick his own team, I'd been one of his platoon commanders, and – there you are.'

'Or rather, here *you* are. Is he in Metz now?'

'Couple of days, he will be. He knows you will be, he told me to get you there . . . Did you get on with the Bish all right?'

'Father Gervais? Yes, of course . . . Why call him that?'

'If they don't make him a bishop one day, there's no justice. All right, who says there *is* . . . Michel was finding stuff out for you, wasn't he?'

She'd nodded. 'He was going to try to.'

'He has. I think. In fact I know . . . Smoke?'

'Oh, I've got some—'

'Here.'

Gauloises. She took the packet, lit two – Father Gervais had left her his box of matches – and passed one back.

Also the packet. 'Thanks. D'you happen to know what he's found out?'

'No, sorry . . . You've made a great recovery, Rosalie.'

'I think the powder Michel gave us made all the difference. He said it worked miracles, and he was right.'

'Sulphanilamide. Yeah. In the field, it's a blessing.' Frowning at her: 'Your hair wasn't that colour, was it?'

'Certainly was not. Thérèse dyed it for me – because they might be looking for me still.'

'Well – they *are*.'

'What?'

Taking a long drag at his cigarette: smoke curling from nostrils then. 'Don't want to alarm you—'

'Come on, what—'

'Posters. You and another girl – Michel said she might be one you'd mentioned to him, got away when you were shot?'

Silent: staring at his profile. He glanced at her quickly, shook his head: 'Doesn't necessarily mean they're actively searching *now*. A month ago, after all – posters do sometimes just get left up.'

'But I'm—'

Speechless – for the moment. Stunned . . .

It meant she'd got away. Or – at least – thinking fast, and hardly believing it – seeing the river, and the chains on her – they didn't get her. Not there and then, anyway. And if they had since, or if her body'd been found—

Posters wouldn't be up now. Not the way *they* did things.

'Luc – are they separate, or posters of the two of us on one sheet?'

'Two of you together.' Easing over, giving room to a herd of goats in the charge of a little girl with a stick, who waved to them. Rosie waved back. Luc nodding: 'Posters all over Metz, and also in Nancy, we've heard. Anyway –'

looking at her again – 'I dare say dyeing your hair may help. Although – must say, it looks a bit – peculiar.'

'Thanks.'

'No, heavens, I don't mean—'

'It's all right. The scarf's supposed to be covering my hair anyway. Snag is, these papers say I'm nearly twenty-seven – which would be OK *except* for the grey hair. So to any quick-witted Boche – at a road-block, say, or—'

'Not so good. Will you dye it back?'

'And look like the bloody posters?'

'No. Well – a different colour, maybe. Red – or blonde—'

'Ugh!'

'Anyway, get new papers. Talk to Raoul about it. Raoul de Plesse, guy we're supposed to be working for. He'll solve it for you. Yeah, don't worry. But hang on . . .' Cigarette-stub between his lips, right hand up twisting the rear-view mirror so that she could see herself, to adjust the scarf. 'How's that?'

'Fine. Thanks . . . God, what a *sight* . . .'

That amazing thought again, though: that Lise must have got away. At least, might still be *alive* . . .

'Morehange, this place is called. We cross a larger road just here.'

Slowing for it. Poplars between them and the sun giving a signal-lamp effect as the rays stabbed through. Rosie asked him, shielding her eyes from it, 'If we were stopped – OK, destination Metz and you're giving me a lift to the hospital, but why taking a long way round?'

'Because from here the next village is – Faulquemont. Some distance yet. I'm delivering these tyres to a farmer there. And if they stopped us beyond Faulquemont I'll have picked the tyres up from him, he's trading 'em in for better ones.'

'*Very* clever.'

'Well – wouldn't want to boast . . .'

'Are you naturally a good liar?'

'It's one of the acquired skills, isn't it?'

'Isn't it, just. Mind another question?'

'Many as you like.' Braking, at the main road they had to cross. Glancing at her: 'Question for question – all right? You ask one, I'll ask one. Whichever catches the other out in a lie's the winner, smokes the loser's fags all the way to Metz. OK, you shoot first.'

'Michel's camouflage is his missing arm. What's yours? Why shouldn't you be recruited into some labour battalion, or the Milice or LVF?'

LVF stood for *Légion des Volontaires Français*. French fascists in German uniform. Luc pointed out, 'You didn't mention the Waffen SS. They've been recruiting Frenchmen into that too, you know.'

'Recruiting Alsaciens – Thérèse told me that – but others can volunteer, can't they. Anyway what's your let-out?'

'Problem with my lungs.' Flicking ash away. 'I could seize up and drop dead any minute. Don't worry, I won't, but I've medical papers to prove it, and meanwhile I'm pursuing a useful occupation. Papers to prove that too.'

'You look healthy enough to me.'

'Open-air life does that.' Looking right and left: but the road wasn't all that busy. Into gear, driving on over and into the continuation of their route to Faulquemont. Nothing on the road ahead except two horse-drawn carts. 'My turn for a question now, though: you married, or engaged?'

'As good as engaged. Not formally, but once all this is over –' she held up a hand with fingers crossed – 'all things being equal—'

'What's his racket?'

'Officer in the Royal Navy – in motor gunboats in the Channel. Well – he's on shore at the moment, as it happens, and I hope they keep him there. He's been wounded twice.'

'Deserves his luck, then.' A shrug. 'Well, well . . .'

'And you, Luc? Fiancée pining her heart out somewhere?'

'Yeah. *Likely.*'

'What d'you mean?'

'Oh. *Was* a girl – in London. Polish, as it happens. But –'
a gesture – 'nothing special. At least, not to her, I don't
believe.'

'How about Michel – is he married?'

'Michel – *married?*'

Tone and glance of surprise: beginnings of a laugh . . .

'You mean he's not.' She shrugged. 'Were you stationed
near London?'

'No. Only there on leave, couple of times. No, we were
in Ayrshire, Scotland. Two French para battalions, as part
of—'

He'd checked. Glancing at her. 'You could be Mata
Hari.'

'So I could. With a bit more flesh on me than I have
as yet.'

Silence reigning again, then. Smoking another Gauloise
and thinking about Lise, and the 'Wanted' posters. Not
good at all, about the posters, but fantastic about Lise. If
one could believe it . . .

They came into Metz from the east, on the main road
from the direction of Saarbrücken, coming in towards the
centre by way of what Luc told her was called the *Porte
des Allemands* and a bridge across the Seille, then turning
right, on a wide anticlockwise curve with the town centre
and the cathedral as it were at the hub, off to their left. Over
two divided streams of the Moselle then, two bridges, and
on into an urban and industrial conglomeration – signs of
bomb-damage here and there, rubble-littered open spaces
and some burnt-out buildings. A district or suburb somewhere ahead of them had the peculiar name of Woippy –

at any rate for a while it was part of the name of the road they were on. Luc didn't know Metz all that well, though, was having to concentrate on making the right turns – overshooting at one of them, having to turn and come back a kilometre or two; explaining that he and Michel weren't here all that often. It was their base, that was all, their work was all in the field. Well, obviously . . .

'But we're getting there. Getting there, Justine, don't worry.'

Turning left: then right. Warehouses, or factories: and another flattened area. A gleam of water between buildings like aircraft hangars. Couldn't be river there, must be a canal, she guessed, probably barge traffic on it. But now left again . . .

'Oy, oy . . .'

Slowing. Military vehicle ahead. A half-track, going their way, filling more than half the road's width. Luc reducing speed still further: he wasn't going to try to overtake it.

Then: 'Oh. Jesu!'

'Uh?'

'Don't look now. We're being followed.'

By a *Wehrmacht* truck. Small one, half-tonner or whatever, with yellow-and-black military insignia painted on its front mudguards. Behind it then – rounding the corner into this straight thoroughfare – it wasn't the Avenue or Rue de Woippy, whatever he'd said it was called, she knew they'd left that one some time ago – a heavy lorry in the same camouflage paint, splash of the same colours on the outer front mudguard: then yet another, identical, rounding the same corner – and a third, for God's sake, on that one's tail.

'Convoy.'

'Yeah.' They were down to about 15 k.p.h. The half-track in front, this other stuff crowding up behind. Luc squinting into his rear-view mirror again. 'Convoy. And we're in it . . .'

Motorcycles: two outriders, coming up screaming fast, swinging out around the big trucks, then up to this one. Powering forward to check on whatever was making them all put the brakes on, no doubt. One of them seemingly tucking itself in close behind them – close enough to be fairly deafening – and the other decelerating but slowly overhauling. Getting a look inside . . . Rosie keeping track of events now only through her ears, definitely *not* looking back: she had at first, but with the bikes this close hadn't again. And *now*, that one was dropping back. Squinting out of the left corners of her eyes she'd seen Luc push out his left hand, either waving them on or – just a friendly wave . . . Rosie began: 'What—'

'Hang on.'

Hanging *back* – leaving a gap of about twenty metres between the *gazo*'s nose and the Boche half-track's rear. Troop-carrier, whatever it was. Machine guns of some kind, probably Spandaus, one each side under canvas covers. Luc telling her – hunched over the wheel, pale eyes fixed on that thing's rear – 'We'll be dropping out of this shortly. Any second now. *There.*' Stabbing a forefinger towards an entrance coming up on the right. Slowing even more. Half-track pulling away ahead, half-tonner closing up astern: the outriders gunning their engines suddenly, swerving out and passing – on the outside, of course, the left, the side away – thank God – from Rosie: despite which she'd put her hands and forearms up to obstruct any view of her as they shot by. Luc shifting gear: and swinging the wheel over now – hauling the *gazo* – rather too fast, so as not to impede the Boches behind them any more than he had already – off the road and into this open gateway. Fence of wire mesh on iron uprights, gates similar, and a painted sign DP AGRICULTURAL ENGINEERS. The heavy trucks were pounding past behind them as they nosed into a concreted yard with tractors parked here and there – also some cars and lorries. Further in, she saw a house that might have been converted from a stable building: L-shaped, actually quite pretty, a country-cottage look, although the base of the 'L' looked *un*converted. Luc drove straight through and pulled up outside that bit, which seen in close-up now consisted of workshops or stores, with what looked like living-space above them. He switched off, lifted both hands in a gesture of helplessness . . . *'Sorry, Rosalie.'*

'What for?'

'Well – military depot just down the road there. Stuff's always passing. Should've damn well *thought!'*

'Then what?'

'Put you on the floor. Blanket over you.'

'Thanks. In *this* weather . . .'

The outriders had checked the company name on the tailgate, seen they had every right to be coming here, therefore had had no reason to stop them. Even if they'd seen *her*: a truck-driver could have a woman with him, without posing much threat to the continuance of the Third Reich. She put a hand on his arm: 'Luc, you've done marvellously, I'm grateful.'

The big surprise of the evening came at bed-time.

Rosie and Luc had had supper with the de Plesse family in their cottage, and Luc had stayed down there, having business to discuss with their host, while she'd gone up to bed. At least, to her room: but intentionally, to bed. It had been a long day and by that time she'd been feeling it. Hadn't enjoyed the evening much, either. Her room, previously used by Luc, was in the flat over the workshop; there was a larger one which had been Michel's and to which Silvie, Raoul's wife, had moved Luc's gear; the two men would share, when Michel turned up. It was known as 'the mechanics' flat', could be entered from the first floor of the cottage but also had its own entrance/exit by a ladderway down into one of the workshops.

The de Plesse family consisting of Raoul himself – a short-legged, big-bellied man, three-quarters bald, mid-forties, with shrewd, watchful eyes: the look of a peevish dachshund, she thought – and at that, with a strong sense of his own importance – and his wife Silvie – tiny, with straight fair hair fading into grey, and a tendency to speak only when spoken to, at any rate in her husband's presence – and a daughter, Roxane, who was plump, blonde, shy – and son Maurice, aged fifteen, afflicted with a crippling stammer but according to his father a technical genius. Rosie had thought to herself during supper that he probably had to be, poor kid. Chip off the old block, was the implication. He was expected to get into the university in Nancy to read engineering, and meanwhile his out-of-school hours were spent working in the business, which consisted largely of supplying and repairing farm machinery, particularly tractors. New ones being unobtainable, it was a matter of salvaging wrecks, either rebuilding them or cannibalizing them for spare parts, also converting diesels and petrol-fuelled machines to *gazo*. Converting motor vehicles of other kinds as well. It was obviously a successful business, which of course would also allow de Plesse and his people virtually unlimited scope for getting around, pursuing more covert interests.

She'd been anxious for a chance to discuss her own situation, but the first chance she got wasn't until after supper, when she managed to catch him alone for a minute. He'd seemed surprised that she'd wanted to discuss anything at all, before Michel's arrival; but he confirmed that at Michel's request he'd initiated enquiries about a firm of manufacturing engineers by name of Marchéval.

'That's *your* interest, I believe?'

She'd nodded.

'Well – Michel has been following up on what I was able
to tell him. He was going to visit a certain individual – a
résistant – who if anyone can help at all—'

'Whereabouts, exactly?'

'Well, that's a major factor – Marchéval's is near Troyes.
Not south of Paris as you'd indicated.'

'*Troyes*—'

'Michel will tell you more. He'll know more than I do,
by this time. But he won't be with us long – you realize?'

'Luc said that.'

'And you'll want to move rather quickly, I imagine.
Which brings me to the question of your papers – which
Luc was telling me are – unsafe . . . Well, as I've understood
it, your plans are by no means certain, so I suggest waiting
until Michel gets here, when presumably you'll decide what
you *are* going to do. All right?'

'You think he *will* be here in two days?'

'About that.' A shrug. 'But – who knows . . .'

'My own priority is to get in touch with London. I don't
want to delay that now if I can help it. Michel said you'd
put me in touch with local SOE?'

'Yes, he spoke of that. And it could be arranged. Not
here, but in Nancy. A problem however is that you'll have
to go there yourself – so the business of your papers again
becomes important. To be on your own – in that town at
all, in your situation . . .' Shake of the head: 'Not without its
hazards, Mam'selle. I think the answer can only be to wait
for Michel. Sleep on it, eh, talk again in the morning?'

She wasn't sleeping on it yet, only thinking about it, in her
room in the flat. On edge, rather, moving around. Apart
from the hour or so she'd spent on her knees she'd been
sitting all day in any case. Tired, certainly, but her feet
weren't; and she doubted whether if she turned in now
she'd sleep.

Troyes, for God's sake. She'd been visualizing a factory in some Parisian industrial suburb.

She thought that in the morning she'd try to push de Plesse into arranging a meeting with the SOE organizer in Nancy right away – *not* wait for Michel. Or maybe – with this thing about papers – the SOE man could be persuaded to come here. She'd already done a lot of waiting, things could be moving fast elsewhere, and Michel's 'two days' this last time had stretched themselves to a month. OK, no blame attaching, obviously, he had a lot on his plate, but this was *her* business and SOE's, no one else's.

Talk to de Plesse again in the morning: explain the urgency, get out of him anything else he might have discovered about Marchéval's – to give Baker Street as much background as possible, in case they wanted her to do anything about it. To which she certainly wouldn't be averse. Michel's musing rang in her memory: *But how you'd get to him* . . . Then the bit about when the shit hit the fan – i.e. when 'Hector' went on the run. When, and/or if. There might be a *chance* of nobbling him, that was all: and for herself, a chance to clear up that unfinished business, at least assist in the nobbling process, conceivably instigate it, even carry it out – if Baker Street opted for that, would allow it, didn't have plans laid already . . . In which case – well, forget bloody 'Hector', leave him to others. Send up a prayer of thanks when they caught or killed him, but meanwhile – midnight pick-up, magic carpet home.

Within just *days* . . .

Home – with Ben. *Safe.*

Why think for even a split second of anything else?

Eyes shut, for a moment: remembering from previous occasions the bewilderingly sudden transition to safety – which only in recent years one had learnt was the ultimate, stupendous luxury.

People didn't realize – at least, outsiders didn't. Might

guess, but could never really get near it. Since of course
one never told them.

Ben knew, through having virtually shared her nightmares. Holding her sweat-slippery body, stroking her,
murmuring into her ear – calming, comforting. Time and
again she'd woken out of sheer terror into that urgent
reassurance, taking a few moments sometimes to recognize
this as the reality – Ben's voice, hands. Ben's love. There,
now, waiting for her: all she had to do was get back to
it . . . She'd been perched on the edge of the bed but
was up again and moving, putting her mind back to the
present situation's realities and needs: one element of its
bloodiness being that she didn't much like Raoul de Plesse,
and guessed from *his* reactions that she might have been
unguarded enough to have let him see it; another, perhaps
more easily solvable but only with that man's help, the
problem of how to get by in Nancy for some period of time
with papers that wouldn't stand close inspection and one's
portrait on 'Wanted' posters all over town: having to be
there at least several days, first seeing the *réseau* organizer,
then waiting for an exchange of signals, and maybe further
signals, elucidations.

Get Justine Quérier's papers doctored? Maybe just a few
essential alterations and up-datings would be enough, if
they had someone here who could handle it. Getting new
papers forged would take too long. Easy and quick in
England, where SOE had a suburban house equipped and
staffed by expert forgers. But even here, with papers already
existing and needing only slight adaptation – changing a
date or two, replacing a passport-size photograph with
a new one, duplicating the rubber stamp that had been
applied to Justine's . . .

Brain flagging. Not yet back in anything like peak condition, either mentally *or* physically. Although the heart –
pulse-rate – seemed OK at the moment. Another *temporary*

condition – please God . . . Should have thought before of getting changes forged into these papers, though. Couldn't have expected Luc to have – he was a soldier, not an agent. And Raoul de Plesse wouldn't have, she supposed, because Luc would only have told him this evening that they weren't up to scratch.

De Plesse was probably all right. You couldn't expect to like every single person with whom you found yourself working. Up to now, no doubt at all, she'd been extremely lucky.

But also, up to now, hadn't had to sit around waiting for other people . . .

A tap on the door, so soft she barely heard it. Then a murmur: 'Rosalie?'

Silvie de Plesse. Trying again, more audibly: 'Rosalie? Are you awake?'

'Yes. Hang on.' She'd been turning down the bedclothes, went now to unlock the door. 'Something wrong?'

'You're still dressed. How fortunate. My dear – Michel—'

'What about him?'

'Well – he's here!'

Staring at her: while that sank in. Then – masking a surge of relief – 'I'll come down.'

'*Such* a surprise! Only *just* beating curfew – he's been here half an hour, they've been talking in the study, but he's having some supper now. We wouldn't have disturbed you, only—'

'One moment.' Going quickly to the mirror that was on the chest of drawers, and smoothing out uneven, patchy-grey hair with her fingers. Not that it made much difference to it . . . The whole outlook was different though, suddenly: no more waiting about – touch wood . . . She faced Silvie again: 'Still awful, isn't it.'

'Your hair?'

'Better than it was, but—'

'It's not all *that* bad, dear.'

The hell it wasn't. She was acutely conscious of it . . . Out into the passage, shutting the bedroom door as her hostess opened the one into the main part of the house. Glancing round with a solicitous, motherly look: nice enough, kind et cetera, but out of her element in all this – *and* under that sod's thumb. Telling Rosie, 'With professional attention – your hair that is, Roxane and I were talking about it – we do know someone who'd come. I mean, someone – safe. If you like, I'll ask her?'

'Terrific. If you could. Except I should mention I've no money. Although of course my people will—'

'Don't even *think* of it!'

They were in the living-room then: Michel getting up from the table, coming to meet her. Very much as she remembered him. Memory had worked reasonably well, considering how it had been that night – the state she'd been in, and having seen him only in semi-darkness. A big man, over six foot and powerfully built, with a lively, humorous expression – which she realized she had not seen in the oil-lamp's glow in Thérèse's attic. Big nose, wide jaw, and that smiling – slightly *wild* look. Thatch of rough, black hair. His hand – the one and only – was extended towards her as if to take hold of her arm or maybe slide behind her shoulder, as would have been a natural movement if he'd been about to stoop to kiss her – as he *had* been, she realized; seeing him register – at the last moment, holding back – that they weren't on such terms, in fact barely knew each other.

If he *had* kissed her she wouldn't have minded.

Because he'd saved her life – the feeling that at some depth she *did* know him?

'Rosalie.'

She'd put her hand in that one of his. The other shirt-sleeve was missing, had been removed, the shoulder sewn up. She'd taken that in without consciously looking at it, certainly wasn't seeing it now . . . 'Very nice surprise, Michel.' A new, rather startling thought had formed in her mind just in that moment, but she hadn't time for it. 'They said two or three days. You've done *far* better!'

'I had a good reason to cut it short, where I was. But you're looking a lot better too, thank God.'

'Thank Thérèse.'

'Oh, Thérèse—'

'And your sulphur powder?'

'That – yes. While I think of it, though – sorry I couldn't get back as I said I would. Several reasons, I'll explain . . . But this shocking business of Thérèse—'

'Did you just hear of it?'

'At the weekend – through Raoul here. In code, you might say – at first I hoped I was getting it wrong. How lucky you were outside the house, though. Luc was telling me. And the Destinier place close by—'

'Marie Destinier was superb. But what anyone can do to help Thérèse—'

'Nothing. If news of her did leak out we'd hear from Marie – that's to say, Raoul would. But I've a lot to tell you, Rosalie – truly *vital* stuff—'

De Plesse cut in, 'Finish your supper first, then we can really get down to it?'

There was a place set at the table, where Michel had been sitting and went back to now. A plate of left-over rabbit stew, Rosie saw, a bread-loaf and a glass of red wine. The food and the wine would be black-market, she supposed. Would have to be. De Plesse well able to afford it – despite most of the populace especially in towns being on near-starvation diets. In Paris, one had heard, a lot of people literally *were* starving.

Michel murmuring to Silvie: 'Apologies – letting your delicious food get cold.'

'Finish it, then we'll talk.' De Plesse, looking at Rosie, smiled in a slightly more friendly way than he had before. 'Sit down, girl. He eats like a wolf, this fellow. Even if he has another helping it won't take long.'

Michel admitting as he began to eat, 'It's a fact, I was slightly famished.' Movement of the head towards Rosie: 'As *she* was, when we got to the Michon place that night. They'd starved her in the prison – *and* whipped her, the swine . . .' Glancing back from her to de Plesse: 'Killing their own generals now, did you hear?'

'The bomb-plot generals, you mean.'

'And working down from that level – God knows how many'll pay for it. Like a pogrom with the victims all his beloved Aryans. He's raving mad, of course.' Switching to Rosie again then; she'd parked herself at the end of the table, beside Luc, Silvie had asked her whether she'd like coffee, and she'd said yes, *please* – Michel telling her, 'It's not going to take long now, Rosalie.' Meaning the war, not coffee or what passed for coffee. 'Not here in France, that is. I mean, if you want to get that creature before he disappears?'

'You've been investigating. I hear. I'm grateful – and surprised you'd have remembered, let alone spent time and—'

'Big thing on *your* mind, wasn't it, but it rang alarm bells in mine too – danger to us all – at any point of contact, it *is*. Therefore – logical reaction – eliminate it, if there's a way of doing so. Should say, *help Rosalie* eliminate it. But now there's more, *much* more – it's a big thing you've started. I've been to see a man I was put on to by Raoul here. Who incidentally may have told you the business is near Troyes, not where you thought?'

'Yes.'

'Making it easier for me, as it happens – made this recce possible, only a slight diversion from what would have been my route anyway. In fact, *two* diversions, because after I'd left him I was near Dijon, he was able to get a message to

me through mutual friends, and I went back there. Where
I've come from now, you see – because the sooner you heard
this, the better. I take it you're still of the same mind – to go
after that *vendu*?'

'Go after him.' Nodding – but uncertainly. *Vendu* meant
a person who'd sold out. Michel's dark jaws chomping.
She explained, 'Standard procedure would be to recall
me. And they may have something on the go already
– or after they hear about it from me may *set* something going. They'll want him tracked down, for sure
– and whatever you've found out, I'll pass on – obviously – when I make this contact in Nancy – which I
hope—'

'We'll go into that presently.' De Plesse had cut in without
looking at her, but with a glance round at the other members
of his family – the boy doing homework, Roxane just
sitting. Silvie with sewing on her lap but hands folded
on it. His glance might have been to tell them that their
presence could be dispensed with shortly, if not sooner . . .
Adding, 'When you've had that second helping, Michel.
That is, if you wouldn't prefer to put this off to the morning, er – Justine – or Rosalie, if that's what we call you
now . . .'

'Rosalie is my real name. Justine's the one on the papers.
No – I'd like to hear about it now.'

Silvie put in, 'You *are* looking tired, Rosalie.'

'Twice the girl she was, believe me.' Michel studying
her. He had kind eyes, she thought, but a moment ago
you wouldn't have thought so. He'd noticed the way de
Plesse had cut her short, then the slightly contemptuous
Or Rosalie, if that's what we call you. She'd seen a flicker
of warning: that second time, she'd thought for a moment
he wasn't going to let it go. But he was wiping the last
of the stew out of his plate with bread – quick shake of
the head at Silvie's offer to refill it, then glancing back

at Rosie: 'Hair's grown a lot, too. Can't say the colour suits you.'

'Disguise, supposedly. Since I'm featured in street posters?'

A nod. 'I've seen some.'

'But the good thing – *marvellous* thing – at least, if I'm reading it correctly—'

'I can guess – the other girl they're looking for. The one you told me you were hoping might have escaped, by way of the river?'

'It *must* be her. If they're looking for her as well as for me – maybe assuming we'd be together—'

'Might well assume that. I think in their shoes *I* would. Putting you together on the same poster – an encouragement to reward-seekers—'

'Reward?'

'A million francs each. But – yes, she must have got away. Only thing is – to be completely realistic, Rosalie – if they'd caught her since—'

'She might still be on the posters. Rather than reprint them with me alone.' She nodded. 'Even if they haven't caught her, though, there's the question of how far she'd have got – where she might be *now*.'

'In any case it's closer to good news than the other kind.' Michel took a swallow of wine. 'But –' pointing at her with his head – 'tell you, Raoul – to my dying day I'll remember it – with the most intense – well, astonishment, for one thing, but also – you know, a very *happy* thing? To have found that lifeless body – *almost* lifeless – and now after just a month, hey presto, to have with us this highly personable young lady – alive and kicking and – in my view, much more than just *attractive*—'

'Oh, please—'

'And I may say extremely brave. What this young lady did – on top of the horrors she'd already been through –

I personally would call the height of courage. So to have had the privilege – Luc and I – of being *responsible* for this – this miracle—'

'Hear, hear.' Luc had been quiet, just listening. He raised a glass with no more than a drip of wine left in it: 'To our foundling!'

Enfant trouvé, was the expression he'd used. Michel watching her over his own half-empty glass: Rosie meeting that calm regard, appreciating that the exaggeratedly complimentary remarks he'd been making would have been largely for the benefit – or rather, reproval – of de Plesse, a counter to his rudeness. Michel was a man and a half, she thought. Asking her as he put his glass down, 'The bullet-wound in your shoulder – turned out all right, has it – no bones smashed, or—'

'Collar-bone was fractured – so the *sage-femme* told me. The bullet passed just grazing it, was actually diverted downward slightly.'

'I don't believe *that*, Rosalie.'

'Well – it's what she found – said—'

'Did she say you had *steel* collar-bones?'

'All I know is it went in here, behind, and came out lower down – here—'

'I remember very well how it looked. But that's nonsense, what the woman told you. Angle of entry might have been downward, I suppose – if you'd been angled backward at that moment – sort of staggering, might have been?'

'Might have. Doesn't seem likely, but – one doesn't remember every split second. And the *sage-femme* was quite certain.'

'Quite wrong, I'd say. Fixed you up well enough, obviously, but I'd guarantee the collar-bone wasn't touched. A bullet would have smashed it, not been deflected, you'd have been in a far worse state. Of course it would have *hurt* badly, having torn through muscle – you'd have *believed* her—'

'Not sure I still don't – despite your own obviously extensive knowledge—'

'I know a little. Rudimentary – as one needs in the field, rough and ready – just to get by.'

'It's true.' Luc nodded. 'Enough to get by.'

She'd smiled at Silvie. 'May they both *continue* getting by.'

'Hah.' Michel picked up his glass. 'Let's drink to her again. Here, Luc, I'll spare you a millilitre of this . . .'

The family had gone to bed, and Luc went up too. He was leaving in the morning, for Verdun and St Mihiel, ostensibly on de Plesse company business. Michel would be leaving too but not so early.

Luc had kissed her hand. 'Goodnight, and good luck.'

'You too. And thanks – for everything, including getting me here.'

As he'd told her earlier, he was taking over the top Maquis-liaison job from Michel up in this area – in whatever stretch of territory it was. They had other paras out there in the field, she'd gathered, instructing and organizing. Watching them from where she was sitting at the table – Luc on his way to hit the sack, Michel crossing the room beside him with a hand on his shoulder, talking quietly, a thought which she'd had earlier came back to mind – the similarity between him – Michel – and Lise's Alain Noally. Michel was younger of course – Noally's wiry hair had been grey as well as unruly, in conformity perhaps with what she'd learnt was his public image – as an artist of some stature, a sculptor, well known in France even before the war apparently. By the time of his betrayal and death a couple of months ago he must have been at least in his middle fifties. Twice Lise's age, therefore.

Noally and Michel could have been brothers – with that gap of age between them, of course. But it wasn't only a physical likeness – from as little as she knew or had known either of them, they'd have been brothers under the skin as well.

Tell Lise, she thought. One day. Touch wood . . .

He was coming back to them. De Plesse pushing a chair out for him with his foot: Michel's hand on the table then, taking his weight as he let himself down. All three were smoking. De Plesse leant across, moved a saucer-ashtray to where they could all reach it.

'Go ahead, Michel.'

A nod. Sitting back, exhaling smoke, dark eyes on Rosie. 'First thing – Troyes. On the Seine, one hundred and eighty kilometres from Paris. Southern end of the district of Champagne. As I said, I've just come from there, from this man Dufay. Incidentally, I'm working a patch of country to the south and east – Dijon at its centre, more or less. You're thinking I needn't have told you this, but it's relevant, in a way. First though – *most* important for you to know, is that there is no SOE presence at all now in that region. There *was* a *réseau*, a very active one I gather, but – gone.' He drew deeply on his Gauloise. 'Tell you also, Rosalie – in the weeks since we met I've had some idea of co-opting you as my pianist. Damn cheek, eh? But not really – I'd have asked you first, obviously, and then – if you'd agreed – asked my people in England to approach SOE. You told me you're a pianist, and we're short of them – as Raoul here knows. Anyway –' shake of the shaggy head – 'it wouldn't have worked. I'd thought it might have suited you, a basis on which they might have allowed you to remain in the field – only for a few weeks, you see. But it wouldn't have worked, because of the distances involved – which is why I'm going up to Luxembourg tomorrow.' Addressing this to de Plesse. 'Collect one pianist. Leaving Luc with one fewer in his area. Too bad . . . Anyway – the Marchéval factory, Rosalie. Not in Troyes itself but to the west of it, a village called St Valéry-sur-Vanne. Little place on a little river with Marchéval's, you might say its beating heart. To be honest, someone else said it.' A nod to de Plesse: 'Your man, Dufay. Incidentally, Rosalie, it's also close to the Forêt d'Othe.'

'Maquis country?'

A nod. 'So I was told. But another thing Raoul discovered for me through his business connections, before I went down there, is that the factory has been on war production for the Boches right from the start, and still is.'

'To be expected, surely. Proprietors of manufacturing industry don't have much option?'

'None. Well, except – Peugeot, for instance – down near Montbéliard – they were making turrets for Boche tanks. London ordered it blown up, and who helped? Well – Robert Peugeot . . . Anyway – next item: this guy Victor Dufay is a leading *résistant* with a business similar to Raoul's, only he specializes in borehole pumping systems. It was he who told me that the SOE *réseau* had folded. He also gave me the name of a colleague of his who's more closely on the spot, in St Valéry-sur-Vanne. A Resistance colleague, that is – in fact an hotel-keeper, proprietor of L'Auberge la Couronne. His name's Jacques Craillott, his wife Colette is also an active *résistante*. In the morning, Rosalie, I'll jot all the names down for you – unless you've already committed them to memory?'

'Might check in the morning, see they're still in it.'

He'd nodded. 'Auberge la Couronne, Jacques and Colette Craillot. *If* you should happen to be there, and need a safe-house. Which I imagine you would. Introduction to them would be made by Dufay. OK?'

'As I said, it's unlikely they'll let *me*—'

'In which case you'll soon be in London briefing others – huh?'

She nodded. 'Maybe . . . What sort of age are the Craillots?'

'He's in his forties, Dufay said. I didn't visit St Valéry. Time, distance – had to push along. I have a sketch of the place, though, which Dufay made for me, on this second visit . . . Oh, by the way, Luc mentioned the papers we got for you aren't so good, you'll need new ones?'

'Actually, may not. At least I *hope* . . .'

'Sounds like she's going to save you trouble, Raoul.'

'Well – good . . . But – Michel – you found you had a good connection with Dufay, you were saying?'

'Yes.' Michel turned back to her. 'I'll tell you where to find his place in Troyes – or Raoul will. But just for more background information – my crowd have run some clandestine operations from time to time, and one not long ago was to knock out the Radio Paris transmitters at Allouis, near Melun. The sortie was commanded by a good friend of mine, and Dufay was at this end of it, met them when they dropped. It was a long-range job – not from Troyes, long way north of there, but still several nights' hard slog to the target, lying up all day, so forth. Those transmitters had been jamming RAF signals; our boys blew up the main pylons and got away again without a scratch. Well – success and a mutual friend makes for a good *rapport*, which Dufay and I now have. I told him you might turn up and that you were – something special, so – use my name as the password, you'll be welcomed. OK?'

Looking at him: 'So what is it?'

'What?'

'Something more than just Michel?'

'Oh.' He laughed. 'Michel Jacquard.' A frown: 'Do I know yours? Other than Rosalie – which you say is—'

'Justine Quérier?'

'Ah. If you stick to *that*—'

'I think so.' A glance at de Plesse: 'If a few small changes could be made. The photo – a new one, obviously – also date of birth, and the paper's date of issue?'

He shrugged. 'If that's all . . .'

'If it could be done quickly, though. Tomorrow? Wouldn't be more than a hour or two hours' work, would it, for an expert? Except for the photo. And conceivably one or two of the forms may have been superceded – which your expert would know. Well – *you* would. But even the photo could be done in a day – I would have thought—'

'It's possible.'

'And your wife said something about a hairdresser.'

'She did, did she?' Slight shrug. 'Well, we'll make that her department.' A glance at Michel: 'Go on?'

'Yes. Well . . . As *you* ascertained, Raoul, Marchéval's are primarily makers of metal tubes – pipes, cylinders, so forth. And the factory's never been bombed. One reason is that it's part of the village, workers' cottages all around it – in an air attack there'd be women and children killed. It wouldn't be an important target anyway – right? Dufay thought not, anyway. Important to them locally, but that's about all. There's never been any sabotage either – not that he knows of, and this he thought would be accounted for by (a) the target's lack of importance, (b) sabotage brings reprisals, and in a small, isolated place like that – well, we know how they handle such things, huh?'

'A *ratissage*. Shootings, burnings.'

'It's been known, hasn't it? But now listen. After my first visit, Dufay thought he should look into the situation at St Valéry. And we're lucky he did – that my visit got him off his backside to that extent. D'you know what they're turning out there now?'

De Plesse shrugged. 'How would I?'

'Rocket casings. For some weeks now, apparently. There was some re-tooling and a break in production a few months ago, now it's going full-blast. Craillot has had suspicions about it for some time, I gather, but having no channels to SOE at all now – also the problems I've described, difficulty if not impossibility of bombing, even if he *could* get word through, and the local people's disinclination to indulge in sabotage . . . He's not exceptionally bright, Dufay admitted – Craillot, that is. It wasn't said disparagingly, his words as I recall them were that he's a good guy but no genius . . . So there it is, Rosalie. I'd guess – Dufay guesses – that what they're making *might* be casings for Hitler's secret weapon number two, about which we've heard so much. These are very large objects – twelve metres long and two in diameter, approximately. Dufay suggests they might be using factories in France because Germany's being bombed to pieces – and a plant such as this, four years untouched, they might even consider as immune from bombing – eh?'

'Immunity likely to be lifted very shortly.' Rosie leaking smoke, staring at him through it. 'Just have to get the people out of the way somehow. Last-minute warnings. But mind you, if your friend's guess is right—'

'Bombers'd be over that village the minute we were sure of it. No doubt of *that*. But here's another line of thought, Rosalie. Remember I suggested – more or less – staking out the Marchéval place against the chance he'd show up there?'

'When the *merde* hits the fan.'

'Exactly. Meaning then, when our troops get into Paris – or sooner, when the Boches take to their heels. But they might take him along, you know? Or dispose of him some other way. Or, he might take off on his own before that. So I thought, what if it could be arranged for the factory to be bombed or sabotaged? Eh? Which now it may *have* to be?'

'*If* the rocket report stands up.'

'Exactly—'

'Only Craillot's story via Dufay, though – plus guesswork. It's not a lot. If it *does* stand up, of course – well, crikey—'

'Dynamite. And to have turned it up like this – for sure it's last-minute stuff, but *any* interruption of that programme—'

She'd nodded: it went without saying. 'As regards "Hector", though – whether in fact a bombing attack would bring him rushing down from Paris—'

'I agree – an attack on the *works*, that is. This is another angle, now. After my first talk with Dufay I couldn't see such an attack being laid on – for the reasons we've discussed – unimportant target, risk to local families' lives. So I thought then – before anything came up about rockets – why not target Henri Marchéval's own residence? Henri is André's father, I should have said. Mightn't *that* bring your boy running?'

'Maybe it would. If he was able to get there. And heard about it in the first place. One doesn't know how free or otherwise he may be. Might help if there was sabotage – the Gestapo might take him down there with them.'

All speculation . . . Remembering how they'd brought him to Morlaix in the hope he'd identify her; and how in Rue des Saussaies he'd been allowed freedom of movement – apparently – but still jumped to obey when the man with the whip had yelled 'Get out!' . . . She'd finished her cigarette; dropping its remains in the saucer, looking at Michel again across the curve of the table's end.

'This house – *not* right in the village?'

'Little way out, in walled grounds. I'll show you on Dufay's sketch. Quite a big old place, apparently – Manoir St Valéry. Marchéval *père* has been allowed to retain one wing of it, the rest's occupied by Boches.'

'Oh . . .'

'Attractive target, huh?'

'Could be . . . But so are rocket casings. Any idea how they're shifted – by rail, for instance, or—'

'By road. Flat-bed trucks in military convoy. Dufay – or Craillot – couldn't say at what intervals.'

'Still seems barely credible. When all you were prospecting for . . .' She shook her head. 'Do they know anything about the son?'

'Dufay knows of him, and has reason to *believe* he's an agent of SOE and working in the Paris area. I didn't comment, thought it safer not to, but that's his belief and the Craillots', apparently. He *was* educated in England – didn't you say?'

'In Scotland – according to the staff officer who – I told you, conducted my final briefing and swore he – André Marchéval – was straight. You asked about *him*, then?'

'And the answer to that?'

'Oh – not possible. You scared me for a minute, but – absolutely not, Michel.'

'What *he* said about young Marchéval – didn't you say?'

'Different – really, *entirely*. In any case – he was only giving his view. André was being brought home, and if he'd got there he'd have been put through the wringer. Really *would*. Which he'd have been well aware of, of course – why they staged his arrest. OK?'

'If you say so.' A shrug. 'Anyway, the rocket thing's got to be checked out double-quick by *someone* – right?'

Chapter 7

Nancy: Wednesday August 2nd. Mid-morning. The drive from Metz had taken nearly two hours, but the traffic was thinner now. A lot of it had been military and mostly northward, in particular one convoy of heavy trucks which they'd begun to think would go on for ever. Mostly *gazos* and bicycles now, though, in this old town with its maze of narrow streets. De Plesse shifting gear as he took yet another sharp corner. Raoul de Plesse the new man, having been called to order by Michel . . . A wave of the hand towards some ecclesiastical pile ahead and to the left – 'Les Cordeliers. Church, as you see, but also a convent. And this edifice now, right next to it – the Palais Ducal. Nancy was once the capital city of the Dukes of Lorraine – as perhaps you know. It became French in 1766. Having some interest in the history of this region, I am able to give you that date. And the university, by the way, which my boy will be attending in due course, is two hundred years older still.' Glancing at her as if expecting to be congratulated: in some respects he'd pulled himself together but he was still a pain in the neck. Another corner not far ahead, and coming up behind them a black Citroën 15. He'd caught his breath, she'd glanced back, seen it too as he slowed, edged closer to the kerb to let the thing sweep by. He'd gone a bit grey around the gills in those few seconds, during which Rosie had noted that there'd been two occupants, males in civilian suits and – unusually – no hats. Too warm, she supposed: square heads overheating. She told de Plesse – chat aimed partly at steadying his nerve – 'In Paris they're wearing uniform now. Shifted out of civvies at the time of the Normandy landings.'

If the one in the Citroën's front passenger seat had looked into this vehicle *en passant*, he might have guessed that the middle-aged collaborator – de Plesse looked too sleek to be anything else – had picked up a somewhat faded *fille de joie* along the way. Dark-skinned female with bright yellow hair under a white scarf (Silvie's), which emphasized the swarthiness of her complexion. Cold cream with an admixture of boot-polish had produced this effect: recipe devised and supplied by Silvie's hairdresser, whose efforts had also made a great difference to Rosie's hair, not so much in colour as in overall shaping. It had grown enough in the past month to *be* shaped. Having trimmed it here and there, she'd bleached it before the re-dyeing, advising Rosie to keep it as it was now, if possible, since frequent bleaching made hair brittle, liable to break off. The yellow was really *too* bright, though.

Another improvement, of her own design, was the padding in her cheeks, pads cut from a pre-war rubber sponge, which she'd put in to fatten her face before the new ID photo had been taken. The forger had handled the photography as well, and on his way out through the DP yard he'd taken shots of a tractor that had been rebuilt and looked like new: this was for DP advertising purposes, maybe also to justify his visit. Rosie's photo was to be processed within hours, but these would take a few days: he'd told de Plesse, 'Can't do *everything* in a tearing rush . . .'

'You've done a fine job, Antoine!'

'You mean "magnificent". And when have I not?'

Little sharp-faced man in a straw hat that made him look like a dried-out mushroom. He'd fixed all the papers, though, and substituted ration-coupons of the type that had superceded the ones Justine Quérier had had. By trade he was an architectural draughtsman, he'd told her.

She *hoped* these papers would get her by, now.

'Round this next corner is where I'll be dropping you.'

'All right.'

'Also wishing you the best of luck.'

'I'm more than grateful for all you've done.'

'Oh. Very little, really . . .'

Might have been less, too, if it hadn't been for Michel sorting him out, on Monday night. When they'd finished that late-night discussion de Plesse had gone out to do his security rounds of the yard and workshops, and she'd asked Michel whether he'd noticed a certain off-handedness in their host's attitude towards her. Knowing that he *had* noticed it, wondering whether he could account for it.

'I suppose I'm a nuisance to him.'

'More a matter of his attitude to SOE. He's – you might say, on his dignity – in relation to SOE, not you personally. I've had trouble with it before, problems getting him to liaise with your Nancy *réseau* over the transmission of wireless messages – although it was agreed in London that we might call on your people for that kind of help if we needed to. Did you realize, your administration has merged now with BCRA?'

'*Really?*'

BCRA stood for *Bureau Central de Rensignements et d'Action*: the Free French, Gaullist intelligence and sabotage organization. Between whom and 'F' Section SOE at staff levels there'd been a certain frigidity in past years, although in the field cooperation between agents had been more common-sense. Michel told her, 'As of July 1st. Makes us brothers and sisters at arms, eh?'

'None too soon.'

'But the de Plesse problem – I mentioned to you before,

didn't I – on the subject of getting news of you back to your people? Part of it is he doesn't like the Nancy *réseau* being able to contact *him*. Makes him feel exposed. Also – this is only a suspicion, why he *might* have such reservations – there were rumours which some believed – a year ago, about a *réseau* with the code-name "Prosper"?'

'Blown, wasn't it? Usual problem – infiltration. But why—'

'The whisper was that your people had deliberately sacrificed it, as part of some deception plot – connected with the invasion of Sicily, allegedly – and of course there were French nationals involved, who were all arrested. Anyway that's the story that went round.'

'And it's rubbish.' Crossing fingers: she *hoped* it was.

Michel accepting anyway, shrugging . . . 'Could be that he *likes* to bear a grudge. I'll sort a few things out with him. The basis of it with him though – what it comes down to is resentment of foreigners on *his* territory.'

'So who's a foreigner?'

'Good question, Rosalie. I'll bring it to his attention. One thing I have in mind to raise with him is that SOE in Nancy must know of a safe-house where you could stay a few days – and as he's got to fix a meeting for you, he could fix that too. Otherwise it would have to be a last-minute arrangement, which might be difficult. Anyhow – you go on up now.'

'You've been terrific in all this, Michel. I owed you my life already – now all *this* help—'

'As I said, it's as much in our interests as yours. And – in any case . . .'

Leaving it there: words ostensibly without meaning, left hanging in the air between them: *in any case* . . .

Then yesterday morning when they'd been alone for a few moments – he'd given her Victor Dufay's sketch-map of St Valéry-sur-Vanne, also explained where to find Dufay in Troyes – she'd asked him quietly, 'How did you manage

it?' Referring to the already noticeable change he'd wrought
in de Plesse. He'd only shrugged, grimacing slightly, con-
spiratorially: they'd been on their own for no more than a
few seconds. And one final, private exchange just shortly
before he'd left, when he'd explained to her that after he'd
collected his pianist from somewhere in the Luxembourg
direction they'd be driving south to his new area of operations, not stopping either here or in Nancy.

'Sadly, therefore – may not see each other again. At least
for – well, who knows . . .'

'Good luck, Michel. And thank you again.'

'Very good luck to you – with *all* of it.'

She'd suggested – quietly again, the de Plesse son,
Maurice, being possibly in earshot – 'Might manage a
reunion, one day.'

A nod. Eyes on hers, and serious. 'I suppose SOE in
London would tell me where you are – if I asked them
nicely?'

'Don't see why they shouldn't.' De Plesse had come into
the room at that moment. Rosie not looking at Michel then;
but excusing herself *to* herself, later on, by daydreaming
of being with Ben in London, Lise joining them for a
meal in one of Ben's rather boozy haunts, and Michel just
happening along – by her own crafty pre-arrangement, of
course.

Might Lise see the man *she* saw?

Might not. Might not want to. Might hate the very concept
of Noally being replaceable.

In any case, she thought – in de Plesse's *gazo*, getting
into the middle of Nancy now – the Boches having put up
posters with Lise's portrait on them didn't prove she'd got
away. Any more than it did in her own case – she could
have died in Thérèse's house, for instance.

'Here we are. The parting of our ways.'

Easing his *gazo* in to the kerb, and braking. On the other

side a narrow alleyway led off at right-angles between tall
buildings. Shabby, scarred, and the alley itself littered, its
walls streaked. At a glance, she could guess how it would
smell. He nodded towards it. 'Through there. Only a few
metres.'

'Just a moment, though . . .'

Glancing back: her view of two *gendarmes* whom she'd
spotted approaching the last corner, and who'd now reached
it – she'd been watching to see whether they'd turn this way
or the other – was abruptly blanked off by a military van
pulling in beside them. *Milice*: at least, the one getting out
on this outer side was. Khaki shirt, black tie and beret, wide
leather belt and holster.

He'd gone to the rear. De Plesse grumbling, 'Nothing to
do with us . . .'

'And let's keep it that way. If you don't mind.'

Not, in other words, cross the road within a few metres
of them, burdened with her gear and looking like God
only knew what . . . All right for de Plesse – *he* wasn't
on bloody posters all over town. Not that she'd seen any
yet, the way they'd come, although she'd been looking out
for billboards. It was enough to know they were there,
that any of those men – the *milicien* climbing back in
beside the driver and the two *gendarmes* with the rear
doors open – getting in, she supposed – would as likely
as not have likenesses of herself and Lise fairly well in
mind; the posters must have been up for several weeks
now.

The van was backing – past the corner, and across the
end of the side-street.

'All right now – believe me?'

It had stopped, was moving forward again, turning away
into that side-street. She put her hand on the door. She was
going to have to get used to looking as she did, but this first
public appearance was unnerving. She told him – surprising

•

herself – 'I have had considerable experience of this kind of work, Monsieur.'

'Yes, well . . .' Pointing with his balding head towards the alley. 'Up there, and round to the left. Give Rouquet my regards.'

Guillaume Rouquet. Code-name 'Boris'. Memory *was* still working: at breakfast yesterday she'd been able to recite the names from Michel's briefing of the night before: Victor Dufay in Troyes, Jacques and Colette Craillot at the Auberge la Couronne in St Valéry-sur-Vanne. It was a relief that she hadn't lost the ability to memorize: one did *not* want to make or keep notes. Flashback to Rouen a year ago, when she'd had to put everything on paper for the benefit of the man she'd later knifed to death in a train's lavatory. Could have been *ten* years ago . . . She was out on the narrow pavement; de Plesse staying put, watching traffic in his rear-view mirror, making a show of it, she thought, to justify inertia. And of course keen to be on his way, to be rid of her. She opened the car's rear door, hauled out her basket and the old suitcase Silvie had given her.

The basket had a cat in it. Cat trapped in the DP yard this morning by Maurice de Plesse before he'd gone off to school. He'd been rejoicing earlier in the fact that this was the last week of term, summer holidays imminent; he hated book-work, he'd told her, and after the cat's capture she'd suggested to him that if he didn't make the grade as an engineer he could always emigrate to the Yukon and become a trapper: he'd laughed delightedly and begun stammering about wearing the skins of skunks and bears, but Papa who'd been present hadn't even smiled.

'All right?'

'Yeah.' Shutting the rear door by pushing against it with the suitcase, then the front one with her hip. Movements intended to conform with her appearance. Calling to de Plesse then, 'Adieu. Thanks for the lift.'

'I trust the animal will recover.'

That exchange had been for the ears of passers-by: the nearest an elderly man and woman crowding past and staring with undisguised interest at the dusky-skinned artificial blonde and the pompous-looking driver leaning across to wind up the near window. The blonde with a smile on her face, watching him move off. The hairdresser had suggested, 'Those beautiful teeth show to great advantage in contrast with the dark complexion. You should make a show of them, smile a lot, eh?'

'Think that'll help?'

'Sure it will!' She was a woman in her forties, well upholstered, and herself a blonde with a dark parting. She knew her business, and *this* kind of business too, it seemed. Telling Rosie, 'It's your mouth, my dear, not just the teeth, you got a smashing mouth, you know that? Yeah, course you do! See – they aren't thinking hey, this is some *résistante* on the run; they're thinking, boy, get an eyeful of *that!*' Heavy body shaking with mirth . . .

In principle, good advice, though. A *résistante* with a price on her head wouldn't be making a public spectacle of herself, she'd want to be invisible. As Rosie rather wished she could have been now – while aware that it was precisely the impression she must *not* give. Crossing the road, basket in one hand, suitcase in the other. Her skirt – one Roxane had grown out of – was a bit tight. New shoes – another present from Silvie, wooden shoes of course but with articulated soles – click-clacking on the cobbles: and a *gazo* deliberately *not* slowing – might actually have speeded up slightly – so that she only just made it without running. You didn't have to be German, she thought, to be a shit. The cat was moving around inside the basket – Thérèse's, with the central handle and a half-lid each side of it, perfect except that it had more room in it than any normal cat could need, and the balance kept shifting as the animal lurched around. Maurice had tied the lid flaps down for her, warning her that it was wild, a ratter and mouser, a yard-cat, completely undomesticated.

Poor thing. Probably scared stiff. Might have been worth its weight in diamonds though, if those *miliciens* had made a nuisance of themselves. Peculiar-looking woman with a wild cat, taking it to the vet – who'd want to see papers?

The alley was only about a metre wide, and stank as she'd known it would. Passing the side doors of shops that faced on to the street – or might have been entrances to apartments above the shops – then rounding the corner into a back-street – itself too narrow for motor traffic – and seeing the sign-board on her left: *MAGNE ET RACKE, Vétérinaires.*

Two front windows obscured by internal Venetian blinds, and a green-painted door between them. Knocker in the form of an iron horse's head: she rapped with it, and a woman's voice called immediately, '*Entrez!*' She pushed the door open and went in: into a vestibule with a counter like a hotel reception-desk and behind it a short, stockily built red-headed girl in a white coat staring at her. Turning to push the door shut: conscious of that stare and wondering again whether she wasn't a bit *too* noticeable. It was a point they'd discussed at some length, in the de Plesse house: but it was indisputable that the milk-chocolate tint did hide the scarring on her forehead, and for technical reasons – the hairdresser's – blonde was the only colour she *could* adopt, without looking too much like the old Rosie with a suntan.

She'd put her suitcase down, and lifted the basket on to the counter. Surprisingly, no sound or movement from the cat.

'Madame?'

'It's a cat. Monsieur Rouquet knows about it, he's expecting me. I'm Justine Quérier.'

*   *   *

'Mam'selle Quérier to see you – with a cat. She says you were expecting her.'

'I was indeed, Béa.' Sounds of movement in there – a chair scraping back, a drawer pushed shut. The redhead stood aside, wordlessly inviting her to go on in. She – Béa – had taken possession of the basket; asking her now, 'What is its name, Mam'selle?'

She shook her head. 'I don't think it has one.'

She couldn't safely have made one up either, not knowing its sex. But she'd know this man's English name, in a moment – with an effort of memory . . . He was staring back at her, obviously startled by her bizarre appearance, and just as obviously wouldn't have any recall of one of a class of trainees to whom he'd lectured three years ago at Beaulieu in Hampshire, where she'd been in the final stages of her SOE training course and he'd come down as a visiting lecturer. At that time he'd been one of the few who'd already been in and out of France as a *chef de réseau*.

She'd heard of him since then, too. He was one of the stars. Looking older than she remembered him. Light-brown eyes intent on hers, as if trying to read her mind. On his feet, bony hand now enfolding hers. Narrow face with high cheekbones, brown hair. She'd remembered now: first name was Derek. Could have been all they'd been told, in fact. Murmuring. *'Enchanté, Mam'selle.'* Slight frown: 'I'm trying to recall who it was that telephoned. Only yesterday, but – alas, my rotten memory . . .'

'Raoul de Plesse?'

'Of course. Of course . . . And he said he thought perhaps cat flu, but – rather unusual symptoms. One couldn't altogether rule out rabies – as I warned him. Please – sit down.' To the receptionist then, who must still have been in the doorway behind her, 'Transfer the animal to a cage, Béa. I'll take a look at it in a minute. See what you think meanwhile – but be careful, wear your gauntlets.' He was returning to his side of the desk: 'Of course, if it should be rabies, Mam'selle, you realize – only one thing for it.' A shrug: 'But let's hope that is not the case.' The door clicked shut behind Béa, and his eyes came back to Rosie. 'Have we met before?'

'Yes. As it happens.'

'I had that impression – that perhaps I should know you. But – I'm sorry—'

She told him in English, 'The boot-polish probably wouldn't help. Yellow hair-dye wouldn't either.' Touching her cheek: 'Boot-polish mixed into cold cream. There's some scarring on my forehead and it hides it. Your first name's Derek – or it *was*, about three years ago. I was one of a group of trainees you gave some lectures to at Beaulieu. You couldn't possibly have remembered.'

'And would Baker Street recognize the name Justine Quérier?'

'No, they wouldn't. You know of Michel Jacquard, though?'

'I do?'

'Yes, you do. He got the papers for me – ones I have now. My cover-name *was* Suzanne Tanguy, code-name Zoé. I was in Brittany, and – things went wrong, we were making a dash for the Finistère north coast, but – well, the car crashed, I woke up in hospital in Morlaix with Gestapo standing around the bed. Also an SOE traitor code-name "Hector", real name André Marchéval – our former air movements officer?'

Staring at her. As motionless as if paralysed.

'Zoé. Field name Suzanne . . . Am I right in thinking you're – a bit famous around here?'

'You mean the posters.'

'But how – how on *earth* . . .' A long-fingered hand to his forehead . . . 'Where does Michel Jacquard come into this?'

'He found me – saved my life. I'd been shot. I was on a train – a group of us *en route* we thought to Ravensbrück. The train was stopped – because of another on the line ahead which Michel's people had sabotaged – this was in open country somewhere near Baccarat, but where the line runs close to the river – the Meurthe – and – I made a run for it, to divert the guards' attention—'

'So the other girl on those posters could get away.'

'Exact—' She'd cut the word off short. Then: 'You heard of this from Michel, I suppose.'

Shake of the narrow head: 'Haven't spoken to him in weeks. Only to de Plesse. But allow me to surprise *you* now. That other girl – fellow agent of yours, you'd known each other before and then met in Fresnes prison – her code-name was Giselle, real name Elise or Lise?'

'Yes, but –' leaning forward, hands white-knuckled grasping the desk's edge: 'But what—'

'She was sitting in that chair –' pointing at it with a nod – 'well, August 2nd today, must have been three, four weeks ago. A Monday.' Exercising memory: 'July the tenth. I arranged a pick-up for her. Hudson, from Tempsford. Which is what you'll want, I imagine?'

Looking for her affirmative, but not getting it: she was still staring at him, hardly daring to believe it. Thought *en passant*, Hudson because you'd be out of Lysander range here, for the return trip. Asking him – almost incredulously – 'And she went – *was* picked up?'

'Certainly. Later that same week, what's more!'

Lise not only alive, but in England – for three weeks now. A derivative of which was that Baker Street must already have the low-down on 'Hector', one wouldn't need to explain anything like as much as one had envisaged. *And* they'd have taken action to warn any agents in the field who'd still been in the clear but might have had contact with him at some stage.

Lise *alive* . . .

He was offering her a Gauloise. 'You're supposed to be dead, you realize. Baker Street will shortly resound to the popping of champagne corks.'

'Or they'll be reaching for the smelling-salts. Thanks . . .'

He'd smiled. 'Lise was *certain* you were dead.'

'I thought *she* was.' Leaning to the match. 'How did she get to you?'

'She'd holed up with some people – middle-aged artisan couple – down where you mentioned, roughly – offered them a lot of money, the man's wife talked to a friend who knew someone who was an active *résistant*, and a colleague of his had had dealings with my courier. Who checked, very cautiously, and – there we were. Didn't take long at all . . . Extraordinarily enough – this really does take a bit of getting used to – it's only the Boches who've had some reason to believe *you*'d survived – that poster, a million francs—'

'No body, near the train – and there should have been, they knew they'd shot me. But Michel had carted me off. And Lise having vanished too – which they couldn't have discovered until later, I imagine—'

'She was back in England before the posters went up. She'd told me all about you, of course. She was quite positive – that you'd been shot – and I might add deeply distressed.' Shaking his head – in his own lingering disbelief – staring at her across the desk . . . 'Zoé – field-name Suzanne. Mind telling me your real first name?'

'Rosie. Christened Rosalie.'

'Yes. Lise said that. Tell me one other thing – when and where did she get to know it?'

'In the train.' She nodded. 'By which time that sort of security detail didn't seem to matter any more. You're thinking I might be an impostor.'

'Not seriously. Considering it – as an outside possibility.'

He spread his hands. 'In fact, it's highly improbable and not all that obvious what purpose might be served – by what would have been a fairly tricky ploy – although it *would* of course explain the heavy make-up.'

'So do the posters. But – the purpose – *your* head on the block, to start with?'

'They'd have had to have known, to send you to me in the first place.'

'Uh-huh. De Plesse knows all about you, obviously. I could have fooled *him*. So his head and yours, and of course any others of your *réseau* to whom I might be introduced. Plus maybe a Hudson and its crew shot up as it lands, and the reception team bagged or killed.'

Such things did happen, had been known. His slight shrug acknowledged it. Rosie added, 'I wouldn't trust de Plesse further than I could spit anyway. I mean if they put the screws on him.'

'You could be right.'

'I can put your mind at rest about *me*, anyway.' She leant towards him across the desk – head tilted sideways, cigarette into left hand, pushing the white scarf up above her ear with the other. 'See the groove? Hair's covering it quite well now, thank God. This one knocked me out, I think. See it?'

'Crikey.' His fingers replaced hers: the tip of one fore-finger gently traced the line of the indented scar. 'A couple of centimetres to the left, you and I would not—'

'No, we wouldn't. But the most damaging one was in the back of this shoulder.' She sat back in the chair. 'Came out here. Sheets of blood. Probably what fooled them into thinking I was dead. A *sage-femme* fixed me up, in the safe-house Michel took me to. Where I spent a month, in fact. He left us some sulphur powder too. Sulphanilamide, some such name?'

'I've heard of it.'

'I'll tell you the rest, just briefly. Michel was in the vicinity because he'd blown a train ahead of the one we were on – why ours stopped, how Lise and I escaped the crematorium. He and Luc – his number two, another para – heard there'd been some shooting, came looking, and took me off to – well, other side of the Vosges mountains. Close to the Natzweiler camp, as it happens.'

'And eventually transferred you to Raoul de Plesse.'

'There was a stop in between, but – yes. What do *you* think of de Plesse?'

Slight grimace . . . 'Awkward to deal with. Great opinion of himself. Wields influence in Resistance circles, therefore has his uses. But you're right, I'd say he values his own hide above all else. Absolute phobia about using the telephone, for instance. Fair enough as a matter of general principle, but—'

'Michel called him to heel over his attitude to us. To SOE generally, was Michel's analysis, but it seemed to me at the time it was directed at me personally. He read him the riot act anyway – don't know what he said, I wasn't present.'

'The root of the trouble is that he has political ambitions. De Plesse, I mean. That's enough to make him anti-foreigner. Playing to the gallery – you know? But he wouldn't want to fall out with *Forces Françaises de L'Intérieur* or the Free French army or de Gaulle – especially not at this juncture – so I suppose Michel *could* crack the whip. Michel's FFI title incidentally is Commandant, First Maquis Liaison Group – if one needed to refer to him in any communication with Baker Street, for instance. But what *are* we going to say to them . . . Something like *Agent code-name Zoé previously believed dead has recovered from wounds and is in the care of this réseau. Request pick up soonest* – and I'll specify the landing-field. Anything more than that?'

'Yes. A lot more. A lot to explain—'

His telephone had rung. 'Damn it.' Snatching it off its

hook: eyes on her, frowning . . . 'Yes?' Listening, he'd sighed. 'All right, put him through . . .' Hand over the mouthpiece: 'Won't take long – I *hope* . . . Yes, Guillaume Rouquet speaking . . .'

He'd had to rush off, and Béa had produced coffee. The cat was in good health, she said – temperature at forty degrees a little high, attributable to stress, but it had been released into a spacious cage, given milk and a fish-carcase. If any enquiry should be made, it was being kept here for a day or two for observation. Béa was an insider, obviously, but it was better to leave it at that, not ask questions. Meanwhile there were comings and goings – white coats here in the building, rough working clothes on others arriving or departing, all seemingly in a rush. Virtually all the work was with horses, cattle, sheep and pigs, Béa told her, very little these days with domestic pets. Guillaume was absent for about an hour, then rejoined her: his 'coffee' was stone-cold, and Béa brought more for both of them.

'So – let's hear it – finally?'

'Yes.' First drag at a new cigarette . . . 'First – to put it all in perspective – how I've come to know all this – there's a lot to explain, I'm afraid—'

'Take your time. We won't be interrupted again, officially I'm out of town.'

'Right. To start with – the traitor – "Hector", real name André Marchéval – was with the Gestapo in Morlaix when they visited me in hospital, *and* then in Rue des Saussaies—'

'You must have told Lise all this.'

'She told *you*. Good . . . But when you think – the know-ledge he must have had – *has* – details of *réseaux*, individual agents, landing fields, dropping-zones – escape lines too, probably – when you *think*—'

'It's staggering. Fortunately London will now be cognizant of it, through Lise.'

'Which helps a lot, yes. But it's what I've learnt *since* – I'll come to it . . . She may have mentioned that "Hector", at a stage or two removed, was almost certainly responsible for the death of her Organizer in Rennes – then her own arrest?' Guillaume had nodded: she explained, 'The relevance of it is that from her point of view as well as mine it's – quite personal, this "Hector" thing.'

'But we'd *all* agree – the sooner we have him behind bars—'

'On a rope, would be my preference.'

'All right. Or in front of a firing-squad. But he should be able to tell us plenty first. In particular what's happened to a lot of agents who've disappeared without trace. *Then* – by all means, due process of military law.' An eyebrow cocked: 'Where is this leading us, Rosie?'

'There's a lot of it. I did warn you. I can't give it to you in a dozen words.'

'All right . . .'

'At the safe-house in Alsace I told Michel about "Hector" – André Marchéval – including the fact that his father has some sort of engineering works somewhere south of Paris. Which *I* was told in London – by Bob Hallowell, incidentally. Michel's reaction was instantaneous – "Hector" should be knocked off, immediately, if not sooner, and he'd try to find out exactly where the factory is. Idea being that when the Boches pull out that's where he'll turn up – *chez* Papa. Papa's name is Henri, by the way.'

'Has Michel located the factory?'

'Has indeed. West of Troyes, village called St Valéry-sur-Vanne. And he visited – intro by courtesy of de Plesse – a *résistant* in Troyes by name of Victor Dufay who runs yet another agricultural engineering business, and – well, the background is, Marchéval's is under Henri M's management but Boche control, they've been turning out pipes and cylinders to Boche requirements right from the start, couldn't be bombed without killing workers' families because the works are integral with the village itself, and the workers wouldn't want to go in for sabotage either, for fear of reprisals. Boches are on the spot, apparently, occupying most of Marchéval senior's house, a manor-house *outside* the village.'

'So – bombing ruled out, and sabotage unlikely: and the product's not particularly important anyway—'

'Well, wait . . . After Michel had talked to Dufay he pushed on – some new brief he has now – to Dijon, and Dufay decided it was time he updated himself on the St Valéry situation – only reminded of the place's existence, it seems, by Michel's interest.'

'Some distance from Troyes, is it?'

'Yes – but anyway, Dufay then got in touch with Michel in what must have been a bit of a flap, to tell him the Marchéval product is now rocket-casings – allegedly, for Boche secret weapon number two.'

'Christ! Whose allegation, though – Dufay's?'

'I think a man by name of Craillot, a *résistant* who runs an *auberge* there. But now bombing *can't* be ruled out – right?'

'Not if this is confirmable.'

'They did produce some detail – overall measurements, might give *some* clue – and Michel seemed fairly convinced. But it'll have to be checked, obviously – on the spot, and preferably by a pianist, who could then report to London *from* the spot. I gather we've no SOE presence in that area now?'

'Regrettably, not.'

'*Réseau* blown eight or ten weeks ago, I'm told. Maybe another "Hector" casualty. But going back a bit – what I *would* have proposed to Baker Street anyway was that they might leave me here long enough to stake out Marchéval's and/or St Valéry on the off-chance of "Hector" turning up

– when, or if, the Boches dispense with his services, or whatever. It was Michel's idea originally – and he then suggested having the works or better still the manor-house bombed. Manor preferably because no villagers'd get killed and it'd be more likely to bring André running to Papa.'

'If the Gestapo let him go.'

'He might have more freedom of movement than you'd expect. He's not a prisoner, he's sold out to them. But – a chance, that's all.'

'Chance of what, precisely?' Stubbing out his cigarette. 'OK to call you Rosie, by the way?'

She'd shrugged: 'Wouldn't you agree the sooner he's dead the better?'

'You mean that if he did put in an appearance, you'd kill him. *You* would?'

'Well – if I was there on my own—'

'You know what Baker Street will say?'

'I can guess what *you're* going to say.'

'They'll say pick-up coming, Rosie, get yourself back here double-quick!'

'Although in these *new* circumstances—'

'Obviously the rocket issue'll be taken care of – if it's confirmed. *If* it is, it's – putting it mildly, top priority, obviously. As far as "Hector"'s concerned, though – OK, if it was thought necessary to knock him off because he was still imperilling agents in the field—'

'Isn't he? As far as we know?'

'You see – if your aim was simply to track him down, make sure he doesn't just bloody vanish or if he does we'll know where to—'

'Baker Street would support *that*, you think.'

'When the Boches pull out there's going to be chaos, isn't there? Gadarene swine stuff. Thousands on the run. Odds are he *will* go to ground.' Tilting his chair back, fingers drumming on the desk, eyes on the high, ornately decorated ceiling. 'But not for ever. Not even for very long. He'd surface when the waters calm a bit – a Frenchman under French jurisdiction – right? – and foreigners by then strongly discouraged from poking their noses in. You can bet on *that*. Gallic bullshit'll rise like a dense fog – out of which I can see Marchéval emerging, presenting himself as one of about forty million totally bogus heroes of the Resistance – alongside the *real* ones, of course – indignantly denying any charges we lay against him.' Looking at her again: nodding. 'I'd say there definitely is something to work on here, Rosie. Baker Street *would* go for it.'

'Good!'

'Unless of course they've taken steps already. They may have – Lise having got back and spilt the beans – thanks to you, and as you intended. I may say I admire what you did enormously. But whether they'd let you stay in the field for any purpose at all, after all you've been through . . . Frankly, I doubt it. They'll want the job done, but not by you. I think if I was advising them I'd say pick her brains – whatever she's found out – and drop in a small team, commando-style. Find him, grab him, fly him out.'

'Fly them in when and where, find him and identify him how?'

'Well—'

'You see, being a pianist, I could go down there, check the rocket-casing report – using the pub that man runs as my safe-house, incidentally – do the groundwork on the bombing – which as you say would be top priority – then deal with "Hector" – Marchéval – *if* he shows up. Point is I *know* him – I've spoken to him, been spoken to *by* him, I could pick him out in a crowd—'

'Well – makes a *degree* of sense—'

'I'd *like* to see it through, too. Where this started, you realize – in the train, talking with Lise, *en route* Ravensbrück – then the chance came up, a faint hope she might get away,

purpose being precisely what she and I had been talking
about – ensuring bloody "Hector" does *not* live happy
ever after!'
'Baker Street would agree wholeheartedly in all respects
except that of leaving it to *you*.'
'Despite the time factor?'
'Well – I don't know. But – it's going to be their decision,
anyway, I'm only guessing. Look – we might say something
like *Zóe proposes – as alternative to recall* . . . But – do you
honestly think you're fit enough?'
'Yes. I do. Am.'
'Another aspect – has it occurred to you that it would suit
Marchéval down to the ground to see *you* dead?'
'Hadn't thought about it.' Blinking at him. 'But – yes, I
dare say . . .'
'He knows all about you – must do. And it's odds-on
he'll know you've escaped. When you met in the Gestapo
building, would he have known or guessed that you knew
who *he* was?'
'He'd have realized I'd catch on, I think. There and then,
of course, he wouldn't have given a damn either way – I was
as good as labelled "Ravensbrück" – which he couldn't *not*
have known.'
'He'd know now, therefore, that if he went on trial you'd
be *the* key witness.'
'But they're looking for me anyway, aren't they? The
Gestapo, I mean.' She gestured dismissively. 'He's only
their stooge, he's *nothing*.'
Guillaume thinking about it, gazing back at her across
the desk. Giving up, reluctantly . . . Shaking his head as
he reached for paper and pencil.
'My bet stands – they'll recall you. But let's see now . . .'
Eyes down: murmuring it aloud . . . '*Agent code-name Zoé
previously believed dead has recovered from wounds and is in
the temporary care of this réseau* . . . Might follow with: *If*

immediate recall is decided upon, suggest early pick-up from Xanadu, subject confirmation. Glancing up: 'Xanadu is the field Lise went from. Reasonably easy reach from here. Confirmation depending on my courier taking a bike-ride to check that in the last couple of weeks it hasn't been littered with tree trunks or concrete blocks.'

She nodded. That sort of check was standard procedure. He went on. *But as alternative to her recall she proposes that she might be left in the field in order to track movements of the former agent 'Hector'* . . .

'How soon will this go out?'

'Oh.' He paused in his scribbling. 'Next scheduled transmission would be tomorrow night. So – emergency procedure, for this. This afternoon, I expect.'

'Emergency procedure' meant the *réseau*'s pianist having to conduct a two-way exchange with the home station – making contact, then getting confirmation that the signal was coming in intelligibly, then again that they'd received it, and there was always a heightened risk of such transmissions being picked up by German radio direction finders. Which was a steep enough risk in any case. Long-range detection to start with, then radio-detection vans positioning themselves for more accurate fixing, sometimes men on foot with headphones and radio packs. Then, the black or grey Citroëns, thugs in ill-fitting suits and soft hats . . . But she'd used emergency procedure often enough herself – recently in Brittany for instance, sending urgent requests for *parachutages* of weaponry for Maquis groups. Tapping the messages out in roadside ditches, mostly, the transceiver powered from a *gazo*'s battery, aerial-wire strung out between trees.

And old Dr Peucat as look-out, puffing his pipe . . .

Guillaume was having trouble drafting this signal. Scratching several lines out . . . 'Here, Rosie – you've got it all clear in *your* head . . .'

'OK.'

She picked it up from the words *movements of former agent 'Hector'* – and added in her own rounder hand, *by observation of Marchéval engineering works at St Valéry-sur-Vanne near Troyes, where he might be expected either when Rue des Saussaies evacuated or sooner if the factory or family residence were bombed or sabotaged. Factory is part of village so bombing would endanger workers' families, whereas residence is isolated and occupied by German officers as well as by Marchéval senior. A safe-house in St Valéry is known to Zoé and she has introductions to local résistants. More importantly, research in last few days has elicited a report that the factory is now producing rocket casings believed by Resistance informant to be for V2s, casings' approx dimensions length 12 metres and diameter 2 metres, which are shipped into Germany in Wehrmacht truck convoys at intervals as yet unknown. Suggest this calls for immediate investigation and, if confirmed, for early bombing attack, targeting residence as well as factory, which might also result in surfacing by 'Hector'.*

She pushed it back over to him. Adjusting the soft-rubber padding in her cheeks while he looked over the lines she'd written; telling him as he finished and shrugged approval, 'If they did give me the job, there'd be some things I'd want. For instance money, a pistol, cyanide pills, Mark III transceiver. And I think I might *ask* for a Eureka beacon.'

'Lug *that* around with you?'

The 'Eureka' was a ground responder navigational beacon, which came to life when triggered by a device in an aircraft called a 'Rebecca' on-board interrogator. It was in use all over France; but you could hardly have carried it on a bicycle, for instance. Rosie acknowledged, 'I know – it's a problem. Might make do with an "S" phone. With a Eureka I'd do without any battery, anyway. Scrounge one locally – or something. But incidentally, the American Eureka – PPN1, I think they call it – isn't all that big. If one was available, of course.'

'Common or garden variety weighs about fifty kilos, doesn't it? "S" phone – what, about seven kilos.' He paused. 'Well – *if* they gave you the job – and in my book this is still only a matter of going through the motions – we'd do better to ask for the drop here, and make arrangements to get you and the gear moved down to –' checking the draft of the signal – 'St Valéry. Maybe with help from de Plesse. If Michel Jacquard's strictures are still an influence . . . What about Michel himself?'

'Gone. Unfortunately. Might ask de Plesse just to lend us a *gazo* – which he'd get back. I could drive myself down there and leave it with the man in Troyes.'

'Wouldn't advise it. On your own, and "wanted". Not even if your papers are a hundred per cent. Are they, by the way?'

'Maybe not quite a hundred, but—'

'Anyway – as far as *this* is concerned' – the draft of the signal – 'I'll mention that if they were leaving you in the field there'd be a shopping-list to follow.' Shake of the head: 'Won't be, but – notionally, Rosalie: transceiver, "S" phone, cash, pistol.' He'd begun roughing out a list. She prompted, 'PC capsules.' 'PC' standing for potassium cyanide, suicide pills. He'd grimaced slightly: 'Here and now we'll just say, *If Zoé's proposal that she should remain in the field is approved, a parachutage of transceiver, codes, "S" phone, cash, pistol and capsules etc. will be requested.*'

Glancing up at her: 'What kind of pistol would you ask for?'

'Llama, please.'

He looked surprised. 'I'd have thought something lighter, easier to carry hidden. Summer clothes, after all. A Beretta .32 for instance – reason I ask is it happens I've one here you could have.'

'Thanks, but Llamas suit me, and 9-millimetre's easier to find than .32.'

Quizzical smile: 'Wouldn't be fighting a battle, Rosie!'
'No. But still . . .'
Thinking, *Just killing one man.* Reaching to the desk,
touching wood.

Chapter 8

She was smoking too much, she knew. One just crushed out and the next match flaring – in this small apartment above the hat-shop to which Guillaume had brought her an hour ago. He'd left her a whole pack. Black-market, obviously – the ration being only two packs a *month*, for God's sake. Smoke-haze hanging in a thick layer: she got up, slid the nearer window further open to let some of it out. This was his pianist's flat and she worked in the hat-shop under it: her employer owned it but had a house on the other side of town, apparently. Rosie had known, leaving the premises of Messrs Magne et Racke after a snack lunch of hard biscuits and cheese in Guillaume's office, that they were going to visit the pianist, but he hadn't mentioned her name or anything about a hat-shop; one could have been arrested in the street *en route* and interrogated until the cows came home, wouldn't have been able to tell the bastards anything. So with no option *but* to hold out, you'd have suffered . . . Anyway, Guillaume had only said, 'All right – if you're ready?' – and to his girl-assistant, Béa, 'I'll be out for a couple of hours, but I'll probably call in at old Vasco's stables – leave a message there if anything's really urgent, eh?' They'd left by way of the alley out to the street where de Plesse had dropped her, and turned left, heading further into the shopping centre. Southward: noting street-names where any were visible, walking beside Guillaume with a hand on his arm, about three steps to every two of his, Roxane's skirt making that inevitable. Conscious again of her awful hair and make-up, pink blouse, new shoes noisy on the paving, Thérèse's rain-jacket incongruously shabby but with room for her papers in its capacious inside pocket. Would have room for a 9-millimetre Spanish-made Colt-action Llama too – in due course – subject to decisions to be made in London, any minute now.

She'd left Michel's sketch-map of St Valéry-sur-Vanne in Guillaume's desk. It had no words on it, a snooper wouldn't have made head or tail of it, but if it had been found on Justine Quérier she'd have been expected to explain it.

How? Mental exercise, while waiting to cross a road. *Gazos*, bicycles in streams. Over then, and turning left. Thinking of interrogation, how one might or might not stand up to it, because being out and almost on one's own now, in a town where one's face was plastered on street corners – and being in something less than the very peak of condition: knowing also that if she was caught again they'd make damn sure she stayed caught – *unless* she could convince them in the first five minutes that she wasn't who she might have been. Explanation of that map, therefore – say it was the district of Sarrebourg – no, Souillac, where she'd been living with her sick mother. Sketch made to show a locum doctor, stranger to the district, how to find their terraced house in the Rue Celeste. There were a lot of people about, many just sauntering, idling away their lunch-breaks. Two *Feldgendarmes* shouldering through from behind: they seemed always to patrol in pairs, and there were far more of them on the streets than there had been a year ago in Rouen.

Releasing second-line troops who'd now become front-line, maybe?

Say priest, not doctor. Priest who'd offered transport to the hospital.

'Over the road there – see?'

Guillaume pointing with his chin. They were passing through a more or less triangular *place* that had a railed grass centre; the *Feldgendarmes* had turned in at a stone portico that jutted out ahead here, with a swastika banner drooping from a staff above it. Opposite, across the street and behind those railings, was a hoarding crowded with official notices. Guillaume gesturing again: 'This end – one from the end?'

Black and white. Others were framed in red – red and black being the Nazi colours, as on that filthy banner – and those were familiar enough, she'd seen dozens, wherever she'd been, notices of 'executions' carried out. The black-and-white poster on the left, though, at eye-level halfway up the hoarding – two side-by-side images – that they were of females was about all one could make out from here – with a caption in large black capitals and some lines in smaller print below that. Guillaume had muttered as she craned round, 'See? Proof of your fame.'

'Could we cross over?'

'Better not.' Tugging her along. '*Feldgendarmes* head-quarters we just passed. Only take one of them goofing out of a window – wondering how to kill the next hour or two, getting *you* in his sights as you trip over to admire yourself . . .'

'Any chance you might get me one?'

'A poster?' Nearing the end of the square. 'Over here and then to the right there . . . I suppose – if they're still on show when the balloon goes up.'

'Get two, if you can? One for Lise – please?'

'I'll try. There *will* be a few other things going on, mind you. Along here now – Justine . . .' To the right. She saw a tin street-sign, Rue St Jacques. Then they were passing a jeweller's window – necklaces of amber and lapis lazuli in a small central display, second-hand items of costume jewellery around it. And next-door, now, a milliner's.

'We're here. Keen on hats, are you?'

The inscription on the shopfront was *Pauline Delacroix, Modiste*. Guillaume was giving Rosie time to scan the contents of the window, telling her quietly, 'Pauline is a good friend, a *résistante*, and Léonie works for her and lives up there – over the shop.'

'Your pianist – Léonie, right?'

'Right. Makes hats too. Come on, plenty more inside. They make 'em out of everything you can think of.' Pushing the glass-topped door open: 'We're in luck – I'd thought they might have been shut for lunch. In you go . . .'

Into a powdery, hot-house atmosphere in which an auburn-haired woman, fortyish with an hour-glass figure wrapped in a smart black dress, was holding a pink, cloche-shaped hat in her two be-ringed hands, offering it – for Christ's sake, they were in the shop and it was too late to back out now – to a tall Boche officer who'd glanced round sharply – irritably, even – as Guillaume pushed the glass door closed shutting out the street's noise . . . He – the Boche – had thrown them that quick glance, then turned back to the woman. His long-peaked *Wehrmacht* cap, Rosie saw, lay on the glass-topped counter, incongruously close to a wide-brimmed, floppy-looking flowered creation. A Boche was about the last thing you'd have expected to run into, in here: getting off the crowded street had felt like arrival at some place of refuge – just for a moment, with what Guillaume had been telling her about this rather voluptuous woman, and the girl they hadn't met yet. She felt breathless suddenly, and was trying to keep her face averted. Although Guillaume was taking it calmly: lifting a hand in greeting to the woman, who'd flashed him a smile and made a lightning scan of as much as she could see of Rosie in that same swift glance. Horrified by even that much, Rosie guessed – but showing nothing, switching the smile back to her customer, assuring him huskily, 'It's an excellent choice, Herr Colonel, I'm certain the lady will adore it. And for your daughter what do you think of this little model? Extremely *chic*, don't you agree, while also definitely *young* – for a young girl as you've described her?'

Guillaume was steering Rosie away to the left, into a longer, narrower part of the shop. The German muttering behind them in accented French, 'This one I'm less sure of. But – come to think of it, I wonder . . .'

He'd turned this way just as Rosie had risked a look back over her shoulder at them: thinking that she should *not* have been taken so much by surprise. France was full of Boches, there was no way you *wouldn't* run into them here or there . . . Guillaume's hand on her arm though, turning her back again – towards a nearer display of hats. 'How about this one?'

Made of velvet, a hideous shade of green. He couldn't have meant it seriously. Hadn't, of course; only didn't want the Boche making any closer study of her than he might have done already. She touched the green hat: shook her head. 'Not really . . .'

Guttural French behind them: 'Do you think, Madame, you could persuade the young lady to assist us? There's a slight resemblance to my daughter – *very* slight, I suppose, but – it might give one some idea . . .'

Imagining this?

'Guillaume.' Pauline's throaty tone . . . 'Did you hear? *Might* the young lady be so kind?' Clicking of her own articulated wooden soles as she approached: Guillaume had put himself on that side of Rosie, shielding her.

'Much as I cherish our friendship, Pauline, I do *not* believe your customers should—'

'But I don't mind.' Rosie patted his arm: had come up beside him, facing Pauline and beyond her the German.

This wasn't avoidable, had better be taken head-on. The German's smile was as symmetrically curved as a child might have drawn it, on the round, pink face. Rosie added to Pauline, 'Long as it doesn't take too long.'

'Extremely kind, Mam'selle . . .'

'Although I wouldn't have thought my suntan –' addressing Pauline again, but the Boche cut in, 'It's primarily the hair-colour, also the general – should I say, combination of youth and – how to put it . . .' With his hands, was the answer, outlining her size and figure. Presumptuous sod . . . Pauline and her scent in close-up then, though: 'May I?' Removing the scarf, and settling the little hat on Rosie's head; adjusting its angle slightly, then stepping back. 'There, Herr Colonel . . . *Quite* entrancing?'

He was giving Rosie a long, hard stare. Studying *her* more than the hat, she thought.

Wondering what might be familiar about her?

Guillaume protesting, 'So happens we do *not* have time to waste—'

'But – please –' Pauline's lashes fluttering – 'just another tiny *instant* . . .'

It didn't look like suntan. She knew it didn't. Wouldn't even to this bastard – couldn't possibly, not for long, such close inspection . . . Could have been oil or cream of some kind *on* tanned skin: that had been how the hairdresser had suggested she might explain it. She glanced at Guillaume, forced a smile. Praying that the creature currently feasting its little gimlet eyes on her might *not* have studied the posters, *not* be straining its memory . . .

If they *had* memories. One could wonder as one might about dogs: did they actually *think* – or see in colour, or just in black and white?

Snap of its fingers like a pistol-shot. 'I'll take it.'

A nod to the proprietress, and a small bow to Rosie: 'I am greatly obliged, Mam'selle.' Guillaume turned away, looking annoyed and making a show of checking the time again, as Pauline lifted the hat carefully from Rosie's head, purring, 'So *very* kind . . .'

He'd acted his part well, she thought. Affronted and impatient, but in a subdued manner, natural enough in the daunting presence of the Boche. And her own reactions had only *really* become noticeable – to herself anyway – after the event, when they'd got up here. The need to smoke as voraciously as this, for instance . . . She was glad of that, that at the time she'd managed it all right. She squashed out another stub, committed herself to waiting ten minutes now before lighting another. For one thing, cigarettes were rationed and not all that easy to come by unless one had black-market connections and money to spare. Which Guillaume probably would have. Her pulse-rate was still much too fast. Time now, ten minutes to two. The pianist, Léonie Garnier, should be getting the signal out by now, might even have sent it and signed off. *Zoé proposes that as an alternative to immediate recall . . .* Guillaume had told them he'd be back here by three thirty. Using emergency procedure and when a reply was called for, you'd get it exactly one hour and ten minutes after the operator in the communications centre in Sevenoaks had received your signal. She could see it all happening – having worked in that establishment as a radio-operator herself, before Johnny's Spitfire had been shot down into the Channel and she'd applied to be accepted for training as an agent. Initially they'd turned her down: Johnny had been killed only the day before, and the interviewing officer had suspected her of harbouring some sort of suicidal impulse; then shortly afterwards apparently had second thoughts and called her back. She'd heard later that in fact Maurice Buckmaster, head of 'F' Section, had just about blown his top at hearing of the rejection of a candidate who was already a trained wireless operator as well as a fluent French speaker.

But she did know the Sevenoaks scene intimately: could hear the clicking of the Morse key as the operator acknowledged receipt of message and signed-off with the letters AS, meaning 'Stand by', simultaneously buzzing for the message in its five-letter groups to be rushed to the cipher room where it would be translated into plain language and passed to Baker Street by teleprinter. Supposing Sevenoaks had received it at 1350, say, it would be chattering through on Baker Street's teleprinter in plain language by two fifteen, and 'F' Section staff would then have twenty minutes to think about it, reach a decision and draft a reply: so by 1440 the decision affecting her own future movements would be rattling off the teleprinter in the Sevenoaks establishment, where ciphering would then take twenty minutes and Léonie Garnier, somewhere in Nancy, with her ivory-white skin and blue eyes, near-black hair and delicate, artistic-looking hat-making hands would have it at 1500.

What she'd get first would be a code-group meaning *I have a message for you, are you ready?* to which she'd tap out in reply *QRV – K:* 'Ready. Over . . .'

Wherever she was. Couldn't be far because Guillaume had arranged to see her back here at three thirty, which meant Léonie couldn't be more than half an hour away – across town or out in its fringes somewhere. You could get a long way on a bicycle in half an hour. Delivering a hat, no doubt, or collecting one. She'd taken a hat-box with her on the bike anyway. And she'd have had the set hidden in some loft, or a church tower, or – factory building, empty office or roof-space or a friend's apartment which if she was wise she would neither have used before nor use again.

Nice-looking girl. A year or two younger than Rosie – twenty-two or three. Rather shy, quiet manner, smiles that were slow in coming as if she didn't like to waste them. Rosie had apologized for putting her in such danger: the emergency procedure routine, especially in a town, wasn't much less chancy than a game of Russian roulette. The German radio detectors would have caught that first transmission and the rapid acknowledgement from England, there'd be Boches listening out now for London's further response and they'd know the SOE procedures well enough to be expecting it – as Léonie was – after the seventy-minute interval. So they'd be listening for *her* brief 'Ready. Over' and 'message received' transmissions – having perhaps got somewhere near to pinpointing her from the earlier exchange.

Could have watchers down in the street by then. She'd be acutely aware of it, and very, very cautious; checking whatever might be visible from the windows before she emerged, and so forth. Even then knowing she wasn't anything like safe, but emerging into the street casually like any other citizen going about her normal business, while taking every possible precaution to ensure she didn't have a tail.

Tailing her back *here.*

Two o'clock. Reaching for another cigarette. Pulse-rate still faster than it should have been, but – improving. She *wasn't* anything like properly fit: couldn't have hoped to be, after a whole month just sitting around. Emotional disturbance was what upset the rhythm, she supposed. Tension, fright, in other words. One was scared half to death, quite often. It had always been more or less OK, she remembered, when one was on the move and things were actually happening; the worst strain had always been before and after.

So think about something else – *now.* How it might be in 62–4 Baker Street, for instance, with the arrival of this signal, reactions of friends and colleagues, all of whom would earlier have written one off as dead. There'd be astonishment, even disbelief and suspicion of the authenticity of the message. But the rush to sort out the options, come to the right decision in a situation that might be complicated by factors of which *here* one had no knowledge – such as measures which might already have been taken with regard to 'Hector' – and with the rocket element in particular making for real urgency – having to tie it all up in twenty minutes flat wouldn't allow for much jollification.

But *then* there'd be some whoops of joy, she thought. Tonight, maybe, the pop of a cork or two. At least, *a* cork. Smiling to herself, thinking: *Damn well* better *be . . .*

They'd pass the news to Lise, of course, right away. Glancing at the clock, thinking *Might have already . . .* Except Lise might not be in Baker Street, might be in one of SOE's country-house establishments. Might even have been sent on leave. Wherever she was, when the news did get to her she'd be pole-axed.

And Ben?

Better if they didn't tell him, she thought. At least, not unless the decision was to recall her forthwith.

At three twenty there was a rap on the door: she opened it to Guillaume, and he locked it again behind him.

'All right?'

She held up two crossed fingers. 'You're early.'

'Had a date with a horse and it took less time than it might have. So –' he flopped on to the sofa – 'here I am, playing truant.'

'Do your partners – Racke and Ruin, whatever – they know you have these outside interests?'

'One of them does. The young one – son of Racke. The other's – well, frankly ga-ga.'

'Were you a vet before the war?'

'Oh, yes.' Reaching to the pack of Gauloises. 'Mind?'

'They're yours, why should I?'

'No – your very own, a present from the management.'
Peering into the pack, 'Been going it a bit, haven't you?'

'I'm afraid I have.'

'Nerves?'

'Well. You know. Time heavy on one's hands.' She saw a
hint of mockery, and admitted, 'That Boche downstairs—'

'You coped marvellously. Should give you confidence in
your disguise, eh?'

'I'm sure he was wondering where he'd seen me before.
And if he sees a poster *now* and it jogs his memory—'

'Mistake to give the imagination too much rope, Rosie.'

'Only thing is – you were with me, and you're a friend
of Pauline's – which would have been obvious to him . . .
But OK, you're right, spilt milk . . . Were you a vet here in
France?'

'No. England. Boyhood and some schooling here though
– hence the lingo.'

'I suppose you and Son of Racke were students together,
something like that?'

'Something like it, yes.' He'd lit their cigarettes. Sitting
back now, checking the time again. 'Come on, Léonie . . .'

'Not actually late yet, is she?'

'Well – not quite . . .'

'There you are, then. What's *her* background?'

'Rosie – you know better than—'

'Anyway, she's nice.'

'Understatement of the week. What I *can* tell you is she
was born and brought up in Belgium, father a Venezuelan
who skipped home in '39. In the oil business – or was.'

'What about Mama?'

'Skipped too. *Not* as far as Venezuela, fortunately.' Checking the time again. 'Now, she *is* late.'

'Using a bike, is she?'

'Yep.' He got up, went to the window, then pulled back

from it. 'What's *that* specimen holding the wall up for, I wonder.'

'Where?' Beside him, and seeing the object of his interest. A man in exceptionally shabby clothes, propped with his back against the wall close to the door of a baker's shop. Dark-blue cap, pale blob of a face, head forward as if dozing. Guillaume had taken a step back from the window: the ceilings were low, on this upper floor you weren't all that far above street level.

The man was obviously waiting for something, or some*one*. Or to see who came and/or went. Rosie said, 'One thing I mustn't forget – that shopping list, pistol and cash and so forth – another thing I'll ask for is a wristwatch.'

'Boches pinched yours, I suppose.'

'Didn't have it when I came to in the hospital at Morlaix. The *Feldgendarmes* who I was told picked me out of the car-wreck must have taken it.'

'They would have.' Looking round at her, shaking his head: still at the window but she'd gone back to her chair, perched on its arm. 'But Rosie – in your shoes, I really would grab at the chance of getting home. The more I think about it – after all *that*—'

'*All that* is over and done with. And I feel I *need* to. For instance – lacking a watch hasn't bothered me because I've been in other people's hands all the time – like a child . . . All right, I'm very grateful to all concerned, *very*, but—'

'I'm still betting Baker Street will recall you.'

'In which case – as I said—'

'You've no husband, I imagine . . . Any boyfriend who matters?'

She shrugged. 'I keep getting asked that. There's a man who wants to marry me, yes. Australian.'

'Are you *going* to marry?'

'Probably. As of this moment, he most likely thinks I'm dead. I *imagine* they'll have—'

'Hey.' Pointing down at the street: Rosie moved up beside him again. A woman had come out of the baker's shop, stopped on the pavement looking round as if she'd lost someone, while the man who'd been leaning against the wall had straightened – head up, and right behind her. Then – he must have spoken or yelled, right in her ear – and she spun round . . . He was laughing, she moved as if to swing at him with her shopping bag but he stepped inside her guard, and they embraced: were on their way then, his arm round her shoulders. About to pass out of sight behind a parked *gazo* van from which crates of cabbages were being delivered to a café-restaurant.

Cabbage soup tonight, she guessed. In her mind, she could smell it. Guillaume asked her, 'This Aussie'll be thinking you're dead, you say.'

'Probably. Since Lise's got back. He'll have been in touch with Baker Street, badgering them for news of me, and—'

'He'll be in for a surprise now, then.'

'Won't he, just . . . *You* married?'

'Me?' Quick glance at her: shake of the head. 'No.'

She looked at the clock: three forty-two. Way past schedule. Sitting again, visualizing Léonie on her bicycle. She thought Guillaume might be the girl's lover – or shaping up to be. That 'understatement of the week': and his tone, expression when he'd said it. Also that sharpish denial of other attachment: as much rebuttal as denial. And the look of him *now*: leaning across the low table to stub out his cigarette, he'd frozen in that position – head up, motionless, eyes on the door.

Like a pointer. Even to the extent of having one paw still raised . . .

Scrape of a key being pushed into its lock: the first sound *she*'d heard, but he must have heard the girl coming up the stairs. He was at the door unlocking it and jerking it open, then she was inside – he might have yanked her in, was reaching past her now to push the door shut, simultaneously hugging her: 'At bloody *last* . . .'

'There was a hold-up. On the Sarreguemines road.'

'And?'

'Nuisance, that's all. They were searching lorries and vans mostly, and car drivers' papers. I showed them the hat, wasn't even asked my name. There's a heck of a lot of military traffic heading north, by the way.' Disengaging herself, she smiled at Rosie. 'Hello. Sorry you had such a wait. I've got London's answer, all we have to do is decode it.'

She'd fetched her one-time pad – a pad of microfilm pages, rice paper, easily destructible, even edible, each page for use only once – and a pencil and paper, magnifying glass for reading the micro-lettering, her own personal alphabetical table printed on a silk handkerchief, and Baker Street's message; she'd pencilled it on the inside of a used envelope which she must have opened up and then re-folded into envelope shape again – so that it looked like nothing *but* an old, used envelope. She'd had it in her pocket with a receipted butcher's bill stuffed into it.

'OK. Key . . .'

Three groups each of five letters to form the top line, in capitals. Rosie did the writing-down, Léonie dictated; Guillaume was in the kitchenette making what might pass for coffee. The cipher-text as received from London had to be written letter by letter horizontally below the key; translation into plain language came from reference to the table printed on the square of silk.

The message wasn't a long one.

All here are overwhelmed with joy and send Zoé our love and congratulations. Include shopping-list in your Thursday transmission, also confirmation that Xanadu is usable. Listen out tonight midnight CET for detail of special courier visit probably

Saturday with pick-up Sunday for courier with or without Zoé depending on further deliberation and investigation at this end.

She'd called it out, word by word, commented as Guillaume came from the kitchen with mugs of coffee-substitute, 'Seems as if they're keeping their options open.'

'Does, doesn't it.' He put the mugs down, took the decoded text from Léonie. Muttering to himself, '*What* investigations at that end . . .'

'The rocket dimensions – if there's any Intelligence data?'

'Ah. Yes.' Glancing at her, then: 'Keeping options open, mind you, doesn't mean they'll give you your head . . . But – all right – first thing is to be listening out at midnight, Léonie. From here, huh?'

She'd nodded. Rosie asked her, 'Spare transceiver here?'

'Yes.' Movement of her smooth, dark head, pointing upwards – attic or roofspace up there. 'Receiver only – in case I was ever tempted to take a risk.'

'Wise.'

A shrug, as she gathered up her bits and pieces. 'Careful, anyway.'

'*Better* be.' Guillaume smiled at her. 'But listen – it might be best for Rosie to stay here with you – d'you think? Tonight anyway, with more guff coming in?'

'Yes – definitely. If that couch would do you, Rosie? I've slept on it, it's quite comfy.'

'Do very well. Yes – thanks . . .'

'Better all round.' Guillaume was dispensing sugar-substitute. 'Save time and a lot of running to and fro. Also exposure of you to the outside world. I'll have to fetch your suitcase, that's all. And I'll bring some rations. Later on, Léonie. On second thoughts, I'll send Willi with the case.'

'I should be downstairs earning my living – *now*, I should. Rosie, you could let him in when he comes?'

'Of course—'

'Rather a big lad, Rosie, answers to the name Willi and looks savage, but he's harmless – to his friends, anyway. Some time around five, when he knocks off – OK?'

She'd nodded. 'Is he your courier?'

'God, no . . .'

And he wasn't telling her who *was*. Béa, maybe. She shrugged: 'Anyway, thank you both. Where *would* I have been staying?'

'A rooming house – west of here, other side of the railway station. We need to keep in touch though – with this message coming in tonight, and ours with your shopping-list out tomorrow. Better finalize that, hadn't you? *And* it's best to keep you off the streets as far as possible.' He turned back to Léonie. 'I'll check the Xanadu field myself. I've business in that direction, and I'll have a word with the Déchambauds – family with a cottage out that way, Rosie, it'll be handy if this courier's to be with us for a day. We could move *you* out there too. Now that's a good idea. Directly from here to there – Saturday evening, say, in my *gazo* – then you'll have your day with Baker Street's courier, and either go back with him or – well, from there to wherever you *are* going.'

'How?'

'What?'

'How – from your friends' cottage to St Valéry-sur-Vanne?'

He nodded. 'Have to think that out. Easier if you went back with the courier, of course.'

She'd been dreaming that Marilyn Stuart was on the blower to Ben telling him that she, Rosie, would be back in London within two or three days, while she was screaming that it wasn't true – and grabbing for the telephone, fighting, yelling – Marilyn cool as a cucumber, fending her off easily and laughingly, having of course the advantages of height and reach. Rosie bawling at her that she had no business raising his hopes when they both knew it wasn't true, in fact that she might *never* be back – and Ben's voice suddenly booming over the line, 'What in hell are you drongoes *at*?'

Ben's Aussie voice, all right, but not his face. *Michel*'s face. Marilyn taunting her, 'Don't know one from the other, do you!'

'*Bitch!*'

'Hey, hey . . .'

Léonie: with a hand grasping Rosie's shoulder . . . 'Rosie, hush. Dreary old nightmare . . . Over now, you're awake, OK? Listen, I'm on my way up to take in this message . . .'

To the attic, to listen out for Baker Street's midnight call. Murmuring in the semi-dark – the only light was coming through from the half-open bedroom door, Léonie a black cut-out against it – 'Too much cheese for supper, probably. Like in that Will Hay film, feeding the old man cheese to make him dream . . . Will you be all right now?'

'Yes, of course. Sorry . . .'

'I'll take the key, lock you in – then if you fall asleep—'

'I won't, I'll wait and—'

'Won't be long – touch wood.'

Baker Street and Sevenoaks permitting, she wouldn't be. But how, even in a dream, confuse Ben and Michel, Rosie wondered? Echoes of it still in her mind. Or how see Marilyn as such a bitch? Marilyn who, when she'd been seeing her off on the Lysander flight from Tangmere a few months ago, had actually wept! Wet-faced in the dark – having thought the darkness would hide it, no one would see her tears, so what the hell – forgetting the goodbye kiss, the contact of a damp cheek, and Rosie wondering then *why*, why *this* time? Thinking third time *un*lucky, maybe? One would never have expected tears – or any lack of emotional control – from Marilyn, of all people: she was a tall, cool blonde, had come to SOE from the Wrens,

in which she'd been – still was – a Second Officer, and in
'F' Section she'd started as an agent but then been taken
her out of field work because her French was so appalling.
Strictly English-schoolroom French, grammatically correct
enough but the accent of a *vache espagnolle* – as someone had
rather cruelly described it – cribbing that from the Rattigan
play *French Without Tears*, of course.

Brainwave striking, then: they might send Marilyn as the
'special courier'?

Might well. Short visit, minimal need of conversational
French. *She'd* go for it, sure as eggs – not only because
the two of them were as close as they were, but because
behind that cool façade she'd loathed being confined to
admin and training work, sending *others* into the field. Just
as Rosie herself had felt at one time – between deployments,
when Ben had been begging her never to go back. But
Colonel Buck would approve, for sure: he thought highly
of Marilyn, one knew, and he'd see the sense in sending
someone with whom Rosie was in close *rapport*.

Bet on it, she thought.

And London – or rather Sevenoaks – would be on the
air by now. Léonie up there crouched over her receiver,
having paid out the thin, matt-black aerial wire from a
window. Listening out on a frequency pre-set by her own
personal quartz crystal – the night-time crystal, not the
one she'd have had in her transmitter this afternoon –
and *only* listening, doing nothing that might attract the
Reichssicherheitshauptamt boffins' attention. Crouched with
the headphones flattening those small, neat ears and shiny
dark hair against her head while she jotted down the
message stuttering from the Sevenoaks operator's transmitter key. Baker Street maybe saying they'd changed their
minds, would be making other arrangements about the
rocket-casings – for instance, having that village flattened,
without any confirmatory check? It was – conceivable.

The rockets would be what mattered now – mattered *most*. 'Hector' mattered quite a lot, but compared to the rockets he was very much an SOE domestic matter; the War Cabinet, for instance, or the Chiefs of Staff or the top brass of SIS wouldn't have heard of him, wouldn't give a damn about him one way or the other even if they had, but they'd know all about the threat from 'Hitler's Secret Weapons', which the Boches were still claiming were going to win the war for them.

She lit a cigarette – partly to stay awake, not slip back into that ridiculous dream. Hardly a nightmare, as Léonie had called it: nightmares had to do with torture and mutilation. They had since Rouen, last year. As Ben knew, having on occasion vicariously suffered with her . . . Picturing him in her mind, in the smoke curling up from her Gauloise and melting into darkness under the low ceiling where the light from Léonie's bedroom door didn't reach; *seeing* him, recognizing him as unquestionably the most important factor in her life.

To have and to hold. Cling to like a bloody limpet.

Scrape of a key in the door. Rosie holding her breath, watching as Léonie slipped in, closed the door softly and re-locked it.

Expelling a lungful of smoke . . . 'All right?'

'Far as I know.' Flipping a sheet of paper out of the pocket of her gown. 'Want to help?'

What Baker Street was telling them in this message was that subject to the contents of Léonie's transmission on Thursday night – tonight, it was Thursday *now*, of course – the 'special courier' would be dropped by parachute on the Xanadu field on Saturday half an hour before midnight and collected by a Hudson at 0200 Sunday morning. Confirmation of both the paradrop and the pick-up two and a half hours later would come on Saturday afternoon/evening in a *message personnel* stating 'Gaston has become the father of twins'. And – as one had more or less expected – the courier would have Baker Street's authority to decide whether Zoé should remain in the field or return to London in the Hudson.

That was all, except for detail of recognition signals to be used between the aircraft and the reception team. The main change from their earlier, off-the-cuff response was that the courier would be on the ground for only a couple of hours instead of twenty-four.

Léonie was putting her bits and pieces together. Rosie asked her, 'What time did Guillaume say he'd get here?'

'Seven thirty, or thereabouts. Then he'll be going out to inspect Xanadu, of course – so I can give them an OK on it tonight. The other thing I'll need is your requisition list.'

'I'll get down to it first thing. Money's one problem – how much to ask for . . . I've guessed who the courier'll be, by the way. In Baker Street, ever meet Marilyn Stuart?'

'Marilyn . . . Yes. But is she a parachutist?'

'Yes. *Was*, and she's kept it all up – she's done refresher courses at Ringwood. I happen to know because I did one with her.'

Guillaume arrived on the dot of seven thirty, had a light breakfast with them and left soon after eight. He'd drop in again when he got back from his visit to the country, he said, but if he failed to show up – i.e. had run into trouble – Léonie was to make her transmission with Rosie's shopping-list in it and the warning that no reconnaisance of Xanadu had been possible. If he still didn't appear – by Saturday, in which case it would be obvious he was in *real* trouble – Léonie was to arrange for their courier to take Rosie out to the Déchambauds and supervise the reception of Baker Street's parachutist.

'Then the usual team – Déchambaud would get them together for him – for the reception of the Hudson.'

Muster them for *him*, Rosie had noted: so Guillaume's courier was not the veterinary receptionist. She commented, 'We're looking on the black side rather, aren't we?'

'Wouldn't you agree it's wise?'

'I suppose . . .'

'Things *can* go awry. And in this situation you'd be stuck, wouldn't you.'

'Certainly would be if Baker Street cried off too.'

'Well.' A shrug. 'In my hypothetical situation there'd be no reason they should. It also assumes that having collared me, the Boches weren't immediately rounding up the rest of you as well. I admit that's no better than a fifty-fifty chance. But – in this hypothesis you wouldn't set out for Xanadu without hearing first about Gaston's twins, would you? And if there was reason you knew of to call it off, Léonie'd talk to Baker Street.' Looking at her. 'Knows her onions, this kid. But I'm a wily bird myself, Rosie, don't worry. Matter of thinking ahead a bit, that's all, having some notion how one *might* react.'

Léonie went to work at eight thirty, came up for an early snack soon after noon, and told Rosie she'd be out for a while.

'Moving your transceiver to wherever you'll be using it tonight?'

'Hah. Aren't *you* the wily bird!'

'Not really. Being oneself a pianist, and damn-all to do all day except put two and two together.' She paused, then asked her, 'Guillaume's a good one, isn't he?'

'How d'you mean?'

'Well –' dissimulating, somewhat – 'a good man to work with?'

'I enjoy working with him, certainly. He's – considerate, usually a step or two ahead, and one does feel – well, if things did go wrong, (a) he'd cope and (b) his priority would be to look after *us*.'

She nodded, thinking about it. You could tell, she thought – the ones you'd trust and the ones you might have when you were green but with experience wouldn't.

Léonie was getting ready to depart. She added – as if she'd been pondering whether or not to say this – 'But answering your question about Guillaume – that's as far as it goes. I mean, professional relationship, mutual liking and respect – that's *it*. What you were really asking, wasn't it?'

'Well—'

'I'll tell you anyway – strictly *entre nous*. He's in love with Pauline. She is with him, too. It's the real McCoy, they're crazy about each other. Look, I must run . . .'

Guillaume came by in the early evening bringing them a fowl for boiling, half a dozen eggs and some potatoes. Booty from the countryside – enough to have got him arrested if he'd been caught bringing it into town. The Xanadu field was clear, he said, and the Déchambauds would gladly lend Rosie and her visitor their sitting-room on Saturday night: unless, he added, she and the courier might prefer to save time, conduct their interview right there on the field. Because allowing for the arrival and for the departure preparations they'd be unlikely to have more than an hour, hour and a half for actually conferring. Rosie suggested, 'Best just to see how it goes.' By 'it', meaning Marilyn's parachute landing – might be quick and neat, on-target, might not. People out of practice broke legs sometimes, for instance. Guillaume agreed, said he'd provide a Thermos and sandwiches just in case they decided against trekking back to the cottage.

'All on foot, will it be?'

'Use a cart probably, coming away with the gear. We've

used Xanadu several times like that – softly, softly. It's a good field, I wouldn't want to compromize it.'

'So if it was a large-scale *parachutage*—'

'We've had a couple. Used farm-carts, trans-shipped the stuff to lorries elsewhere. But listen – if it's decided you're staying on, I'll take you as far as Troyes in the office *gazo*. Leave the Déchambaud place at six, be there – well, middle of the day, roughly. But using minor roads or even *routes blanches* where possible. I'll check the map, see how best to plan it.'

'But that's marvellous!'

Routes blanches meant unpaved roads. Not only to avoid checkpoints, he explained, but for his own cover, ostensibly visiting some farms. He asked her, 'You do know where to find this man in Troyes, do you?'

'Yes. Michel gave me all that. Guillaume, this is *very* nice of you.'

'Frankly, the sooner you're out of Nancy, the better. Not that we aren't enjoying your company—'

'Oh, goes without saying . . .'

'From Troyes onwards, you'll be on your own. I can find spurious reason to be there, but not any further west.'

He'd been taking Léonie away with him then, dropping her off at whatever address she'd moved her transceiver to. Wherever it was, she'd need to be installed there before curfew cleared the streets, and he'd pick her up and bring her in with him in the morning.

'So I'm afraid you have a lonely evening ahead of you, Rosie.'

'Dare say I'll survive it.'

'And a fairly boring Friday and Saturday too. But it really is much safer for you not to go out at all – agreed?'

'Being so famous.'

'Seriously, don't be tempted. No runs round the block, or—'

'I'll do my exercises. Press-ups, sit-ups—'

'You might give some thought to a cover-story for use if we get stopped on the way out of town on Saturday. Could be chancy – they're going to look twice at young females *leaving* town. Meanwhile, stay away from windows, and if anyone comes to the door don't go near it, don't make a sound. OK?'

On the Friday, Léonie came and went, from time to time. So did Guillaume. Léonie's transmission had gone out all right. Baker Street would have all Friday and most of Saturday in which to organize the shopping-list. Guillaume was asking for the container which they'd be dropping to have its otherwise empty compartments filled with mainly sabotage materials that he wanted for his own *réseau*: and one rather fiddly part of Rosie's list, which Marilyn would probably attend to even if she wasn't to be the parachutist, was to collect a few items of clothing from the flat in North London which Rosie shared with another girl, and have any English labels removed, if possible French ones substituted. Marilyn knew the flat and had a key to it; she'd also have a good idea of the sort of things Rosie would want.

Get rid of some of *this* awful gear, then.

Saturday, at last. The hat-shop was open in the morning, but shut at midday. Rosie and Léonie lunched on what was left of the boiled chicken, and Guillaume joined them just after seven in the evening, in good time for the BBC's French-language 'personal messages' programme. Léonie's illegal domestic wireless was plugged in in the kitchen – the most sound-proof corner of the apartment – with the volume turned low, and eventually they heard amongst a confusion of assorted gibberish as well as bursts of jamming and static that Gaston had fathered twins.

'Good for him.' Guillaume stubbed out a cigarette, and kissed Léonie's cheek. 'Bless you. Come on, Rosie.'

Chapter 9

They'd driven north out of Nancy on the Metz road, then crossed the Meuse, heading west towards St Mihiel. Rosie thinking of Lise having come out over this same route, in this *gazo* and with the same driver hunched over its wheel, only a few weeks ago, and wondering whether it might conceivably be her they'd send tonight.

Possible, she thought, but not likely. Although a reunion here, in the light of all that had happened, would have been – sensational, in a way. Both of them 'Wanted' . . . Something to remember in one's old age – if one had any such thing. But Baker Street wouldn't send Lise – *especially* not if they knew about the posters – which Guillaume would have reported, she guessed. Lise might not have wanted to come, anyway. Would anyone, in their senses? Thinking of herself then, with the easy option of going home but choosing – if she was to be allowed a choice – to stay on . . . Glancing at Guillaume's profile – prominent cheekbones, deep-sunk pale-brown eyes, light-brown hair starting well back on the narrow forehead, as he swung out to pass a farm-cart, raising a hand in greeting to the old man plodding at the horse's head. Could have been some English pastoral scene: could *easily*. Buckinghamshire, where her mother lived, in deeply rural surroundings . . . On the point of asking Guillaume whether London knew about the 'Wanted' business, the rewards on offer, she decided to leave it, to prolong the silence. Leaving town and for the first half-hour or so they'd talked a lot: about Léonie for instance, whose mother had a dress business in London, somewhere north of Oxford Street, and Guillaume's own post-war hopes of a veterinary partnership in Wiltshire, where he had an ancient father still alive. Chat-time over, though, for the moment; time for private thoughts and enjoyment of a lovely evening, near-empty roads . . . They would *not* send Lise, she decided. If only because she wouldn't have the degree of authority that Marilyn had – or, frankly, the necessary detachment. Lise, who believed in Fate, would tend to be guided more by her emotions than by her head.

There'd been a lot of people about, when they'd been leaving town. Guillaume had counted on it, on crowded streets and pavements making them less conspicuous. In the event – leaving Rue St Jacques – there'd been one short period of anxiety, and before that the surprise of Guillaume having an off-duty Boche soldier apologize to him. He'd just dumped Rosie's suitcase in the *gazo*'s boot, and the boy had come dashing across the road to join friends he must just then have spotted and was looking at – calling to them – instead of where he was going; and he'd collided with Guillaume. In dull-green uniform, heavy clumping boots, forage-cap with a coloured patch on it: and wide-eyed, flushed with embarrassment – could have been an English face, English country-lad type . . . Guillaume had muttered something to him, and she asked him as he slid in and jerked the door shut, 'Ticked him off, did you?'

'Far from it.' *He*'d looked embarrassed, then. 'He begged my pardon, I said no, *my* fault.'

She'd laughed. '*Really* . . .'

'Ludicrous. Absolutely . . .'

And in slight contrast, seconds later, *Schutzpolizei* on the corner, watching the flow of traffic and pedestrians around

them, one of them focusing on the *gazo* as Guillaume
brought it slowly up to stop at the intersection and wait to
turn right. Both with pistols in holsters on their belts. Rosie
was on that side of the car, of course – sitting there trying
to look prim and proper with her handbag – which Léonie
had given her at the last moment, as they'd been leaving
the flat – on her lap. The Boches were concentrating their
attention on *her*, she realized: maybe taking in Guillaume
too, but she was getting the brunt of it.

As bad as those few minutes in the hat-shop.

'*Damn* it . . .'

'It's all right.' She *hoped*. 'I think they're only—'

'I know, I know . . .' Craning forward, watching traffic
streaming from the left. Meaning he was aware they were
only *Schutzpolizei*, semi-military traffic cops. But they could
still read 'Wanted' posters. He was drumming his fingers on
the wheel . . . 'Rosie – if it looks like they're making any sort
of move—'

'My papers are good enough, and the story'll hold water.'

'I was going to say don't react, don't *see* it. Stop looking
anxious, wind that window down a bit—'

'Gap coming!' Thinking: *He* can talk – about looking
anxious . . . 'Guillaume – *now*—'

Her blurred sideways view of the two Germans whipped
away – out of the corners of her eyes and into memory,
history – as the *gazo* swung out into the busier road.
She'd said after a moment, in a degree of relief that was
a reflection of how tense she'd been, 'You'd think *they'd*
be feeling the strain. Boches, let alone – I was thinking
yesterday, seeing *miliciens* down in the street – French
collabs and suchlike . . . I mean, with Allied armies on
the move now – and surely they must realize there can
only be one end . . .'

'I doubt they're hearing much about it. And it does
seem to have been a long time practically static – since

the landings. *Still* does . . . OK, the fighting's obviously grim . . . Did you get any news earlier on?'

'Yes – meant to tell you. Yanks have taken Laval and are advancing on Le Mans. Which I suppose could be the thrust that's going to encircle Paris – Michel's theory, a long right hook he called it. Around Paris and down the Seine to Rouen. Then let's hope eastward and over the Rhine. But Laval's real progress, surely.'

'Are such things as counter-attacks though, aren't there? And the Boches aren't *bad* soldiers. Also "Secret Weapons" – such as your rockets, maybe. They'll be putting their faith in something of that sort.' Nodding to himself: 'I'd say that's your answer.'

'Clear sky, thank God.'

'Yes.' She agreed. 'We're lucky.'

It was a fact: it could have been overcast, or the wrong time of the month, and the Special Duties Squadrons needed a moon for the clandestine operations. She'd had this in mind all week, remembering there'd been a newish one at the time of the disaster at Thérèse's place, which meant it would be near-enough full tonight.

'How far now?'

'About half an hour. Smoke?'

'Thanks.' Gauloises again; she took out two, gave him back the packet. 'Thought you'd never offer . . . Light yours, shall I?'

'By tomorrow you'll be able to buy your own, eh?'

'*If* I'm to be left here . . .'

'But now listen – I doubt we'll be stopped, out here, but if we are I think we should change the story slightly. Forget the cousin in Commercy – too close, a *gendarme* might come from there himself and and ask some question you'd make a hash of. Let's say I'm on veterinary business, just brought you along for the ride. I still met you when you brought your mother's cat in, all that business. OK?'

She'd lit both cigarettes, passed one to him. 'Along for the ride . . .'

'Yes – but – if you don't mind – easily believable?'

'Since I look like a tart anyway?'

'Not *at all*. You're very attractive, was what I was implying. Even under a layer of boot-polish. The fact your turn-out's a bit garish—'

'I'll look better with the stuff I hope Marilyn's bringing.'

A sideways glance, through smoke: 'Who's Marilyn?'

'Tonight's courier. My guess is it'll be Marilyn Stuart, Second Officer WRNS. "F" Section admin, mostly.'

'Don't think I've had the pleasure . . . Here's our turn, now.'

Off to the right – uphill, unpaved road, vistas of woodland ahead and on his side. He added, 'That's the St Mihiel road we've just left, you realize. St Mihiel mean anything to you?'

'Should it?'

Luc had been going there, she remembered. Nothing else. The *gazo's* tyres drumming noisily on this rough surface; and the thought of Luc bringing a fleeting image of Michel. Guillaume telling her 'In the last war – September 1918 – there was a battle here, the first large-scale American involvement. There was an enormous German salient – the St Mihiel salient – a bulge westward, in other words – and this first-ever all-American army got the job of eliminating it, straightening the line. Yanks under General Pershing, who was under Marshal Foch of course – and they didn't see eye to eye, exactly. By the time they'd argued it out, they used only seven US divisions, instead of fifteen – divisions twice the size of ours or the French, admittedly – and six French, and the tactic was to attack simultaneously in two prongs – a pincer-movement – one on the salient's western

flank and the main one here in the south – to squeeze it
out like a boil, and trap thousands of Boches in the middle,
they hoped. Huge artillery support, nearly three thousand
guns, mostly French; and the air element all British, RFC
and RNAS. As it turned out, the Boches knew it was coming
– everyone in France knew – and began to pull out before it
started. So a lot of the bombardment fell in empty trenches
and not as many were trapped as they'd hoped. But the
salient was eliminated. Wasn't much resistance, the whole
front was crumbling by then. Am I boring you?'

'Not in the least.'

'General Ludendorff had launched his great offensive too
soon, you see. *Because* the Yanks were coming in. By the time
they did, he'd really shot his bolt. Troops exhausted, morale
at low ebb. Whereas the Yanks were fresh, keen as mustard,
only just getting into their stride.' Guillaume waved a hand
towards the countryside ahead: 'Where we are now would
be where the attack went in, on the salient's southern flank.
The Yanks' right-hand pincer. Corps commander by name
of Ligget – brilliant soldier, finished up commanding their
First Army. And up *there* – see those woods? That's where
we're going – another turn-off just over this rise. Paved
road there again. Déchambaud's place is – well, a hamlet
on a crossroads, just a few dwellings and a blacksmith's
shop, his cottage and small-holding a few hundred metres
down the road. He's a retired railwayman, runs a few sheep
and grows vegetables, and his wife has a market-stall in
Commercy. His first name's Fernand, and hers is Ursule.'
A sideways glance: 'Consider yourself briefed.'

Déchambaud came plodding to meet them. Guillaume had
parked his *gazo* in an open-fronted barn about fifty metres
up a track which led up from the lane, beside the cottage.
It looked as if space had purposefully been left for him;
there was a donkey-trap in the barn and another had

been taken out, parked in the entrance to a field on the other side. Unkempt hedgerows crowding over, rickety shed with missing boards, that field-gate held together with baling-twine: now this slightly stooped old man – sunburnt, craggy face, fringe of grey-white hair, and a long arm extended to Guillaume: 'Monsieur Rouquet!'

'Fernand, *mon vieux* . . .'

Rosie's turn then to shake his hand.

'Mam'selle . . .'

'Monsieur Déchambaud.'

Distantly, the sound of a train. Not all *that* distant. Guillaume commented, jerking a thumb, 'Be a good day when that goes off with a bang!'

A grunt: a nod that was upward, like a horse tossing its head. 'Not long now, please God.'

'Scheduled for destruction.' Guillaume told her, 'The Paris to Metz line. Part of Michel's brief – that and a few others all at once. Fernand will be taking a hand in this one. Do it now, they'd have ample time for repairs – and reprisals, searches and so on. But all at once, and when they're either running or trying to reinforce—'

'Michel's set that up?'

Déchambaud glanced at Guillaume: 'She knows Michel, uh?'

The name *was* effectively a pass-word, she thought – as he'd said it would be with the man in Troyes. If one ever got there. That train was still audible, maybe at about its closest, and she could see it in her imagination: Paris to Metz, whereas the one she'd been on had been Paris–Nancy – and doubtless continuing into Germany. Via Saarbrücken, she supposed; out of memory interpreting the distant hum into the rhythm of the wheels as they'd pounded in her brain all that frightful day – *Ravensbrück. Ravensbrück. Ravensbrück* . . . Hour after hour. Hot, urine-scented compartment in which they'd embarked at the Gare d'Est: herself and Lise

– long-limbed, dark cropped hair and by that time almost
skeletally thin – and the Belgian woman and her daughter,
and middle-aged Edna, who pre-war had been a school-
mistress, and Daphne – flame-red hair, as much as they'd
left her of it, and in a defiant but also hopeless way still
elegant; and Maureen, the baby of the party, who at some
earlier stage had wet herself. Chained, doomed, knowing
beyond doubt or hope that the end of the road was an
extermination camp, *Vernichtungslager*; if not Ravensbrück,
which was the most likely prospect, *the* women's hell, then
one of the others. Remembering one of her fellow prisoners
– it had been Edna – speculating as to where they were
being taken, and Maureen holding up her manacled wrists,
wondering too 'Yes, *where*, in all this finery?' Suggesting
then 'Ascot, d'you think?' and Daphne's drawled '*Wouldn't*
we just wow 'em!'

All dead, by now. Except for herself and Lise, almost
certainly all dead.

The cottage door banged open. Guillaume urging her,
'Come on.' A hand on her elbow: adding in English, 'Wakey
wakey!' She'd been lost, walking the fifty or sixty metres
with them like a zombie. Couldn't hear the train now: only
Déchambaud calling into the kitchen, 'Ursule, our friends
are here—'

'Heavens, haven't I got eyes and ears?' Pushing out past
him. 'Monsieur Rouquet – ah, you're welcome. *And* the
young lady. Please, come in!'

Short and stout, with enormously thick arms and a hand
that felt like a lump of warm dough. Hairs on her chin:
nice smile, though. She had supper ready for them, she
was saying – pigeon pie. Guillaume thanking her profusely,
but checking the time and saying it was important they
should hear the nine thirty broadcast of *messages personnels*.
Anyway there'd be time to eat first.

*   *   *

The pie was delicious, and they'd wiped their plates clean well before the time of the broadcast. Plans were discussed, during the meal. Guillaume had an 'S' phone here which he'd brought on his Thursday visit and would be using tonight; and Déchambaud had arranged for three helpers – whom he named, and Guillaume evidently knew – to meet them at the Xanadu field at 2300, by which time they'd have reconnoitred the surroundings and approaches. One of them – name of Groslin – would be bringing a *gazo* van.

'Could have used a cart, Fernand.'

'Too slow, I thought, on this occasion, with so small an interval of time. And Groslin's used to driving without lights.'

Ursule nodding: 'A fox, that man!'

'We'll need transport anyway – I've asked for some stuff for ourselves, as well as the – special delivery, you might call it.'

'A van's ideal.' Rosie cut in: 'Load the stuff into it, and perhaps the courier and I could do our talking in it. Better than in a ditch. Then either transfer it all into the Hudson, or have – Groslin, is it? – drive us and the gear back here.'

'Good . . .'

'You see.' Their hostess nodding to the men, and tapping her own head. 'When you want clear thinking – uh?'

By nine forty they'd had the final confirmation of Gaston's twins. The wireless went back into its hiding place – some dark hole elsewhere in the cottage – and Déchambaud brought the 'S' phone in its green carrying-case. Guillaume checked it over. Webbing harness, headset, microphone, collapsible dipole aerial; all of which, plus its ten rechargeable batteries and vibrator power-pack, were contained in canvas pouches on the harness.

'OK.' Indicating a Morse lamp, which Déchambaud had now produced. 'You handle that, Justine?'

'Pleasure. Recognition letter's R, isn't it?'

'R for Rosie, maybe. The Stens next, Fernand?'

Two of them, Stens Mark II, each in its three component parts, wrapped in sacking. Rosie assembled one of them, squinting down its short barrel before fitting it: Guillaume telling her, 'Sorry we only have these two here. I've a pistol with me, though – the Beretta I mentioned. Have that if you like.'

Madame – Ursule – lent her a sweater to wear under Thérèse's rain-jacket. They'd be out there several hours, at least until 2 a.m., and with the sun down it was already turning cool. Guillaume strapped on the 'S' phone harness, shrugged on a raincoat over it, and slung the Sten over that. One magazine in each gun, two spares each, twenty-eight rounds per magazine. Magazines held thirty rounds, but compressing the spring too far increased the likelihood of jamming.

'All set?'

She was carrying her own suitcase, formerly Silvie de Plesse's. She'd put the signal-lamp in it, and the Beretta and one spare clip in her jacket pockets. It was a neat little weapon: might keep it, she thought, take it along as well as the Llama which Marilyn – or someone – should be bringing. *If* she was going anywhere. Guillaume looked huge in his bulked-out raincoat; she suggested, 'I could relieve you of the rations?'

'Dare say you could.' Thermos of coffee-substitute and sandwiches intended for Marilyn – or whoever. The case still wasn't heavy, and they only had a kilometre and a half to cover, to the rendezvous. Madame Déchambaud kissed them all goodbye – Rosie first, then Guillaume, then her husband. He assured her, 'I and Monsieur Rouquet and perhaps the young lady will be back by two thirty.'

'God willing.'

'Or say three at the latest. You know how it is.'

* * *

Out from the back of the cottage, through a field of low-growing vegetables, and keeping in the shadow of the hedge: Déchambaud leading, then Rosie, Guillaume as rearguard. Cool and quiet, with the almost full moon still low in the southern sky. Over a gate then, into a field that had sheep in it, and following another hedgerow along to a wire-mesh fence, which they crossed and were then entering woods. About ten thirty now, she guessed – visualizing a black-painted Hudson on the airfield at Tempsford, Marilyn in a jump-suit padded out with a sweater or two, parachute harness over all that. Recalling her own similar departure from Tempsford, her one and only action-drop, which had been into woods near Cahors. She'd worn a top-coat over her other clothes, trousers pulled up over the coat's skirts, handbag on a string around her neck and hanging inside the jump-suit. Sweating inside all that, and with that uncomfortable tightness in her gut, she'd remarked to Marilyn, who'd been seeing her off, that she now knew what a barrage-balloon felt like.

Jokes as camouflage of inner tension, jumping nerves. It was pretty much the same every time, but at least one had learnt that one *could* handle it.

Trees thick all round now, hardly any moonlight penetrating. Déchambaud glanced round now and then, and each time she followed suit, checking Guillaume was still behind her. Shifting her suitcase to the other hand, and forging on. Burdens could start virtually weightless and get heavier in direct proportion to distance covered: it was a phenomenon with which she'd become familiar during training, especially on Scottish mountainsides. No strain, though, this far – touch wood, no heart problem. Touch wood again – plenty of it within reach – her heart *might* have slipped back into gear. Wouldn't have to tell Marilyn any lies, therefore. Lise would

have trekked through these same woods, she supposed –
when she, Rosie, had still been at Thérèse's farm. Imagining her here beside her now – tall, long-striding . . . A surprising aspect of having come out of all that alive – when
one thought back to how it had been in the train, that
total hopelessness, not so much actual despair in one's
conscious thinking as resignation to the inevitability of
it – finality as one *fact*, and loathing of the creatures who
were responsible for it as another – and reminding oneself
that when one had gone into training as an agent, one had
done so in full awareness that the chances of survival
were no better than fifty-fifty. They'd all been told so over
and over. So OK, you'd gone into it with your eyes open,
and here it was: so *shut* your eyes, say your prayers . . .

Stopping abruptly – because Déchambaud had. He'd
looked back – with a hand up. She crouched – as he
had now. Motionless, listening. Heart thumping a bit hard
but steadily. Seeing him quite clearly, although behind her
Guillaume was invisible. Trees more sparse ahead there . . .
But – that train business, and Fresnes prison before that, and
the Gestapo in Paris – thinking about it now, and having
talked about it with Léonie, was like looking back into
a sort of underworld from which one had escaped only
by sheer luck – and which was still there, an abyss into
which one single stroke of *bad* luck could very easily see
one slipping back.

Here and now, maybe the darkness and unfamiliar-
ity with one's surroundings contributed to that feeling.
Déchambaud up again, and two others – one already with
him and the other just materializing, forming and solidify-
ing out of shadow. She could make out the shape of a Sten
in the crook of that one's arm. It wasn't just that the trees
were sparser there, she realized, that was the end of the
wood, edge of open ground under a pale wash of moonlight.
Guillaume closing up from behind calling softly 'All clear,

Fernand?' She'd had the Beretta in her hand, thumb on its safety-catch, slid it back into her pocket as she went forward close behind him.

Sitting with her legs drawn up, hugging her knees. Guillaume beside her, but standing; he'd taken off his raincoat, put it on the ground with his Sten-gun on it, had the 'S' phone headset on and the microphone covering the lower part of his face. Both mike and earphones were soundproof externally, so that nothing he heard or said was audible to her. No aircraft audible yet, either. Open ground all around them; the clearing was about seven-fifty metres deep by five hundred wide – more than adequate for a Hudson to land and take off, let alone for a *parachutage*. It was high ground too, not overlooked from anywhere. Groslin's van was parked under cover of trees over on the far side, where he'd driven it up off a forest track; stony there, Déchambaud had said, there'd be no tyre-tracks for snoopers to find in daylight. Groslin, a short, fat man who dealt in second-hand goods, which was what he used the van for, was at a paced-out distance of fifty metres to Rosie's and Guillaume's right: facing the same way as they were, i.e. down-wind, with Guérin a hundred metres from him in that down-wind direction, Lemartin another hundred on from Guérin, and all three with red lamps ready to shine skyward. They'd switch on when they saw Rosie's white lamp flashing the recognition signal. The aircraft, flying into the wind, would pass over Lemartin and release its parachute load when it was over Guérin; all being well, the point of impact would be somewhere between Guérin and Groslin.

Now she *could* hear it – that faint throb. Not the Boche-type throb, which by now every school-child in Britain could identify: a steadier, more constant note. Expanding – already much less faint. That plane's navigator would have the 'S' phone's beam triggering response in a receiver-dial in his cockpit: the beam, which he'd be homing in on, had a range which depended on the aircraft's height, could be as much as a hundred kilometres if it was flying at three thousand metres or as little as sixteen or twenty if it was hedge-hopping. The pilot would have gone up to about five thousand, probably, to pick it up at longish range, but he'd be diving now to a hundred and fifty or two hundred. The latter was the height Marilyn would drop from. Or Lise, or whoever. Could even be top brass – Bodington for instance, Buck's 2i/c. Sound mounting rapidly: by now Guillaume and the pilot would be in voice-communication, which had a range much shorter than that of the beam.

This was something bigger than a Hudson, though.

'Flash "R" Roger, Rosie!'

He'd pulled the mike clear of his face to yell it. Rosie already had the lamp up and aimed, began flashing short-long-short, short-long-short. The three red-covered lights were burning, red pinpricks halo'ed pink, from here in descending order of brightness according to distance. To the pilot's eye, she thought, they might take a bit of spotting: although they might be clearer from above than at ground level. Guillaume shouted, 'Dropping one container on this pass, one body next time round!' Volume of sound expanding fast, and the bomber over the top then – deafening and for a second or two discernible in black outline against stars and moon – no Hudson but a Lancaster and the 'chute whipping away astern of it. Gone – racket fading as swiftly as it had grown – to circle around and come over again on the same path. She heard the surprisingly close-sounding thud as the container hit the ground: containers fell faster than bodies, of course. As she recalled it, dropping-time from two hundred metres – or it might have been a hundred and fifty – was fifteen seconds. Messrs Guérin and Groslin would have that container's position marked, but for the moment they'd stay put. The Lanc circling – travelling from right to left now, westward. Guillaume doubtless still chatting to its pilot. Safe enough – 'S' phone transmissions couldn't be picked up by any monitor on the ground more than a mile away. That drop would most likely have been from a hundred and fifty metres, this next one would be at two hundred: giving Marilyn an extra second or two in which to compose herself, remember the drill as she prepared for impact with mother earth. Rosie visualizing again: seeing her normally immaculate, elegant friend trussed-up in the harness, sitting long-legged on the bomber's cold metal deck. The despatcher hooking her 'chute to the static line: maybe encouraging her with a grin and/or a thumb-up sign – if she was looking his way, not peering down through the round aperture in the deck through which in a few seconds she'd be launching herself. Narrowed blue eyes up again from the fast-moving rush of moonlit woods, focusing on the row of lights telling her and the despatcher: Stand by – stand by – *go!*

He'd have bellowed it. And that spewed-out white flash – *Marilyn?*

Lanc thundering over: Rosie on her feet, Guillaume with one hand on the mike and the fingers of the other on the volume-control, the power-pack on his chest: the vertical aerial jutted from that. He and the pilot no doubt exchanging goodnights, good lucks. Parachute open – thank God – and within seconds a light thud and a shrill whistle – from Groslin, who was already up and running, Rosie on her way too.

'Flabbergasted *might* be the word.' Marilyn scrambled into the van; she'd divested herself of the parachute harness, which with the two 'chutes would go into the now empty container. Its other contents – the last of them now – were being loaded into the van, Rosie's in one pile and the *réseau*'s up against the forward bulkhead; Groslin had spread a tarpaulin over that lot and now got out, shutting and bolting one of the rear doors. Guillaume offering Marilyn the Thermos of pseudo-coffee and package of cheese sandwiches; she told him, 'Sweet of you, but I had a meal only a couple of hours ago at Tempsford House. Honestly couldn't face more.'

'Well – these fellows will dispose of it, I'm sure. We'll leave you to yourselves now. One and three-quarter hours – then I'll give you a shout.'

The second door shut quietly; Guillaume's retreating footsteps then, over hard ground and the litter of last winter's leaves. He and the others would be standing guard out there for the next hour and a half. Here in the van they'd been left a lantern with a stub of candle in it and a more or less intact spare candle; there was a roll of musty-smelling carpet to sit on. Marilyn gazing amusedly at Rosie: blonde eyebrows hooped, blue eyes, perfect skin and at least the *impression* of every strand of hair in place. A short laugh: 'Flabbergasted plus . . . Here – some time since you had a *decent* smoke?'

'Oh, boy . . .' A packet of twenty Senior Service: she took one, eagerly. Marilyn had a lighter ready, told her as it flared, 'There I was, semi-stunned and not knowing who or *what*—'

'Referring to the fact I look like a dog's breakfast?'

'Well –' peering through a drift of blue smoke – 'Since you mention it . . . But I mean when I banged down. You could've been a phoney, deceived our "Boris". Your return to the land of the living wasn't all that *probable*, after all. And "Boris" hadn't ever seen you – only heard of you, from Lise?'

Rosie nodded. 'He and I discussed this when I first descended on him, as it happens. I even showed him some of my wounds, as proof of identity.'

'*Did* you . . .'

'But if Baker Street had such doubts, for all they knew they might have been dropping you right in it – uh?'

'Not really. Any doubts were – really, theoretical. Anyway, I volunteered. Lise did too.'

'How is she?'

'Fine. I'll tell all – when you have. But as I was saying – I hit the ground, wondering *now* what happens, and what I get is your casual "Hello, Marilyn, how's tricks?"'

Both laughing. Rosie admitting, 'I'd rehearsed it. I guessed it might be you they'd send.'

'I'd imagined you would have. But—'

'I'd *thought* of asking "How's Richard?"'

Trying it on. Richard had become hush-hush several months ago, although he'd still been there in the background. Evidently still was: all Rosie got was a funny look and a dismissive 'Thank you, he's fine.' What she knew was that he was a senior RAF officer; she *suspected* he might be married, hence the security clamp-down. Marilyn becoming business-like now: 'But down to our *moutons*, Rosie – time being so limited. Start by telling me how you got away from the train, et cetera?'

'All right. But first you tell *me* – St Valéry-sur-Vanne, am I to take that on?'

Twitch of the blonde head. 'You're under no obligation to. In fact *I'd* be happier if you didn't. Lise'd rather you didn't, too – she'll be at Tempsford when I get back, hoping I'll have you with me.'

'How about Colonel Buck?'

'His view is that if you're up to it—'

'That's it, then.'

'If you're set on it. But we've got an hour and a half, decide *then*. The rocket thing's desperately urgent, of course, and you're sort of half into it already – that's Buck's reasoning, plus the great confidence he has in you. But there *is* a lot of ground to cover, Rosie, and I'd like to have recent events clear, to start with. Tell me what happened to you?'

Expelling smoke: she'd been smoking greedily and the air in the van was already fairly thick. Couldn't risk opening a door, either. Candle-lit fog: peering at Marilyn through it. 'You'd know it all from Lise, up to the point when she and I made our break for it?'

'*You* made the break. She thought you'd gone nuts, only went along with it because there wasn't time to argue. Now, in her view you're Joan of Arc!'

'Oh, Lord . . .'

'And Buck has put you in for a George Cross. What's more, he's heard from number 82 that you'll be getting it. Look – no more digressions – you ran from the train, there was shooting—'

'George Cross.' Staring at her. '*Me?*'

'Number 82' meant 82 Baker Street – Michael House, SOE worldwide headquarters, a building belonging to Messrs Marks and Spencer. Marilyn shaking her head: 'I was told to tell you, that's all. We all love it – especially now it doesn't have to be posthumous. Honestly, Rosie, we're all cheering for you. But I don't want to start blubbing – or waste any more time than—'

'George bloody *Cross*. It's – *ridiculous* . . .'

'Colonel Buck doesn't think so, nor do the powers that be. That's what counts, not what *you* think. Rosie – come *on*. They were shooting at you, Lise heard it. Quickly, now – we've a *hell* of a lot to get through – huh?'

She'd nodded. 'I was shot in the back – here – and the side of my head – this groove, this one knocked me out, so I was – I suppose sort of corpse-like, smothered in blood – exit wound here, incidentally, near-miss of left bosom . . . Anyway, they left me lying there, it got dark, I was like a loose light-bulb, sort of on and off, you know? More off than on, I suppose. Then – here's the miracle – two Free

French para officers – Michel and Luc, Michel's a major, Michel Jacquard, Guillaume told me his military tag is Commandant First Maquis Liaison Group.'

'We know about him.'

'You do?' Stubbing out her Senior Service, on the van's metal floor beside the candlestick. Marilyn telling her, 'There's a lot of cooperation going on – you'd be amazed.'

'Michel said something about that.' She was shredding the stub, which if it was left here and the van was searched might get Groslin a one-way ticket to Buchenwald. 'It was also Michel who found out where the Marchéval factory is. I'd told him about "Hector", and he offered to – his notion entirely. Then he visited a prominent *résistant* in Troyes by name of Victor Dufay. You memorizing this?'

'Hope so. Go on.'

'After Michel had been to see him and asked about Marchéval's, Dufay realized it was a long time since he'd been in touch with a Resistance friend of his in St Valéry – proprietor of L'Auberge la Couronne, which I'm hoping will be my safe-house down there. Jacques and Colette Craillot, both active *résistants*. They must have tipped off Dufay about the rocket-casings, and he immediately got hold of Michel again – Michel being off on some new brief.'

'We know about it.'

'*Do* you . . . But am I right in thinking at least part of the reason nobody's heard about the rockets until now is there's no SOE *réseau* in that area?'

'Probably.' Marilyn nodded grimly. 'Another "Hector" effect.'

'Effects plural, surely.'

She looked puzzled for a moment, then nodded. 'Several individuals, yes.'

'Including one or two who were on that train with us?'

Another nod: 'Does seem so. Not from *that* area, but—'

'Rather underlines the need to do something about him, doesn't it?'

'*Doesn't* it, just.'

'Could you spare another fag? I can tell you the rest in about thirty seconds flat. Michel and Luc took me to a woman – war-widow, Thérèse Michon – who was part of an escape line on the far side of the Vosges Mountains. I say she *was* part of an escape line because she's since been arrested.'

Roughing out the picture – names and places. None of it mattered in practical terms at this stage, although it would when the Boches were driven out and the time came for people to be thanked and recompensed; Baker Street needed to have it on the record, for future reference. Rosie finished, 'You know the rest. Guillaume's pianist got the signal out that afternoon. Must have given you a nasty turn?'

'Floored us, Rosie. Absolutely floored us. You see, that was the afternoon of August 2nd, this last Wednesday, only the day after I'd invited Ben to come to Baker Street to meet Lise, hear her story and – well, hear from me, first, that you were dead.'

'I'm sorry you had that job.'

'So was I. Wish I hadn't, too – if I'd delayed it just two days—'

'Have you told him yet I'm *not* dead?'

'No. For one thing, there's hardly been a minute. Lise's seen him a couple of times during the week—'

'She has?'

'From the meeting we had in Baker Street, he took her to lunch. I'd have been with them, but I couldn't, I got called away.'

'Leaving them to cry on each other's shoulders.'

'Well, sort of. Metaphorically more than actually, though. She *is* stricken. Her *chef de réseau* – Alain Noally – you met him, didn't you?'

'He was more than just her *chef de réseau*.'

'So I gather.'

'He was really something. I mean *really*. Quite a bit older than her, but – for her, the beginning and end of everything. As it's turned out – well, I hope not, but maybe even *literally* . . . You say Ben's seen her – a few times?'

'I think exactly as you say, to cry on each other's shoulders. Although she doesn't show it much. She's shattered, but it's – you know, locked in. Although she and I have had long talks – right from the start, she was under medical supervision for a couple of weeks, and of course de-briefing, and our relationship's been helped by the fact I've known *you* so well . . . Anyway, we decided – or rather I did – that for the moment we wouldn't tell Ben anything. One *couldn't* be sure it wasn't a hoax – and you see, if you were coming back with me tonight fine, no reason *not* to—'

'You mean that as I'm not, you might find yourselves having to break bad news all over again.'

'Lise thinks we should tell him. This was only – God, yesterday morning. There *hasn't* been time. She'd had supper with him on Thursday night and – look, I'm not keeping secrets from *you*, Rosie—'

'I'd hope not!'

'He unburdened his soul to her, apparently. I might have mentioned, he was pulverized by what we'd told him. One keeps using that word "shattered"—'

'Go on?'

'He told Lise there's some woman he was involved with – long before he met you, apparently – who married his CO mostly because he, Ben, wouldn't marry her – if *that* makes sense—'

'It does, actually.'

'Well, that marriage has broken up now—'

'She's in the wings again, is that it?'

'Seems so. Ben – well, he's been *crushed*, remember. It might seem like – I don't know, but when you're – you know, floundering—'

'She was after him, all right. And I suppose if I'd ceased to exist—'

'Exactly. Rosie, we've got to move on, but first two questions – one, *should* we tell him you're alive?'

'Yes. *Please*. And tell him I'm sorry I didn't get to say goodbye?'

'Well – you *couldn't* have. But all right – I'll have Lise tell him tomorrow. Second question – in view of what I've told you – about this other woman – want to change your mind, come back on the Hudson?'

'No. Once he knows I'm *not* dead—'

'All right.'

'But don't tell him you've told me anything about Joan Stack. Lise needn't have told *you* . . . Is he stationed in Portsmouth still?'

'London – back in his old St James's Street job. Since soon after you took off. Anyway, Lise'll tell him tomorrow – as fresh news, it'll still be less than a week old – and I've been out here checking it – which is *true* . . . I'll tell him you send your love and hope to be back – within a few weeks, say.'

'Better say as long as it takes. Otherwise he's going to be camping on your doorstep, isn't he?'

'I suppose – yes. Rosie, you *are* completely recovered, are you?'

A nod. 'Completely.'

'There was talk in Baker Street of sending a doctor with me to check you over, but parachute-trained quacks don't grow on trees.'

'I'm fine. What's next?'

'We'll go through this stuff I've brought you, presently. And associated detail. Hope I picked the right clothes. I've got the make-up you wanted – Max Factor, pancake. Not as dark as whatever *that* muck is . . . Oh, we're giving you a new code-name – as of now you're Masha.'

Lise's influence, perhaps – she being of White Russian parentage. Or an abbreviation of Marchéval? Easy way to remember it anyway, in case of memory failure. She'd shrugged: 'Masha. All right.'

'I've brought the A Mark III, plus one-time pad, et cetera, set of three crystals, and a note of your new radio checks for you to memorize. Here, with the small fortune you asked for?' A package she'd had inside her jump-suit. Thirty thousand francs, in there – or should be; she'd be able to afford her own black-market cigarettes now, at least. Marilyn telling her, 'As soon as you're there and functional we'll expect a message, *Masha on line*, followed by any news you have for us. Thereafter, listening out and transmission schedules as you'll find listed with the radio checks, but initially listen out every night midnight to 0100 – after you've set the ball rolling. Emergency procedure transmission *any* time, of course.'

'I'll destroy the notes before we push off for Troyes in the morning.'

'So you'll be in Troyes – or even St Valéry-sur-Vanne – by tomorrow evening?'

'Depending on Victor Dufay and transportation. Or getting a bike, maybe. But I'll have rather a lot of gear for that. You'll hear from me when you hear from me, that's all. Guillaume's taking me as far as Troyes in his *gazo*.'

'Good for him. But now – pushing this along a bit, Rosie – subject of the rocket casings. The measurements you gave us do tally, roughly, with other received Intelligence. This is confirmed by SIS – your old chums, who wouldn't normally want us within miles of a job like this, but Buck told them he hoped it'd be you doing it and they're happy. Measurements of the *completed* rockets – warhead *and* casing – are forty-six feet long, diameter five feet six inches.

Diameter over the fins eleven feet seven inches. Your casings won't have fins – presumably – one imagines they'd be made somewhere else, assembled somewhere else too – but allowing for the length of forty-six feet including warhead, your casing length of about twelve metres could be about right. The body diameter's a bit out. So – confirmation of dimensions, plus detail of screw-holes or fixing points, or whatever for fins and warhead. And where the casings go when they're shipped out, either for partial or final assembly – it'd be terrific to know where – and how many per flatbed truck, how many trucks per road convoy, and how often. Notice of departure of a convoy, if we knew its route, could lead to RAF intervention – straffing by Mosquitoes for instance. We have a very recent air-recce photo of the village, by the way, a good one. I didn't bring it – you wouldn't need it, and it would be compromising.'

'Not knowing who'd be receiving you. This is much more an SIS than an SOE job, isn't it?'

'Vital we should all muck in, anyway. There's *extreme* concern at the highest level, I can tell you – at the V2 threat. Incidentally, the Germans have given it a code-name "A4". If you hear or see that designation anywhere around, we'll know what we're on to right away, mightn't need any other checks. But – *enormously* important, this, Rosie. Especially as it seems unlikely we'll over-run the launch sites before the damn things are ready. Obviously the Marchéval factory won't be the only source. SIS *had* assumed it would all be happening in Germany. They're *highly* destructive missiles – so much so that numbers might be limited by cost – each one's said to be six times as expensive as a Junkers 88. *Far* more of a menace than the flying bombs.'

'What's the picture with them, now?'

'Not as bad as it looked to start with. Eighty per cent are being destroyed in the air, AA batteries have been shifted to

the coast, double benefit through leaving the air inland free
for RAF to operate. Fighters have been shooting them down,
even tipping them over with a wing-tip. *Slightly* hazardous,
no doubt. But you can see them coming, shoot them down –
with the V2s no such hope, straight up into the stratosphere
and down at Christ knows what speed soundlessly and
invisibly, no warning, just a huge, devastating explosion.'
    'Totally indiscriminate.'
    'Oh, yes. It's a terror weapon, nothing else. Anyway
– the Marchéval factory. If we can be certain those are
casings for V2s, we're guaranteed an air-strike – code-name
"Jupiter" already allocated, night-bombing attack in sufficient strength to wipe the place out – targeting the manor
as well. Manor's shown clearly in our photograph – taken
by a Spit on Friday, incidentally.'
    'Well – all *I've* got's a rough sketch. I made this copy
for you, but obviously you don't need it.' She'd had it
in a pocket. 'Dufay drew it, for Michel.' Unfolding it . . .
'There. That's the manor. Match the photo, does it?'
    Marilyn was turning it, to see it from a western per-
spective – the way the attack would go in, presumably.
Nodding: 'Yes, near-enough the same. This squiggle's the
Vanne – right? Which flows into the Yonne – out here.' Off
the paper, a long way west of St Valéry. 'Hereabouts, place
called Sens?'
    'Exactly. Good. I was looking at a map too – Guillaume's
pianist's. Sens *is* the place. The Yonne flows north into the
Seine, of course. I was imagining they'd come down east
of Paris, find Sens and turn sharp left, on course for St
Valéry. They'd pick up my "S" phone beam pretty well
immediately. I'd be *here* – not far from the manor, *that* side
of it, the approach side . . .' Glancing round to where her
stuff was piled. '*Had* thought of asking for a Eureka beacon.
But if I can I might have a bonfire lit, somewhere between
the manor and the factory – i.e. the village, same thing. I'd

have to confirm all that before the event, of course; not having seen the place yet, one's flying blind.'

'Don't put yourself *too* close to the manor.'

'And get bombed oneself, you mean. But we do want the manor hit. There'll be no lights visible, obviously – with Boches in residence – and a smallish target – trees all round it, by the look of *this*. Be over it before they saw it. I know the factory's the big thing, but "Hector"'s not *un*important, is he?'

'Certainly is not. Although that's only a fairly long-shot hope. As you say, priority has to be the factory. And remember your last bombing target, Rosie, Châteauneuf-du-Faou – Château Trevarez. I can tell you a lot more bombs fell around it than on it. They hit it all right, but—'

'Bombs falling round it *should* have dropped on a fair concentration of Boches who were expecting a Maquis assault, not the RAF.' The night she'd had to run for it, night of the car smash. 'Didn't they?'

'Yes. As it happened. You saw it from a distance, we heard.'

'Heard how?'

'SIS man you were with – crashed that car?'

'So he made it back . . .'

'He was devastated at having to leave you. Could hardly have carried you, though – what, sixty or seventy miles. We got the whole story from him, of course: and then from Morlaix that you'd been moved to Paris by the Gestapo. Christ, but you've been through it, haven't you . . . Once again, back to the point – bombing's not always as accurate, and if you're swanning around in the manor's grounds—'

'I'll put myself a safe distance west. Terrain permitting. Due west, and the "S" phone beam on the reciprocal of the manor's bearing from me. According to this sketch the line'd be about five degrees south of due east, and I might aim to have a bonfire – well, say *here* – depending on access, et cetera?'

'Otherwise just the "S" phone. Should be enough for them, surely. But – OK . . .' Lighting her own second cigarette; Rosie's was barely stub; she wasn't wasting any. Marilyn nodded. 'We'll listen out for you on your night-crystal frequency – tomorrow evening'd be a bit soon to hope for, let's say midnight to 0100 Monday and Tuesday. If we hear from you Monday night, you'll hear from us on Tuesday – otherwise Wednesday. Listen out on the night after your first transmission, and let's assume that'll be Tuesday at the latest – *Masha on line* plus whatever you have for us. If it's positive, we'll send you "Jupiter" with a date and time, and you acknowledge confirming the target-marking detail.'

'What about a *message personnel* for "Jupiter", while we're at it?'

'Why not. Let's say "Even in mid-summer the nights are sometimes cool."'

She repeated it. Flattening her cigarette stub; the candle wasn't going to last much longer either. 'One other thought, though. Do we need to be completely certain that the casings are for V2s? Since it's so urgent and important mightn't we just assume they *are*?'

Decisive shake of the head: Virginia tobacco-smoke pluming. 'For one thing the RAF's at full stretch. Aircraft, crews and other resources not to be wasted on what may be – well, *anything*, Rosie – boilers, ventilation trunking – portable urinals for Hitler Youth, for God's sake – and second, there are sound reasons quite apart from plain old-fashioned humanity *not* to blast a whole French village into kingdom come just as it were on spec.'

She nodded. 'All right.'

'Another point is urgency. Shouldn't take you long, should it? Your *auberge* proprietor must have contacts in

Marchéval's, let him work on them, and let's hear from you *soon* – OK?'

A small smile. 'Yes, Ma'am.'

'It does happen to be as important as any brief you've ever had, Rosie.'

'I realize . . .'

'So – next on the agenda – André Marchéval.'

'Where we came in, you might say.' Shaking out another Senior Service. 'May I? Local things are going to taste foul after this . . . Anyhow – Guillaume's view is you'd want the sod caught – apprehended, not killed.' Leaning to the flare of Marilyn's lighter. 'Because there'd be information to be got out of him – primarily what's happened to agents who've disappeared. But would he know? I mean once the swine's shopped them—'

'In some cases he might. Potential value to us being one, remote chance of tracing an individual to some camp or prison where he or she *might* have survived, and two, arrest and trial of those responsible. But *how* you'd "apprehend" him—'

'Exactly. Especially as according to Dufay the locals think well of the father – Henri Marchéval – and some – including Dufay I think – believe his son's an agent of SOE. I know, how secure can you get? But it could be difficult for an outsider to get much cooperation, on that basis – might even be safer not to ask for it.'

'How about the couple at the *auberge*?'

'Don't know.' A shrug. 'See how it turns out. But I don't have to ask anything about André, don't have to know of his existence. Only thing I'd like to have clear – now – is if he does show up, am I authorized to kill him?'

Marilyn removed a shred of tobacco from her lip. Perfectly manicured nails, as always. Telling Rosie carefully, 'We want him alive or dead, and appreciate that taking him alive might be very difficult. So – yes. But bear this in mind, Rosie – if he knows you escaped and that you're still at large—'

'Guillaume was going on about that. But he *can't* know, none of them can. I could have done a flit like tonight's weeks ago – or I could be dead!'

'Could easily. *Too* easily. God's sake don't push your luck, Rosie. *Don't* ask about him in the village. Just don't be tempted. From what you said, he'll still have friends there – not to mention a father. If he heard even a whisper he'd only have to mention it to his Gestapo chums – very much "Hector" style, wouldn't have to show his face.'

'But – minuscule as the chances are – in the event he does show up, and the even unlikelier one he agreed to be brought back for debriefing—'

'Fifty to one against?'

'At least, but—'

'All right – a *réseau* in that area – "Patriarch", shut down a few months ago. Organizer was a Frenchman named Lambert – used a field known as "Parnassus". Unless you gave us reason not to, we'd use that.'

'As always, you've done your homework.'

'I have, naturally, but – easy, both starting with "P", and those a's. That's it, anyway – a call for urgent pick-up from "Parnassus", we'd have a Hudson there either that night or the one after. Say between midnight and 0200, the pilot'll be expecting "S" phone reception, and for a *message personnel* let's say, "*The beech trees are at their best in autumn.*"'

'If there was time for *messages personnels*.'

'Of course. Better change this candle, hadn't we? Rosie – whatever you do, I mean *à propos* "Hector" – *extreme* discretion, obviously . . .'

Chapter 10

She'd asked Marilyn, soon after they'd lit the new candle, what Bob Hallowell's standing in 'F' Section was now, following the revelations about 'Hector'.

Out in the field called Xanadu now, waiting for the Hudson, and thinking back to that discussion, in particular racking their brains for anything they should have discussed and hadn't. Guillaume standing ready with the 'S' phone, Fernand Déchambaud beside him with the white signal-lamp, Guérin and Lemartin out on the flanks of what would be the Hudson's landing run. Groslin was patrolling around the field's perimeter, in the cover of the trees, and no doubt keeping an eye on his van. Rosie and Marilyn were sitting on the container, which in due course would be loaded into the Hudson.

That question about Hallowell, though: he was the major on 'F' Section's staff, who in Maurice Buckmaster's absence at the end of April had conducted Rosie's farewell briefing on the day of her departure on this last deployment. He'd insisted that, despite rumours, 'Hector' was entirely trustworthy. He'd known him a long time, had every faith in him; he was being brought back, he said, only to clear the air – he'd described it as 'going through the motions' – adding that he happened to know 'Hector''s chief accuser was motivated by sexual jealousy, 'Hector' having pinched that individual's girl.

'Always did have a bit of a roving eye. Doesn't make him a traitor, does it?'

And since everyone now knew he *was* a traitor, that disastrously wrong assessment would surely have become a crisis issue.

Marilyn had told her, 'He's on indefinite sick leave. Official line, anyway. He may be facing a court-martial.'

Rosie remembered Michel asking her in Thérèse's attic, 'Any doubt of *him*?' Raising the possibility of treachery right there in Baker Street: and her own sense of shock at the very notion. She'd dismissed it even as a possibility when Michel had brought it up again in Metz, just recently. Marilyn explaining, 'Question is how "Hector" wasn't rumbled a lot sooner, and another *was* how Bob went on sticking up for him.'

'You say a question *was*. Meaning it's been answered?' Wondering also whether 'sticking up' might mean 'covering for' . . . Meanwhile, during this part of their talk she'd been going through the things Marilyn had brought with her. The clothes were well chosen, and had no English labels. Shaking her head: 'Hard to believe *he's* a traitor – secret Nazi, or—'

'No. Not that, quite.'

'What, then?'

Visualizing him as he'd looked to her that day of the briefing. A thin man with a grey, pinched look; she hadn't known him at all well, had never had much to do with him, but she knew he was a dug-out, with an MC from the '14-'18 war. Vintage about 1900, she guessed, straight from school into that war in its last year or two.

Marilyn had been lighting a cigarette. Telling her now, 'The answer's *cherchez la femme* – in the person of Helen Marchéval.'

'André's mother? Who wert in Scotland?'

'*Art* in Scotland. Aberdeenshire, in her brother's house

– brother's in the Eighth Army in Italy. Wouldn't be surprised if that's where Bob will hole up now – if he's at liberty to. Not Italy – Aberdeen . . . Rosie, Buck let me hear this in confidence, so – under your hat? Bob H. was being interrogated at the time, in one of our places in the country – soon after Lise got back, and while she was being debriefed. Buck had just seen some preliminary report. But apparently they were lovers – Bob and Helen Marchéval – before the war, and I think the inference was that they still are, and that it would have been at least partly why she left her husband and came back in 1940. Even if at the time it might have looked like just getting out from under. She'd been spending as much time in Scotland as in France in any case; and André was over here too of course – university and after. Papa trying to get him back to France to join him in the business, and he wouldn't go. Unlike the daughter – André's sister Claire – no, I hadn't heard of her before either – but according to Bob she never got on with her mother and disapproved of her liaison with Bob. *Probably* would have – could have been the primary reason for their "not getting on". Apparently she – Claire – never left France at all. But do you remember Bob telling us in that briefing session that André wouldn't go back to join Papa because he was enjoying himself too much over here? Thirty-eight, thirty-nine that would have been. And he presumably *didn't* mind about his mother's carrying on – which might indicate a somewhat feckless character?'

Rosie nodded. 'But rather surprising Buck telling you all this?'

'He had a few of us together to see if we had any contributions to make. Bob's social life, et cetera. I didn't – I'd never seen him outside the building.'

'I'd hardly have thought he was capable of it, frankly. I mean the romance thing. Dry old stick . . . But is the

conclusion that he was covering for "Hector" – knowing
he *was* a traitor?'

'I'd say not – Buck seems to think not. One wouldn't
want to think it, of course. You're right, though, it's very
much the question that needs answering. My guess is he
honestly believed in André. OK, *stupid* – perhaps blindly
loyal to Helen—'

'Anyway rotten judgement.'

'*Unacceptably* rotten judgement. So rotten it's cost lives.'
Looking at Rosie, reading her thoughts and nodding, in
the candle-light: 'Caused agonies. Horrors – as well as
organizational disaster here and there. If "Hector" had
been pulled out of the field three or four months ago,
as he should have been, lives would have been saved
and several blown *réseaux* would still be in place. Look,
briefing *you* that day – you were flying out to the field
where "Hector" was *supposedly* waiting – huh?'

'I've thought about that a lot.'

The bastard *had* known she was going to Rennes – where
she'd met Lise in a public place. Noally had been so
right . . .

Rosie had been unwrapping the Llama pistol at this
point in the palaver. It lay in her hand for a moment:
flat, black and heavy, though not as heavy as a Colt.
Sliding the magazine out, counting the seven rounds in
it, then working the pistol's action to ensure there wasn't
one in the breech as well. There wasn't. She'd slipped the
magazine back in, clicked it home . . . 'What's *that* now?'

'Unwrap it and see.'

'Like Christmas . . .' Fleeting smile. Candle-light flickering slightly in a sudden draught that also set Marilyn's
cigarette-smoke swirling. Rosie had slid the Llama into her
left-hand jacket pocket – the Beretta was in the right-hand
one – and reached for this small object, pulled the wrapping
off it . . .

Lipstick holder. Marilyn said, 'It's silver. Belgian-made. Try unscrewing the bottom end.'

The end, when turned, acted in the usual way, winding the pink lipstick out and pulling it back again. But the bottom part that turned had a gnarled ring at its base. She couldn't unscrew it, though. Marilyn told her, 'It's a reverse thread. Undo it by screwing *up* – clockwise. But be careful – don't spill—'

It came off easily – a cap about the size of a sixpence. Up-ending it then, to tip its contents into a cupped palm, and guessing in that second what they'd be. Two cyanide capsules. The normal issue was just one, but on this last deployment she'd asked for two – which had been taken from her in the hospital in Morlaix. There was just room for them in the little secret chamber between the pink stuff and the base. She'd looked at them for a moment, cupped in her palm: thinking that Justine Quérier surely wouldn't have had a *silver* lipstick, very likely wouldn't have had one at all. But OK – Justine's mother's just pegged out, this was among her few effects . . . Glancing up at Marilyn: 'My dear – what I've *always* wanted . . .

She'd keep one capsule in the lipstick, decide on a different hiding-place for the other. No point having two if you kept them together. But think about that later . . . There'd been a wristwatch too, which she'd asked for in the signal. Marilyn's own watch: she'd had it on her right wrist, with a newer, smarter one on the other; this one was suitably *un*smart, but Swiss-made – strictly neutral – and Marilyn had assured her it kept perfect time.

'Also luminous, please note.'

'I'll treasure it—'

'Oh, it's no *treasure*!'

'– and I'll bring it back.'

'It's a present. Just bring *yourself* back.'

*   *   *

No Hudson yet. Should have been on the ground a quarter of an hour ago: by now in fact should have been *off* the ground again and homebound. Delay made one feel nervous: as if there had to be a limit to good luck. Wait long enough, you'll wish you hadn't.

Moon still well up, anyway. They were sitting on the rough grass now: a lot softer than the container.

Marilyn yawned. 'I'm not too happy about your papers, Rosie.'

'Better than they *were*, believe me.'

'I'd avoid road-blocks and checkpoints if you can. I mean, obviously you wouldn't go *looking* for them – but try to use minor roads, and so on.'

'Luckily they've only got to see me through for a few weeks. Touch wood. And once I'm in St Valéry, probably not moving around much—'

'Extraordinary to think of, isn't it? Just a few weeks . . . And *probability*, no pipe-dream . . .'

Prospect of France in French hands, cleansed of Boches, 'F' Section therefore redundant, its staff and surviving agents demobilized. Marriage to Ben – like two new people in a new world – in many ways strangers to each other. Different people, really, they'd have to be . . . Lise had talked about this in Rennes, she remembered; about herself and Noally – whether things could possibly be as good between them as they had been in the bizarre, often terrifying circumstances they were used to, had become one might say their natural habitat. She'd postulated then, 'Could be I can't see us in another kind of life because we *won't* be?'

Springing from her belief in Fate. Whatever that was . . . But having lived this kind of life, it became about ninety per cent of what you were. Everything you knew, or – in Lise and Noally's case – shared. Each of *them* in a way a refuge for the other. For herself and Ben it should be all right – she believed – because although they hadn't been together *in* it he'd known all about it, certainly lived *with* it. Wouldn't expect her not sometimes to scream in the night.

Lovely Ben . . .

Who'd better bloody not have committed himself to the Stack woman. Although he might have done – in reaction to shock, desperation – needing *something*. Even *that* crooked bitch.

Marilyn said – emerging perhaps from some similar line of thinking – 'You'll need to find some new challenge, won't you – when this does all suddenly come to a grinding halt. Even if you do marry Ben – which I'm sure you *will*—'

'Were you head girl, at school?'

'What makes you ask *that*, heaven's sake?'

'Just you sound like it, sometimes.'

Soft laughter, in the moonlight. 'Must stay in touch, Rosie. Whatever happens to either of us—'

'Stand by!'

'*Ah* . . .'

Guillaume, fitting the mike back over his face. There *was* a thrum of aircraft engines, she realized, so distant that at this moment it was more a trembling in the night sky than actual sound. They were on their feet: and it was already clearly sound, the kind they'd been waiting for. Guillaume with a hand out grasping old Déchambaud's arm, warning him to be ready with the signal lamp but not start yet. It would be the letter 'R' again, as it had been for the Lanc. When the flashing started, Lemartin and Guérin would switch on their red lights, and the Hudson homing in on the 'S' phone's beam would put itself down to taxi in midway between them.

'Rosie.' Marilyn had put an arm round her shoulders. '*Certain* you don't want to hand over to someone else?'

'Hell, *yes*!'

'OK.' Tighter squeeze before she let go. 'Only asking.'

Rosie reflecting that it would have been too damn late

anyway – her suitcase and other gear being in the van, couple of hundred metres away. They'd be wanting to save seconds on the ground, let alone minutes. Groslin trotting up then, pushing his Sten-gun strap over his shoulder; he'd be needing his hands free to help loading the container. He and Déchambaud; the other two would stay out there as markers for the take-off.

'Make "R", Fernand!'

Engine-noise loud now, its note as well as volume rising. Rosie half turning from the lamp with a hand up to shield her eyes, save her night vision, but still getting the aura of the dot-dash-dot, dot-dash-dot. Seeing also then twin red pinpoints glowing: the Hudson was coming in, coming down, a flash of reflected moonlight from the Perspex canopy over the pilots' cockpit – just that brief glimmer before it dipped into shadow below the tree-line.

Invisible touch-down: then in sight again, the moonlight flickering on its twin props; the rest of it shiny black, stubby-looking, rumbling up this way between the red markers. Guillaume shouting – holding the mike away from his face, looking round at them – 'All set – Marilyn? Got the bumph I gave you?'

'Right here.' Patting her chest, a bulge in the jump-suit.

He'd nodded, yelled, 'Good luck!' The 'bumph' was paper-work from him and/or others to Baker Street. The Hudson racketing up close, bigger now, slowing and stopping, then lurching around to point back the other way; Marilyn set off at a run towards the tail-section – this port side, the passenger door – and Rosie trotted after her. Déchambaud and Groslin were hefting the container: empty, two men could handle it easily enough, even run with it. The door in the rear of the fuselage had been opened from inside by one of the four-man crew: pilot and co-pilot staying put up front, tail-gunner visible in the moonlit transparence of his dome on top, machine-gun barrel jutting blackly,

ready to cope with interference. Guillaume would still be
in communication with the pilot over his 'S' phone. Marilyn
now waiting clear of the open doorway while the two
Frenchmen lifted the container up to it and others inside
grabbed hold. Could have been passengers – a Hudson
had room for twelve, this one might well have made other
pick-ups or deliveries, or have others yet to make before its
return to Tempsford. It would be an hour before the moon
set. The container was inside, and a man in khaki reaching
to give Marilyn a pull up: then the door swinging shut and
the plane already moving – starting back to where it had
landed, from where in about half a minute's time it would
take off this way, into the wind and over Rosie's and the
others' heads. When it did come roaring, hoisting itself into
the night sky, destination Tempsford – where Marilyn had
said Lise would be waiting – the thought was inescapable
that in some ways it would have been *fantastic* to have been
up there too.

In other ways, though – less so. If she *had* gone, she'd
have been kicking herself by now and maybe for ever after
for having chickened out.

'Because –' she'd told Guillaume, in the van on the way
back to the Déchambaud place, Groslin driving without
lights and slowly enough to be able to swerve off the track
and into the cover of the trees if necessary – 'I've got to fix
this awful hair. The dye I asked for? Make-up too. I've got
to arrive there looking as I'm *going* to look, haven't I?'

'Of course. Hadn't thought. But you'll get hardly any
sleep at all. We *must* start out pretty early.'

'Sleep in the *gazo* on the way. Unsociable, but—'

'Nonsense!'

'If we were stopped, I'd have been up all night with my
dying mother.'

She used the Déchambauds' kitchen for the hair-dyeing

and drying. Déchambauds upstairs in their own bed or beds, Guillaume on a pallet on the floor in the 'small front-room', as they called it. There was an armchair in the kitchen in which Rosie could relax when she'd finished: or at least doze, while her hair was drying a light chestnut-brown. It was an easy change from the scarifyingly bright yellow, and a welcome one, halfway back to her own naturally deeper brown: and wouldn't look any different as far as the photo was concerned. The other priority job was to get the dark-tinted grease out of her skin and replace it with the Max Factor pancake make-up which Marilyn had brought. The light in the kitchen – two oil-lamps – wasn't good enough to be sure, but she *thought* it was a huge improvement. With the rubber pads back in her cheeks she didn't bear all that close a resemblance to Rosie Ewing either.

Wouldn't matter so much in Troyes anyway – probably still less in St Valéry-sur-Vanne. There'd hardly be posters of her and Lise that far from where they'd lost her. It was possible, but she didn't think there would be. All right, you could still run into bad luck: if Justine's papers looked phoney to some sharp-eyed Boche who then checked with Paris, say. But those were the risks everyone took all the time: and her papers weren't *that* bad.

One thing she had to decide was where to carry/hide the cyanide capsules. Or anyway one of them. She'd set out on this deployment with tiny pockets sewn into the hems of the two blouses she'd brought with her; still had them – the blouses, not the capsules – when she'd been moved from the Morlaix hospital to Fresnes prison – and had hung on to them, despite the problem of laundering without soap and under a cold tap, and sharing cells with thieves – so she'd been wearing one in the train and when she'd been brought blood-soaked to Thérèse's farm. Thérèse had soaked it off her, but it had been bullet-holed front and back, hadn't been worth trying to mend so they'd torn it up and used it for bandages. She'd come away from Thérèse's with three others – one on, and two in the basket, all umpteenth-hand and much mended – and now had two more which Marilyn had brought . . . OK – decision time: leave the old ones here, take only the two fresh from London; and as time was short and one wanted to get some shut-eye – and with this poor light and not having a needle – just improvize, for now: open a little slot in the front hem – try it on one blouse anyway, see if you could insert a capsule then slide it along a bit.

Kitchen knife. Using its sharp point to pick out a few threads. Working with narrowed eyes and a lot of concentration, close up against a lamp. OK so far . . . The seam was ironed flat, but the capsule could be worked along with one's fingertips – a few centimetres, say. Must have ironed this blouse herself: an age ago, in that other world – in which Marilyn would be, by now – and she, Rosie, *could* have been. Shaking her head, lips compressed; fixing the second blouse the same way. Might borrow a needle and cotton from Ursule at breakfast-time, make a job of it – stabilize the access slit and put a stitch in a few inches along so the capsule couldn't work round and get itself out of reach. When one needed to get at it – seeing this in her imagination quite easily, having been in such situations – one would be fiddling nervously, apparently out of terror but actually fiddling it round. As long as they'd left one's hands free. Otherwise back in the cell, *after* the first session . . .

She'd fixed the second blouse. Whenever she changed into a clean one she'd transfer the capsule. Crossing the room now to rummage the lipstick out of her jacket pocket: she unscrewed the cap, tipped the capsules out on Ursule's tall pine-wood dresser and took one of them to insert it into the blouse she was going to wear. Working it round a

few centimetres – a pinching action, as envisaged. Fine . . .
And might as well change into this now – in fact change
completely, underclothes and skirt as well – (a) while one
had this privacy, (b) to be ready then for the breakfast call,
not have to do so much in a rush.

She had to more or less unpack the suitcase, to get out
the things she wanted. Disrobing then: Ursule's sweater on
the table, and the rest of the stuff she'd been wearing – and
didn't ever want to see again – in a pile near the stove for
Ursule to dispose of. Starkers for a moment: then dressing
quickly: but pausing again, half-dressed, her eye caught by
the lipstick-holder on the dresser. Wondering what to do
about it.

She didn't think much of it. First because no Boche
who realized it was silver would leave it in a prisoner's
possession. Some craftsman on SOE's payroll had made a
neat job of it, she thought, but rather pointlessly. Marilyn
couldn't have given it much thought either.

So where, *how* . . .

Handkerchief?

Marilyn had brought her three, plain white cotton. Might
sew one capsule into a corner of one of them?

They'd leave you a handkerchief, probably. If you were
sobbing into it – and they'd see it was no more than it
seemed, a plain little *mouchoir*, no map or code printed on
it. Seemed almost too simple, she thought. But it might be
as good a way as any. Quicker than most, at that: corner of
handkerchief into mouth, bite on it. Cyanide killed instant-
aneously, one had been assured several dozen times.

Later, then, fix that up – in Troyes or St Valéry, when time
permitted; and rather than borrow needle and thread, ask
Ursule if she could spare some. Meanwhile, stick to the
lipstick-holder – which one might take in the normal way
in one's – Léonie's – handbag. Old scuffed leather bag on
a carrying-strap. Some time on Saturday morning she'd

muttered to herself *damn*, forgot to ask Baker Street to send a bag, and Léonie without a word had put this one aside for a parting gift. You'd have looked wrong without one – and God knew, she'd been looking wrong enough as it was.

Looking around, as she finished dressing, asking herself what else. Apart from letting her hair dry – which it would still be doing while she slept. (You couldn't towel freshly dyed hair that was still damp, the dye'd come off on the towel. The hairdresser in Metz had put her wise on this.) There was something to be said for having such short hair, anyway. Another peek in the mirror on that dresser: even allowing for the rotten light, it didn't look too bad. Wouldn't want to arrive in London and meet Ben, looking like this, but – for present purposes . . .

What she did have to do now was re-pack her suit-case. Better do it now too, not leave it to struggle with by first light. Should have slept all afternoon, she told herself, instead of sitting around smoking and gossiping with Léonie. The suitcase was on the floor, open, a pile of stuff on its lid. To start from scratch was the easiest way – everything out, – beginning by putting her new wireless codes, cash, the Beretta and the Llama and spare mags for both on the bottom. The inside of the case smelt faintly of *eau de Cologne*. She'd had the Llama in her jacket pocket, considered transferring it or the Beretta to her handbag but decided against it, at least on this trip today. To be caught with it at a road-block would mean instant arrest: and trying to shoot your way out of that kind of situation wouldn't get you anywhere – not anywhere you'd *want* to be . . . She was packing the rest of the stuff now, had got about half of it in, then paused for a moment, cursed, took it all out again, and made a new start, this time wrapping the guns and magazines in a pullover and a striped towel which had never belonged to her – her flatmate's, probably. But searchers of baggage just felt in with their hands sometimes

– when they were only searching perfunctorily, as at a checkpoint, for instance.

Now all the rest. And still the radio schedules to be memorized, then burnt.

Pity Silvie de Plesse had had no key for this case. Although locked items were always of greater interest to searchers than *un*locked ones. Just as luggage in plain sight drew their attention less than items you'd locked away in a car's boot, or covered with a rug.

Sleep now. She'd turned out the oil-lamp that was on the dresser, could reach the other long-armed from the chair. Checking the time, first, on Marilyn's watch: should get damn near an hour.

Had had fifty minutes – according to the watch. Unbelievable – it felt like five – if that . . . Grey light of dawn, and this colossal din, Ursule raking ashes and clinker out of the stove. She hadn't said a word – as far as Rosie knew – was evidently relying on the racket she was making to wake not only Rosie but Guillaume too in the next room. Guillaume, who'd have been luxuriating in about three hours' sleep, having the gall to yawn as he shambled in and stood blinking, first at Rosie then at Ursule's enormous black-draped rear where she was stooped with the ash-can and a shovel. She must have opened the curtains before she'd started: greyish light, no sunlight in it at all although that was an east-facing window. Guillaume eyeing Rosie's closed suitcase: 'If that's ready, I'll take it out to the *gazo* with me now . . . Look – Rosie – there's a pump in the yard. Ursule will be needing the sink, and we don't want to hold things up, do we. I mean breakfast. You know where the privy is?'

The outside WC. Of course she knew. And caught on to what he was proposing: he'd take the case and some other things to the *gazo*, in the meantime if she made use

of the privy and cold water from the pump she'd have it
to herself and might have finished by the time he returned.
He'd be refuelling the *gazo*'s charcoal burner and flashing
it up while he was out there, he added, so they could start
as soon as they'd had breakfast.

'All right?'

'Of course.'

On her feet, stretching and yawning, blinking at him.
Guillaume as it were re-focusing on her suddenly: 'Hey,
Rosie! You look like a new woman!'

She *felt* like something recently dug up. Managing a
smile: 'OK, is it?'

'Transformation, absolutely!'

Ursule growled without looking round from the stove,
'She's a real beauty now, you're right. I had a close look
before she woke . . . Giving you porridge, that do?'

'Couldn't think of anything better, Ursule.'

She hadn't got the pads in her cheeks yet: wouldn't have
until she'd rinsed her mouth out. No toothbrush, of course:
make do as she had for a long time now with a forefinger.
She went out – pulling Thérèse's jacket on – into a drizzly,
overcast morning. Total change of scenery in just these few
hours. They'd been lucky, anyway, that the weather hadn't
broken any sooner.

Privy first: then the pump, sparingly. Then breakfast –
porridge, bread baked by Ursule, home-produced honey.
While eating, studying radio scheds. Déchambaud had
been outside seeing to the animals, in a dark serge suit
and white collar; he and Ursule were to attend Mass in
Commercy, would be leaving in the trap shortly after
Guillaume and Rosie were on the road. He'd remarked
to Guillaume, 'Mam'selle is looking even more charming
than before', and Rosie had murmured, 'You're very kind,
M'sieur.' Shake of the grey head, telling her seriously, 'I
only tell the truth as I see it. Is that not so, Ursule?' His wife

had sniffed, towards him, but then smiled at Rosie: 'It's the truth *this* time, anyway.' Still over breakfast there was talk between the two men about a meeting of *résistants* in two days' time at some neighbouring farm where there was to be a further distribution of weapons and ammunition. Then Guillaume showed her on a creased map with a lot of pencil jottings, the route they'd be taking today: first south for about fifteen kilometres to a place called Toul, then on minor roads with occasional *route blanche* diversions until just forty kilometres short of Troyes, a place called Brienne-le-Château: those last forty kilometres would be on the main route between Troyes and Metz – or Nancy.

'Not that there'll necessarily be checkpoints on it. And only forty kilometres out of – oh, getting on for two hundred.'

'Far as *that*?'

A shrug. 'Hundred and ninety, maybe.'

They were out at the *gazo* by about six fifteen, Fernand going out too to see them off and also to harness some horse or donkey into the trap. The charcoal in the *gazo*'s burner was glowing red, ready to go. Rosie had brought out her new A Mark III transceiver, in its own small suitcase, Guillaume having picked up her 'S' phone, still in its protective wrapping.

'Where's best to put what, d'you think?' She'd caught them up at the *gazo*, having been delayed in farewells with Ursule. 'Boot, or—'

'Well, look here . . .'

A carton, from the boot, prominently marked BREUVAGE – which meant 'drench', in this case cattle-drench. He opened it on the ground inside the shed, removed the eight or ten bottles of pinkish fluid from it, substituted the 'S' phone and tied the lid down again. It could go on the rear seat, he suggested, along with her suitcase.

'You can hang on to it if you like. I mean when we

get there. Your transceiver's best in the boot, I'd suggest.'

Also in the boot, as well as a sack of charcoal, was his own vet's kit in a Gladstone bag. And the *breuvage* bottles, which he laid in straw in an open wooden box that had once contained Moselle – that went in the boot too.

'See – at a glance, obviously all veterinary equipment.'

It was true. You hardly noticed the transceiver. If you did, you'd assume it contained the vet's tools, or maybe his personal gear. Bottles of drench, a bag such as a doctor carries, in a litter of excess straw; and in full view on the back seat her own suitcase and the carton.

Rosie shook hands with Déchambaud; he and Guillaume embraced each other. 'Tuesday, then.'

'As you say.' His whiskered face appeared at Rosie's window, as Guillaume started and revved the motor. Guillaume hadn't shaved this morning but old Fernand probably hadn't for a week. 'God bless you, Mam'selle.'

'And you and your comrades, M'sieur.'

Backing out . . . Guillaume commented, 'Couldn't have gone better, could it?'

'Rosie. Justine, I should say—'

She'd been dropping off, jerked awake now. 'Huh?'

'Woke you. Sorry. But look – we'll be in Toul in a minute, should have our stories matching, in case of road-blocks. I'm me, on vet business – easy. You brought me that cat because your mother'd died and you didn't know what to do with it. I've said I'll find a home for it, but meanwhile had to make this trip, and you'd told me you wanted to get to Troyes, on the track of a relation and her husband who have a farm somewhere in that area. You're hoping they'll let you stay, work there perhaps. You don't know where it is exactly, but there's someone in Troyes you think you'll be able to find, and he will know.' A sideways glance and a shrug: 'You hope.'

'Sounds vague enough to be true.'

'Why can't you go on living in Sarrebourg?'

'They let my mother stay on in the house because she was sick, but there was so much rent owing – which *I* certainly couldn't pay—'

'You don't understand these things very well, do you? Why you couldn't easily have got a job. You were hurt, concussed et cetera, in that air-raid on Rouen.'

'Hardly remember any of it. I was working in a kindergarten, I remember *that*, but—'

'This trip now – it so happened I was going almost as far as Troyes, and you being such a pathetic object I thought well, just an extra few kilometres—'

'What'll you do with me when we get there?'

'Oh – release you. Like a stray cat. Shove you out with your gear and bugger off quick!'

'Callous swine . . .'

'I'm a working man, I've farms to visit!'

Indignant: as he would have been, justifying himself to some nosy *gendarme* or Boche. Rosie expanding on her own act then: 'The relation I'm looking for – it's never been a close relationship. Not at *all*. My brother married her sister. He's – I've no idea where now, but he was in the French navy, may have been killed, we never heard from him – or from her either. So Colette – that's the name my mother mentioned when she was telling me I should go and – like I'm doing now – you see she didn't know exactly *where*—'

'Excellent. They'd have heard more than enough, by now.'

Rosie asked him, 'Talking about stray cats, what'll you do with it?'

'Telephone de Plesse, tell him it's OK now and ask him to come and fetch it. Poor bloody animal . . . This is Toul now. The Moselle skirts it to the east, but we won't see it, the water you'll see ahead of us in a minute is a canal. Have to cross that – twice. Then out of town on the road to Vaucouleurs. Rosie, if we *were* stopped and questioned, we started from Nancy, nowhere near where we *have* been.'

'So how to explain being on the Verdun road now?'

'Took a wrong turn. Realized I was heading north instead of southwest, turned back. There, see the water ahead? Quite a nice little town, this – the river, and a cathedral—'

'Will we be mostly on *routes blanches*?'

'Tell you the truth, hardly at all. I'd thought it'd be better than it is. But short of travelling in great zigzags—'

'No point.'

Head back, eyes shut. Justine exhausted, wouldn't have taken much interest in her surroundings anyway. Opening her eyes again then: 'Know your way through the town and out, do you?'

A smile. 'Go to sleep.'

'I'm very grateful to you for all you're doing, Guillaume. Really, you've been a rock.'

'Well.' Turning right. On the left, a Nazi banner drooped from a jutting flagpole. Guillaume easing the wheel back . . . 'It's been a pleasure. *And* – as I said before, I think – I'm not sorry to be seeing you on your way, (a) before some Boche recognized you in the street, (b) before we get really busy here. There's a lot in preparation. So – glad *you're* happy. But tell me – or don't, as the case maybe – what's your brief now?'

'To check on the rocket-casing business.'

'And "Hector"?'

'Secondary. Rocket-casings first. That's what's vital and urgent.'

'Must be long odds against the sod showing up, in any case. But if he does, are you cleared to – er—'

'They'd prefer to have him "apprehended", but appreciate that might be very difficult.'

'Ah.' A glance at her: eyes quickly back on the road. '*Carte blanche*, then. I was wrong.'

'But as you say, long odds.'

'Any other fascinating news from Baker Street?'

'Not really.'

Could have told him about Bob Hallowell, but didn't feel inclined to. Too much detail, explanation, but a degree of shock still lingering in the thought that for recent disasters Hallowell might bear almost as much responsibility as 'Hector' did. What she might have told Guillaume about was the George Cross business. She'd have liked to have been able to talk about it, get *his* reaction, but it would also have been embarrassing. Privately, in a way shaming – as well as so startlingly improbable that she felt she might only have dreamt it . . . She'd never given a thought to being given *any* medal. Why *her*? It would be for the train escape, obviously, for the sheer luck that had made that hairbrained stunt work, allowed Lise to get the truth about 'Hector' home to Baker Street. Perhaps they'd give Lise a medal too. *Then* it mightn't be so bad. Should have asked. But not only Lise: what about Edna, Maureen, Daphne? Seeing them again on her memory's screen – especially their eyes, during the long rocking silences against the background of the train's drumming, remorseless rhythm, that shared or replicated, anyway virtually identical, locked-in desperation . . . Oh, give *them* medals! And never forget them. *She* wouldn't, she knew it, wouldn't ever *not* have them with her. She was trying to open Léonie's handbag, to get a handkerchief; damp-eyed, her view of a flock of cyclists they were passing misted, out of focus. Awkward damn clasp – until one got the knack of it . . . Harsh intake of breath as unexpected as the tears: and Guillaume's quick 'Rosie—'

'Hm.' She'd got the bag open, found the handkerchief. Using it: managing, 'It's OK.' Then a smile, of sorts: 'Drive on, my man.'

She'd slept, woken again. They were on unpaved road through undulating farmland, the track potholed and stony; it could have been the vibration that had woken her. Guillaume was smoking, and lifted that hand: 'Want one?'

'Oh, please . . . But I owe you lots. Might get some in Troyes – if you don't *have* to rush off?'

'It's Sunday.'

'Oh, God, yes . . .'

'Farm road, did you notice?'

Lighting the cigarette, nodding. 'Where are we?'

'I turned down at a place called Gondrecourt-le-Château. Here.' The map. 'Next comes Germay. Pretty country, eh? But the villages tend to be dull. You've slept through a couple. Straight lines of drab houses and that's that. Not like Alsace, they don't pretty them up at all. Got Germay?'

'Yes . . .'

'Next, Poissons. Then rather a major crossing at Joinville – back on hard road before that – see? And at Joinville we cross the main Reims to Chaumont highway. This is the only bit of *route blanche* we'll get, I'm afraid . . . Sure you're all right?'

'I could drive, if you like, give you a rest.'

'Thanks, but—'

'One thing I thought of – when you see de Plesse, if I come into it at all would you let him think you put me on that Hudson?'

'All right.'

'Just that I'd rather he didn't know where I am. I don't suppose he talks to Dufay all that often.'

'He a chum of Dufay's?'

'He put Michel on to Dufay.'

'Ah . . .'

They'd rejoined the hard road, crossed the Marne and were approaching Joinville where this one intersected the bigger, busier one that came south from Reims to St Dizier and Dijon. Dijon being one of the centres mentioned by Michel as being in his new territory, she recalled. But from Joinville there'd be about a hundred kilometres to go; so they'd come about halfway. Rosie as alert as Guillame now, watching the road ahead as buildings – houses, and factories, a builder's yard, motor repair works – began to crowd in along the road.

'You'd think it was a big place.'

'Not by the map, it isn't. But I suppose communications aren't bad – not a bad road we're on, and this more important one we have to cross.' Slowing; entering the village; there was what looked like a queue of traffic ahead. Several lorries, and a crowd of dismounted cyclists. 'Bit of a hold-up . . .'

Time – by Marilyn's watch – just on nine thirty. Three hours and about a hundred kilometres gone. Guillaume edging out a bit from the right-hand side to get a view past the lorries . . . 'Damn.' Pulling in again. '*Wehrmacht* convoy on the main road, looks like.' Braking, stopping close up behind a lorry loaded with timber. 'Solid line of heavy trucks moving left to right, and a motorbike parked, rider doubtless controlling traffic. *Gendarmes* on the corner too.'

'So – may not be for long—'

'Hah. Never said a truer word . . .'

Because the lorries ahead were already beginning to move forward. He pushed the *gazo* into gear. Cyclists on the move too, some of them walking, others mounting, wobbling at slow speed. The sky was lighter than it had been, clouds higher, the drizzle having passed on eastward, she guessed. Lorries picking up speed: Guillaume shifting into second.

'Could've been a lot worse, couldn't it?'

A whistle shrilled. The lorry ahead of them put its brake-lights on, then off, and began moving faster; it was being waved over rather frantically by a Boche trooper in field grey-green and helmet; machine-pistol slung from his shoulder. His bike was parked in the other lane of this road, near the corner. That lorry had been the last he was letting over, he was ordering Guillaume to stop – hand up, palm towards them. Guillaume jamming on his brakes and cursing . . . Short, stocky Boche with the helmet jammed low over his forehead, a cartoon-like figure with booted legs apart: lowering that arm now, turning away. Beyond him, heavy military trucks already filled the road again, pounding northward nose to tail.

'Looks like a big movement.'

'Doesn't it.'

'Reinforcing or evacuating, I wonder?'

The Boche had called something to *gendarmes* on the left side of the road, the narrow pavement there; he'd gestured towards this *gazo*. Guillaume asked her, 'When d'you think you'll make your first transmission?'

'Soon after I get to St Valéry. Possibly tomorrow night. Depends on Dufay, largely. Guillaume, *gendarmes* coming over.'

'Don't want to seem concerned about it though, do we . . . Look at the map – quickly, if you can – tell me a place nearer Troyes where I might be visiting a farm?'

She was *very* quick on it: and as it happened, spotting a possible short-cut by *route blanche*, too. 'Brevonnes do?'

'Brevonnes. Fine.'

'On what looks like *route blanche*, a short-cut that'd miss out Brienne-le-Château.'

'Oh, yes. Did notice that one earlier, I'd forgotten.' Winding the window right down. 'Bonjour, Messieurs. Are we likely to be stuck here for long?'

A shrug of thick, sloping shoulders. 'Probably not. There are breaks between units or detachments of whatever they are, from time to time. Your papers, please?' Glancing into the back, at her suitcase and that carton. Grey hair, florid complexion, grey moustache. The other one was younger, ratty-looking; he'd moved towards the *gazo*'s bonnet, maybe to get a more direct view of Rosie. She'd folded the map while they were still on the way over, had glanced at them without interest and was now watching the procession of heavy transport on the main road.

'Vet, uh?' Nodding towards the rear, focusing on the word BREUVAGE. Guillaume shrugged slightly.

'As you'll see, in those papers.'

'Going where?'

'Immediately, a village called Brevonnes. Farmer near by by name of – oh, damn it—'

'And the young lady?'

'Giving her a lift. Her mother just passed on, she's in search of a relation somewhere near Troyes—'

'Does he want to see my papers?'

Reaching inside Thérèse's rain-jacket . . .

'No, we won't bother.' Returning *his*. The other one had called something, pointing down the main road to the left; this one said, 'Seems you're in luck.' The Boche meanwhile had moved out in front of them again: a gauntleted hand raised, a warning to be ready but not move yet. Guillaume asked the *gendarme*, 'Big troop movement, by the looks of it?'

'Is indeed. Going on since first light. Must be – oh, God knows – at least a division, maybe several. And we had tanks through here yesterday – Panzers, dozens of 'em.' He lowered his face closer to the window. 'Coming from Lyon

and west of there, we heard. Ask me, they're clearing out
. . . There you go now!'

The trooper was waving them forward – impatiently, as
if they'd kept *him* waiting. Tail-end Charlie of the file of
big trucks just clearing the intersection. Guillaume looking
to his left as he drove over, Rosie leaning forward to see
that way too, see the next lot coming. More of the same. He
muttered, 'No end to 'em . . . What I was asking, Rosie –'
he was across the intersection and shifting gear, putting his
foot down – 'when you're transmitting, reporting arrival
and/or whatever else, might be worth mentioning a very
large troop-movement northward towards Reims, said to
be from Lyon and points west.'

'And Panzers yesterday.'

'Glad he didn't want to see your papers.'

'Had one like him just the other day. But he'd got the
message that I was mentally retarded.'

'Some message *that* was . . . What was upsetting you,
earlier on?'

'Upsetting?'

'Coming through Toul.'

'Oh.' She shook her head. 'Thoughts. About – you know
– friends.'

'Ah.' Glancing at her again: and passing her his half-flat
packet of Gauloises. 'Light one for me too?'

'OK.'

'I'll tell you what my wish for you would be, Rosie. Clean
up this rocket thing, and *not* have "Hector" turn up.'

'Well.' Extracting two Gauloises, lighting them both and
passing one to him. 'Very likely how it *will* be.'

Chapter 11

Dufay's place wasn't hard to find. They'd stopped to ask directions once, a few kilometres short of the town, and one of a group of women dressed for church had put them right: left at the next crossroads and after about five kilometres turn right: they'd cross the Seine then, and after following their noses for another two kilometres would find themselves at the Buchères intersection. It was Buchères that Guillaume had asked for; from there on, Michel's directions had been explicit enough, in fact probably had been even up to that point; they could have taken a wrong fork in the last few kilometres. Rosie had been distracted, though, during that brief halt, by wafts of martial music on the westerly breeze from Troyes, drums and brass unpleasantly reminiscent of a Sunday rendezvous three months earlier with a frightened informer in a public park in Quimper in Brittany; she'd been trying to allay his fears, keep him up to the mark, while in their immediate vicinity the Boche garrison's band was having its Sabbath outing – drums, brass and jackboots, and that filthy emblem in red, white and black floating at the column's head.

Sound and sight in memory still set her teeth on edge. With an accompanying recollection that it had been that informer cracking under interrogation which in the long run had put her on the train to Ravensbrück.

They had to be getting close now.

'Right at the next crossing, is it?'

A nod from Guillaume. 'Should be.'

'What if he's not at home?'

'We stop, eat our sandwiches and think it out.'

'What sandwiches?'

'Stale ones. Ones I brought for your friend Marilyn. Also a Thermos of coffee, so-called, which will now be lukewarm at best.'

'I thought you were giving them to Groslin and the others?'

'Had second thoughts. They're in my bag. Anyway you'll get a meal at your *auberge*, I imagine.'

'So you can have the lovely sandwiches all to yourself.'

'Maybe. If Dufay's here, and willing to take you on.'

'Otherwise? "Think it out", you say, but—'

'There'd be no option, really, I'd take you myself.' Preparing to take the corner. 'But there's no reason he should *not* be there.'

On the straight again: a narrower road, leading roughly north, northwest. It was still overcast, no sun for guidance except very vaguely, an area brighter than the rest. He shook his head: 'My problem would be fuel. I've some spare in the back but I'll need to top up with that here, at Dufay's. With the extra distance – if I did take you on – plus two hundred and something kilometres back to Nancy. And it's Sunday.'

'What's happened to *gazos* running on bottled gas? I've seen one or two, but—'

'Most have gone over to charcoal because it's easier to get and cheaper. There wasn't ever a bottled gas depot where you wanted it. Cleaner, of course.'

'Next left?' She saw his nod, and added, 'And he *will* be here.'

'Sure he will. Contingency planning, that's all.'

'Also known as looking on the dark side. There's the turning.'

With a *Wehrmacht* despatch rider belting out of it, sweeping into this road and curving left – away, the direction of Troyes she supposed. A cloud of exhaust fumes hung blueish where he'd re-opened his throttle after the turn; Guillaume muttered, slowing, 'Noisy damn things.'

'I had one, once.'

'You did?' Shake of the head. 'You're full of surprises, Rosie.'

'My uncle bought it for me. English uncle, I adore him. Adored the bike too, but I had to sell it when I got married.'

'You say – married?'

'Fighter pilot. Shot down in the Channel, February 'forty-two.'

'Oh. How *bloody*.' Turning left. Reek of petrol in the wake of that DR . . . Dufay's place was supposed to be on the left here, about a hundred metres up. There were plane trees along both sides and open fields behind them; nothing like the industrial area she'd expected.

'Now what . . .'

A parked truck: soldiers were unloading the makings of a road-block – trestles and striped poles. On the left, a wide-open space like a very large garage forecourt with a large building set well back and a small, drab bungalow the other side of it. Two other *Wehrmacht* vehicles: one, a smaller truck – half-tonner maybe – parked close to the front of that central structure, which was of concrete and corrugated iron – with DUFAY ARROSAGE in white lettering above its doors – and the other what might have been a staff car – nearer the bungalow. Both camouflage-painted.

Guillaume said, 'Going to have to stop. At least – show willing.'

Because it was obvious they were about to erect a road-block: to take advantage of the fact that it wasn't yet in place might not be the cleverest of moves. This was a crisis situation, clearly recognizable as such, had come up as swiftly and unexpectedly as crises usually did. She agreed – aware of having suddenly become short of breath – 'Show willing, by *all* means.'

Wouldn't have helped to have had the Llama in her pocket, she told herself. Natural to think of it, but it wouldn't – except maybe to avoid being arrested, get shot instead – which in another time and place *had* been a procedure she'd considered. Maybe should again: *if* one got out of this. Guillaume said quietly, 'We're looking for the road to Villeneuve-l'Archevêque. Came from Nancy, of course.'

In case they were separated; what *he* was going to say. Slowing . . . Villeneuve-l'Archevêque was a village on the road west just short of St Valéry, she remembered from his map. Archbishop Villeneuve. Rather striking name, which was probably how he'd remembered it, but she thought she'd have picked some other road to be looking for. Although at instant notice like this – when some might have panicked, forgotten their own names even – well, who'd quibble . . . There were men standing around on the concrete between the bungalow and that building; mostly soldiers, but two in plain clothes. One of those had a trooper each side of him and the other – wearing a hat – facing him. The one under guard and being questioned had to be Victor Dufay.

Grey-headed, burly . . .

Guillaume had slowed to a crawl: on the off-chance of being allowed to go on by, winding his window right down.

'Halt!'

The one in charge had his hand up. Nazi salute, almost. Guillaume had jammed his brakes on.

Schmeissers, and helmets. But ordinary troops, not SS. She'd suspected they might be SS since the man in the hat had come in a *Wehrmacht* car, might therefore have been SD – *Sicherheitsdienst*, the SS Security Service. Gestapo used Citroëns, nearly always grey or black. Guillaume enquiring politely with his face in the open window, 'Messieurs?'

A sergeant: pale, very young face under the helmet, but a peevish expression. A jerk of the machine-pistol: *'Raus!'*

Meaning get out. One knew that much. But he'd addressed it to Gauillaume – anyway not *clearly* meaning she should get out too . . . *Sit tight. Once you're out, you're out* . . . Guillaume murmuring with one hand on his door, 'Relax, Justine.' Calm, reassuring look. 'Someone else's trouble, not ours.'

The longer-term future – like not having Dufay to help now – was a problem so dwarfed by the immediate one that it was out of sight. This was *now*. Guillaume out in the road, producing papers from an inside pocket; the sergeant snatching them and flipping though them, Guillaume telling him affably, 'I'm a vet. *En route* to visit a farmer near a place called Villeneuve-l'Archevêque – got problems with his milking herd.' Pointing with his head at the carton on the back seat – containing Rosie's 'S' phone – then listening to some question in the sergeant's Germanic French. He'd nodded: 'Aiming to get on that road without going through town. Don't know the area well, see.' Glancing round: 'Trouble here, is there?'

One of the others was peering in at her, now. Calling something to the sergeant.

'What's she, then?'

'Giving her a lift, that's all. She has relations in the area.' From this back view of him she saw his shoulders hunch, and guessed he might have winked. 'Anyway – company . . .'

'Why wouldn't they get a *local* vet?'

A lorry had stopped behind them – French civilian lorry but with the inscription *Au Service de l'Allemagne* across the forefront of its cab. The sergeant had pointed, telling the man from Rosie's side to see to that one: then yelling at the others to get a move on with the barrier. Glowering at them: might not have been a sergeant very long, she guessed. He'd turned back to Guillaume, who'd paused in his answer to that question, told him now, 'The man at Villeneuve-l'Archevêque has a vet he says is useless, tried another who wouldn't come out on a Sunday, then remembered my senior partner – name of Magne – who didn't want to sacrifice *his* Sunday—'

'All right.' There were some dismounted cyclists behind there too, now. 'Go on, clear out . . .'

Her eyes had been on the mirror: jerked back to Guillaume, hardly daring to believe it was *him* being told to 'clear out'. Seemed so, though: Guillaume taking his papers back from him, turning at the same time – his manner admirably casual – to see what was happening in Dufay's yard. Rosie sneaked a look that way too – natural enough to show some interest, in fact unnatural *not* to, especially having been so to speak cleared, having therefore nothing at all to do with whatever was happening here. Then she wished she hadn't: the civilian they'd been questioning was disappearing into the back of the truck – pushed in by those soldiers she guessed, and by the way he'd moved, in handcuffs. The German in the hat had left him, was strolling into the open front of the garage-type building. Looking around – at pumps and piping, she supposed; Michel had said boreholes and pumps, and *arrosage* meant irrigation. Might be other things as well, of course. An arms cache, for instance, wouldn't be a bad place for one. She knew how Dufay would be feeling. Empathy was total, virtually as if it were happening to *her*. Her own sense of relief, the sudden removal of the threat to her and to Guillaume, had in a sense made way for this; otherwise it would still have been for herself she was sweating. Dufay's predicament would have been peripheral to that. Guillaume was back in his seat, jerking the door shut. Glancing at her, murmuring 'Poor sod. But – God, what a near-miss . . .' As much to himself as to her, as he pushed the *gazo* into gear and began to edge out around the truck. '*Bloody* hell . . .'

'You handled it pretty well.'

'Sheer luck. Slight contrast to Dufay's . . . But that fellow not bothering with you, especially.'

It would be the men's camp at Natzweiler as likely as not for Dufay, she thought. But if they kept him in prison for interrogation long enough – and he survived *that* – the beatings and whippings, starvation, drowning, whatever else they thought up – he might have a hope. Guillaume had got by the stationary truck, and behind them the barrier had been put across – black-and-white poles horizontally across the road between white trestles – two lengths of pole, three trestles, so they could open either lane if they wanted to while keeping the other shut. She thought the tactic was wrong though: they should have been off the road, on Dufay's concreted yard with the others, *watching* the road, not blocking it. Not so competent, that lot. Guillaume said, shifting gear, 'Next stop St Valéry. Get back on to the road we *were* on, if we can.'

'Hoping nothing like this is happening there as well.'

'No reason to believe it would be.'

'Unless they know of Dufay's links to the Craillots. From what Michel said, it must be of long standing. And having shown his face in that district again just recently—'

'Rosie, all things are *possible*, but—'

'What about the fuel problem?'

'In the short term there's *no* problem. Longer term – I don't know. Manage somehow . . . Let's smoke?'

'Oh, you genius . . .'

Light-headed, suddenly: despite the visual memory of
Dufay being shoved into the back of that truck. Guillaume
demanding: 'You do realize how extraordinarily lucky
we've been?'

'Not to have been there with Dufay when they arrived.
Yes.'

Imagining it . . . Her fingers holding the match were
reasonably steady, though. Maybe she *was* more or less
back on form. Foreseeing possible hazards ahead wasn't
any symptom of cold feet, only a matter of keeping on
one's toes, not walking into traps. She passed Guillaume
his cigarette, and drew deeply on her own. 'If we make it
to the Craillots—'

'Of course we will.'

'– I'll buy you a few packs.'

'Ah, *well*.'

'But not only if we'd got there sooner – suppose we'd
come an hour or two later. When they've searched the
place they'll leave it open, won't they – a few of them
inside waiting for anyone like us. Which could happen –
anyone just blundering in – as we'd have done?'

'*Ergo*, warn Michel.'

'Ask de Plesse to get word to him, soon as you get
back?'

Emphatic nod. 'That's what I will do. Now – some sort
of junction coming up. The Craillots, by the way, may be
a bit dicey now. Strangers on the doorstep telling them
Dufay's been arrested, *would* have vouched for us?' Peering
ahead: toe off the accelerator; *gazo* slowing. 'Now – eenie,
meenie—'

'Left would mean detouring too far south, wouldn't
it?'

'H'm.' Slowing even more, thinking about it . . . 'Maybe.
Whereas *this* way at least before we get right into town we
must cross the road leading west.' Foot down again. 'When

we're in the straight I'll stop and refuel. Get the sandwiches out at the same time, if you like.'

During the fuelling stop they heard the band again. Guillaume pointed with his thumb: 'Mad about the old oompa-oompa, aren't they?'

'Do you loathe them as much as I do?'

'Loathe . . .' Hefting the sack out. 'Well, yes . . . But only the way you'd loathe cobras if you were in a house full of them. Once we've cleared 'em out I don't suppose I'll give much thought to it.'

'The things they've done? What they're doing *now*? To Victor Dufay at this moment, even?'

A nod. 'Your own recent experiences, of course. Wouldn't exactly warm the cockles of the heart . . . Incidentally, would Dufay have had your name or anything about you from Michel?'

'I'm sure not. There was no certainty I'd be given the job, even.'

'On the other hand the Craillots – whom he *does* know—'

'You mean Dufay does.'

'And you're likely to be with them.'

'Michel seemed to think well of him, anyway. Dufay took part in a sabotage operation led by a friend of Michel's, a fellow para. I got the impression of – you know, mutual respect, so forth.'

'So – fingers crossed. And Rosie – sandwiches and Thermos in that bag of mine. It's not locked.'

They found the road that led west – it even had a sign on it, which was a rarity now, almost as much as it was in England where all signposts had been taken down in '39 or '40 when invasion had been expected. This one pointed west and read ESTISSAC – which she'd found on Guillaume's map, a village about twenty kilometres from Troyes. St Valéry

would be about another thirty from there, the other side
of a place called Foissy-sur-Vanne. Distance to St Valéry
now therefore, about forty, forty-five kilometres. Time,
one thirty.

'Any fresh thoughts on the charcoal problem?'

'Only that I might have to stay the night at your *auberge*.
Unless Craillot knows where I'd get some on a Sunday.'

'Sorry you've been lumbered with this. Even taking me
to Troyes was a bit over the odds.'

'In for a penny, Rosie.' A sideways glance at her. 'In for
a penny . . . But – it's a pleasure. Truly is.'

Bumping over a railway crossing – the line from Troyes
to Sens. Until now it had been on the right-hand side of
the road. Rosie said as they picked up speed again, 'Wasn't
such fun at Dufay's though, was it?'

Having had time to appreciate how close a call it had
been. If that young sergeant hadn't been feeling harassed,
for whatever reason: if he'd taken the time to check her
papers, as he should have done, or even had a close look
at *her* – at the dark make-up camouflaging scars. With a
Gestapo officer there to refer to: doubtless with ready access
to their file of 'Wanteds'.

She'd have been where Dufay was now, and this time
it'd be for keeps.

'Any cigarettes left?'

'Masses. Well – to be precise, three. Two for you, one for
me.' Extracting two, and lighting them. 'I really *will* try to
get you a few packets at the *auberge*. Even if Sunday's not
a legal day for selling them. Please, don't let me forget?'

'Tell me about the uncle who gave you a motorbike. How
old were you?'

'Sixteen – the legal age for it. I'd been on about saving
up for one. My mother took a dim view, I may say. He's
a sweet man, though.'

'Your mother's brother?'

'Yes. But nothing like her. He's lived on one lung since 1918, when he got caught in German gas.'

'Poor devil.'

'Half his platoon died of it.'

Shaking his head. 'Hasn't been used in this war, thank God. Although we have huge stocks, and I'm sure they must have too. Tell me, how old were you when you married?'

'Twenty-one. In May of 'thirty-nine. Johnny was a regular – squadron leader, when he was killed.'

'Rotten luck again, Rosie.'

'For him, yes. Well – for us both, *maybe*. Things could have got better, I suppose. What I'm saying is it wasn't any great shakes as a marriage. Doesn't make his being shot down a happy event exactly, don't get me wrong, I'm only saying – well, I survived it all right, that's all.'

Estissac, when they got to it, wasn't much. The Vanne put in its first appearance here though, several strands of it merging and then looping westward, now and then but by no means always in sight of the road. It was in a dip on the left – where the railway line was now too – with the land rising on its far side towards forest. Forêt d'Othe: inhabited by Maquis, Michel had said.

She was smoking slowly – trying to – to make this one last. Recalling that last night she'd been smoking Marilyn's Senior Service. Seemed an age ago now, a distant, momentary – respite, almost.

'Funny to think of Marilyn at her desk in Baker Street now, isn't it?'

'Work on Sundays, do they?' He shrugged. 'Of course, they *must*.'

'She'll have reported to Buck this morning, and apart from any other crises looming, she's bound to have work to catch up on. This business will have taken up several days, and she's very conscientious. But she'll have spoken to Lise by now too. At length, in fact – Lise was going to be at Tempsford. To welcome *me* back, was the idea.'

And Lise would have spoken to Ben. Who'd know she, Rosie, was alive. He'd have to break it to the Stack woman. Preferably not feeling *too* sorry for her. Ben was a kind man and when he felt sorry for anyone – for an attractive female, anyway – he'd been known to take it rather to excess, especially if he felt himself responsible in some way. In what way, precisely, in the case of Joan Stack, was a matter for speculation. Marilyn, Rosie thought, might have been a little guarded – or diplomatic, she'd have called it – in her account of whatever Lise had said about Ben and Joan. One line in particular stuck in her memory and seemed to call for elucidation: *He's been crushed, remember. Might seem like – I don't know, but when you're – you know, floundering . . .*

Sounded like apologizing for him, excusing him for something. Suggesting that she, Rosie, should make allowances.

There was a crossing in sight ahead, the first for several miles, a *route blanche* leading up into forest on the left and over cornfields on the right. Children at the roadside waved; she and Guillaume both waved back to them. The bridge there across the Vanne was decked with railway sleepers.

All dry as a bone. Hadn't rained *here*, this morning.

It wouldn't matter, about Ben and Joan Stack. It would be over, now. Tough on la Stack, no doubt, but – *finis*.

'When you go on the air, Rosie – one, this morning's troop movement, two, tell them about Dufay? It might get to Michel via Baker Street more quickly than through de Plesse on the home ground here.'

'You're right. Might even be worth a transmission on its own. Guillaume – something coming up behind us.'

'Snap.'

He'd seen it in the same moment. Car, coming fast, at this moment just about where those kids had been.

'Nothing to do with us.'

'Couldn't be.'

'But if it was – same story. Farmer near Villeneuve-l'Archevêque. Can you see any place a few k's off this road but near there?'

'Courgenay. A right turn – *at* Villeneuve-l'Archevêque.'

'OK. We'd be turning short of St Valéry anyway. In case there's any sensitivity over Marchéval's. I mean arising from Dufay's recent interest in the place. Christ, there's an outrider, too . . .'

'Aiming to turn right at Villeneuve, then, making for this place about five kilometres north of there.'

'Fine.'

'There's a flag on the car!'

'Pendant. Boche general, probably.' He was keeping well in to the right, tyres almost on the grass verge, and he'd slowed a bit to make it easier for the car to pass. The hedgerow was taller here, you couldn't see far ahead although the bend looked shallow. Telling her, 'Definitely *not* after us. Generals hardly ever—'

'*Two* outriders!'

The first flashed past them. Car fifty metres behind. Khaki-greenish paintwork, red-and-white triangular pennant whipping on a staff on the left-front mudguard. Guillaume said, 'Must be bloody Rommel . . .'

'Isn't he in Normandy?'

There were two men in the back: one in uniform, details undistinguishable, and the other in plain clothes. In front, a soldier-driver with an officer of sorts beside him. Young: and the only one who went so far as to turn his head and look at them. Actually, at Rosie. Second outrider now – taking no interest in them: blast of sound, and he was gone. Guillaume murmured, easing the *gazo* further out into the road, 'May not be long before the bugger's coming the other way just as fast if not faster. But listen – I was thinking –

if I get back tonight I'll ask Léonie to report Dufay's arrest. You may well not be in a position to transmit this soon – and the sooner we *do*—'

'I'll still mention it when I go on the air.'

'Yes. Good.'

Another *route blanche* crossing, On the right, a lot of the corn had been cut. Harvesters either at lunch or sleeping it off, she supposed. In the countryside people didn't do so badly – hence the townspeople who came foraging for chickens, rabbits, game, eggs, anything they could get. Women and girls on bicycles with capacious baskets, mainly. With so few able-bodied men about, women were the providers, had to do whatever they could to feed their broods.

They passed through several villages before Villeneuve. One was unidentifiable, and seemed not to be marked on the map: another with a roadside sign still legible as Benoist-sur-Vanne. The river was still down-slope on the left, in the dip and at this stage not visible. Then a place called Vulaines: not much of it. At Villeneuve-l'Archevêque – a much larger place, dull and gloomy, could even have been deserted, but with an interesting old church off the road to the left – they trundled over the railway track, putting it to the north of the road thereafter.

Beyond it – and to the south as well, over the river – was woodland. Guillaume muttered, picking up speed again after the railway crossing, 'River's closer to the road now.' Eyes front again as he steered around two slow-moving hay-carts. It wasn't a *wide* road. 'Heck, what's *this* metropolis coming up?'

When they'd barely left the strung-out glories of Villeneuve . . . Rosie checking the map. 'Must be – Molinons. They're joined, almost. See what you mean about the river, we really *are* sur Vanne here, aren't we?'

'And *tout de suite* will be in St Valéry?'

'Not all that *tout de suite.*' Glancing up from the map:
the narrow road shaving around a crumbly old church
that was virtually right on it. Back to the map – such as
it was . . . 'About three kilometres, Poissy-sur-Vanne, and
our turning's about half a k beyond it.'

'Switch to Dufay's sketch, then.'

'Yes.' The thought of Dufay again, what might be happening to him. The most common start would be a general
beating up, the prisoner with his hands tied and a thug, or
team of thugs, using fists and boots – and buckets of water
to bring him round when he passed out. SOE's standard
expectation was for an agent to hold out for forty-eight
hours before telling them anything, the object being to give
his or her colleagues that much time in which to disappear.

But if you had a job to do, how could you?

Passing through Poissy-sur-Vanne. Turnings to right and
left matched those shown on the map.

'Half a kilometre, you said.'

'Probably a bit more than that.'

She flicked the small, damp stub of her last cigarette
away, and took another look at the pencil sketch. There
was going to be a turn-off to the left, a bridge over the
Vanne after about a hundred metres, then a fork; bearing
right would bring them into St Valéry, and the Craillots'
pub would be well into the middle of the village on the
right. She asked Guillaume, 'What if the Herr General's
car's parked outside L'Auberge la Couronne?'

An airy gesture . . . 'What d'you think? Let its tyres down
and sing "God Save the King"?'

'Seriously, though. There are Boches living in the manor,
he could be visiting them – rocket-casing business?'

'More likely still he'd have been on his way through Sens
to Fontainebleau and Paris. Coming from, say, the Dijon,
Chaumont direction, it's the route you *would* take.'

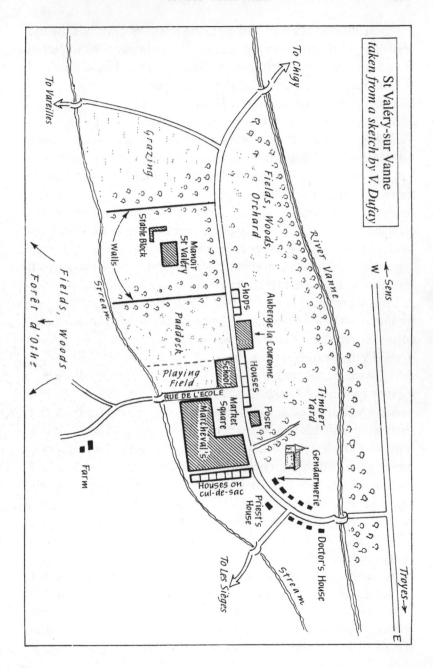

St Valéry-sur Vanne
taken from a sketch by V. Dufay

Dijon where Michel had said he'd be. She remembered
also that Marilyn had said Baker Street knew what Michel
was doing: she'd meant to ask about it when they'd covered
the essentials, but it had slipped her mind.

Marilyn might not have told her anyway. Since Michel's
activities weren't any of her business now. Guillaume was
slowing, railway line crossing the road ahead again. 'Rosie
– I'm praying this'll go well for you.' The *gazo* jarring over
. . . 'In case we don't get a chance to speak alone again –
be *bloody* careful, eh?'

'Bet I will.' Glancing at him: those last words, he'd
sounded just like Ben. Really, could have *been* Ben. She
said, 'Hope your end goes right too. But listen – to get
anywhere with the Craillots we're going to have to put all
our cards on the table, aren't we? Barring any mention of
André Marchéval, that is. But the option of bombing, for
instance – there'd be no other answer, or reason I'd have
come. Be fatal to give them some flimflam that won't stand
up – d'you think?'

'Agreed. But start by telling 'em about Dufay.' Pointing
forward with his head: 'Looks like the turn.'

Also what looked like a German military sign on the
corner of the side-road, a square of tin painted yellow
with the numerals 18 on it in black. Guillaume slowing,
turning – right-angle turn into a much narrower road, but
the corners had been cut back and gravelled, presumably
to make it easier for larger vehicles. On a down-gradient
then, with a stone bridge in sight fifty or sixty metres
ahead. Shifting gear again, and humping slowly over it.
Forty metres of bridge: say thirty of river under it. Wider
than she'd expected. And pretty – a shallow, tumbling fall
of water over rocks – clear, clean-looking water, and further
downstream on this side – the right – a parting of the ways
where it split in two around a small island. Guillaume said,
'Trout in it, bet your boots.'

'Are you a fisherman?'

'Have been. May be again, touch wood. But here we are, Rosie – St Valéry-sur-Vanne. Doesn't *look* like a place you'd build a factory, does it?'

Little hideaway place. Trees and undergrowth thick along the verges of both road and river. After the bridge, a lush-looking field around which the lane curved right-handed: the fork off to the left would lead to a place called Sièges, according to Dufay. Apple orchard now on this side, then a row of cottages with cabbages, tomatoes and what looked like currant bushes crowding their front gardens. All very compact and close together then, the village's component features coming up fast although Guillaume was driving very slowly. Another half-dozen cottages on the right here, and a larger house on its own amongst trees and shrubs on the other side. This side again – the right – a church set up on a rise some way back from the road, and a track leading away through trees. On Guillaume's side, an alleyway led off at right-angles between a terrace of small houses – workers' houses, as shown on Dufay's plan – and a high brick wall that was the eastern enclosure of the factory area. On the right, a yellowish building that looked semi-derelict – flaking plaster and rotten woodwork. There was no sign on it, but Dufay's sketch identified it as the Hôtel Poste. It was across the road from the market square – after the front wall and entrance to the factory – at which she was looking back, attempting a double-take – at human activity around that entrance; having hardly registered it at first glance, since it was on Guillaume's side and she'd been trying to look both ways at once, had now a retrospective impression of people dressed for work – not just Sunday strollers – crowding through a door set in one of the big timber gates. Anyway – too late. Market square now: cobbled, with a roofed structure like a band-stand in the centre. The impression was even more strongly of a tight-packed, tightly enclosed village – walls, trees, house-fronts all crowding in on and around this narrow street; virtually the only open space had been that market square. *Too* small, *too* compact – recalling Michel's comment *There'd be women and children killed . . .* There surely would be. Another quote – Michel quoting Dufay, describing St Valéry as *a little place with Marchéval's as its beating heart.* That described it well too – the village was virtually wrapped around that factory.

Factory *at work* – at lunchtime on a Sunday, in rural France?

School – on the left here, the corner after the market square. So obviously a school that you could almost smell the chalk and ink. A lane ran down beside it, edging the square. Some more of the factory wall was visible again down there. The rectangular market 'square' was in fact a corner cut out of a larger square comprising the factory area. This was clearer on Dufay's plan of the village layout than it was from a passing view of the place at ground level. *Had* passed it now; on the right, Rosie's side, was a terrace of maybe half a dozen small dwellings, stone frontage patched pale-greenish and fronting on to a pavement no more than a metre or so wide. As wide a pavement as the street could spare: any more so and two vehicles could hardly have scraped past each other.

Guillaume pointed: 'There's your pub, Rosie.'

L'Auberge la Couronne. On the right, this side – an oldish, not antique but attractively weathered building. Clinker-strewn track up this side of it between it and that row of houses – to a yard and/or maybe outbuildings behind. Guillaume passed that, drew in and parked behind a trap with a tired-looking grey pony in its shafts. He'd bumped two wheels up on the narrow pavement: she'd have barely enough room to get her door open. Just enough actually to peer up through the wound-down window at the frontage of creeper-covered stone and an inn-sign above the door depicting a golden crown. Making a quick check then in the rear-view mirror – the pancake make-up, and the pads in her cheeks. Hair OK – more or less . . . She brushed cigarette ash off her skirt, and squeezed out. Not all *that* much squeeze about it though; she wasn't the skeleton she'd been in her pre-Thérèse period, but there wasn't any excess of flesh on her either.

Never had been – or would be, if she could help it. Pulling her clothes straight, tucking the blouse in: feeling for, and finding, the small shape of one cyanide pill in its hem. Looking up at the *auberge*, meanwhile, seeing there was one upper floor of bedroom windows and smaller ones above them. Couldn't have many rooms. Unpainted wooden shutters, and Virginia creeper. Really quite attractive.

'Not bad, eh?' Guillaume was standing in the road; speaking French for the first time in hours. 'See if they can do us lunch, shall we?'

'Let's.' She came round the front of the car to join him. 'Did you notice the factory's at work?'

'Seemed to be, didn't it. Overtime.' He changed the subject: a wave of one hand: 'Pleasant outlook too.' Looking across the road, over a low wall and a paddock in which a carthorse and a pony grazed. Trees thick to the left: going by Dufay's sketch, hiding a wall that surrounded the manor-house. Some distance along the road to the right one could see there was a much higher wall . . . There was a stream down there in front though, with more fields and woods beyond it, patches and fingers of woodland which in the further, hilly distance massed together into forest. The stream had to pass close behind the factory; they'd get whatever water they needed from it. An offshoot of the Vanne, she supposed: glancing to her left as a *gazogène* puttered by. White-haired, red-faced driver with a white-haired, white-faced woman beside him. Then voices from the *auberge*, and two men emerging from its front door: a priest first – thin, dark-faced, sharp nose and chin, whites of his eyes showing as he glanced up at the patchy grey overhead. Turning: 'Thank you, Jacques. Excellent meal, as always.'

'Oh, next to nothing, Father!'

'Your wife's clever at making fine meals out of what you might call next to nothing . . .'

His voice fading, losing the thread: distracted by noticing his host – who with the name of Jacques could only be Jacques Craillot – staring at these strangers. Taking in first Rosie, then Guillaume, and the *gazo*. Priest and hotelier shaking hands then: 'Until soon, *mon vieux*.' Priestly smile for each of them in turn: crossing the road then, heading towards the village centre. Craillot approaching, meanwhile, asking Guillaume, 'Perhaps I can be of service?' A glance at Rosie, and an inclination of the head: 'Madame.'

'Mam'selle actually, M'sieur Craillot.'

'Ah – *pardon* . . .'

Surprised, suspicious look: on guard, suddenly. But she had to handle this – take the lead. It was her brief, she was going to need a certain degree of authority here and she didn't want the Craillots to get the impression she was Guillaume's subordinate. Craillot, she guessed, must be a few years on the right side of fifty. About five-ten, fit-looking, with curly dark hair greying around the edges. A pleasant-enough face – even though it could have done with a shave. Guillaume asking him, 'We were hoping – we aren't too late for a meal?'

'Ah, well.' Transferring his gaze from Rosie. He was wearing dark, rather baggy trousers, a striped waistcoat over a blue shirt, white tie. 'There's sausage, and there's cheese. You'll have heard Father Patrice then, but that was fish pie – all gone. Bit late now, we were busy earlier. May I ask – you know my name, but –' a glance towards the *gazo* – 'just passing through, M'sieur?'

Rosie cut in: 'You *are* Jacques Craillot?'

'Yes – as it happens—'

'If you'd provide us with a meal – sausage or cheese would be fine – somewhere where we could talk with you and your wife privately? My name's Justine Quérier; you won't have heard of me, but Victor Dufay may have told you there'd be someone coming. I'm here by his direction, you might say.'

'Dufay.' A hand to his brow – looking puzzled . . . 'I'm not sure I recall—'

'He came here after he was visited by a man you *have not* met, by name of Michel Jacquard. Dufay may have mentioned him to you. You gave him – Dufay – certain information which he was able to pass to Michel, who passed it on to me. That is –' quick glance round before she murmured it – 'to SOE. I'm sorry to be so – direct, but I'm trying to save time here. Because – look, here's the bad news. This morning we came by way of Troyes – Buchères, actually – from where I was hoping Monsieur Dufay would have brought me and introduced me to you personally, but our arrival there coincided with his arrest. At about midday, we saw it happening just as we arrived.'

Shock had been visible momentarily: he'd absorbed it now. Shaking his head: 'Since I don't believe I know this person—'

'If we'd got there an hour earlier they'd have caught us too. We were *very* lucky.'

'Indeed.' Gesturing helplessly. 'I confess I'm – at a loss . . .' Turning to Guillaume: 'Monsieur—'

'Rouquet. Guillaume Rouquet. I'm a vet, in Nancy. That's a fact, but also –' he'd looked round as Rosie had, seen there was no one near them. 'As my colleague said, we're cutting corners – nothing else for it – in view of what's happened. I just have to tell you – I'm *chef de réseau* of SOE in Nancy. And Michel, whose visit to Dufay started this off, is Commandant, First Maquis Liaison Group.' He checked round again: the nearest passers-by were on the other side of the road. 'You understand, Dufay would have brought Justine down here and introduced her to you and your wife. Would have made this a lot easier, obviously. As it is, I'm acting as delivery boy, and somehow we've got to convince you we're who we say we are. May we come in and talk – please?'

Colette was making the running now. She wasn't more than thirty-five, Rosie guessed, a good ten or twelve years younger than her husband. Hour-glass figure – in a white blouse and dark skirt – attractive, heart-shaped face, tiny little ears, hair almost the colour Rosie's was naturally, without the dye. Cleverer than her husband – perhaps – as well as younger. Michel had quoted Dufay as saying that Jacques wasn't any too bright; he didn't look or sound exactly stupid either, but he did seem to be leaving most of this to her. She asked Rosie now, 'Who made the arrest? Gestapo?'

Dufay might have been prejudiced for some reason, she thought. Shrugging: 'A Boche in plain clothes – he'd come in a *Wehrmacht* staff car and my guess was SD, but he could have been either.'

'And they'd set up a road-block but just let you through it?'

Pushing the dish of sliced sausage towards her. There was no hostility in this questioning, only a perfectly understandable caution: questions for the sake of questions – taking soundings and giving these strangers a chance to trip themselves up. They were at the kitchen table, the four of them. The Craillots had two daughters still of school age who were spending this part of their summer holidays with relations in Châtillon, Jacques had mentioned – while still insisting, although more quietly than his wife, that he didn't know *anyone* by the name of Dufay . . . Rosie answering Colette's last question: 'They stopped us, and had Guillaume out of the car to show his papers. They didn't look at mine. The barrier wasn't even in place, we were the first through.'

'Why set it up at all, one might wonder?'

'To net certain individuals, perhaps. That's a point, though – if you know anyone who might call there or try to contact Dufay—'

'We don't. I've told you, my husband has told you—'

'The fact is we were very lucky. If we'd got there earlier, for instance, been with him when they arrived—'

'Have *you* ever been arrested?'

'Yes.' They were eating sausage with home-made pickle and bread and butter; Rosie taking advantage of her mouth being full, not to reply immediately. Knowing she *could* convince them she wasn't an infiltrator, but concerned not to divulge certain things. About the 'Wanted' posters for instance – in case it scared them to the extent they wouldn't risk taking her in, and because of the price on her head. One knew – from Dufay – that they were *résistants*, but nothing more than that, nothing at all about them as individuals – and a million francs being a lot of money. She'd nodded, swallowing. 'Yes, I have. But listen – if we were caught and *you* were interrogated—'

'Have you some reason to think it's likely?'

'We all know it can happen. If they knew of your connection with Dufay, for instance – if he let them know of it—'

Jacques shook his head, frowning. 'He wouldn't. Damn *sure* he wouldn't.'

'Oh, Jacques – heaven's *sake*!'

Rosie smiling at him, Colette glaring. Rosie deciding she rather liked him. OK, so he wasn't the brightest spark around – what the hell . . . He'd flushed with embarrassment. She went on – to Colette – 'If the worst did happen and you were obliged to tell them anything, quote me as telling you I arrived by air from England last night. It's all I *would* have told you. None of what I'm about to tell you now – which incidentally I can prove.'

'Be glad to hear it, then.'

In manner and looks Colette was not unlike Pauline, the milliner in Nancy, Guillaume's girlfriend. Rosie was distracted for a moment, hearing Jacques Craillot telling Guillaume, 'As much as you want. I collect from the burners in the forest, stock it here and distribute all over. It's a useful side-line and it gets me around, of course – especially out there, you know?'

'But that's wonderful . . .'

'Fetched up in the right place, eh?'

Colette shushed him, and prompted Rosie: 'You were about to say?'

'I'll cut it as short as possible. I was in Fresnes prison. I'd been arrested – by Gestapo – after a slight débâcle in Brittany. Actually I'd been in a car smash – these scars, d'you see? They don't show much now, but it's why I'm wearing dark make-up. Anyway I was pretending loss of memory. From Fresnes I was taken to the Gestapo building in Paris, Rue des Saussaies, and they flogged me – demanding all sorts of information which I didn't give them – instead I fainted. But my back's still striped from it, that's part of my proof. I mean I'll show it to you. An infiltrator wouldn't get herself whipped, would she? Then from Fresnes they put me and some other SOE women on a train for Ravensbrück, it was stopped in Alsace by Maquis sabotage of the line, I made a bolt for it and I was shot. Here – this side of my head – feel it?' Leaning to her, across the corner of the table. 'This graze knocked me out, I think, but I was hit in the back too – back of this shoulder, the bullet came out *here*. So I was unconscious, blood all over, and they left me for dead, but Michel – the man who later went to see Victor Dufay—'

'We're supposed to *believe* this story?'

Jacques was staring at her too: but intently, not cynically . . . Guillaume told them, 'She passed through two other safe-houses and ended up in my office in Nancy. Just four days ago. The reason she made a bolt for it, from the train, was to divert the guards' attention so another girl could get away – under the train and into the river Meurthe. That one passed through my hands too, we got her away to London – with very important information, which was Justine's reason for doing what she did. We'd have arranged a pick-up and sent her back to England too, but your news about the rocket-casings reached us through Michel, Justine offered to take on the job, London agreed, and that's why she's here. In my own opinion she deserves a medal, Madame, not disbelief.'

Rosie glancing at him quickly: reminded, and still far from comfortable with it. It was – a curiosity, more than anything: if it turned out to be untrue – if Marilyn had jumped the gun for instance and in the interval they decided against it – well, almost a relief . . .

She asked Colette, 'Want to inspect the scars?'

'Perhaps in a moment. Tell me this first. Monsieur Rouquet said you offered to "take on the job". *What* job, precisely?'

'I'm a pianist. My brief is to investigate whether these are or are not rocket-casings, and inform my people in London.'

'Then if it's as we believe it is, they'd send bombers?'

'If they did, we'd know in advance, and when the time came we'd have to get everyone out of their houses some-how. In fact right out of the village – I realize this having seen the place, it's so hugger-mugger, isn't it? But we would, we'd have to – with your help, of course, as a stranger here I couldn't set it up. But – *you* provided this information, remember – and if it's true – for God's sake, those are weapons of mass destruction, there'd be thousands of lives at risk – and with *no* warning. Could change the course of the whole war, even – if they made our ports unuseable, so we couldn't supply our armies? That's the Boches' hope and belief, isn't it?'

'Yes – apparently. But—'

'And admittedly knocking this lot out won't scotch that threat – only contribute to countering it – save a few hundred lives, maybe a thousand—'

'And what about *here*? Heavens above, all our friends – and their children, even—'

'I said, we'd warn them, get them out. With your help – *somehow*—'

'I don't know . . .'

Gazing at Rosie: then at her husband. He muttered, 'We've no option. You know we haven't. She's right, we started this, we *have* to!'

'Have to what?'

'Well – see it through. Co-operate, whatever's—'

'What I'm asking –' Rosie interrupted – 'is for you to let me stay here – help out in any way you like, in return for board and lodging. Actually I'd pay my way. You'd pass me off as a sort of distant sister-in-law who'd been going through a bad patch and needs help – I was hurt in an air-raid, had slight brain-damage. I'm – you know, slow. But my brother married your sister—'

'If I'd even *had* a sister! As everyone here knows I never did!'

'You might invent one? One you've never let on about because you couldn't stand her, or – brought up by some other relative, maybe?'

'My God.' Spreading her hands, glancing at her husband. 'And she says she's *slow*!'

'We could make it a cousin, couldn't we?' Jacques spoke quietly, reasonably. 'For instance if your aunt Adèle—'

Rosie agreed quickly, 'A cousin would do. In fact better . . .'

Chapter 12

She was woken by the noise of a car tearing through the village. Petrol engine, therefore Boche – evident not only from the sound, but from the scent of exhaust moments later in the still night air. Decidedly cool night air, to a body straight out of a warm bed. She'd tumbled out of it to the window barely awake, in fright that it was Gestapo coming *here* – and as background to it a vision of Dufay breaking under interrogation, naming the Craillots, L'Auberge la Couronne . . . Half-asleep logic insisting – why else turn off the main road? Nothing *else* here . . . The car had rushed by though, westward, the noise at an explosive peak just as she reached the window: she barely saw it, had only an impression so vague it too could have stemmed from her imagination, that hurtling shadow in the moonlight.

Gone. But the engine-note falling suddenly, steeply . . .

Turning into the manor? Of *course* . . .

Crouching at the window, listening: getting her breath and heartbeat back under control. The gateway to the manor was only just along the road there, two hundred, two-fifty metres away, no more. She heard the scrape of tyres on gravel, then the car's engine picking up again, driving on – into the manor's walled and wooded grounds. Colette had said the house wasn't visible from the road, and trees were indicated on Dufay's map. She checked the time – by moonlight. Just after four. Shivering, dragging the lower part of the sash window shut. The sky had cleared since she'd come up to bed at about midnight, and the land down to the stream and beyond it was patched in black and silver. Full moon, she guessed – somewhere overhead, out of her sight, but it had been as near as dammit full the night before. And before it was much less than full, St Valéry-sur-Vanne might look very different. Certainly the village centre, all around the factory. *If* it was acceptable as fact to London that the tubes were rocket-casings – as Jacques and Colette firmly believed, all the more so now that the factory was working three shifts, seven days a week, with completed casings – *'les tubes'*, they called them – rapidly filling up available under-cover storage space. The time to hit the place, she thought, would be *now* – destroying not only the works but perhaps more importantly the past few weeks' production before they got it on the road to Germany. Colette's explanation, in their talk last evening around the kitchen table, had been, 'Shortage of trucks, they're saying. Tied up maybe collecting from other places. Must be that, because these are specially fitted ones. Mind you, we're hearing from all over that there's a mass of heavy transport on the roads; also that with most of the Seine bridges blown or bombed a lot of it's being abandoned, up north. Vicinity of Rouen, particularly. They could be stuck in that lot. But you're right – needing the things so badly – which they must, wouldn't otherwise be keeping Marchéval's so hard at it, would they – they aren't idiots, aren't going to leave them here, are they?'

'Squeezing all they can out of Marchéval's while they can.' Jacques, smothering a yawn. With supper – soup, bread and cheese – they'd drunk red wine out of bottles without labels. On their own, the three of them, the *auberge* being shut on Sunday evenings. He'd added, 'Writing's on the wall for them, and they must know it.'

Colette had crossed her fingers. 'Soon, please God. Paris first, then –' flapping her hands like shooing chickens – 'to the Rhine – into it or over it, eh?'

'What are your plans, for when they pull out?'

A grunt from Jacques: 'Celebrate! What else?'

Colette had sniffed, thrown him a caustic glance. Telling Rosie then – in a designedly adult-to-adult manner – 'Maquis'll come out fighting, ahead of the first troops getting here. There's a *message personnel* to come: *Martin's uncle breeds horses that win races.* That's what will trigger it. I should tell you, we're in frequent touch with the boys out there. Jacques and his foraging for charcoal, you know? Takes them whatever they need that we can get. A lot of help comes from local farmers. They pay for their charcoal in produce too – suits *us*, what makes it worthwhile, you might say. But the boys are well armed – we've helped with that – and they had weaponry instructors flown in – oh, six months ago. Moved on, since . . .'

It had been a late supper; by the time they'd sat down to it Guillaume should have been back in Nancy. He'd left at about three in the afternoon, with ample supplies of fuel and two packs of Gauloises supplied by Rosie. He'd refused to accept more than two.

She'd asked the Craillots, 'Are you sure there isn't any proof you've overlooked that they're rocket-casings?'

'Proof, no. Indications, however – *yes*. One is the speed-up in production – which seems to match the military situation – don't you agree? As Jacques said, squeezing what they can out of the place *while* they can. Another's the very fact that *still* nobody's allowed to know what they are.' She'd shaken her head. 'It's *not* proof. And I'll tell you – Justine . . . All right, we'll help you. But if your people aren't convinced, I won't be shedding tears. I don't *want* bombing – nor does Jacques – eh?'

'If it could be avoided – no. But – look, we're saying

it'll only be a week or two, and so on – it may *not* end that quickly. The Allied advance could be stalled. Boches might counter-attack – meanwhile, Marchéval's still churning those things out. I see entirely that if it *can* be stopped, it *must* be.'

Colette tight-faced, shaking her head. He asked her, 'Don't hear the sound of the guns yet, do you?'

'That's silly. Armies move fast, in modern war. This isn't 1914, heaven's sake!'

Rosie intervened: 'One thing that doesn't quite add up, by the way – you gave Dufay the casings' diameter as two metres – but according to another intelligence report they've had in London—'

•'The true figure is fractionally less than –' Jacques tapping his forehead in the effort of recollection – 'one hundred and seventy centimetres.'

He'd surprised Colette too, with this. She'd asked him where the hell he'd got it from.

'From Guy Fortran.' Aside to Rosie: 'He's a foreman in charge of the loading and reception bay. Quite often in here. The tubes are of a size that you can't waste a centimetre – two abreast on a flatbed, I'm talking about – without making the load too wide for the road out of here. Especially the bridge. Anyway, they've adapted the flatbeds so they *can* get two abreast – even using a smaller-diameter securing wire than they started with. That's how tight it is.'

'Did he volunteer this information?'

'Right in the bar here. General conversation. It's of considerable local interest – we'd heard the Boches were going to put in some new type of bridge made of steel, flat thing. I suppose they'd just plonk it down – which'd mean blowing up our fine old stone one, been there a hundred years. On an issue of that kind, naturally there's public discussion.' He'd shrugged. 'Didn't occur to me, at the time . . .'

Diameter of five feet six inches, Marilyn had said. Rosie had worked it out there and then, on paper, and the figures tallied. She'd looked up at Jacques, across the table: 'That's a lot better. Matches what came from the other source.'

'Take it as proof, then?'

'They might, I suppose. I think *I* would. But it's London's insistence there should be no doubt whatsoever . . . Jacques, they put two on each truck, do they?'

'Was two, now it's four. Managed that by building a sort of staging, so there are two above two – double-decker. The weight's all right, apparently, that's another thing came up in relation to the bridge.'

'Any idea how many finished tubes sitting there?'

'Must be at least a dozen. Fifteen, sixteen by now.'

'So one convoy of four trucks could clear the lot out in a single trip . . . You don't know anything about screw-holes where the fins are fitted, or for attachment of the warhead, anything like that?'

'No. And if we were to ask questions of that kind—'

'I wouldn't suggest it. Another question though – any idea where they're taken to in Germany?'

'Good question – bomb them there, not here. But you'd only get it from the drivers, and who's going to ask *them*?'

'Boche drivers?'

'Some. Others we heard have been French in Boche uniforms.'

Colette broke in. 'You must understand, we're not intelligence agents. Although we *have* worked with your people – when we had means of contact, Vic Dufay for instance—'

'Of whom you've never heard . . . But seriously – you've been in this village right from the start, have you?'

'Oh, for ever!'

'So you're trusted, must have good friends of long standing—'

'We have, of course.'

'It does seem extraordinary – this is a comment, not a criticism – that there should be not even one single informant in the entire work-force. How many employees are there, by the way?'

'Sixty – full-timers. But – it's the situation here, you see. Well-paid jobs, nice houses, a good school for their kids – and dead safe, as long as they keep their noses clean – so they do, they just get on with it, they don't rock the boat!'

Colette had been out of the room at that stage, Rosie reflecting in the pause that 'just get on with it, don't rock the boat' might typify the outlook of about nine-tenths of the population; therefore maybe wasn't all *that* extraordinary. Jacques putting a match to his pipe, squinting at her over it . . . 'Started by interrogating *you*, this afternoon, now you've turned the tables. Better at it too than we were, eh?'

'There's so much to ask. Stuff I don't know anything at all about, and really need to. For instance, how did you first get the idea these might be rocket-casings?'

'It was Colette, not me.' Expelling a cloud of acrid smoke. Like old Destinier in Alsace he grew his own tobacco; tawny leaves of it festooned on a clothes-drying rack above the stove, in the open despite the fact that growing it for one's own consumption was illegal, apparently. He added after another puff, 'She was alerted to it by the *patron* himself.'

'The *patron*. You mean—'

'Henri Marchéval. Not that he stated it in so many words. In fact we didn't catch on to the significance for quite some while.'

'So what exactly—'

'Ask her, she'll be back in a minute.'

'All right. But – on good terms with him, are you? What's he like? Does he ever come here, to the *auberge*?'

'How many questions in one breath?'

She'd gestured: 'Sorry.' Helping herself to a cigarette. 'But

– right at the centre of everything, as he must be – *if* he's – accessible—'

'Oh, he is.' A shrug. 'But your first question – are we on good terms with him – yes, you could say so – say it of most of the village, and as it happens Colette's known him since she was a little girl. He comes in sometimes, yes. Has a beer, or a cognac on the days we're allowed to sell it. Passes every day in any case – on a bike, unless it's raining, then it's a *gazogène* . . . Hey, *chérie!*'

'What now?' Pushing in, letting the door flap shut behind her. Winking at Rosie: 'Calls me *chérie*, don't know *what* he might have in mind.'

'He was saying Henri Marchéval put you on to the rocket theory.'

'Well – that's the conclusion it led to. What he gave me was an indication that they were something – not to his liking.' Shaking her head as she sat down. 'Poor man.'

'How, "poor"?'

'Several ways. For instance he has a son – André – and a daughter, Claire. The son – you ever meet him or hear of him, by any chance?'

'No. Didn't even know of his existence.'

'In your SOE?'

'Are you saying that Henri Marchéval has a son who—'

'Who is – or *was* – in SOE. Yes, it's a fact.'

'But that's astonishing!'

'I suppose you wouldn't necessarily know all your colleagues?'

'Not by any means. But – good Lord—'

'Another fact is that about three months ago he was arrested.'

'The son was?'

'His father hasn't heard from him since. But Claire also – of whom you won't have heard either?'

'No, I haven't. But you don't mean she as well as her brother—'

'A few months before André was arrested, *she* was. In her case we don't know the circumstances – I don't believe her father does either – but Jacques and I have known for a long time that André was one of your people. Well – from the time he showed up here again – the end of 'forty-one. He's – he *was* – a gutsy young man. Even as a kid, things he got up to . . . Perhaps after he came back he recruited his sister to work with him – would that be possible?'

'Might be. But – I hate to say this, but if it's months since they were arrested—'

'I know.' A grim nod.

Jacques murmured, 'Wouldn't say it to their father.'

'I'm sure *he* knows darn well—'

'Did André know you're *résistants*?'

'Yes, he did. When we heard of the arrest, that gave us some sleepless nights. But – unnecessarily, obviously he managed to keep his mouth shut. One respects that, as well as –' a shrug – 'feeling gratitude. The confidences between ourselves and him were mutual, you see. Natural. Having known him since he was in nappies, we were – really quite close, despite the fact there'd been a gap when he was at college in England. Several years, he was away. His father wanted him to come home, but – his mother's influence, is my guess. She's English, I should mention.'

'She here?'

Colette shook her head. 'She went to – Scotland, I think. Claire stayed, and worked for her father – office work, accounts, so forth. Then when André returned – which was a happy surprise for all of us, I may say, although in the circumstances somewhat alarming initially – he became the company's representative in Paris. Liaison with Boche government agencies, they said. In reality that would have been mostly just his cover – wouldn't it? He was supposed to have come back from Marseille – I don't know, some story they'd concocted. He took an apartment in Paris, and Claire had one in Fontainebleau. She moved out from the manor after the Boches moved in – there was one in particular who never let her alone. A shame – she was always very close to her father – more so than André. Maybe André *did* recruit her – it's possible, it wasn't until after his return that she moved out – and if that's the case and Monsieur Henri knew about it, it might explain that move. I mean, her departure must have been a blow to him, but as far as we know he didn't try to stop her.'

'Easier to have done something about the Boche, you'd think.'

'No. Not Monsieur Henri's style. Regrettably. But we're getting to the point now. When Claire was arrested – early in the New Year, this was – it was André who brought the news of it—'

'How was that?'

Colette nodded. 'Another pointer, isn't it? But what I was saying – Monsieur Henri reacted as if her arrest had been aimed at *him*. You know – to blackmail him. Jacques and I, I may say, considered this unlikely. He'd always thought first of the welfare of his workers and their families, he could have gone to England with his wife in 'forty for instance, but he wouldn't run out on them – as she ran out on *him* . . . What I'm saying is he'd have gone along with no matter *what* demands.' Shrugging . . . 'I know – may not seem exactly honourable. But one can understand it, eh?'

Rosie had wondered whether Henri M. might not have been as concerned to safeguard his own business and livelihood as to look after his workers' families. Treading carefully, she didn't moot it. Colette continuing, 'We thought – Jacques and I – they'd have had some simpler reason to arrest her – that maybe she *had* been working with André, or in that field.'

'Did her father actually *say* she was a hostage?'

'Effectively, he did. I'd gone to the manor, at his request
– I should explain, he's asked me a dozen times if I'd work
for him, so many hours a week – but it's not possible, I've
more than enough to do here, especially with Jacques out
a great deal attending to other business. But on occasion,
I've helped out. Oh, another thing is there's a man and
wife by name of Briard who live and work at the manor
– mostly for the Boches. Briard outside and his wife inside
– cleaning, cooking, laundry, all of it. They live above the
stables. The thing is, Monsieur Henri doesn't like them, and
he suspects Madame Briard of spying on him. He's found
his correspondence disarranged – that sort of thing.'

'Couldn't he fire her and get – if not you, someone
else?'

'He'd like to. But the Boches employ the Briards, she'd
still be there, and if he got someone else she'd make it
hard for them. She's a mean bitch, I tell you. The Boches
have more of the house than he has – although it's his, of
course, all of it – and she bows and scrapes to them . . . And
Monsieur Henri – of whom we're all extremely fond, there
are many very likeable things about him – he's not what
you'd call a *resolute* man. Where he went wrong with that
wife of his, in *my* view – let her walk all over him. Now he's
over sixty, not physically robust, and he's under the Boches'
thumbs. There again – one of them, a captain, his name's
Wachtel and he's an engineer – he oversees everything in
the factory. Monsieur Henri still runs it – on the face of it
– but it's Wachtel who says OK, we'll work an extra shift
from now on – huh?'

'How many Boches live in the manor?'

'Three officers – Wachtel, and a lieutenant – Klebermann
– and Major Linscheidt. He's the boss. In the view of many,
not a bad fellow. Only one eye; he was a tank commander.
Under them they have – oh, two sergeants, one of whom's a

mechanician, and maybe a dozen others. Drivers, orderlies, sentries. That's all, but patrols come through from Sens too – road and forest patrols, you never know when or where you'll run into them. They could muster a substantial force very quickly if they needed to. In fact larger bodies of troops have inflicted themselves on us a few times – conducting sweeps of the forest is the usual thing, searching for Maquis. It hasn't occurred for several months now, one might doubt whether it will again, but at such times they open up the Hôtel Poste.'

'That place that looks as if it's falling down.'

She'd nodded. 'They hang a swastika on the pole in front, crowd the place out and bivouac on the waste ground behind it. French troops sometimes – LVF, *that* filth. The Boches prefer to use French to hunt down their own kind – some reason . . .'

'I'm surprised you'd need a hotel and an *auberge* in a place as small as this.'

'The answer is you don't. That's just it.' Colette explained, 'We do quite well here, most of the time. Not only from local custom, but people come down from Paris, for instance for fishing holidays. Not far to come, and the fishing's excellent – trout, last summer there were record catches. Just at this moment people are staying put – for obvious reasons, and it's why we're empty. But the Poste was originally a large farmhouse, it was Monsieur Henri's father who decided to turn it into a hotel – again, for fishermen, that was the great idea – when he built the manor for himself, you see. It was a very large farmyard there, where the factory is now, he'd made his fortune in some engineering business in Paris – used to come down here sometimes, loved the place, so—'

Looking at her husband. 'Something the matter?'

Craillot took the pipe out of his mouth. 'The family who had the Poste at the beginning of the war, Justine, were all murdered – what the Boches call "executed" – lined up against the front wall and shot, with the whole village compelled to watch. The parents and both sons they shot, the younger boy only eleven. An officer of the SS had been found dead – someone had shot *him* – and for some reason that family were held responsible.'

'When was this?'

'Christmas of 'forty-one.'

'Were these same Boches here then?'

'Oh, no . . .'

'Were *you* – in this *auberge*?'

'Yes. And –' a movement of the head – 'in the crowd at this – spectacle. We were rounded up and they held guns on us. It was then I became actively a *résistant*. Colette too. She'd inherited this place from an aunt who'd died only a few months before.'

'Aunt Adèle?'

Colette smiled. 'Another one. Adèle lived her whole life in Paris.'

'Ah. One other question—'

'Only *one*?'

'Well – for the moment . . . Does Monsieur Henri know you're *résistants*?'

Jacques was tapping out his pipe. 'Almost certainly. Although –' to Colette – 'I personally haven't discussed with him—'

'At least, not since – well, right at the beginning.' She shrugged. 'Although of course since we were quite open with André—'

'Yes. Things *were* said. For instance after the business at the Poste. But what I'm saying now is – time for bed, eh?'

'Yes.' Rosie agreed. 'Very good idea. Only first – Colette, just quickly – you were going to tell me what happened after Claire's arrest – when you went to the manor, you said—'

'God, yes. Got side-tracked—'

'Side-tracked *yourself*, chérie!'

'I know . . .'

'Nothing unusual about that either.'

'What it was, Justine, he wanted me to put away some clothing Claire had left. After her move to Fontainebleau she'd still stayed a night or two sometimes, so she'd kept some things there. But – she'd been arrested, and André had put in a surprise appearance the day before – came down from Paris – to break the news to his father. How he'd have known about it, unless she *had* been working with him – well, that's still my guess . . . Never mind – Monsieur Henri wanted her stuff put away, some of it had to be washed and ironed first, and he didn't want the Briard woman to lay a finger on it. I was to pack it away, he said, "against Mam'selle Claire's safe return". He was – quite tearful. Really, a miserable day. But I got it all done, and on the point of leaving I said something like "Perhaps it'll turn out to be not so serious a matter, and they'll release her." I was just – felt I had to say *something* – as one does – and then wishing I hadn't because it made it worse, he turned away with his face in his hands. All that, all over again . . . Then when he'd found his voice he told me – I can hear him now – "Pray for this filthy war to end, Colette. As long as it lasts I'm tied hand and foot." He repeated it – staring at me, his face all – you know, contorted . . . "Hand and foot! Why, those things we're having to turn out for them now—"

'He'd checked himself. Trembling, shaking his head, tears still welling, muttering only "My God. My God." Over and over . . . I asked him, "What are they, those tubes? Nobody seems to know –" and he shouted, *"Don't ask! I tell you, don't!"*

'He wasn't going to explain. I told Jacques I thought he was having a nervous breakdown and maybe our Doctor

Simonot should see him, but he wouldn't – I mean Monsieur Henri wouldn't . . . And that was all we thought of it, until later we began to put two and two together – with the secrecy about the tubes continuing as it has. Indeed we came to the conclusion that if it was so secret and important they *might* have arrested poor Claire as – what you said, a hostage.'

'You didn't pass any of this on though, until Dufay visited you just recently?'

'I'll tell you – there was a man by name of Lambert, a livestock auctioneer from Montereau, who also saw André quite often. We were waiting to tell *him*. He'd asked us never to try to contact him ourselves, he'd come by often enough in the course of his business.'

Lambert, whom Marilyn had mentioned. She commented, 'But he hasn't, all this time.'

'Nor did André. Then we heard he'd been arrested. Early in May?' Jacques had nodded, and she went on, 'But Joseph Lambert we still expected. We'd had dealings with him – mostly *parachutages* that he arranged and Jacques helped with. Lambert had stayed here for the night a few times. He brought his wife with him once – a very beautiful young woman. So – he was the man to talk to, and we waited for him. Nothing else we *could* do. Except we discussed with –' a jerk of her thumb in the direction of the forest – 'Jacques' friends out there – possibilities of sabotage, blowing up the factory. But in the first place we were only guessing about the tubes – we had to admit that much – and secondly there'd have been reprisals. Also the policy in recent months has been to arm, train, be *ready*, not—'

'Dufay told Michel that action by local *résistants* was out of the question because Marchéval was such a popular employer, no one'd lift a hand against him. *And* the prospect of reprisals.'

'Exactly.'

'Which accounts for our present intentions . . . Lambert, though – may have been chief of the *réseau* that was blown a few months ago?'

'Ah – we know *now* it was blown. Didn't until Victor Dufay told us, when he finally showed up.'

So Claire had been arrested in January, Rosie thought. (Having been back in bed for some while now – and glad to be, Marilyn's *message personnel* about cool nights in mid-summer being nothing but the truth.) And by January the first rumours about 'Hector' had been filtering through to Baker Street. Bob Hallowell ignoring them, attributing them to some other agent's sexual jealousy. But – she thought, in reference to 'Hector', a.k.a. André having brought his father the bad news – he might even have shopped her himself?

Dear André – of whom she'd never heard, until last night . . .

Although another possibility was that the Boches might have taken Claire to give themselves a bit of extra leverage on *him*.

Go on the air this evening, she thought. Tell them it looked highly probable, not yet 100% certain but in her opinion virtually so. Transmitting not from here – *definitely* not . . . The forest might be best – Boches well aware, obviously, that it was lousy with Maquis, which might help to confuse the issue in the minds of the *Reichssicherheitshauptamt*'s radio-detection boffins. Make the transmission from the vicinity of some other village: nearer some other one than this, anyway. Borrow a bike from Colette – or from one of her daughters – or get a lift from Jacques. Yes, *that*. Especially as it was months since she'd ridden a bike, and she wasn't anything like as fit yet as she should have been. *And* didn't know her way about – especially in the forest. Try Jacques anyway. *Gazo* battery to power the transceiver being a major advantage, no need to take its own battery along. And code up a message telling Baker Street: (1) Dufay arrested – essential warn Michel, (2) rocket-casings' diameter now reported to be a shade less than one hundred and seventy centimetres, (3) twelve to sixteen finished casings awaiting collection from the factory by flatbed trucks, each capable of carrying four, but route or destination in Germany unknown and probably not ascertainable, (4) factory working round the clock seven days a week, and (5) hours-long troop convoy yesterday through St Dizier from direction of Lyon towards Reims, tanks reported on same route Friday.

But how to get any more positive confirmation – when the Craillots from their insider position hadn't managed it over a period of months . . . Maybe no way: maybe the information one had now was as much as one was going to get. And Colette's soul-searching notwithstanding, one did *not* want London holding off now: one wanted the factory and the manor hit – for dear André's sake, André-of-whom-one-had-never-heard's sake . . .

Add a sixth item to the signal, to the effect that evacuation of the village immediately prior to an attack was considered feasible.

Monsieur Henri might be one's best bet, she thought. Propose oneself as a candidate for the job at the manor? She'd thought of this when Colette had been telling her about it. At least, might get to see him, talk to him. The proposition might even make sense locally – if no village women would contemplate it for fear of ructions with Madame Briard, whereas this slightly dim and distant cousin (a) wouldn't know anything about la Briard, (b) needed a paid job, which the Craillots couldn't offer?

It would have to be Colette's idea. But then what?

He wasn't going to agree to having his factory wrecked, was he? Going by what Colette had said – and one's own instinct. Especially if the daughter *was* a hostage for his good behaviour.

It was still attractive, the idea of being right there, *chez* Marchéval.

This room was on the *auberge*'s second floor. The Craillots' daughters had rooms up here, but Jacques and Colette were on the floor below, where there were also three other guest rooms and the only bathroom. When there were paying customers they moved up here, apparently. The rooms weren't bad, only smaller and with lower ceilings, and there was a lavatory with a hand-basin in it. There was also – across the passage from Rosie – a boxroom full of junk, amongst which yesterday afternoon she'd hidden her transceiver and the 'S' phone.

Cash, codes and pistols were still in her suitcase: which didn't lock. She'd hunted around for a loose floorboard, but hadn't found one. First time ever: there'd *always* been loose boards . . .

Sleep now, though. Concentrate the mind on Ben. Who might be lying awake himself, on this first night of knowing she was alive.

Breakfast consisted of 'coffee' and bread with home-made jam; she ate it in the kitchen with Colette, Jacques having already had his. By now he'd have swept the pavement in front of the *auberge*, Colette said, would be tidying up in the bar and cellar, then delivering some loads of charcoal in Villeneuve-l'Archevêque and some other nearby village, while she'd be doing this, that and the other, including later on some cooking. Also there'd be a scrubbing and cleaning woman arriving within the next half-hour, a Madame Brissac whose husband was a fitter in Marchéval's.

'I'll give her the story we agreed. That'll be a quick way of putting it around the village . . . Did you sleep all right?'

'Until that car rushed past at ninety kilometres an hour, about four a.m. You hear it?'

'Of course. Woke us up. Wasn't it a cold night? Ridiculous, in August! A wind from the east, Jacques said. But that car turned into the manor.'

'Which I'd like to see. Are we going on our tour of the village, some time?'

'If you want. Yes, we decided we would, didn't we?'

'Will we see the manor?'

For a preliminary check on distances and bearings as they'd relate to positioning herself with the 'S' phone. Colette was less than certain, though. 'I could ask Monsieur Henri, if we might go in and walk around . . .'

'I was thinking, you see – lying awake after that car roared by—'

'Boches returning from a night out, it must have been. Dining with their friends in Sens or Troyes . . . You were thinking what?'

'That if I could get to meet Monsieur Henri – what you said last evening, that he'd like to have someone other than Madame Briard work for him?'

'*You?*'

She nodded. 'Being a total stranger, I wouldn't know anything about the Briard woman, and if you played it down – you'd like the idea of getting me out from under your feet, and as an old friend of Monsieur Henri—'

'You realize there are Boches all over that place?'

'So what? Seeing as it's his house and I'd be there on his authority?'

'As an escaper you'll be listed, surely.'

'Oh, yes. In Metz and Nancy my face is on "Wanted" posters. Was, a few days ago. But it's got to be a thousand to one against my being recognized down here. I got away with it *there*, for heaven's sake . . . Aren't any Gestapo here, are there?'

'In Troyes and in Sens there are.'

'Anyway, my papers are in order, and you're giving me

perfectly good cover. If Monsieur Henri did want to hire me, I could surely apply for a *carnet de travail, carte de séjour,* et cetera. If they're even bothering now . . .'

'What would you hope to achieve?'

'Well – to get to know him – talk to him, listen to him.'

'You think he'd tell you just at the drop of a hat what he won't or can't tell *us*?'

'I might pick up something, that's all. Look, you've had your bar full of Marchéval employees, and you've heard practically nothing. The odds are I'd hear even less, I'd be wasting time sitting *here*. Two angles, aren't there? One, the factory itself, two, the tubes already made. If anything they're the most important – because with any luck this place'll be over-run by Yanks within a couple of weeks or so, the factory won't have long to go in any case.'

'Well – please God—'

'But the tubes could be collected today, tonight, tomorrow. Damn little chance they *won't* be, in fact. Wouldn't Monsieur Henri have to know when the trucks were coming?'

'Maybe.'

'Well, if he could be induced to let *that* slip, I'd be on the air to London right away – road convoy of however many trucks plus escort leaving here Wednesday, Friday, whenever . . . It *is* a chance, isn't it?'

Colette silent for a moment, gazing at her . . . 'Even to the extent they might leave the factory alone?'

'Well.' Spreading her hands, eyebrows raised – '*Maybe*. With time as short as we *hope* it is?'

'Perhaps I'm hoping for the moon, but –' shaking her head – 'I'll tell you something. Jacques and I feel we've been – stupid. Your questions last night, why we didn't get word out sooner – or *do* something about it sooner. We should have, should have realized – maybe pressed harder for sabotage action—'

'If you could have. But you explained—'

'It's only because of this that we can even *contemplate* involvement in any bombing. I want you to know that. It's not only the lives at risk, it's all these people's way of life. Ours too, for that matter. Well – that's *our* lookout . . . Anyway, I'll speak to Monsieur Henri.'

'You'll call him?'

'Yes.' She glanced at the clock. 'Now, in fact, might just catch him before he leaves for work.'

'You do think that if an attack was laid on we could get everyone out of their houses?'

'Oh – I'd make it a condition of helping you at all!'

'I think *I'd* make it a condition.'

'If you could. You mean you'd *like* to. But – yes, we could get word round. Jacques would arrange for say a dozen people, two or three taking each group of houses, maybe an hour before the start. Maquisards, and maybe others who'd say they'd been visited by Maquisards and ordered to put the word round. Jacques and I were talking about it after the car woke us up – when you say you were doing *your* thinking. There's a danger some individuals might run straight to the Boches or the *gendarmerie*, of course—'

'Wouldn't stop the attack coming in. They'd be endangering *themselves*, that's all.' Rosie put her hand on Colette's. 'I *am* sorry—'

'I believe you. But it's not a *nice* position to be in.' She took her hand back, and got up. 'My prayer remains that it won't happen. Listen – that thought of having them hit the convoy on the road instead – it's possible that even without any tip-off from Monsieur Henri *some* notice might be given.' On her feet, looking down at Rosie for reaction: Rosie thinking of the problems and complications, mostly unpredictable – such as availability at short notice of a suitable straffing force, and locating the convoy after its departure: also that if London were taking any such action they'd probably also want to target the factory. While what *she* wanted hit – as much as anything – was the manor. Colette had turned away: 'I'll try to get Monsieur Henri.'

He sounded excited – *before* she'd told him about Justine. Then there was a fall-off, hesitance, he certainly wasn't jumping at it. He said, 'Naturally I'd be happy to meet a cousin of yours . . . But look here – come tomorrow, not today. Colette, my dear, in any case I'm so glad to hear from you!'

'Why, *patron*? What's special?'

'Well – it's *always* special . . . By all means bring the young lady along – but I'll *particularly* look forward to seeing *you*. Anyway—'

He'd checked. Only buzzing on the line . . .

'*Patron*?'

'Just thinking I might stop by the *auberge* later on.'

'Well, do!'

'No. It's not a good idea. Tomorrow. Definitely, you come here tomorrow.'

'What time?'

'Would you mind making it rather early? *This* sort of time?'

'Seven thirty?'

'Really, seven o'clock. I'm just leaving now for the factory, you see, I don't like to be late and we'll need more than a bare five minutes.'

Colette found Rosie washing up the breakfast things.

'Believe it or not, tomorrow at seven a.m. – at the manor. Something's up with him – God knows what . . .'

'Was he interested?'

'To be frank – no, he wasn't. Delighted to make your acquaintance, I should bring you along, and so forth, but –' she shrugged – 'he's in a state. Excited about *something*. Tomorrow at seven all right with you?'

'Of course. And thank you . . .' Reaching for a dish-cloth. 'One other favour – could I borrow a needle and white cotton, please?'

'I expect so . . . Oh, Jacques—'

'Just off – delivery round. Three calls in Villeneuve-l'Archevêque and one in les Marchais. Morning, Justine – sleep well?'

'Very well, thanks.'

'That's good . . . What is it, chérie?'

'Don't forget the rabbits from Plassat's – on your way back, eh?'

'I swear. See you both later.'

'Might I have a word, though?' Rosie added as he paused, looking back at her, 'I'll come out with you – won't hold you up . . .'

Madame Brissac arrived at that moment: a big woman, dressed in black. Jacques went on out; Colette said, 'Go on, have your word, I'll introduce you when you come back.' Rosie, following Jacques, heard her beginning to explain the distant cousinship, et cetera. Jacques was holding the door for her – a side door. He was in overalls and still hadn't shaved.

'What can I do for you, Mam'selle Justine?'

She explained that she wanted a hiding-place, preferably outside, for her transceiver and a box of other equipment, and she'd wondered whether the outhouse where he kept his charcoal might be suitable and if he'd mind . . .

'Do better than that. You'd be filthy with charcoal dust every time you fetched it or put it back.' They were scrunching up the alley that led up this east side of the *auberge* to a yard at the back. A *gazo* pick-up truck was parked there, already fired-up, a red glow and the familiar hot smell from its burner. He told her, 'My workshop's the place. So much litter you'd never notice a bit more.' Opening the door of what had been a stable. 'Anywhere you like. No lock, see, you can always get in here – night-time, whenever. Is it night-times you do it?'

'Depends. But this is perfect.' Looking around, remembering a similar but less chaotic workshop which she'd been allowed to use for the same purpose at Châteauneuf-du-Faou. She looked back at him: 'Jacques – talking about that – fact is, I do have a message to send. Any chance of a trip for more charcoal later in the day, taking me along?'

'Transmit from the forest?'

'As good as anywhere. At some distance from here. Transmissions can be pinpointed, you know.'

'All right.' He checked the time. 'Say four o'clock. Have to be back by six, that's all.'

Touring the village then, with Colette: turning left out of the *auberge's* front door and following the narrow pavement past terraced houses – which had gardens behind them, she said, then woodland and low-lying orchard and pasture reaching to the Vanne – while on the other side of the road was the school and then the market square, with Rue de l'Ecole running south out of the square's bottom right-hand corner. Looking down there – across the road, and past the side of the school – goal-posts were visible, this end of a playing-field which adjoined the paddock opposite the *auberge*. Rosie thinking that might be a good site for a bonfire, on 'Jupiter' night – bonfire to mark this end of the factory area, as she'd discussed it with Marilyn. The bombers' line of flight *would* be near-enough due east – over the manor where she'd be with her 'S' phone, and four or five hundred metres – she'd pace the distance out, when time permitted – to the factory.

Colette had stopped to speak to a youngish woman scrubbing her doorstep, and introduced Rosie; two others joined them, and Justine Quérier's history was trotted out yet again. It was some time before they were able to move on.

'The place we were telling you about. Hôtel Poste.'

Even less attractive, now one had heard that story. Across the road the market square was much more pleasing to the eye: two or three shops, and a vegetable stall under the heavy-timbered, roofed structure in the centre, women moving around with baskets. A few waves, greetings from across the road . . . Bicycle traffic – no other kind.

'Not exactly humming, is it?'

'Well – Monday morning.' Colette shrugged. 'But – all right, we're a backwater here, in any case. Most wouldn't want it any different.'

'The kids, I'd have thought—'

'Well – why mine like to go away in the holidays, of course. But there are several larger villages in easy reach, you know, they have a lot of friends around.'

They'd passed the grim-looking so-called hotel.

'Where does this lane go to?'

'Timber-yard. And here's our church. Right *there*, however—'

'Yes.' Across the road, the entrance to what Dufay had referred to as the village's beating heart. Big timber gates, really massive, with the personnel-access door set in one of them.

'When the trucks come, is there room in there for them?'

'Drive one in and load it – or unload, when it's a delivery of steel plate for instance – and if there are others they park in the market square, wait their turn. Then the first one out – drive in, back out – and the next one in . . . Justine, I was thinking – if you wanted a watch kept for a convoy arriving at night – there'd be an excellent view from the Poste, and boys *have* got in there – playing games, showing off to each other, I suppose. They can get in at the back – so my daughters have said . . . But see the lane there? It's a *cul-de-sac*; the wall's the boundary of Marchéval's, and those are more workers' houses.'

Click-clacking on, on their wooden shoes. Graveyard up behind them on their left, where the ground sloped up to surround the church. It wasn't an *old* church. Colette pointed ahead: 'These were farm-workers' cottages originally, when the factory *was* a farm. All the other housing's of more recent origin. Those in the *cul-de-sac* were built in Monsieur Henri's time for instance, not his father's. This end one though – here, the old farm cottages – that's our *gendarmerie* now. We have a sergeant and one *gendarme*. Boches use it too – at least the lieutenant, Klebermann, spends time there – signing permits and so forth. Major Linscheidt seems to leave it all to him – doesn't as far as anyone can see have anything to do himself. But while we're here, why don't we call in there, register your arrival?'

'Uh-huh. Don't have my papers with me.'

'But you *should* have, Justine!'

'I suppose. Anyway – later on, or tomorrow . . . What's this now?'

A staff car, camouflage-painted, stopping at the *gendarmerie*: soldier-driver jumping out . . . She did have her papers, but still didn't trust them. In particular the *feuille semestrielle* – a document issued twice a year, entitling its holder to renew the various categories of ration card – was a bit of a botched-up job. At a glance, quick check at a road-block, it might get by, but detailed examination at leisure in an office – no. If she could avoid the registration procedure altogether, she *would*. At least delay it as long as possible . . . The driver had pulled a rear door open for a young Boche officer to alight. Fifteen or twenty metres ahead of them. Colette said quietly, 'Lieutenant Klebermann.'

Bat-ears under the tall peaked cap: long legs in shiny boots, striding into the *gendarmerie*. Rosie tugged at Colette's arm: 'Since I don't have papers with me and he might only be in there a minute – might cross, go back on the other side?'

'All right.'

The soldier was back in the car, waiting. Starting over, Rosie pointed to a house directly across from the *gendarmerie*; she'd noticed it in its large garden when she'd passed here in the *gazo* with Guillaume.

'Who lives there?'

'Our *curé* – Father Patrice. Big enough place, for a man living alone?'

'He was leaving the *auberge* when we arrived, yesterday. What are his – er – politics?'

'Well – he's sheltered Maquisards who were sick – and had Doctor Simonot visit them there in that house. And he's been into the forest to say Mass for them – many times. Sometimes Jacques has taken him.'

'And the doctor?'

'Very *much* one of us.'

'Would other villagers be aware of it?'

A shrug . . . 'He wouldn't broadcast it. But – it might become known. The fact most of them are – passive, one might say – doesn't make them pro-Boches, or informers.'

'Do the Boches appear in church at all?'

'There was one who did. Happens that none of them at the manor now are Catholic. In any case they'd go into Sens on a Sunday – all that parading, beating drums?'

'So you don't see much of them. Although Monsieur Henri must?'

They'd crossed over, and turned back. Factory gates coming up on their left. Machinery noise from inside, smoke rising vertically from the tall chimney. There was no wind at all, now; in Thérèse's jacket, Rosie was feeling the day's increasing warmth. Colette telling her, 'He says – Monsieur Henri, I mean – that the one in charge, Major Linscheidt, isn't at all bad. A plain soldier, he calls himself – only one eye, and he's lame, but he takes a gun out sometimes, for pigeons and rabbits, and on occasion he's given some to Monsieur Henri. I don't know much about Klebermann. Wachtel – the engineer – is fairly poisonous, one hears.'

Rosie said, 'Granted that some may be less poisonous than others. I don't think I'd differentiate much between them.' She touched Colette's arm: 'Could we turn down here?'

Down the west side of the market square. The school, she saw, had a playground immediately behind it, *then* the playing-field with its goal-posts. Low wall along that side, Marchéval's high one on their left. A side-door, she saw, in the factory wall: it was shown on Dufay's sketch. And on this side at the bottom end of the concreted play area, a timber shed – pavilion, it turned out when they were closer to it, with a veranda facing the field.

Set fire to *that*, on 'Jupiter' night? It was ideally located, and easily accessible over this waist-high wall. A bottle of petrol and a match was all you'd need. All *someone* would need . . . Colette was saying, 'At the bottom here there's a bridge over the stream – the track goes on past farm buildings you can see from your bedroom window. But there's a path along the stream too, and a good view of the manor from just along there. No trees or wall this side of it, just garden, Monsieur Henri's father wanted the view south to the hills and woods. I don't want to be all day, but—'

'I'd very *much* like to see it . . .'

Chapter 13

'We go left here.'

Woods thickening around them. Leaving St Valéry Jacques had proposed, 'Thought we might go by way of Chigy, to woods on high ground between les Clérimois and Fontaine-la-Gaillarde. Unless you've any better idea?'

'None at all. But how far'd that be?'

'Only seven or eight kilometres. Near a guy I collect stuff from, though: and if you were based in Sens, even, you might choose that area. No reason the detectors should think of St Valéry or Marchéval's.'

'Sounds good, then.'

Chigy was only a few minutes from St Valéry, and still on that side of the Vanne. A small bridge, narrower and planked, not paved, carried the road across the river; Jacques slowing again then to bump over the railway line, which must have crossed the main road between the St Valéry turn-off and this one. Rosie saw what looked like a station building – a halt, at least – half hidden in trees to their left.

'Could the tubes not be sent east by rail?'

'Marchéval's did use the railway, before. But as you'll have noticed it's single-track – and they're short of rolling-stock, the line's been bombed or blown up several times – not here, but on the Paris side of Sens – and near Troyes, come to think of it . . . Each time, no trains then for days

. . . And you see, on a line like that – well, a truck can get off the road, but a train can't get off its tracks – huh?'

'In any case that bridge isn't up to much, is it?'

'Ours at St Valéry is the only one that *is*. Even at that they were talking about replacing it. As I told you. The only alternative's hardly practical – a long way round with some very tight bends in narrow roads – especially right in the villages.'

'So if the St Valéry bridge was blown up—'

'Don't suggest it, please!'

A sideways glance, showing the whites of his eyes. There was a heavy growth of stubble on his cheeks by this time. Eyes front again: they were on the so-called 'main' road now but he was slowing again, preparing to turn off to the left. Adding, 'In any case they'd soon put another one across – the steel thing they had in mind before. You wouldn't isolate Marchéval's for long.'

'For a while, though. If one needed to. To hold the trucks up for a day, even – if an air attack was coming in?'

'I thought bombing was what you were talking about – smashing the bridge as well as . . .' Turning: and the side road looping back immediately in a sharp left-hand bend, to cross yet another small bridge. Not the Vanne, though – unless it had split into two streams, one each side of the road . . . Jacques finished: '– the bridge as well as the factory.'

'I was thinking of PE. Plastic explosive. Which the Maquis must have – by way of the *parachutages* you've helped with?'

'Have, I'm sure. When the whistle blows they'll be using it. Railway lines, primarily.' Another glance at her: 'You handy with explosives?'

'Oh, yes. Comes into our training.'

A grunt. 'Just don't practise on our bridge, eh?'

'You have strong feelings for that bridge.'

'I'm a fisherman. You'll be getting fish for your supper

this evening that came from the Vanne. One of the best pools is close by there – where the river divides around a small island.'

'I saw it. Guillaume said he thought there'd be trout.'

'Guillaume?'

'The man who brought me here. *He*'s a fisherman.'

'And a *chef de réseau*, he said. Had eyes for you, huh?'

'Oh, nonsense . . .'

'It was plain enough to me – and to Colette. Reminded me of the way André Marchéval used to watch *her* all the time.'

'*Colette?*'

'Despite her being ten years older than he is. Or was. But that's André for you. Joseph Lambert really had it in for him, I can tell you. Well, Joe's wife's a stunner – or she was. Huguette. He told me she was spending more time than was justified in Paris and he was certain it was André she was seeing. Her parents live there and her father had had a stroke, it gave her good reason to visit them. Supposedly visit *them*. Joe felt sort of helpless – he was still crazy about her.'

'Did Colette know?'

'Uh-huh. Reckons young André's the bee's knees. Not that *she*'d have—'

'I'm sure—'

'I *know* it. Shouldn't be gabbing like this, should I. Don't mention it to her – please? Joe spoke to me in confidence – desperation, you might say. Oh, he was explaining why he'd brought her with him that time. Yes, that was it.' Nodding . . . '*Shouldn't* talk about it. For all we know they could both be dead, poor sods – she wasn't exactly isolated from Joe's work, they'd have hauled 'em both in, wouldn't they. Bloody tragic . . . Got a cigarette, have you?'

'Of course . . .'

'Another kilometre or so, we'll be in les Clérimois. Turn

left there. What are you telling them in London – if I'm allowed to know?'

'Telling them that in my judgement the Marchéval products *are* V2 rocket-casings, and giving them your figure of a hundred and seventy centimetres diameter.'

'Just *less* than—'

'Yes. And that we could evacuate the village before an attack. And – finished casings, a dozen or more, awaiting transport. Also – although they may know it already – about Dufay being arrested.' She paused: match flaring. 'Here.'

One ready-lit Gauloise . . . Jacques took it delicately in blunt, calloused fingers. 'Thanks.' Placing it between his lips: eyes on the road, both hands back like clamps on the juddering wheel. It wasn't a good surface – dirt and gravel, pot-holed and ridged. Rosie with her head back, inhaling the pungent smoke and remembering Bob Hallowell telling her in the SOE flat in Portman Square, back in April, *Happen to know the motive's nothing more than sexual jealousy. A Frenchman 'Hector' himself recruited and whose girlfriend recently transferred her affections – to 'Hector', d'you see . . .*

For 'girlfriend' read 'wife'? Otherwise like all professional liars sticking as near as possible to the truth?

She asked Jacques, 'Do you know, was Lambert recruited by André Marchéval?'

Whites of eyes again . . . 'I *wouldn't* know.'

Could have been some other agent, some other girl. Jacques' reminiscence had rung that bell, but it didn't *have* to dovetail so neatly. Hallowell again: *Always did have a bit of a roving eye. Doesn't make him a traitor, does it?*

Made him a shit as *well* as a traitor, Rosie thought. Visualizing him as she'd seen him first in Morlaix and then in Paris: average height – five-ten or eleven, maybe – slim, dark, she'd guessed between twenty-five and thirty. Swarthy complexion, smarmy smile, a way of crinkling his eyes. And a voice that had sounded artificially deep – as if he worked at it, the way he *liked* to sound: that was the impression she'd had.

Lambert reporting on 'Hector' to Baker Street, maybe, 'Hector' then shopping Lambert to his Boche friends? Which might have involved shopping the pretty wife as well?

'This les Clérimois we're coming to?'

A nod. Wet-looking Gauloise clinging to his lower lip. 'We go left – on a smaller road, believe it or not. Listen – if we should be stopped – unlikely, but could happen – well, everyone for miles around knows who I am and what I do – you're just along for the ride – OK?'

She shrugged, glancing away. 'Heard *that* before . . .'

A kilometre or two westward from les Clérimois there was a wide area where loggers had been at work, thousands of tree-stumps and the litter which accompanies tree-felling giving an impression of general devastation. Jacques said, 'They moved from here a month ago. Started on the other side now. Give it a few years – well, twenty or thirty, say – Christ knows *what* this place'll look like.'

'Beautiful rolling farmland, maybe.'

'Whether the idea's to re-plant, or to grub out the stumps . . . *Could* make farmland eventually, I dare say.' Nodding ahead, pointing: 'I'll be turning up the far side of this lot, OK?'

'Anywhere you say.'

'Sort of place a couple with necking in mind might pick on, eh?'

'Or with charcoal-collecting in mind.'

'That track you can see now . . . Yes, sure – charcoal-collection as cover to our *real* purpose, is the idea they should get if we ran into a patrol, I'm saying.' Shake of the dark head: 'Not likely we'd run into any, mind you. Week by week lately they've been fewer and further between. I'd guess they're scraping the barrel for men they can put in the firing-line. Here we go. Up there, I'll turn into the trees.'

It wasn't a steep slope, more like one of a succession of wooded undulations. Just as well, considering the smoothness of the pick-up's tyres, which she'd noticed in the yard at the *auberge*. Battered old wagon, by the look of it converted to pick-up from an ordinary saloon, also converted to *gazogène*, with its burner and chimney right behind the cab. Lurching and crashing over ruts as he swung off into a thinnish copse of beechwood.

'Mind opening the bonnet so I can clip my transceiver lead to your battery?'

'Sure.'

The transceiver in its fitted suitcase was under her seat. This would be an emergency procedure transmission. i.e. calling the Sevenoaks station and getting a go-ahead from them before passing her message – which she'd coded up in her bedroom earlier in the afternoon. Also at that time she'd found a good hiding-place for the one-time pad and other items including the Beretta. The Llama and its spare clips were with the 'S' phone, in that carton, but this indoors cache was in the boxroom, an old trunk containing amongst other things a wedding-dress that reeked of camphor, and a lace-up corset; the coding materials, cash and the pistol had gone under those, nestling among God knew what – bloomers, maybe. Now she'd got the transceiver out of the car, and by that time Jacques had opened the bonnet; she gave him the business-end of the power lead, spring-clips for attachment to battery terminals, put the case on the ground on the blind side of the *gazo* from the road – or rather track – and then walked away into the trees paying-out the aerial wire in a more or less straight line. Twenty metres of the very fine, dark-coloured wire: over lower branches where there were any, looping it around trunks when there were not.

Back to the *gazo* then. Jacques was leaning against it, stuffing a pipe and keeping an eye on the road and surroundings generally. Rosie sat on the ground and pulled the set on to her lap. Switch on: a glimmer of red light and a quiver of the needle in the ammeter. When she began to transmit she'd adjust the output to forty or forty-five milliamperes. She'd inserted the appropriate quartz crystal – the 'emergency procedure' one – before starting out: that crystal pre-set the wavelength, made it distinctively hers – 'Masha"'s – which would be picked up and trigger immediate response from 'her' operator in North Kent – touch wood. Key, now: she plugged it in: and the headset. The key itself, capped with black plastic, had a pleasantly familiar feel between two fingertips and the thumb. Now the message in its five-letter groups – from an inside pocket in Thérèse's jacket, smoothing it out left-handed on her knee. OK. Switch to 'Send': headphones over her ears . . . Starting then, tapping out 'QTC 1' – meaning, *I have a message for you*. Then 'QRK, interrogative' – *Is this reaching you intelligibly?* And 'K' – *Over*.

Switch to 'Receive', and wait . . .

Two seconds: three . . . A thin squeaking in her ears then: she was turning it up, Sevenoaks stuttering 'QRK . . . QRV . . .' *Intelligible . . . Ready to receive. Over.'*

Magnifique . . . Except they'd be alert in the Boche radio-detection centre in Paris too: lights glowing, tapes running, direction-finders seeking jerkily this way, that way . . . With the switch at 'Send' she opened with Marilyn's stipulated self-identification *Masha on line*, followed by a group indicating that no reply was expected: otherwise with emergency procedure there'd be the seventy-minute deadline, Baker Street frenetic. Whereas in quite a bit less than seventy minutes she and Jacques would be back in the *auberge* – she hoped. Eyes on the message, the rows of capitals with Masha's personal security check included in the form of a corrupt (misspelt) seventh word. There was a 'bluff' check too, which didn't add up to much and could legitimately be revealed under torture.

Last group dot-and-dashing out. A pause, then 'AR' – end of message. And immediately from Sevenoaks 'QSL' – *I acknowledge receipt* – and 'K' – *Out*. Rosie switched off, disconnected the key and the headset, extracted the crystal: it went into a little bag, in her pocket, could be ditched in an emergency. She called, 'Finished, Jacques. Unclip, roll the lead up?' Neither wasting time nor taking risks you didn't have to take: it was done, the thing now was to clear out, quick. Quickly through the trees unstringing the aerial wire, whipping it around a card on her way back to the *gazo*. Slotting it and the power-lead into the case: then the case back under her seat. Jacques was already on board, with his pipe between his teeth and a hand on the gear lever, waiting for her to shut the door.

She did so. 'Thanks. *Great* help, Jacques.'

'Easy as that, eh?'

She smiled: 'Nothing to it.'

'When you know how, I suppose . . .'

'Think what you've told them will result in bombing?'

'Oh, I don't know. Ball's in their court, we wait and see.'

'How long, wait?'

'I'll be listening out for a message tonight and every night this week. Normally, I'd keep to a schedule of three nights a week.'

'Going out at night to do this?'

She reassured him: 'From my room in your *auberge*. Won't be transmitting, don't worry – just listening, between midnight and one a.m. The transceiver's in two parts, one for transmitting and one receiving, and I'll take just the receiver bit in with me.'

'And the person sending it from England knows you'll be getting it?'

'Yes. They know I'll be listening on that wavelength.'

'So you might hear tonight?'

'Might. More likely tomorrow, I'd guess.'

She was lighting a cigarette. They were back on the road now, heading for les Clérimois. She explained, 'It won't be solely an SOE decision. Much higher level. SOE present the facts and the proposal, top brass say yea or nay.'

'But *you've* recommended bombing.'

'What I told you, that's all. What you and Colette have told *me*.'

Sucking hard on his pipe: then turning his head to spit out of the window. Pipe bubbling audibly . . . He glanced at her, licking his lips. 'Listen. Another thing Colette and I were asking ourselves. If the bombers come – factory's smashed, also some houses, although please God not many casualties . . . Well – if it's a few weeks before the Boches are driven out – or even if it's less – it's not unlikely there'll be reprisals—'

'Not necessarily. An air raid, after all—'

'– and *certainly* investigations. You say "not necessarily", but won't they guess someone here called for the bombers – sent out word what was being produced here?'

She thought, *If someone had lit a bonfire* . . .

Jacques added challengingly, 'How would families have been warned to leave their houses, otherwise?'

'By Maquisards, surely.' Maquisards would have lit the bonfire too: they were the answer to *all* of this. She asked him, 'Wouldn't it be? Colette and I were talking about it, *she* said so. Maquisards knocking on all the doors. In fact she was thinking others might help as well – saying they'd been ordered to – but I'd guess it might be better if no villagers knew anything at all until it happened. Not even your doctor or the priest. All right, the

Boches may stage some sort of offensive against the Maquis
afterwards—'

'My belief is they'll be nosing around us too, Justine. And
what I set out to ask you is this: after the bombing, what do
you do? Vanish? Have an airplane pick you up?'

'Frankly, I hadn't thought.'

'So think now. This young woman shows up just before
the bombing – total stranger, allegedly a relation of Colette's
– so the Craillots say. Then we have the bombing and –
pouf, she's gone again. How do they look at these damn
Craillots *then*?'

'It's a good point.' She nodded. 'The answer is that Justine
Quérier's come to live with her cousins – needing a roof
over her head, all that – and she'll stay as long as they'll
have her. Bombing or no bombing. Speaking of airplane
pick-ups though – when you were helping Lambert, was
there a particular field around here you used?'

'Little way south – near a place called Villechétive. He
called it "Parnasse". They dropped some weapons instructors off there for Guichard, the last time.'

They were back in the *auberge* well before six. Colette was
in the kitchen, Madame Brissac had gone home. There
were no customers in the place at that stage, but some
were to be expected, apparently. Colette asked Rosie if
she'd like to have supper rather early, before things got
busy; supper would be fried trout with boiled potatoes and
haricots verts. Rosie said she'd eat a supper like that at *any*
time. Six thirty, then: Colette would have it with her, in the
kitchen. She'd already set tables in the dining-room, there
was nothing Rosie could help with. All of which was fine,
she'd have time after the meal to do her sewing and get a
few hours' sleep before midnight, when she had to set radio
listening-watch. She took the receiver upstairs and put it for
the time being in the trunk that had the wedding-dress in it,

and on the spur of the moment she took the Beretta, with a clip in it but not cocked, and pushed it under her mattress – for no reason other than the thought that it was pointless to have a pistol at all if you couldn't get at it quickly. Then she had a wash and went down to keep Colette company until supper was ready. There were some men in the bar by this time; Jacques of course was barman. Rosie asked Colette if there was an alarm-clock she could borrow: she explained what for, Colette having assumed that she was concerned about waking up in time for their early appointment at the manor with Monsieur Henri. Whom she'd seen passing on his bike, she said, but he hadn't stopped as he'd half said he might.

'Got your message away, eh?'

'Yes. And learnt a certain amount from Jacques, along the way. About the village and so forth.'

'He likes to gabble away, my husband.'

'Well, I was glad of it. I'm getting a feel of the place – beginning to. Not least, Colette, from my guided tour this morning. I must say, the manor's situation's lovely.'

'It's a fine house, too. The old *patron* didn't stint himself, I'll say *that*. As you'll see for yourself . . . Look, you'll find an alarm-clock in Yvette's room. Even *with* it, that girl's bad enough at waking for school. Solange manages to drag herself out all right, but Yvette – my God . . . Hers is the first room on the left – nearest to the stairs.'

'Thanks. This trout's delicious . . .'

'What we still have to do is check you in at the *gendarmerie*.'

'I know. I will.'

'Do you expect to have a decision on the bombing over your radio tonight?'

'Doubt it. More likely tomorrow, or the night after that. By the way – Jacques mentioned that you were worried I might just vanish somehow, after a bombing attack if there

is one, so then you'd be under suspicion for having har-
boured me. But I won't, I promise. As long as you can put
up with me, I'll stay. All right?'

She didn't answer immediately. Picking a fish-bone off
her tongue . . . Nodding then: 'Perfectly all right.'

No great enthusiasm: Rosie had expected at least some, if
that really had been worrying them.

Not a good idea to go into the woods with Jacques?

See about a bike, for future trips. Ask Colette tomorrow.
Weight off her mind, maybe. Although it might be only
her continuing anxiety over the bombing threat. Which
was entirely understandable: a credit to her in fact that
she was steeling herself to go along with it at all.

She did her sewing, making a cyanide-pill slot in one
corner of each of two handkerchiefs, and putting a few
stitches in the hems of the two blouses, including the
one she'd worn today. Replacing the capsule then in the
clean blouse. Do some laundering tomorrow, probably.
The second capsule was still in the silver lipstick holder,
in Léonie's bag: she unscrewed the cap and tipped it out,
fitted it into the slot in one of the handkerchiefs. It would
be secure enough, she thought; the capsules were made of
hardened gelatine, not glass, wouldn't break without being
bitten quite hard. She got into her pyjamas – old blue ones
Marilyn had brought – then went along to clean her teeth
and brought the radio from the boxroom, put it under the
foot of the bed. She'd already set Yvette's alarm for a few
minutes to twelve. She switched off the light, opened the
curtains and pushed the window up. Draw the curtains
again at transmission time; she'd need a light for it. It
was a clear night, very still, starry sky, moon not risen
yet. Much warmer than last night. Despite which she put
Thérèse's all-purpose jacket handy on the foot of the bed.
It was about nine now, would be cooler by midnight and

she'd need the window still at least a crack open, with the aerial-wire hanging out – in a loop, otherwise it wouldn't clear the ground.

Clock under the bedclothes, so as not to wake the Craillots. She slid into bed. Escape, now – concentrate on Ben. Who at this moment might be thinking about *her*? Lovingly, please God, happy in the knowledge she was alive. Lightly fingering the scar above her left breast, that bullet's exit wound: acknowledging to herself that how he reacted to his first sight of it was going to be fairly crucial. She didn't think the other scars would matter much, any more than the ones on her knees had, but this one might.

Please God though, *wouldn't*. Ben still being Ben?

Over 'coffee' in the kitchen just after six-thirty she told Colette no, nothing had come in from London. She hadn't expected anything, had only listened out because her instructions via Marilyn had stipulated that she should. Although Marilyn had said there was intense concern at high levels over the V2 threat, there'd be other considerations too – the progress of the Allied armies, for one thing. If American spearhead units might be probing into this area within days rather than weeks, for instance; and if there was such close liaison with the Free French now, maybe *they*'d have a say in what was or was not bombed. Talking with Colette – who looked as if she hadn't slept much – Rosie speculated that if there was such chaos on the roads – hundreds of heavy trucks being abandoned, et cetera – straffing from the air might stop *anything* much getting through to Germany: they might settle for that, leave this place alone . . . She'd checked the time: 'Ought we to be starting?'

'Oh, no rush. It's ten minutes' walk at most.' Colette covered a yawn. 'Although you're right, he won't want us to be late.'

'Reminds me.' Rosie put her mug down: the stuff was too hot to gulp yet. 'Talking about walking – I was going to ask you whether there's a bike I could borrow – I don't mean now, but next time I have to go somewhere to transmit. Rather than be a burden on Jacques, is there one I could use?'

'Mine, if you want. Or Yvette's, while she's away. But what about the radio?'

'I've had that *and* a suitcase on bikes – dozens of times, with a carrier on the back and a basket in front. The transceiver's in what looks like a small suitcase – I've passed through road-blocks often, never had to open it.'

'If you had, you wouldn't be here now?'

She admitted, 'Probably not.'

'Better let Jacques take you. Quicker – safer.'

'If he really doesn't mind – and if you aren't left with too much on your hands here—'

'If either of us minded, we'd tell you . . . Listen, you could use Yvette's bike now, we'd save some time.'

She'd wobbled a bit, starting off, but then was back in the way of it, no problem. Following Colette – past the butcher and *boulangerie*, which were on the same side of the road as the *auberge*, and with the manor's wooded grounds behind a high wall on their left. Then the imposing gateway: stone pillars, iron gates standing open and the wall continuing westward. Colette dropped back, was beside her for a moment: 'I'll do the talking. There'll be a sentry inside but they all know me.'

Nothing coming: no traffic at all, nothing audible except the rattling of the bikes, tyres scrunching on the dirt edging to the road and then on gravel as Colette swung across and turned in, Rosie following. An elaborate 'M' for Marchéval was carved into each pillar, she noticed: seeing the guard-hut then, a black-painted shed with a helmeted Boche soldier in its open doorway. Colette shrieked, 'Visiting Monsieur Marchéval, he's expecting us!'

Presumably he understood French. Staring at Rosie, now. She smiled politely, kept pedalling, glanced back and saw him still goofing – hadn't said a word, or moved. The drive curved left, then right, then straightened, with a narrow view of the house ahead: pale stone, Colette had said it came from some local quarry. Rhododendrons and other shrubs edged the drive, trees towering behind them. Colette looked back, flapping her right arm: 'Round that way . . .' The view ahead widened: there was an oblong of grass – orchard-length, not lawn – with a flagpole set in concrete in the middle, the sand-coloured drive encircling it and extending right and left around both wings of the house. No flag on the pole. A small truck and she thought three cars were parked down there on the left, the side they were *not* going, and beyond the grass patch and the flagpole a soldier with a slung Schmeisser was patrolling the area in front of the main entrance – a wide flight of steps under a pillared stone canopy. There were several deep-set windows each side of that, and a couple more in each of the protruding wings. Above were towers and chimneys – a lot of chimneys, and rectangular towers, although in her view from the south yesterday she'd seen round ones with conical tops – as well as the chimneys, some of which were massive. Round towers on the south-facing frontage, square ones on this north side: and the central part of the house had a steeply ridged slate roof with dormer-type windows in it. It looked better from the south, she thought, less pretentious. But it was more *château* than *manoir*. Pedalling in Colette's tracks, thinking what a pompous ass grandfather Marchéval must have been. That soldier had halted, was facing this way, watching them, but they weren't going anywhere near him. Henri Marchéval's entrance evidently being at the side, front door strictly for the Master Race;

while the drive swept on around the protrusion of this
west wing into a stable-yard the size of a couple of tennis
courts, cobbled, the stables themselves a substantial, mostly
two-storied L-shaped building bracketing it on that side and
at the end. The dreaded Briards lived 'above the stables', she
remembered Colette saying.

Colette was dismounting, gliding up close to a porch
sheltering the side-door. Rosie followed suit, propping her
bike there too. Colette at the door by then with a hand up
on the iron-ring knocker, looking round at her: then two
thuds, on the solid oak – and *immediately* a man's voice
calling from inside: 'Is that you, Colette?'

'Yes, *patron!*'

Sound of a bolt being pulled back: door opening inwards.
It was still a few minutes short of seven, but he'd either been
waiting at the door or maybe seen them from a window,
hurried down to it . . . Framed in the opening doorway
then: less old-looking than Rosie had expected. Less tall
than his son, too – about five-eight, five-nine. Hair thin
but still dark except around the edges, large brown eyes
with dark pouches under them, sallow complexion. Eyes
flickering to Rosie, back to Colette.

'Come in. Come in. This must be—'

'Justine Quérier, *patron*. Justine – Monsieur Henri Marchéval.'

'It's a pleasure, Mam'selle.'

'For me too, M'sieur.'

'You're a cousin—'

'Distant – by marriage. My brother—'

'We can talk better sitting down. This way . . .'

If you'd had to name it you might have called it a
back-staircase hall, into which the door opened. A big room
with a dining-table in it, stairs slanting up the opposite
wall from right to left. Two doors in the left-hand wall:
Monsieur Henri was guiding them towards the further

one, which stood open. Wooden-soled shoes loud on the plank flooring. There was a door near the foot of the stairs too, leading she guessed into the main part of the house – *verboten* area, no doubt.

'My *petit salon*. Servants inhabited this wing, before. Come in. This particular room was I believe the *majordome*'s private den. Pokey little hole – but there you are, beggars can't be choosers. Sit down, please.'

Colette said, 'It's not such a bad room, *patron*. And the day can't be far off when the entire house will be yours again. Can't happen too soon, huh?'

'In *there* –' pointing, to the room next door – 'it's even pokier. As Colette knows, I use it as an office.' Rosie sat down, on a sofa; Colette did too, on the other end of it. Monsieur Henri, on the point of sitting facing them, hesitated . . . 'Colette – speaking of the office – I wonder if I might have a word with you, in there?'

'All right—'

'Nothing to do with your interest in coming to work here, Mam'selle Quérier. Only a rather private and urgent matter I've been anxious to discuss with my old friend here.'

'Perfectly all right.'

'But in regard to that proposal – frankly, I have to admit that at this juncture it might be a little difficult. There's a Madame Briard and her husband who both work here—'

'Colette told me. What gave me the idea, in fact.'

'We might do something about it later on. But – give us a few minutes, please. Excuse us . . .'

He shut the door behind them. Rosie looking around at the clutter of furniture – too much of it for the room's size. Big old pieces too, some of them. Whatever he'd been so anxious to talk about in private, she'd guessed, must relate to whatever he'd sounded excited about on the telephone to Colette yesterday.

Boches pulling out – or planning to?

Seven minutes gone, Marilyn's watch told her. It felt like more than that. Eight minutes. Nine . . .

The door opened: Monsieur Henri standing aside, for Colette to enter. Pushing it shut then behind him: he looked surprised – or alarmed – gazing past her at Rosie. Colette was beside her then, a knee on the edge of the sofa, and grasping Rosie's hands: she looked excited about something . . . 'Justine – I've got to tell him who you are and what you're here for!'

Elated, even . . . Rosie frowned, shook her head. 'He *knows* who—'

'Listen – Jacques and I were telling you about Monsieur Henri's son – remember all that?'

'Of course, but – so what?'

'He's *here!*'

'Who is?'

'For God's sake.' Colette's hands tightened on hers. '*André!* André Marchéval!'

'My son.' Perching himself on to a chair facing them. Peculiar-looking chair – probably antique, but ugly, she wouldn't have given it house-room: giving it a moment's attention now though, rather than show astonishment or shock – her mind frozen for a moment in instant flashback to Michel's *Think, girl! When it all hits the fan, isn't his father's place where he's likely to show up?*

Instant *logic*.

And, she realized, no need now to bomb the manor.

Monsieur Henri repeating, 'My *son*, Mam'selle. Though why it should be necessary for you to be apprised of this I have no idea. Doubtless Colette will explain. The fact is, however, that André – who I should tell you was arrested by the Gestapo several months ago—'

'I knew that. Colette and her husband were telling me about you and your family. But your daughter too, they said.'

He'd passed a hand over his face. 'Colette insisted I should tell you this. I do so with reluctance . . . The position is that on Sunday evening, when I was in the factory, I received a message – a scrap of paper – from the hand of a young man who works for me. It was signed by André, saying he'd come here to see me – well, this last night. I was to leave the door unfastened for him – all night, he couldn't say what time. I recognized his writing and signature but I could still hardly believe – not having had a word or any news of him – or of Claire either – in *months* . . . However – I asked the boy where, how, and he whispered – this was in my own office, he'd come in on some pretext, worksheets or some – well, never mind – he whispered, "He's in the forest with the others".'

'The forest . . .' It made sense, probably, from André's point of view. 'Did he come?'

'Yes. Having had this message was of course why I delayed meeting you, Colette. To know first it was genuine – not a hoax or a trap of some kind.' Back to Rosie: 'Colette and I – and my family – the only one I *could* talk to . . .' To Colette again: 'If you hadn't telephoned I'd have been contacting *you*, today.'

'What did your son have to say?'

'He escaped from the Gestapo a week ago and he's with a Maquis group commanded by a man named – Guichard?' A querying glance at Colette: she nodded. Sitting back now; she'd let go of Rosie's hands. Telling Monsieur Henri, 'Emile Guichard. His Maquis name is Tamerlan. Jacques meets him sometimes.'

'Well. The rest of it is that they're planning a sabotage operation against my factory.' An expansive gesture, his arms spreading . . . 'To Colette this is good news. Comprehensible, I dare say – but – perhaps you'd tell me yourself how *you* come into it?'

Colette said, 'I understood you to say not that they're

planning it, but that André is trying to persuade them
to.'

A shrug: movement of his rather small hands . . . Rosie
asked him, 'What's your reaction to the proposal, M'sieur?'

'Before we go further, Colette, I insist I should be told
what this young lady has to do with any of it!'

'Well – Justine—'

'Wait.' Rosie asked him, 'Can I take it you'll keep this to
yourself?'

'Mam'selle, I'm not in the habit of—'

'You aren't on close terms with your Boche colleagues?'

'Are you insulting me?'

'You work for them – have done for a long time—'

'Not by my own choice. They've been holding my son
– *and* my daughter. My poor darling Claire.' His face
crumpling . . . 'Who may be – *dead*, Colette!'

'What are you *saying*?'

'They'd promised André she'd be unharmed as long as
he – and I apparently – well, gave them no trouble?'

'So he's been – co-operating with them, are you saying?'

'Pretending to. "Playing them along", he said.'

'Really.' Staring at him. '*I've* been in Gestapo custody,
monsieur. It's no game, there's no playing – except of course
on *their* terms.'

'Justine.' Colette, in a shocked whisper. 'You're not suggesting—'

'You've told us, Monsieur, Claire was a hostage for your
son's "playing along". What happens to her now he's run
out on them?'

'They told him – just recently – she's been sent east.
Meaning some camp.'

'Oh, *patron* . . .'

A hand over his face again. 'You know, *I'd* almost given
up hope for both of them. But this was why he broke out.
He'd asked one of them what would happen now to himself

and Claire – when they withdraw from Paris – in effect would he and Claire be released – but why not let them go now – so forth. That was the answer – may or may not be true, the man was angry he said, shouting at him—'

'He broke out of where, M'sieur?'

'A prison in the Place des Etats-Unis. What I was saying – Claire *may* still be alive, you know? But look here – I'm giving you answers to *your* questions—'

Colette said flatly, 'She's an agent of SOE.'

Staring at her: brown eyes even wider, dampish. A small face: small-boned, and triangular – small, sharp chin, and that width across the eyes. Like some kind of animal: she had it in her mind's eye but couldn't have put a name to it.

Shaping words: 'Then you'd have known my son?'

'One doesn't know by any means all one's fellow agents. Those one's worked with, obviously – or trained with . . .'

'He was in a key position. Air Movements Officer?'

'*Was* he? But he'd have had a code-name – even if I'd had contact with him, I wouldn't have known his real one. Anyway – having escaped he should have contacted SOE in order to be brought back to London for de-briefing. How long was he in Gestapo hands?'

'About – three months.'

'London would insist on pulling him out – and he'd be well aware of it!'

'Perhaps he had no contacts?'

'As Air Movements Officer? He'd have had dozens!'

'But – in a state of mounting confusion, as apparently it is now, in Paris – talk of imminent German withdrawal – and André concerned about my own situation here particularly—'

'Justine is here about your factory too, *patron*.'

Gazing at her: slow blink. Rosie thinking, a lemur, maybe . . .

'What exactly – *about* my—'

'My brief is to investigate a report that you're making casings for the V2 rockets – ballistic missiles.'

'A report, you say?'

'It was my reason for wanting to meet you. Colette didn't know this, but she'd mentioned your problems with Madame Briard—'

'Never mind that. The report you mentioned – what if you discovered it was correct?'

'I'm sure it *is*. Your son's proposal and your own reaction bear it out too. I've told London that I believe it, and if they're convinced – by certain evidence I've given them – the likely upshot will be bombing.'

'Bombing – here – would be – *frightful!*'

Colette broke in: 'You see why she had to be brought into this – and why I welcome André's plan!'

He'd barely glanced at her. Back to Rosie: repeating, '*Frightful!*'

'But entirely warranted. The V2s are frightful weapons, Monsieur. Aimed at changing the present course of the war, through mass destruction and mass slaughter of civilians – they'd hope, forcing at least a stalemate. Which amongst other horrors would perpetuate a system in which such disgusting institutions as Belsen, Buchenwald and Ravensbrück would continue to exist. The possibility that in our efforts to ensure they don't, your village might be knocked about – and your factory of course obliterated . . . Did you know from the start what they were requiring you to make?'

'No – but then one began to suspect, and—'

'Your son knew these were rocket-casings, did he?'

'He knows *now*.'

'So. If the Maquisards go ahead with it, will you co-operate with them?'

'Yes. I told him so. And now more than ever!'

'Why?'

'*Why?* Because – what you've just told me—'

'Oh – the bombing . . . Co-operate how, though?'

'They'd want a set of keys, he said – to get in silently, plant explosives I suppose—'

'What about the night shift?'

'No more. As from today, no night shift. They want production to continue – up to the last minute, Wachtel keeps saying. He's the Boche engineer.'

'But you're running out of space. May not be enough flatbeds to shift them anyway. When do you expect what you have already to be collected?'

'I don't know. I doubt Wachtel does either.'

'How many casings ready now?'

'Sixteen. By the weekend, with no night shift, eighteen.'

'Meaning five trucks. Do they have that many?'

'I don't know. That's the kind of thing I'm not told.'

'What about where they go in Germany?'

'Again, I don't *know*, but I'd guess Essen.'

'Only guess, or more than that?'

'More a conclusion than a guess.'

Colette put in, 'Doesn't it make sense, Justine? Sabotage rather than bombing?'

'It *would* – if the Maquis go for it, and it's viable, and if London agrees—'

'The Maquis, you're suggesting –' Monsieur Henri's tone was derisive – 'need authority from London?'

'Your son as an agent of SOE does. And as I said, I've provided our people with all the information they need to lay on an attack. The Maquis can do what they like, that *is* the intention, as of this moment. I'm not trying to antagonize you, Monsieur, *I'd* prefer sabotage to bombing – but that's how it is.' She nodded to Colette: 'I'd better meet Monsieur Henri's son. And perhaps more importantly, Guichard. Think Jacques could arrange it?'

Chapter 14

Three forty p.m.: on their way into the northern fringes of the Forêt d'Othe. Jacques hadn't been able to get away from the *auberge* any earlier. Rosie had drafted a message to Baker Street and coded it up, but she'd brought the one-time pad and key with her as well, so as to be able to amend or add to it after meeting Emile Guichard – with or without André Marchéval.

With, she hoped. Get the confrontation over.

They were heading for Chigy again, but would be turning south there, to a village called Vareilles. 'From there on towards les Vallées, but we'll turn off before that.' A hand up to his newly smooth-shaven jaw: 'No certainty he'll be there, remember.'

'No. You said.'

He'd be able to arrange a rendezvous, he'd told her, but not necessarily for today. He'd been referring then only to Guichard; wasn't talking about André much. He'd been like that earlier too – listening to Colette, expressing quiet agreement – shrugging a bit, not all *that* enthusiastic, agreeing that a sabotage operation would be preferable to bombing, but expressing doubt as to whether the Maquis were likely to be persuaded. 'Weren't going to touch it before – remember?'

'Then, it was different. We weren't sure what the tubes were, for one thing – and we do now. So do they – André's

with them – and *he* knows as well as his father does . . .
Jacques, he *said* so – Monsieur Henri did!'

'The fear of reprisals was another factor.'

'It's conceivable the Boches won't have time for teaching
us salutary lessons now. Bigger issues on their hands.
Look how few patrols they're sending out now – you've
mentioned it yourself half a dozen times. In any case –
when the alternative's to be bombed—'

'On *that* you could be right.'

'What's more, when it's the *patron*'s own son who's
urging it?'

Rosie wondering now how she'd handle the *patron*'s son.
For instance – she'd feigned memory-loss in the Morlaix
hospital and again in Rue des Saussaies; might stick to that
line – be vague in her recollections of those encounters –
generally let him think she was giving him the benefit of
the doubt?

What doubt, for Christ's sake.

He'd want this sabotage action, for his own sake and his
father's. There'd be talk for ever after of the Marchévals
sabotaging their own business in the greater interests of
France; and who'd have masterminded the operation but
André Marchéval, hero of the Resistance. Guillaume's pro-
jection of future events, that had been, and it was probably
as accurate as Michel's had now proved to be. But another
Guillaume quote in her memory: *Has it occurred to you that
it would suit Marchéval down to the ground to see you dead?'*

Well. Might *suit* him, but he wasn't going to try anything
in front of witnesses.

Marilyn, who'd also issued some such warning, would
still be having fits. Certainly when she read this signal.

In Chigy now: hearing through her wound-down window the clatter of a train. Her fingers traced the outline of
the 9-mm Llama in her jacket pocket. She'd swapped the
Beretta for it, in the *breuvage* carton; she was more at home

with this one. Glancing at Jacques – who'd turned south out of Chigy, into a lane with tall hedges almost meeting overhead – asking him, 'What sort of man is Guichard?'

Jinking, to avoid an old woman on a bicycle . . . Glancing at her then. 'He was a lawyer, in Paris. Up and coming, well thought of, Joe Lambert told me. He's still a young man – maybe thirty-five, thirty-seven. But he was arrested down south in what was then the unoccupied zone – by Vichy police, or it might have been Milice – when he was smuggling a Jewish family down to Menton – Mentone, as they like to call it – from where they'd have found their way into Italy. They'd have been under Italian jurisdiction in Menton, in any case. Mussolini is not a persecutor of Jews – did you know?'

'Didn't we hear they've had to re-think on that?'

'Well – *now*, maybe. But Guichard was caught on his way back. Someone had informed, they were waiting for him at the line of demarcation where he'd slipped over on his way south. Then he escaped, but in Paris they grabbed his wife. She was very young – part-Italian, her mother I think was Italian.'

'And?'

'The usual thing.' A jerk of the head. 'Lambert told me he'd heard they were French Gestapo who took her.'

'Poor kid.'

'Say *that* again . . . But Guichard's a hard man, believe me.'

'Why his *nom-de-guerre*'s "Tamerlan", no doubt.'

'But he's a nice guy and a good leader. André would have known of him through Lambert, I suppose. All the *parachutages* in which I took part were for that crowd.'

'Big crowd?'

'In aggregate, it must be. He has them split into groups of about fifteen men each, dispersed all over. Got a cigarette to spare?'

Usual routine. She passed his to him, and he grunted thanks. Then: 'You had the pleasure of meeting Madame Briard this morning, Colette mentioned.'

'She gave her a flea in her ear, too!'

'Colette did?'

'When we came out after seeing Monsieur Henri, she was inspecting our bikes as if she thought they shouldn't be there. Looks like a toad, doesn't she? She glared at me, and asked Colette, "Who's this and what do the pair of you want here?" Colette told her it was our business and Monsieur Henri's – and what were *her* plans now that her Boche masters would shortly be on the run. "What'll you do, return to the bosom of the community, where we all love you so dearly, you bitch?"'

'Then what?'

'There was quite a bit more, then Monsieur Henri came out, on his way to the factory. That ended it. I was quite sorry, Colette had her pretty well on the ropes. But at the front of the house the Boches were hoisting their revolting flag – I saw the head one – Linscheidt – and one who Colette told me afterwards was the engineer – moon-faced, with glasses?'

'That's him. But Colette was taking a risk, talking about the Boches running. The Briard woman'll report it, for sure. She's a little – overwrought, just now. Colette, I mean.'

'Anxiety about the bombing. *My* doing. But if Guichard takes up this sabotage idea—' She'd checked: exhaling Gaulois smoke . . . 'One thing, Jacques. I'd sooner no one knew I'm sending any message to London today. They might assume I was passing on news that might stop the air attack – which is *not* the case.'

'Unless Guichard—'

'If he makes a positive decision I'll pass *that* on, sure.'

The draft for the signal as she had it encoded read: *André Marchéval formerly code-named Hector is now with Maquis in*

Forêt d'Othe claiming to have escaped from Gestapo in Paris and proposing sabotage of the factory by Maquis. He has visited his father who is willing to co-operate, but Maquis leader Tamerlan has yet to commit himself. Hector's object is probably to establish himself as active résistant, father no doubt similarly motivated. Father has confirmed to me that the tubes are casings for V2s. Am arranging to meet Hector and Tamerlan shortly, possibly before transmission of this message. Am aware of possible threat from Hector and will take precautions. Targeting of manor being no longer necessary, 'S' phone guidance if required would be from vicinity of factory. Further two items: factory is back on day shifts only, in view of pile-up of uncollected casings, and Marchéval senior believes destination of casings probably Essen.

Intelligence which mightn't be of much practical use, she guessed – Essen being the home of the arms manufacturers Krupps and no doubt being bombed regularly in any case.

They were at Vareilles at about the time their cigarettes were finished. It was a hot afternoon and there was no one on the street. Jacques pointed: 'We go straight through – but what we were talking about before, if the bridge at St Valéry was blown and they used this back way out for the trucks – see how sharp that corner is? Most likely *wouldn't* make it. Even longer detour, then.'

'Trucks must be coming, mustn't they. The fact Marchéval's still producing at all – must be *expecting* to get them away.' She stubbed out the last centimetre of her Gauloise, flicked it through the window. 'By the end of the week they'll have eighteen, Monsieur Henri said. No early shut-down in *his* thinking, therefore. What I'm getting at is, if Guichard isn't prepared to do it, and London's *ready* to bomb—'

'Tell Guichard that. It might help him to make his mind up. Although – between us, Justine – his plan for when the time comes is to take over St Valéry and hold it as a Maquis base – cut the road and the railway and hang on until the

Yanks arrive, maybe spread into villages along the road as
well – depending on how it goes. Consequently he might
not be willing to stir things up now. If they put troops in,
for instance – might, if they foresaw a danger to the road –
their line of retreat?'

'Then we're back to bombing.'

'Which Guichard wouldn't want either – wouldn't want
to bring it on us. So it's a toss-up.' He changed the subject: 'Sounds like Monsieur Henri was talking freely, this
morning.'

'Jittery, I'd say. Unless he's always like that. Colette said
not a *resolute* man. Scared of what he's doing – then *me*, out
of the blue – and the news about his daughter . . .'

They were out of the village, heading about south-
east, forest thickening ahead. Rosie thinking about André
Marchéval again; that it might be best to play it straight.
Have maybe only a vague recollection of Morlaix, but be
clear about the other one. You'd be knocked sideways at
first – having come solely on rocket-casing business, the
name Marchéval not ringing any bells. Although he *had*
told her his name at some point. In Morlaix, she thought.
All right, so a bell *should* have rung, just hadn't. He might
say something like 'I'm supposed to *believe* it's coincidence
you're here?' and the answer would be 'What d'you think –
that I've joined the André Marchéval fan club, following you
around? *You're* the bloody coincidence! Anyway, shouldn't
you have got in touch with Baker Street?'

Plug *that*. Be forthright. He'd recognize trickery – and
he'd be looking for it. Might well want her dead, but his
priority would be for the bombing to be called off in favour
of his own scheme, and she was the only one who *could*
call it off.

Thinking – three or four kilometres nearer le Vallées – of
one phrase in the message she'd coded up for Baker Street:

'*S*' *phone guidance if required would be from vicinity of factory.*
Asking herself *where*, in the vicinity of the factory? The best
she could think of was to put herself at the edge of the trees
almost directly opposite the *auberge*. Due west across the
school playing-field from the factory – maybe two hundred
metres from it. Moving say fifty metres out from the trees
just before zero hour to guide them in, and lying flat as the
planes passed over.

As long as the attack came in reasonably early – around
midnight, say – one could risk moving out into the open
because the moon wouldn't be up by then.

Might pace the distances out, along the road. This
evening, maybe.

'You sleeping?'

Jacques nudged her with his elbow. She'd had her head
back, eyes half shut, envisaging that scene, the release
of bombs just about as they passed over the vertically
aimed '*S*' phone beam, herself by then prone . . . She asked
Jacques, 'Moon isn't rising until well after midnight now,
am I right?'

'About one, one thirty. Why?'

'Just thinking. I wasn't asleep. How are we doing?'

'Turn-off's just along here. It's a track into the woods – a
charcoal-burner I'll be visiting. Probably leave you to wait
there a while.'

'How do charcoal-burners live?'

'This one has a hut, close to his kiln. Also has a wife in
les Vallées – and a bicycle. All he needs, eh?'

'I suppose.'

'He's pretty old.'

'I'll be safe, then.'

'Oh, I'd say so.' His smile faded as she took the Llama
out of her pocket, jerked the top round into the chamber,
thumbed the safety on and slid it back into the pocket.
Nodding: 'I think I will be.'

He'd changed down. 'Without *that*, you would be.'

'Precautionary, that's all. There *are* forest patrols still, aren't there?'

'But I have good reason to be there, and you're with *me*—'

'Might be with Maquisards by then too.' She patted his arm. 'Don't worry. It's only for – *emergency* use.'

Or self-defence. Possibly, self-defence.

He was turning left on to a forest track with trees thick on both sides and a rutted surface of hard-baked earth, drifts of forest litter. Rosie thinking that another location with the 'S' phone might be the stream at the bottom of the Rue de l'Ecole, near that bridge. There was less than a metre of water in it at the moment but its bed was deep, with high vertical banks; standing knee-deep in it, her head would be about level with the top.

Slightly off the flight-path, of course. But that could be allowed for by the navigators or bomb-aimers, whatever. Jacques was taking a right fork: still in first gear, rounding a bend that would already have put them out of sight of the road. Then much sooner than she'd expected trundling into an irregularly shaped hectare or so where trees had been felled: Jacques muttering as he pulled the brake on and switched off, 'Old fellow's name's Guy Trainel. Sit tight while I have a word? There – speak of the devil . . .'

Emerging from what might have been a chicken-shed – a slow-moving, scrawny figure with white hair and beard; he'd propped an axe against the shed's door. On the far side of the clearing the charcoal kiln looked as if it was steaming, more than smoking. The first she'd ever seen: circular, and built of – large stones, it looked like. The old man had started over to meet Jacques, and they were shaking hands: an arm waving towards the far side then, up-slope. Jacques coming back now.

'Best if you'd wait here, Justine. He's a decent old cove,

don't shoot him. I'll be back as quick as I can. Guichard *is* around, he says. Look – any problem, a patrol for instance – keep that thing out of sight?' The pistol, he meant. 'You just came along to see the countryside – I'm conducting my normal business. It's a fact, I *am*.'

'Where will you have gone?'

'Play shy, you don't like to mention it. Why *would* a man go into the trees alone?'

'You'll be only a few minutes, then?'

'Ten – twenty?'

When he'd gone – and the old man had retreated into his hut – she went into the trees herself. Woodsmoke hung like fog. It was oven-hot, with no breeze at all. Sunlight glittered through the branches overhead – the trees were beeches. She came back, climbed into the pick-up and lit a cigarette, but hadn't had more than a few draws at it before seeing movement up-slope, on the clearing's far side. More than *one* man coming . . . She stubbed out the cigarette: reached down to push the transceiver further back under her seat. Pistol – where it was. But that was Jacques, all right: and a taller, bearded man in some kind of smock, old army uniform trousers and a Sten-gun under his arm, slung from the shoulder. The third man had been a few paces behind them, so that she only saw him as the group came into the open, close to the smoking kiln. He was bearded, too. From this distance anyway she wouldn't have thought she'd ever set eyes on him before: but – he was about Jacques' height, and dark, it *could* be . . . They'd paused, looking around the clearing, now were coming on again – Jacques calling to the old man in the hut: 'Hey – Guy?' Rosie pushed the *gazo* door open and got out. At the same time Trainel came out, and Jacques and the tall man were talking to him. Laughing . . . The other one – who might or might not be 'Hector', for God's sake – on his own and staring *this* way.

Coming this way. Wearing dungarees over a khaki-green shirt. Rosie started towards Jacques – the one she knew, *would* head for. To be natural was the thing: despite a sudden tightness in the gut . . . When the time came, show surprise, not shock. With that beard one *wouldn't* recognize him. Mightn't be him anyway . . . Jacques had looked round and seen her, raised a hand; she responded similarly. The tall one with the Sten was obviously Guichard. She'd take Jacques' word for it that he was only about thirty-five; would have guessed he was older. The beard would put a few years on him, no doubt: it was brown, untrimmed, patriarchal. Whereas André's – if that *was* him, what she'd seen this far didn't match the image she'd been carrying in her memory – *his* beard was jet-black and trimmed short around the jawline.

'Justine.' Jacques jerked a thumb. 'Emile Guichard – the man I was telling you about?'

'Justine Quérier.' She shook his hand: it felt more like a lumberjack's than a lawyer's. 'Has Jacques told you what I'm here for?'

'He has, Mam'selle.' He looked younger, when he smiled. Grey eyes wide apart, very light-coloured in contrast to darkly tanned skin. Reminiscent of Michel's friend Luc . . . Hair receding: a lot of sunburnt forehead anyway. He'd nodded towards the other one. 'André Marchéval.'

'Oh.' Turning to him. 'I met your father this morning.'

Staring: and coming closer . . .

'It's not *possible* . . .'

The voice, all right. And the swarthy look. He'd stopped at a range of about two metres: hands on his hips, leaning slightly forward, dark eyes narrowed in concentration. So much for padded cheeks . . . Shaking his head: 'God almighty, I don't *believe* this!'

'What's up?'

From Jacques, that. Guichard watching and looking

puzzled. Rosie had glanced round at them – in surprise, as if inviting help or explanation – before looking back at this – André . . . 'Have we met before, or—'

'Not so long ago, either.' He touched his beard. 'I didn't have this – but—'

'Your father told me you were in SOE – as Jacques will have told you *I* am—'

'Code-name Zoé?'

That stopped her. Staring at him . . . Admitting then, 'It was, at one stage. But I still don't—' Eyes widening: 'Oh, *Christ* . . .'

'We were both prisoners of the Gestapo. First time we met was in a hospital in Brittany. You'd been in a car smash, they told me.'

'I remember *someone* at Morlaix . . .'

Jacques shifting, glancing round as Trainel shuffled off towards his kiln, muttering to himself. André was saying – to her, but with an eye on the others too – 'You were claiming to have no memory. Made no odds, they identified you from a photograph. You had a record of the kind those people least appreciate – you'd killed one of them?'

'Not one of *them*. He was SS – or SD.'

Guichard clapping: 'Bravo, in either case!'

Rosie pointing at André: 'What I do remember – if that *was* you—'

'Well – I just *told* you—'

'I'm amazed you should have. If you hadn't I wouldn't have known you – the beard I suppose – but—'

She'd checked herself: glancing round at the others as if she'd been about to say something, but had second thoughts on *their* account. The Llama's steel was warm in her damp palm: she'd hardly realized she'd been clutching it. Withdrawing that hand from her pocket – aware of Jacques' close observation . . . 'As I said, your father told me you were in SOE – but the name meant nothing.'

'I did introduce myself – at Morlaix.'

'Did you? I've no such recollection. When I was briefed to come here, even, the name Marchéval rang no bells . . . I'd have known you by your code-name, anyway. Air Movements Officer, your father said. Would it have been "Hector"?'

'Right!'

'But in Morlaix I'd no idea . . . And not even the second time, in Paris – in Rue des Saussaies?'

'You were in a bad way, weren't you?'

'They whipped me, you know – shortly after you were sent out of the room. Yes – you *must* have known.'

'*Known*, but—'

'Did they tell you that after that – and a few more jolly days in the Fresnes gaol – I was consigned to Ravensbrück?'

Shock in his face – quite well acted, she thought – and a growl of surprise from Guichard. She looked round at him: 'I'm sorry – not what we're here for, is it. But meeting this – person – the coincidence—'

'Ravensbrück. How—'

'The train was stopped – the line had been blown up ahead of it – and I escaped. Didn't they tell you?'

'Tell *me*?'

She shrugged. 'They might have. Anyway – Monsieur Guichard—'

'Emile, please.'

'Emile. Wasting time, aren't we? Should get on with it?'

'Yes, we should. If you don't mind . . . But let's also sit. I'm going to anyway. We call you Justine, that right?'

'Yes, absolutely.' She sat down too. André squatting on her left, the other two *en face*.

Guichard accepted one of her cigarettes: 'Very kind. We're all scroungers here, we have to be.' Jacques was filling his pipe; Rosie offered André a Gauloise too, but he declined it.

She said, 'The coincidence, I suppose, is simply that you should be the son of Henri Marchéval.'

'Which is no surprise to *me*, of course.' He added, 'To me the surprise is that SOE should be taking this interest in my father's business just at the time *I* come on the scene.'

'Because SOE only just heard about the tubes. Casings.' She looked back at Guichard. 'Sorry, again. After all that, I'll kick off, shall I? Although all I know of the sabotage idea is what I heard this morning from André's father – to whom Colette Craillot introduced me. He said he'd agreed to co-operate.' She glanced at André: 'A matter of providing keys?'

'Yes. It's the only reason for bringing him into it. There are three sets of keys – his, the Boche engineer's and the works manager's. He – Gaspard Legrand – isn't to be relied on, so it has to be my father's set – getting them back to him quick so he can swear they weren't ever out of his possession. The importance of having keys is that we shouldn't have to *break* in – the essence of it should be speed and silence – uh?'

Guichard: 'Why not borrow the keys and get a spare set made?'

'Not possible in the time – unless they were made in the factory itself, which might not be a good idea – sharp eyes, informers, so forth.'

'In any case that's detail.' Guichard looked at Rosie. 'A more basic issue is that you're supposed to be making arrangements for bombing by the RAF. What's the position on that now?'

'*My* position is I was sent here to check on a report that the tubes are casings for V2 rockets, confirmation of it to be followed by an air attack in sufficient strength to destroy the factory. And I *have* confirmed it. As a matter of interest, we'd been told that sabotage on the ground was out of the question, for reasons including the likelihood of Boche reprisals. So bombing seemed the only way, and – that's it, it's in London's hands now.'

'You mean –' Guichard's grey eyes on hers – 'it could happen at any time?'

'Should happen *soon*, because of the completed casings – which London knows about of course, including the fact that transport might come for them at any moment. But it won't happen without my being told. Might hear tonight it's laid on for tomorrow night, for instance.'

'Sooner than *we* could act.'

Guichard had shrugged, glancing at André. Jacques asked him, 'Does that mean you *would* do it – if the bombing was called off, maybe?'

'One point.' André again . . . 'As far as machinery is concerned there's only one would need to be put out of action – the very large plate-bending machine we installed last November.' He looked at Jacques: 'Came in bits in separate trucks, remember?'

Rosie cut in, asking Guichard, 'I suppose you have PE, detonators, time-fuses – or Bickford's—'

'All we need, yes. Thanks to your people.'

'Specifically thanks to Joseph Lambert?'

She saw André's reaction to that name: his eyes flickering to meet hers. She thought Lambert was almost certainly dead by now; and that he – André – must know it. She wondered again about the pretty wife . . . Guichard had nodded: 'D'you know Lambert?'

'Know *of* him. Or *knew* . . . But listen – couldn't it *possibly* be done tomorrow night?'

'Unfortunately not. It so happens my two explosives experts are helping out elsewhere. It would take – well, thirty-six hours to get one of them back, and *then*—'

'Emile.' André interrupted: 'I'm fully competent with explosives.' A gesture towards Rosie: 'So would she be.'

She nodded. 'He's right – we learn it at our mothers'

knees. So if that was the only thing bothering you . . . Look
– Emile – as things are, the air attack *will* be launched –
tomorrow or at latest the night after, I'd guess. Everything
to do with the V2 is high priority, they won't be dawdling.
All right, poor workers' houses, all that, but those workers
have been churning the things out quite happily for months
now and there'll be thousands of people in England killed
by them – once it starts. We're talking about only a tiny frac-
tion of it here, obviously, but even the smallest reduction's
something. A few *hundred* lives, say? Well – I'm not asking
London to delay, let alone cancel, before I know for certain
you're ready to move.' Holding Guichard's thoughtful
gaze: she shook her head. 'It's not blackmail, Emile, it's simple fact – St Valéry might be wiped out tomorrow night.'

She was leaning against the pick-up, had just lit a cigarette.
Guichard, Jacques and André prowling around the clearing.
Guichard between the other two and talking volubly –
about his plans for taking over St Valéry, she'd gathered,
how jumping the gun with a sabotage operation possibly
resulting in reprisals might affect it, et cetera.

André was leaving them, though: coming over here.

Watching him come, she was conscious of the weight
of the pistol dragging on that side of her jacket. Putting
a hand down to swing it back behind her hip: fishing out
the crumpled Gauloise pack then, offering him one as he
stopped in front of her.

He shook his head. 'Thanks, no.'

'Don't smoke at all?'

'Used to. In Gestapo custody I got used to doing without.
Want to talk about all that now?'

'If you like.' Taking a long drag: needing it. 'I think you
can guess what *I* have to say. In a nutshell, that in Morlaix
– and Paris even more so – you weren't a fellow prisoner,
you were working for the Gestapo.'

'No – I was not. I was – having to let *them* think I was. It doesn't surprise me you'd have jumped to that same conclusion, but – truly, it's not so. May I ask why you didn't accuse me in the others' hearing?'

'Because I'm here with a job to do and I don't want complications. Secondly, I'd have to prove it – and these people know you, don't know me. *They* accept you're playing straight, and obviously they need you in on this job. I'd like to sort the rest of it out with you, certainly, but—'

'May I explain – just between ourselves – some background to it?'

She shrugged, exhaling. Trainel had just dumped a sack of charcoal in the pick-up and shambled off without even glancing at them. André told her, 'I had no option but to *pretend* to play their game. To start with they'd arrested my sister – she'd been helping in an escape line, and to my huge regret – in fact *shame* – she was doing something to help *me* out when they caught her. My father doesn't know this, and I daren't tell him . . . Anyway – subsequently they promised me she'd be held in an ordinary prison, nothing worse, as long as I – yes, collaborated. Because in my job with SOE they assumed I'd have direct contacts with *réseaux* all over France. But listen – this is where it becomes a little complicated – almost right up to the time of my arrest I didn't think they knew I had anything to do with SOE. I truly and absolutely did not. Whereas in fact they were on to me – I still don't know exactly how, where or when—'

'So it was solely because of the threat to your sister—'

'*Almost* because of that alone. But the business of SOE – which of course is all that concerns *you* – so happened I never did have all that many contacts in the field. I did have frequent communication with Baker Street, of course – using pianists of several *réseaux* around the Paris area –

whom I may say I was later able to warn, enabling them to disappear – at least I *hope*—'

'And names and addresses of *résistants* handling arrivals and departures on the various fields?'

'Oh, yes.' A grimace . . . 'And before my arrest – as I'd only just begun to realize – with utter horror, I may say – *at that time* – most of the time I was being tailed – and so would – well, quite a number of agents, from the point of arrival onward. They'd have been followed to their *réseaux*. It's a terrible thing to *know*, let alone admit – believe me I'm not saying it lightly. I have to face up to it, that's all – my fault, my colossal – well, *stupidity*—'

'Looking like – something much worse?'

He looked away across the clearing, to where Guichard and Jacques were still in conversation. Shaking his head . . .

'I'm only too well aware –' meeting her eyes again – 'that from an outside viewpoint – from the distance of London, for instance – it might – as you say . . . The *truth* is that I only caught on to what was happening after – well, quite some time. Then I was trying frantically to get warnings to certain others – right up to the last minute. Of course I had a good idea of the danger I was in myself, in fact I'd arranged a flight out by Lysander – not just to save my own skin, but in full awareness that – well, a red-hot skewer applied to a man's eyeball, for instance—'

'Wasn't it London's initiative – to bring you back for de-briefing?'

'That probably was *their* view of it. But—'

She could have ripped into him at that point, drawn blood. There was a risk in *not* doing so, in fact – that he might realize in retrospect if not immediately that she could have, and wonder why she'd been holding back. The answer to which *might* be obvious . . . Dark eyes on hers, watching for belief or disbelief; telling her, 'They arrested me on the afternoon of the day I was supposed to be picked up by Lysander. That very night I would have been at the Soucelles field . . .'

Her cue *then*, if ever there'd been one. She told him – interrupting some detail about the timing of his arrest – 'You'd have been at Soucelles to meet *me*. Bringing me a return rail ticket to Rennes via Le Mans – oh, and a *consigne* ticket for a parcel I was to collect there – at Le Mans. But you weren't at the field, so—'

'Christ – *you*—'

'You didn't know?'

'Know what? Look – I had the tickets and the *consigne* receipt on me when I was arrested! But – *you*—'

'You didn't know the agent you'd be meeting at Soucelles was code-named "Zoé"?'

'I'd been given no name at all. But those rail tickets and the *consigne* slip – I can tell you I was in despair!'

'Fortunately I went by bike instead of train. They'd have had the Le Mans *consigne* staked out, wouldn't they? And I'd have walked into it. Getting through Rennes wasn't without its dangers either. Did you know of a *réseau* that was based in Rennes?'

'I don't *think* so . . .'

'Or of an individual by name of Alain Noally?'

'The sculptor?'

'Also *chef de réseau*. That's to say he *was*.' She let it go: Noally had told her that night that he'd never had any direct contact with 'Hector', and although there was a logical progression of events which she and Lise had worked out, it would have been more easily deniable than provable. 'Hector' shaking his head: 'You went all that way by bike . . .'

'In foul weather, too. And a lot further – long way west of Rennes. But a few weeks later – car crash, hospital in Morlaix.'

'And now, *here*.'

'All one sequence, isn't it – except for it turning out to be your father's factory we're concerned with. That's coincidence, all right – even if it's basically inconsequential. Listen – getting back to that day in Paris – before I even knew you *had* a father – this is *fact*, my memory's quite clear – in that upstairs room in Rue des Saussaies I was strapped to a chair – remember? – waiting to be interrogated, and you tried to persuade me to tell them all they wanted to know? It would have been mainly names and whereabouts of other agents. *More* victims. Meanwhile you were walking around – free, no guards or—'

'Just eyes on every move, ears on every word! Free? D'you imagine I could've walked out into the street?'

'You tried to persuade me that the V1s had England on the point of suing for peace, Allied armies in Normandy were bogged down and about to be driven back into the sea, there was no hope at all for us, I might as well give up, tell them every damn thing I knew!'

'Justine – they had tape-machines in all those rooms. All right – I was doing what I was told – I'm not proud of it—'

'Briefed you on the prisoner's background before each softening-up exercise, did they?'

'I was – rehearsed, you might say, yes. But—'

'*But?*' She laughed, incredulously. 'What do we get now – mitigating circumstances?'

'Justine – you're interrogator, judge and jury, evidently—'

'Perhaps it's as well for you that I'm nothing of the sort. But a number of agents were arrested at that time – as you'd know, of course – and one lot – women – were *en route* to Ravensbrück with me on that same train – and did *not* escape. I remember each one of them quite clearly – I can shut my eyes and – *see* them. I do have – an *interest*, you might say . . . Tell me – when you were arrested, did they knock you about, torture you at all?'

'The answer to what you're really asking is that I told them nothing they didn't already know. They – made *use* of me – in the ways you saw, and in which I was as unhelpful as I could be – but – if it means anything to you at all, my sister's life was still at stake, remember—'

'All right – not much left to say about Rue des Saussaies, is there – let's talk about your sister. You don't mind?'

'I'd like to convince you that – well, you think I was turned, but a better word would be *trapped*. I admit, by my own blundering, but—'

'They told you just recently your sister had been sent east, but there's a chance – your father said – she might not have been?'

Staring at her: then a deep breath, a shrug . . . 'All right. *That* now. Yes – it's a straw to clutch at. He *did* clutch at it. Needs to – she was always his favourite . . . It was a Gestapo major, man called Hammerling – lost his temper. I'd referred to the expectation they'll soon be driven out of France – I was suggesting they might release me *and* Claire right away – and he blew up, screamed at me that I'd be shipped out too, or shot. So – I don't know . . . But I escaped later that same day – it wasn't at all difficult, I simply saw the opportunity, and – I was *out*.'

Hammerling was the Gestapo major who'd questioned her in the Morlaix hospital, she remembered. She could easily visualize that fit of temper. In the hospital he'd had her manacled to her bed.

'You said it was your fault Clare was arrested?'

'Yes. Another – confession . . . She had an apartment in Fontainebleau. She worked at the factory but went back there most nights and always for weekends. On the side, she helped in an escape line that specialized in shot-down airmen. It happened I had two people – a married couple, local employees of a *réseau* in Neuilly, for whom I needed a safe-house for two nights, and I asked her if she'd put them

up. I was to fetch them then and take them to a certain field
we were using near Pithiviers – you see, Fontainebleau was
in the right direction. Well – they may have been followed to
her flat. I'd sent them on their own, simply given them the
address. Possibly they were arrested on the way there and
had the address on them. Whatever – I'd told them I'd be
fetching them on a certain evening – I went along, rang the
bell, and what opened the door was a young Boche. Gestapo
– and two more of them inside, both Frenchmen.'

'But they let you go free – and held Claire hostage?'

'As I was given to understand it then, it was to put
pressure on my father. They told me to go down to St
Valéry and spell it out to him. She'd be all right as long
as he continued to co-operate – keep the work-force in
order and hard at it, and neither ask nor answer questions
– so forth.'

'And what were you to do?'

'Continue as his Paris representative. You see, I truly
thought they didn't know I was SOE, at that stage. Their
questions were all about the escape line – Claire's – actually
not *hers*, but the one she helped with from time to time.
They seemed to take it for granted that I'd been as much
involved in it as she had. But they planted it in my mind
quite adroitly—'

'Planted what?'

'Well – the way I saw it was that they were delighted to
have caught me out – caught *us* out – to have something
over my father, ensure *he* stayed in line. There was no
mention of SOE, none at all. They hadn't caught a sniff of
it, I thought. Made me feel good, actually – running rings
round them, you know?'

'Did you think your father *needed* to have any threat
hanging over him?'

'No, to tell the truth, I thought – using a sledge-hammer
to crack a nut, maybe. On the other hand the importance

of security around the rocket-casing business must have seemed to *them*—'

'Yes. I dare say . . . Did you tell them where you'd have taken that couple, from Claire's apartment?'

'No. I've *never* been an informer, Justine. There was a field we weren't using any more – we'd given it up because I'd thought it might have been compromised – and I mentioned that one. Here's our friend again . . .'

Guy Trainel, with another sack of charcoal; there were several already in the pick-up. The old man was sweating, grunting as he swung the sack up and dumped it in.

Turning to them, this time: 'And that's the lot!'

'Hard graft, eh?'

A snort: *'Used* not to be . . .'

Shuffling off. André told Rosie, 'They'd left me on the loose. I realized later, to have me followed. Every time I went out of Paris, or for instance met some colleague – who might have been a pianist or a courier. I had to make contact with them every few days, and I'd sworn to let them know immediately if I was called on to handle others on the run. In fact of course that didn't happen. I'd told them I didn't think it would – with my sister arrested, and that pair disappeared, sensible people *would* stay clear.'

'You didn't know anything about others involved?'

'No. A voice on a telephone would be all. And for cover generally I had a full social life – my work for Marchéval's wasn't exactly arduous. I mixed with – you know, all sorts of—'

'You mean you had girlfriends.'

'Well – of course. Actually what I'm saying is I *thought* I had adequate cover, for my work for Baker Street. And as I was on my father's payroll, and he was working for the blasted *Reich*, it didn't surprise me to be left to get on with it . . . D'you see?'

She nodded. She'd been thinking of asking him – in

reference to girlfriends – about Huguette Lambert. The chance had gone now – maybe just as well . . . Nodding: 'Yes. Oddly enough, I do.'

'They were clever, the way they induced me to think along those lines – that I was getting away with it, had them fooled – while in fact all the time – God, every step I took – every word on a telephone . . . Then when I did begin to catch on – arrest. D'you see?' Glancing round: 'Seems we're on the move. But they arrested me, you see, because they'd *realized* I'd finally got wise to it!'

Emile Guichard was coming over – leaving Jacques at the hut settling his business with Trainel. Rosie asked, 'One thing, quickly. Why haven't you contacted Baker Street, since escaping?'

'How do you know I haven't?'

'Wouldn't be *here*—'

'Any case – one, no way to do it – not safely. No contact I'd had before could possibly be safe. I know, I know, as bad as *that*. But also, my father's situation – I had to see him. *And* – the whole thing's on the brink, there isn't *time* to – observe formalities, is there. Later, *sure* I'll—'

He broke off, nodded to Guichard. 'Decided?'

'Yes. You get your way. Tomorrow night, and we'll finalize plans between now and then. Justine, it has to be our own plan – André knows the place inside-out, and they'll be my men with him – but you'll want to be in on it, won't you?'

She nodded. 'Mainly so I can send London a first-hand report. But also if you want help with the fireworks—'

'Exactly. And Jacques knows where and when, he'll bring you. Meanwhile, tell your people to lay off?'

Chapter 15

The alarm-clock went off under the bedclothes at five to twelve, and her waking thought was that in twenty-four hours exactly she'd be with the Maquisards, starting off from the timber-yard where Jacques would be taking her at, or by, eleven. No sleep at all, she guessed, tomorrow night. Out of bed by this time, with the curtains pulled shut and the light on, paying out aerial wire. Transceiver now: plugged into the mains and switched to 'receive'. Headset on. She'd fitted the night-time crystal before she'd gone to bed.

Waiting, then; virtually certain they'd have something for her.

She'd added to the message she'd transmitted this afternoon, *Postscript, having conferred with Tamerlan and Hector. Sabotage of one crucial machine and all completed casings still on site is scheduled for night of Wednesday/Thursday. Suggest Jupiter be postponed pending my further report. Will not repeat not be in position to listen out that night. Hector has plausible but flawed explanations of past events and I will try to induce him to submit to de-briefing in UK later.*

Fat chance of that, she thought. Although he'd begun to say he would – then cut himself short, conveniently. But – to put it on the record as one's intention, was all. Marilyn would understand this, and if necessary explain it to Buck.

The message had gone off at about seven; she'd drafted and then encoded the PS in Jacques' *gazo* in the clearing before they'd started back. Guichard and André had left by then, and the old man had been stoking up his kiln; in the *gazo*'s cab the loudest sound apart from her own breathing had been the bubbling of Jacques' pipe. She hadn't intended transmitting from the clearing; he'd had some other spot in mind, which had meant taking a slightly longer route home.

Nothing yet, from Sevenoaks. One minute past midnight. Wednesday, now. One week since de Plesse had driven her to Nancy and she'd dumped herself and the cat on Guillaume. It felt more like a month.

Jacques had commented, when she'd put her enciphering material away and they'd been starting off, 'You and André had plenty to gas about?'

She'd been lighting a cigarette, she remembered: flicking the match away and waving goodbye to Trainel, that comment meanwhile triggering an inclination to tell him *what* they'd talked about; but she'd suppressed it, told him instead: 'SOE business. Putting loose ends together, that's all.'

'I got the feeling you didn't like him and he knew it.'

Exhaling a plume of smoke . . . 'You're astute as well as observant, Jacques. But oddly enough I rather thought you didn't either. Like him, I mean.'

'Well.' A smile. 'Wouldn't admit to it *en famille*, you understand.'

'Colette's fond of him, you mean.'

'I told you about Joe Lambert – and his wife. André used to make sheep's eyes at Colette, too, but—'

'Wouldn't have got him anywhere. No, you said.'

'But to her, the *seigneur*'s son – romantic young spark, you know . . . All I thought of *that* was what a young fool he was. With Huguette it was different. She was a smasher, absolutely, and barely thirty – about André's age – while Joe was twenty years older – and as decent a man as you'd ever meet.'

'You said you thought she'd have been arrested as well as her husband. Do you have any reason to believe it?'

'No. I don't even know where or when they bagged *him* – just that he – you know, didn't turn up again. But they tend to make a clean sweep, don't they – and use the threat to one of them to make the other talk, eh? One's heard of it . . . Physical threat to the beautiful young wife with the tormented husband looking on, for example. Doesn't bear thinking about, does it?'

'But only supposition . . .'

It stirred the other supposition too, though – that Lambert might have been sold out by the man who'd originally recruited him. She'd been tempted to float that with Jacques: in the same breath giving him some insight into her view of André, with the underlying purpose of having him firmly on her side in any awkward situations that might arise in that area. Since this *was* very much André's home ground, his supporters including *le patron* and virtually the whole village – including Colette – and now one might guess Emile Guichard and others.

She liked Jacques; and sensed that the liking was reciprocated. He had the same kind of integrity, her instincts told her, that she'd found and respected in an agent code-named 'Romeo' – in Rouen, more than a year ago. A Mauritian, whom she'd seen shot dead in the glare of floodlights. But the reason she'd restrained herself from giving Jacques any of that background – 'Hector''s – was that it was private SOE business – especially *now* – and if André happened to come to grief at some point and she happened to be anywhere near at the time . . .

Marilyn's advice or warning, in that van on the Xanadu field: her emphatic '*Extreme* discretion, Rosie . . .'

High-pitched Morse in the earphones: Sevenoaks on the air, having given her a few minutes' grace, perhaps deliberately; she mightn't have been ready right on the minute . . . Left hand adjusting volume, the other with a pencil poised then moving swiftly, jotting down the letters as they came bleeping in. Not a lot of them – it was a much shorter message than she'd sent *them*. She'd got it all – end of message, and the operator over there signing off. Rosie switched off too, slid the headset off, took out the night-time crystal and then pulled in the aerial, coiling the thin wire on the card as it came in. Transceiver back under the bed then: and now the paperwork, translation of cipher into plain text.

Your second message received and understood. Jupiter cancelled, repeat Jupiter cancelled. Maquis action heartily endorsed, but extreme caution is urged in respect of Hector.

Extreme discretion, now extreme caution. Leaving one in little doubt as to who'd drafted that message. Smiling to herself, hearing Marilyn's slightly authoritarian tone of voice in the night's surrounding silence. Light off: curtains and window open: back into bed – and glad to be there – but in her mind suddenly, in reference to that advice, whether in the confrontation in the forest this afternoon she should have been more cautious than she had been.

Except that he'd have seen through it. All right, the stuff about the sister's arrest and André being conned into thinking it was only his involvement with the escape line they'd been on to – that had had a ring of truth to it – which she'd acknowledged and actually had believed. Although thinking about it again now, she wondered if he could have gone on being fooled for the best part of three months thereafter. He wasn't a *stupid* man. And wouldn't he have known about at least some of the arrests that had been made during that time, and linked them to his own movements or dispositions? Seeing that even Baker Street had known of them – Baker Street notably in the person of Bob Hallowell, who moreover must have had exchanges with 'Hector' about those disasters and the allegations which by then were being made against him. By Joseph Lambert? Countered by 'Hector' with his own artfully shamefaced admission of having seduced this fellow agent's girlfriend (calculated to seem more innocuous than 'wife'), said agent then making these allegations out of nothing but malicious jealousy, but ending up paying with his life – maybe also his young wife's – for having told Baker Street the truth?

In the clearing, anyway, she'd swallowed André's version of the story. Which had been the best thing to do, she thought. Indicative of readiness to believe, absence of prejudice. In contrast to which she'd been forthright – hostile – in areas where anyone who'd been at the receiving end of it – in Rue des Saussaies, especially – *would* have felt she had a score to settle.

Maybe, she thought, should have pressed it harder. For instance, his having fed her the stuff about armies bogged down and doodlebugs devastating England, and his explanation that everything he'd said was being recorded – she hadn't asked him whether he couldn't have signalled to her that it was cock-and-bull and he was acting under duress. Even just winked, or made faces. They'd been alone in the room, he surely *could* have. Or – re the period after Claire's arrest when he'd thought he was 'running rings around them' and feeling good about it: even if he *had* been fooling them, he most certainly should have told Baker Street what was going on. It would have ended there and then, they'd have pulled him out and a number of agents' lives would have been saved. She hadn't raised this – there and then, shamingly, she hadn't seen it – but it was certainly a key factor. In Baker Street's judgement, would be enough to finish him. That alone . . . All in all, the adjective 'specious' might have been more appropriate than 'plausible', in the postscript to her message.

Time to stop thinking, get back to sleep. Busy day tomorrow: busy night, for sure. She didn't know what part she'd be playing, only that they'd be meeting in the timber-yard behind the church and the Hôtel Poste at eleven. It would be dark by then, and curfew started at ten, but Jacques had said he'd get her there. She pulled the bedclothes up higher, shut her eyes. Trying to doze off, letting her thoughts drift without direction, but instead of counting sheep visualizing black-painted aircraft touching down by moonlight on remote pastures, dropping off agents who were then followed to towns and cities where they, and whoever they contacted, would be arrested – or marked down for arrest after some period of observation and identification of other contacts. She was awake, *wide* awake, staring into darkness and hearing André's voice in the clearing a few hours earlier: *You're interrogator, judge and jury, evidently . . .*

There was fourth role he hadn't mentioned.

Jacques' intention had been to catch Monsieur Henri on his way by in the morning, to make arrangements about the keys, but while they were breakfasting the telephone rang, Colette went to answer it, and Jacques murmured to Rosie, *'Le patron* – I bet you. Ants in his pants.'

'If so, it'll be the second time—'

'Bet you. It's how he is.' Nodding towards the sound of Colette hanging up the phone and now returning: 'See if I'm wrong now.'

'Monsieur Henri—'

'Huh!'

'He says the Briard woman hasn't been into his end of the house since our *fracas* with her yesterday. He'd like after all to come to some arrangement with you, Justine. I said

I thought Jacques might take you along before Monsieur
Henri leaves for work – since you want to see him anyway,
Jacques.'

Checking the time . . . 'Yes. All right.'

'Why don't I go on my own?' Rosie had just about
finished. 'Borrow Yvette's bike again? I could ask him
about bringing the keys this evening – anything else?'

'The keys, yes – but not *ask*, tell him he mustn't fail
us. Other than that, all he needs to know is we're doing
it tonight. Oh, and tell him I've been thinking how to
get the keys back to him, we'll talk about it when he
brings them.'

'Might collect them from us here on his way by in the
morning?'

'Wouldn't care to rely on it. The village may be full of
Boches by then. Don't know *what* the state of affairs may
be. If he couldn't get here, and didn't have his keys—'

'He'd have problems.'

'Might have, mightn't he? But one other thing – ask him
how many semi-completed casings – remember, we spoke
of that?'

Monsieur Henri showed her into the *petit salon*.

'I'd expected Jacques would come with you.' He'd shut
the door.

'But if it's to discuss the possibility of my employment—'

'Frankly –' he was close to her, and speaking quietly –
Rosie wondering, walls having ears? – 'Frankly, I wanted
to hear from him what's going on.'

'We guessed as much. But I can tell you anyway.' If the
place *was* wired for sound, they'd have had an earful at
this time the day before, she was thinking – and she'd
have been on her way elsewhere, most likely in chains
again. She told him, 'Jacques and I met your son and

Emile Guichard yesterday, and – well, it's going to happen tonight.'

'*Tonight* . . . Oh, forgive me – sit down?'

'No, thank you. In any case, if I'm to be your *bonne à tout faire*—'

'*What*'s happening tonight?'

'Sabotage of the large plate-bending machine and all completed or near-completed casings. Incidentally, you said sixteen completed ones, and two more nearing completion – how many others?'

'Perhaps another three.' He was not much more than whispering now. 'But in this case, the bombing with which you were threatening us—'

'Postponed. Could be laid on again if tonight's operation was a failure, of course. And Jacques wanted me to say it's vital that you should leave your factory keys with us on your way home this evening. You'll do that, will you?'

'Say between seven thirty and eight?'

'Fine—'

'When will I get them back?'

'I was going to say, Jacques will talk about that when you bring them.'

'I might call in on my way by in the morning.'

'I thought that, but Jacques pointed out that the place might be swarming with Boches. The factory won't be working anyway – surely . . . But – this evening, talk about it.'

'What time will they be doing it?'

'Well – another point of Jacques' is that the less *you* know about it, the better.'

'All right.' Large, scared eyes shifting away: a murmur of 'He has his head screwed on tight, does Jacques . . .' The eyes back on her then: 'You met my son, eh?'

'And Emile Guichard. But yes – and André and I *have* met before. On two previous occasions. I didn't know his real name, that's all.'

'You knew each other on sight, eh?'

'He knew me. I might have recognized him if he hadn't grown a beard.' She checked the time by Marilyn's watch. 'M'sieur – as a reason for having visited you twice, maybe we *could* come to some understanding about my working for you? Whether or not you really want it—'

'*You* want to, evidently?'

'As I say, for a cover.' (Not to mention continued contact with the Marchéval family, irrespective of what transpired tonight.) 'Entirely valid and believable, if Madame Briard's not coming to you now?'

'Well – nothing's been said, one can only *assume*—'

'You do need *some* help, don't you? Say we've agreed on two hours a day Mondays to Fridays – and Colette will discuss my remuneration. That's something you should know – I'm not all that quick, in my mind. I was hurt in an air-raid on Rouen – it was when I got these scars. I know, you hardly see them now, but—'

'Colette did say something about this, as it happens.'

'Well – fine. It's only – you know, if you were asked about me. After the action tonight there could be a *lot* of questions asked.'

'My domestic arrangements hardly—'

'It could be *me* they were interested in – more than your arrangements. And if you were asked what you were calling at the *auberge* for this evening, it would have been to discuss it with Colette. Your cover *and* mine.'

'Do I take it you'll actually come and work here?'

'Probably – for a while. But you'll have your whole house back before long, one might hope. What about your wife – when the Boches are sent packing will she come back, d'you expect?'

Blinking at her . . . 'You know about my wife?'

'Only that she's in Scotland. Colette mentioned it. Anyway, M'sieur – depending on how things are, I might start work tomorrow. Unless as Jacques predicts getting around is difficult – in which case—'

'Did you get on well with my son?'

He was on his way to the door, and opening it for her. She shrugged an affirmative of sorts. 'Naturally we've interests in common . . .'

'Did he say anything about his sister?'

'What you told us yesterday – that the man could simply have been ranting, when he said she'd been shipped out. He seemed to think there was a reasonably good chance . . . M'sieur – between seven thirty and eight: we'll be waiting . . .'

When she got back, Madame Brissac was washing the floor in the dining-room and Jacques was telephoning customers about charcoal. Colette – in the kitchen – told her there'd been a call from the *gendarmerie*.

'About you, Justine.'

'*What* about me?'

'Sergeant Hannant – our *gendarme-chef* – wants to check your papers and have you complete an application for *carte de séjour* – and *carnet de travail* – as you mentioned yourself, I remember. Word's gone round, you see – if he doesn't look sharp he might get into hot water with his bosses. It would be as well to get it done, Justine.'

'I suppose so.'

Especially before tomorrow, she realized. When one might imagine it really *would* hit the fan. As a stranger here she'd be mad not to have the documents she needed.

Snag was, she wasn't exactly confident the ones she already had would stand up to close scrutiny.

'Justine.' Jacques – letting the door swing shut behind him. 'You're on Jean Hannant's "wanted" list, I hear. Better drop in and see him – I mean today, this morning?'

'I was thinking the same.'

'I'll give you a ride down there, if you like. I've got to get rid of some of this damn charcoal. Thanks to you, I'm over-stocked.' A hand on her arm: 'All right with Monsieur Henri for this evening?'

'Between seven thirty and eight.'

'Excellent. Look – I'll be ready to go in – fifteen minutes. That is, if you *want* a lift?'

'Moral support as far as the door?'

'Well, by all means. Better than that, I'll take you in, introduce you. The sergeant and I are fellow fishermen.' He called to Colette, who'd gone through to the larder, 'I'll be outside!'

She hadn't mentioned to the Craillots that her papers might not be up to scratch. In fact they couldn't be all *that* bad, she told herself: calming her own nerves, or trying to. They'd certainly been improved by the little man in the straw hat, the architectural draughtsman in Metz; she'd been rather pleased with them at that stage – because they'd looked good in contrast to how they'd been before, of course. There'd also been a feeling of having got away with it that far, not having had to show them even once in their earlier state. But – always a first time . . . In her bedroom, shuffling through them. Identity card – which was a forgery – and a *laissez passer* for the journey from Sarrebourg to Colmar and back. A *feuille semestrielle*, meat ration card, fish card, tobacco card, clothing card but no coupons . . . How to account for that, when one didn't have a single item of even near-new clothing?

Tear it up. Clothing coupons stolen – after the air-raid in which a house had fallen on her: might protest that other things including all her cash had been missing when she'd come to in a casualty-clearing station. Her good shoes that she'd been wearing that day too. It must have been a daylight raid – American therefore, the RAF made theirs at night . . . She was checking her appearance in the mirror behind the wash-stand: wondering about the pads in her cheeks, which hadn't stopped 'Hector' recognizing her and which she'd have liked to have been able to get rid of. Had to keep them for the time being, though – the identity card photo had been taken with them in place.

She replaced the papers, minus the clothes-ration card, in the inside pocket of her jacket. (The clothing card would have been all right, she'd realized just after tearing it up: having no money to buy clothes with, she'd have sold the coupons. Stupid – anyone in her position would have.) The 9-millimetre – Llama – was still under her mattress, and she moved it to the tin trunk in the boxroom, where other small-sized items reposed inside the roll of antique corsetry. And she'd moved the transceiver back down to Jacques' workshop before breakfast. Reviewing such arrangements at this point because one had to face the possibility of arrest, which inevitably would be followed by a search.

There was nothing incriminating in the room now, anyway. Only on her person. The silver lipstick-case on the night-table beside the bed shouldn't arouse suspicion: it had been her recently deceased mother's, the only item of any value that she'd inherited. Whereas on her person – well, the suspect papers, and – checking by feel on her way downstairs – one cyanide capsule in the corner of a handkerchief and another in the hem of her blouse.

And, of course – if one were to be stripped and searched – whip-stripes on her back, and the puckered bullet scars. Like brand-marks.

Colette was back in the kitchen, chopping up a cabbage.

'You off, then?'

'If Jacques is ready. But when I get back, if there's anything you'd like done – there *must* be—'

'Windows in the bar could do with a rub up.'

'Right. As long as I *do* get back.'

'Hah . . .'

They went up a concrete path and in through the bungalow-*gendarmerie's* front door, which was standing open. Inside, a wall had been knocked out so that the hallway and what had been the left-hand front room formed a general office with a counter dividing it from a small waiting area.

'Hey, Jean, *mon vieux!*'

The sergeant swung round from a desk behind the counter, nodded to Jacques and looked at Rosie. He was grey-haired, thickset, fiftyish. Stern-looking, but his expression had softened somewhat: 'A quick response. That's good.'

'Mam'selle Justine Quérier, Jean. She's a cousin by marriage of Colette's. Well – as you'll have heard . . . I'll see you when I get back, Justine.'

'Thanks for the lift – and the introduction.'

He lifted a hand in farewell, on his way out. Rosie took out her papers: 'You want to see these, of course.'

'Regulations, more than *want*.' He'd pushed himself up, came to face her across the counter. 'But *you'll* want – if you're intending to remain here with us – a permit to reside here, and also if you're taking up employment—'

'At the manor, I hope. It's agreed for a trial period anyway – I saw Monsieur Marchéval this morning.'

'So I've been advised. Here, now. While I take a look at these.'

He put two different application forms on the counter, and tossed her papers over to his desk. When she'd filled in the forms, she guessed, he'd check her answers to the various questions against what he had there. For instance, place of birth Sarrebourg, date of birth November 13th 1917, father's name Joseph Quérier, father's occupation post-office clerk – mother's name – et cetera.

'Excuse me—'

'Huh?'

'It's stupid of me, but – nothing to write with—'

He grunted, half rising and reaching to give her a pen – wooden, with a steel nib. Pointing at an inkwell at the wall end of the counter.

'Thank you very much.'

Marilyn, she remembered, had checked through her papers the other night and said she wasn't too happy with them – after a very cursory inspection and at that by candle-light. It had probably been then that Rosie herself had begun to feel they weren't too safe. Then again *chez* Victor Dufay . . .

She'd answered all the questions in the residence application. Signing it: in the Quérier girl's unformed hand – which of course she'd practised – then glancing up, seeing the sergeant holding her *feuille semestrielle* against the light from the window, peering at it closely with his eyes narrowed.

That date had been altered. She remembered watching the little man do it.

Heart thumping harder, faster . . . She pushed the completed form over to that side of the counter, started on the other. Similar questions, most in fact identical, but others demanding details of previous employment. The only job she'd had since being hospitalized after the air-raid in Rouen, of course, had been looking after her terminally ill mother. Before that, assistant in nursery schools in Rouen and before that Sarrebourg.

Heavy footsteps were approaching, clomping up the concrete path. She took no notice, concentrating on the form, but the sergeant glanced towards the door and then after a moment's hesitation added the *feuille semestrielle* to the small pile of those he'd already checked. Pushing his chair back now, getting up.

'Good morning, *Herr Leutnant!*'

Rosie looked round, saw the young German of whom she'd previously seen only the back view: long booted

legs and bat-ears. Seeing now broad shoulders, impressive
height and a round, boyish face. He was ignoring her: asking the sergeant in heavily accented French, 'Is everything
in order?'

'It is, sir. In good order.'

Staring at *her* now . . . The sergeant told him, 'Applicant
for residence and work permits, Lieutenant. A cousin of the
proprietress of L'Auberge la Couronne. I have her papers
here . . .'

His tone implied, *If you'd like to cast an eye over them?*

Might then add, 'But this one at least looks like a
forgery . . .'

'Very well.' The Boche was taking another look at her.
She felt slightly sick. Turning back, stooping over the form
she was completing: hands none too steady, body damp
with sweat, heart banging . . . Taking long breaths to calm
it, telling herself *It's OK, he's going* . . . Hearing, indeed, the
German's boots thumping away across bare boards, then a
door pulled open and banging shut. The other front room,
the one to the right as one entered. The sergeant had sat
down and was looking at – she thought, from as much as
she could see – her *feuille semestrielle* again.

'This first one's finished. Still wet, the ink, I've no—'

A grunt as he leant sideways, just getting his short fingers
to it. Rosie carefully not looking at his desk, trying not to
look anything like she was feeling. He was holding the
newly completed form though, running his eye over her
entries while the ink dried. Now – the *feuille* again: and she
was watching him. Identity card, now – which was also—

Don't even think it.

He'd reached into a drawer, brought out a rubber stamp
and a pad: inking it, then applying it to the lower part of
the form she'd completed.

Rosie's eyes down: re-checking *this* form, then signing it
and pushing it over into his reach. Waiting again, then:

also *hoping* . . . Half turning away with one elbow on the counter, to gaze across the office area and out of the window at the end – the window in the side of the house – at a view slantwise across the road, encompassing the top end of the *cul-de-sac* of workers' houses and then the road-frontage and main entrance of Marchéval's. Alternatively from the other window, the front one, one looked directly across to where the *curé*'s solid-looking house stood back amongst its trees and shrubs.

'Mam'selle.' He was trying to reach this second form: she leant over quickly, gave it to him. Grunt of thanks. Rosie turning her attention back to the view from the end window then, while he went through the same procedure – checking, finally rubber-stamping. She didn't want to seem to be watching his every movement: *was* though – intermittently, out of the corner of her eye. On this side of the road out there, just about opposite the factory gates, was the small copse of trees around the start of the track up to the timber-yard: and above and beyond those trees' tops the slate roof of the Hôtel Poste reflecting the blaze of early sun.

Where she'd be after dark tonight. Up that track somewhere. She thought, *Bloody well* better *be good and dark.* Just spitting distance. Well – stone-throwing distance anyway.

'Here we are, then.' Hannant was at the counter again, to give her back her papers. 'Subject to the lieutenant approving the applications – naturally—'

'Naturally.'

'– take a day or two, in any case.' He was dealing her various cards and documents on to the counter between them, one by one. Last item, the *feuille semestrielle*. His thick fingers still on it: frowning down at it, something about it still bothering him. Glancing up then just as *she* did – but looking past her, towards the door of the *Leutnant*'s office. Thinking of referring the doubt to *him*? Pausing for the space of two – three – slow blinks: then meeting Rosie's eyes again. Trying to read her thoughts – read *her*? The smallest of shrugs then: giving the papers a push in her direction.

'Call in again before the weekend?'

'I'm obliged to you, M'sieur.'

He'd turned away. Knowing it couldn't be long now, that he could risk letting her get away with it? Or as a friend of Jacques, reluctant to involve *them*?

Bit of both, maybe.

Outside, there was no staff car waiting for the *Leutnant*. Whose name was, she remembered, Klebermann. Maybe it had brought him and would return for him. Military patrols from Sens called in at this *gendarmerie* sometimes, Colette had mentioned. At night, she wondered?

She spent an hour cleaning the windows in the bar and the dining room, chatted politely with Madame Brissac, and easily persuaded Colette to accept a thousand francs – to cover what she already owed and leave herself in credit. A lot of it was going on cigarettes.

'One might imagine you were thinking of leaving us.'

'Not by choice. But things *can* go wrong.'

'I don't know why you should involve yourself at all. It's André's and his colleagues' enterprise. Even Jacques – apart from the business of the keys—'

'You'd sooner he had an early night.'

'I would, you're right. But *you*, certainly . . .'

'I need to see it through, that's all.' She explained, 'It's what I came here for, after all. In any case, if I can make myself useful—'

'Speaking of that – would you like to do out the girls' rooms? They'll be back at the weekend, and once they spread their stuff around—'

'Of course . . .'

Jacques came back in time for a lunchtime snack of bread and cheese; in return for the deliveries of charcoal he'd brought a shoulder of mutton, some cabbages and a sack of wheat. The 'grey' market, they called it. His hand on her shoulder: 'Did Hannant fix up your papers?'

'Should have them by the weekend, he said.'

'Weekend, huh . . .'

How matters might stand by then, was the question. Ordinarily, there'd be hell to pay, reprisals involving shootings and the burning of property. But if the Boches were preparing to pull out anyway – and this place had no value to them other than its factory, which by then should to all intents and purposes be *kaput* . . .

She looked at him. 'The fact it's a Maquis action – no villagers involved . . .'

'Except *us* – eh?'

'Well – yes . . . Jacques – if *I* – fell by the wayside – the thing might be for Colette to say I'd convinced her I was the long-lost cousin – and had papers showing I *was* Justine Quérier – she had no reason to doubt it, and – took pity on me.'

'As she would have. Although to the Boches, taking pity on the wrong people's a criminal offence. But don't worry, we'll see to it you *don't*—'

'Thank you. Another thing though – I have my coding materials, and other stuff – cash, and a couple of pistols, one of which I'll be leaving here—'

'No shooting tonight, Justine. Quiet as mice!'

'But this stuff – and of course the transceiver and that carton in your workshop—'

'I don't want to know. You've hidden this or that, if it's found I'm as surprised as anyone, Colette even more so!'

'It wouldn't stop them shooting you for having it in the house. And the codes I *beg* you to destroy.'

'Where are they?'

'In the tin trunk in your box-room. Cash too – no point burning *that*.'

'D'you think I'm some kind of loony?' He'd laughed – on his way through to the bar, to take over from Colette.

Monsieur Henri came in just after seven thirty. Jacques had a few customers in the bar, and greeted him with 'Ah, *patron* – you'll have come to talk to my wife, about her cousin?'

'Exactly.' For the customers' ears, this was. 'If it's not inconvenient?'

'She's expecting you. You'd want to discuss it in private – come on through . . . How about a *fine*, while you're here?'

It was one of the days in the week when the sale of brandy was permitted. Jacques poured him one, while *le patron* exchanged a few words with the other men – all of them his own employees – then ushered him through to the kitchen, where Colette was making an omelet.

'*Patron* – excuse me – one minute . . .'

No hands to spare . . . But Jacques came through then, behind him, and Monsieur Henri gave him the heavy bunch of keys. In an undertone: 'You're going to tell me how I'll get them back?'

Jacques nodded. 'It's arranged. They'll be delivered to you at the manor, half an hour after midnight – or thereabouts. Maybe a little earlier. But you don't have to wait up, *patron*, only to leave your door unlocked – as you did for André, uh?'

'And then what, who—'

'Young Charles Saurrat.'

'Saurrat . . .'

The boy who worked at Marchéval's, had a brother-in-law in Guichard's group and had given Monsieur Henri the message from André, that scrap of paper. Jacques explained, 'He has a cool head and he's quick on his feet –

and as you'll have noticed, so thin he's barely visible. He'll
put these on the floor inside, and vanish. If you like you
could be there to receive them, but I'd suggest you don't
speak or put lights on.'

· 'At about twelve thirty.'

'About then. Maybe you should stay up for it – in case
the Briard woman bust in and picked them up?'

'The danger *will* be the Briards.'

'They won't see or hear him. Just let him come and go,
you won't.'

'Very well . . .' Blinking fast . . . Jacques excused himself,
leaving the rest to Colette. Rosie, coming down from her
room, heard her ask him in a normal tone – in contrast to
all the murmuring that had been going on – 'So her pay per
hour – let me think now . . .'

'What?'

He wasn't exactly sharp-witted, Rosie thought. Colette
said patiently, transferring the omelet to a dish, 'The matter of Justine's remuneration, *patron*.' She mentioned an
hourly rate which to Rosie seemed fairly steep, for unskilled
labour. Monsieur Henri glancing at her sharply, then shrugging. 'If that's acceptable to Mam'selle Quérier—'

'Two hours a day Monday to Saturday, the precise hours
to be agreed, and for any meals you want her to provide
you'll get a weekly bill from me.' She dropped her voice
again: 'It's only to have an agreement, *patron*. So we tell the
same story, eh?'

Jacques and Rosie left the *auberge* at ten fifty, out of the
side door into the alleyway and across the yard where he
kept his *gazo*, over a fence and then on grass – an orchard –
Jacques leading and Rosie staying close, at times in physical
contact. She was wearing slacks, old plimsolls, a sweater
over her blouse and Thérèse's jacket over that. Llama in
the right-hand pocket, spare clip in the other.

'Careful here.' Jacques reached back for her hand. A ditch, with wire on its other side. 'I'll go over first.'

'Go on. I'm all right.' She could see the wire, a soft glint by starlight: better in fact than she could see him, in his dark sweater and trousers, dark-stubbled face. Over – *now* . . . Over the wire too. Pausing, breathing the cool night air, scent of herbs and woodsmoke. They'd be somewhere behind the Hôtel Poste, she guessed. Jacques moving on again, with a hand on her arm – diverting about thirty degrees right.

'Here's the track. See, right ahead?'

The track that led from the road between the Poste and the churchyard. It was rutted by lorries or tractors and baked as hard as rock; she was on its high centre, Jacques down in a rut. On the right, beyond a sparser patch of trees, the church's spire a black vertical against the stars. The track curving first left and then right – skirting the churchyard. Rosie thinking about André again – that once this was over he'd have reason to feel pleased with himself, even to believe that with a solid reputation amongst *résistants* in the field he'd have a chance of getting away with past infamies.

Then he *might* agree to de-briefing in England?

'Who's there?'

Gruff challenge – from their left. Jacques stopped, holding her back too.

'Jacques – and Justine. Who're you?'

'Tamerlan. Stay where you are, huh?'

A shape loomed close: closer. Could have been a gorilla, or a bear, going only by its shape. Creature with a weapon of some sort: a Sten, she thought. A Sten it *would* be . . . Jacques asked quietly, 'Duclos, is it?'

A chuckle, and the metallic click of the Sten's safety as he pushed it on. 'Armand Duclos, the very same. *Soir,* Mam'selle.'

'*Bon soir*. But Justine, please.'
'OK. This way, Justine . . .'

Guichard was there, although he wouldn't be taking part
in the action. Shaking Rosie's hand: she managed not to
shake André's, by avoiding others too. Guichard had murmured introductions, gesturing around: 'Masson, Duclos,
de Rommerille, Lescalles. André Marchéval you know, of
course – and this is Charles Saurrat.' All settling down again
then: there were timber-stacks around them, square-topped
against the stars, and some logs to sit on. Six men and the
boy, she counted – as well as herself and Jacques. The
Maquisards all had Stens fitted with silencers, and some
haversacks piled together in the centre obviously contained
explosives. The men had shifted around to make room for
them, were now settling down again: hunched black shapes,
the largest being Guichard. In close-up she'd seen woollen
caps and the kind of jackets they called *Canadiens*. There
was a certain odour.

Charles Saurrat was next to her, on her left, and she
reached to shake his hand. Jacques had mentioned that he
wasn't yet sixteen. 'Heard a lot about you, Charles . . .'

'He'll be your partner, more or less.' Guichard . . . 'Justine
– Jacques – I'll explain what we've mapped out for you.
Starting with you, Jacques. It's as we discussed yesterday,
in fact. In that small pack –' he pushed it with his foot – 'is a
fire-bomb André's made up. I'd like you to hide yourself at
the bottom of the track here, where you can see the factory
gates and along the road both ways. If anything goes wrong
– when the boys are inside, I mean – anything wrong or that
you judge is *about* to go wrong – toss it into the Poste. It
has to be your judgement, obviously – not just for a patrol
passing – right?'

'Right.'

'Well – there's a window at the back with broken panes,

Charles tells me. Worst looks like coming to the worst – chuck it in there. The fuse will give you three minutes – you're finished then, so duck out of it quick, go home – the place'll go up in flames and divert attention from the factory while these lads make themselves scarce. All right?'

'What do I do, pull a pin out?'

André told him, 'It'll have a pencil-fuse, the acid bulb type. Hasn't yet, will have before we separate. You crush the end of it. I'll show you.'

'But I don't stick around to make sure it goes off, eh?'

André – on Guichard's right – snapped, 'Of *course* it'll bloody well go off! Think I don't know my business?'

'So how many charges have you made up for the job in the factory?'

'Twenty. One for the machine – or two maybe—'

'There are sixteen completed casings, two nearing completion, another three less well advanced. That's twenty-one – as well as the machine.'

'We won't bother with the three less well advanced, then. Although if one had been told—'

'Or had had the sense to bring a few spares. We discussed this, you know.'

'It's true, we did.' Guichard, defusing the quarrel. 'Spilt milk now, however. Justine – your part now – if you'll agree to this . . . You know the side entrance – or rather exit – in Rue de l'Ecole?'

'Yes. Opposite the playing-field.'

'That's your station. In fact just over the wall of the playing-field there's a shed you and Charles could use for cover while you're waiting. He'll guide you – to the other side of the Poste first, from where you'll see these five enter the factory – at midnight, and we're working on fifteen minutes as the time they'll need to place the charges. They'll leave then by that side door. You can count them out – the last out will be André, he'll

give the keys to Charles and confirm to you that the
charges are in place. Or are *not* – which God forbid. In
fact I can't imagine anything could have gone wrong that
you wouldn't already know about – arrival of a patrol,
Jacques' fire-bomb exploding, or the boys letting loose
with their Stens – if the Boches had laid a trap for us,
for instance. But your main concern, Justine, is to be able
to confirm positively to London that the job's been done –
am I right?'

'Yes.'

'It's something we want too – to avert any fresh thoughts
of bombing. So – André will have told you it's all set, and
you'll hear the explosions when they detonate at twelve
forty-five. Or twelve forty-four or forty-six, but giving
us all ample time to be away and under cover. For *your*
withdrawal, Justine – again, with Charles as guide, you've
only to get across the playing-field and then that piece of
grazing the butcher owns into the trees on its far side,
opposite the *auberge*. Charles leaves you there, races down
to the bottom, around the end of the wall into the manor
– to return the keys to André's father – while you go up
to the road and slip across. Still well before the explosions,
that should be, maybe quarter of an hour before.'

'How long does Jacques hang around the Poste?'

'Say twenty minutes, Jacques?'

'Leave at twelve twenty then.' Leaning forward to address
Rosie: he was on the other side of Charles Saurrat. 'Took
us ten minutes getting here, won't take me any longer.
We'll just about dead-heat it, maybe . . . Use the side-door,
remember, not the front.'

'Of course.' She turned back to Guichard. 'But I don't
need to delay Charles once he has the keys. I can cross a
field on my own, you know. Don't wait for me, Charles,
just take off.'

'If you're sure, Mam'selle.'

André said, 'When I come out, I have to lock that door behind me. Then I chuck you the keys and *I* take off.'

'To the bottom of the road, over the bridge—'

'Exactly, Justine – and across fields, into woods. Consequently, Saurrat, *I* don't want to be held up either – looking for someone to give the keys to – huh?'

'But I'll be right at the door, Monsieur André!'

Rosie put in, 'So will I.'

Seeing it then. The boy having shot off – she and 'Hector' on their own in that narrow, pitch-dark street.

His plan?

Chapter 16

'All right. Time to move.'

Guichard, on his feet and stretching, tall against starry sky. The others reaching for their haversacks, Jacques for his smaller pack. A few minutes ago he'd muttered to Rosie, 'You needn't have been here – you realize? Could be in your bed, listening for the explosions an hour from now – tell you as much as our friend there will!'

'I did explain, Jacques.'

That in Baker Street's eyes this was her brief, or part of it. She could hardly have stayed away, told them in London later, 'Actually I wasn't there . . .'

'Saurrat.' André – with a haversack slung from one shoulder, Sten from the other – 'You know every blade of grass, you'd better take the lead. All right, Jacques?'

'I'll come last, with Justine.'

'So good luck, lads.' Guichard: 'Keep those *sulphateuses* on "safe", eh?'

Sulphateuses being Maquis slang for Stens or other automatic weapons. In fact they were the chemical sprays used in vineyards. Guichard peering at Jacques: 'No weapon?'

'In my belt – a St Etienne.'

A French-made 9-millimetre. The big man's attention was on Rosie now: '*You* armed?'

'Should I be?'

A grunt: 'You're right. Your business.' Large hand on

her shoulder: and André close by in the darkness. Having thought about it, though, she didn't think he'd try anything, didn't intend to try anything herself either: for one thing, the priority was to conclude this operation successfully: for another, the near-certainty that neither of them would get away with it. Guichard shook her hand: 'We'll meet again, I hope.'

'I hope so too. In any case good luck – now and later.'

There was a low murmuring of farewells. Guichard's line of departure now would be eastward, passing behind the church and through orchard and low-lying pasture to cross the road between the cottages and the bridge, skirt around that end of the village – the way he and the rest had come – and then south to rendezvous at some point in the fringes of the woods, on their way back into the Forêt d'Othe. Rosie, beside Jacques and following the others, looked back to wave goodbye but he'd already gone – or was invisible at a distance of a dozen paces. They were out of the timber-yard then, on the track leading to the road. The plan was that she, Jacques and the boy would wait there with the others, see them sneak over the road and into the factory at midnight – it was eleven forty-eight now – and she and Saurrat would then start off themselves, passing around the back of the Poste to cross the road further along, opposite the market square, while Jacques remained in the trees near the road. He'd only move to the back of the Poste with his fire-bomb if he was going to use it.

In which event, Guichard had suggested, Rosie's best course would be to get out of it, quick – across the playing-field and the paddock, and home. Saurrat on the other hand would still hang on, in order to get the keys for return to Monsieur Henri. Rosie hadn't argued, but if some crisis did arise she'd play it off the cuff, would certainly be disinclined to leave young Charles on his own.

They'd all diverged from the track now, so as to stay

in cover where it broadened near the road. In single file, Rosie following whichever of them it was – Masson, Duclos, de Rommerille, Lescalles – and Jacques close behind her. Jacques with his fire-bomb, which under André's guidance he'd checked – by feel, more than sight – and now had the detonator in one pocket, pencil-fuse in another, wasn't intending to put it all together unless or until he saw trouble coming. The pencil-fuse with the detonator fitted would be only about ten centimetres long, and the bomb itself – a core of PE (Cyclonite) with petrol-soaked wadding around it – was about the size of a Cantaloupe melon.

The men in the lead were stopping. Time – by Marilyn's luminous watch – eleven fifty-five.

André called urgently, 'Car coming!'

From the direction of the bridge: she heard it now. Seeing André moving forward, doubled, creeping closer to the road. Petrol-engined car, no *gazo*. Rosie thinking of the *gendarmerie* – only about a hundred, hundred and twenty metres to the left there – that if it was a patrol it might stop there. In which case – really *lousy* timing – seeing that within the next few minutes these five had to cross the road – André going ahead to unlock the personnel door in those gates.

If it *was* stopping there, nobody was going to be able to move at all.

A lot would depend on how long it stayed, obviously. Since the charges were pre-set to detonate at twelve forty-five.

Whatever this vehicle was, it wasn't coming fast. Might have been coming over the bridge when André or whoever had first heard it – that *sort* of distance – and it wouldn't come into sight from here until it was just about at the *gendarmerie*, on account of the road's right-hand curve. Even at that range its masked headlights wouldn't be more than pinpricks.

Engine-sound growing, but certainly not fast. Unlike the homing Boche staff-car on her first night here. Derivative thought being that waking people in the houses along the road wouldn't exactly improve prospects of all concerned getting away unseen and unheard before the charges exploded. Especially since one of the more tricky aspects, necessitating silence, speed, invisibility et cetera, was that the house at the top, nearer end of the *cul-de-sac*, no more than fifty metres from the factory gates and say seventy from here, was the home of the works manager, Gaspard Legrand, chief toady to the Boche engineer Wachtel. Legrand had been softening his style of late, seeing the way the wind was blowing – so Jacques had said – but was still by no means a friend of the Resistance.

The Maquisards were crouching – taking their cue from André. Rosie did too: and Jacques – on her right now.

A whisper from – Lescalles, she thought. 'André can see its lights. Says it seems to be stopping at the *gendarmerie*.'

The timing on those acid bulb fuses couldn't be altered at this late stage. In any case messing around with them in the dark and in a hurry wasn't to be recommended. All one could do was pray the bastards wouldn't stay for long. Stopping for what, in any case? Maybe just for a break, wake old Hannant to make coffee for them? In which case – what, fifteen minutes?

If they took *twenty*, for Christ's sake – which from their point of view mightn't seem excessive . . .

'It's *not* stopping!'

General murmur of relief . . .

'Coming by us any moment. Stay down.'

Small, dim headlights passing *now*. Rosie half risen, looking over woollen-hatted heads and between tree-trunks, seeing the low-growling shadow crawl by with a weak pool of light preceding it.

It was now passing in front of the Poste.

A Boche driving so quietly out of consideration for the villagers' repose?

Gone, anyway. Would have passed the *auberge* by this time. Checking the time – eleven fifty-eight – she heard André tell those near him: 'I'm starting. De Rommerille, count to fifteen, others count ten.'

Up and not running but moving swiftly, the rest still crouching, watching the dark figure fuse into blackness. De Rommerille meanwhile counting audibly: 'Fourteen – fifteen –' and he'd gone, Lescalles was starting *his* count. The counts were to have been of twenty and then fifteen but André had shortened them to fifteen and ten respectively to make up about half a minute of lost time. Lescalles was on his way: now Masson, and finally, Duclos: like ghosts, nothing out there either visible or audible. Rosie had been watching to the right in case that car might have turned to come back, but it was probably in the manor grounds by this time.

She touched Charles Saurrat's arm. 'Better move.'

'Yep—'

Jacques murmured, 'Take care, both of you.'

'And you. *A bientôt.*'

Up this side of the Poste still in cover, then into the open to cross the cleared area behind it – catching a glint of starlight on windows at the back, one of which had broken panes, would be the one into which Jacques was supposed to throw his bomb. She followed young Saurrat down to the roadside, staying close to the Poste's crumbly wall. He suggested as she joined him, 'Cross together?'

'Yes.' Taking his hand as they crossed the forefront of gravel and weed, then a strip of broken paving. No sight or sound of anyone or anything else moving. Not even a cat. Jacques had told her that in Paris they'd eaten all the cats, but it didn't apply here, she'd seen several. Over the road and into the market square with its central covered area. Darkness here was total: no starlight even. Out of the bandstand then and crossing cobbles, aware that no more than thirty or fifty metres away André and his team would be placing their twenty-odd explosive charges – using torches, she assumed, that would have been supplied in SOE *parachutages*. PE, detonators, Stens and just about everything else the *l'Armée des Ombres* possessed, all by courtesy of SOE, and in this geographic area mostly no doubt by the personal efforts of Joseph Lambert.

Joseph Lambert, deceased. Thanks to bloody André.

At the corner, pausing to look and listen, with a hand on the boy's arm. Imagining that from the other side of the wall, the factory area, there should be *some* sound that would be at least faintly audible in this enveloping silence. But nothing – except from a distance and in the very next moment, owls hooting . . . She whispered, 'Come on.' From cobbles on to tar macadam: and on to the pavement on this side, close to the three-metre wall the top of which Charles had mentioned earlier had broken glass cemented into it. The door in it was about halfway down the road, some thirty metres from this corner. She asked Saurrat in a whisper, 'Do the *gendarmes* never walk round at night?'

'Sometimes – when night shifts are being worked. Never seen them any other time. Once it's locked up, I suppose . . . And the curfew. A patrol might send them out if they thought they'd seen someone.'

'Someone like you?'

A snigger. 'Could be.'

'Doing what?'

'Oh – meeting friends, or – you know, fooling around.' He'd stopped, suddenly. 'Here it is.'

It was a single door, fairly wide but only for personnel – or you could have pushed a barrow through, maybe. Recessed quite deeply into the wall – flush with the inside

surface, she supposed: naturally it would open inwards.
Timber, smooth to the touch; the handle was an iron ring
and there was a keyhole below it.

Twelve nine. Five minutes, say. She leant with her back
against the wall on this higher side of the door, then moved
further up to make room for Saurrat between her and it:
whispering to him as she did so, 'Best stay this side of the
road – d'you think?' He did. The alternative would have
been to take cover behind the low wall opposite, or close to
the shed as Guichard had suggested; but the work might go
faster than they'd allowed for, and she had in mind André's
terse warning to the boy about being on the spot, on no
account to delay him. It was in Saurrat's best interests,
therefore. Also made sense to place themselves on this
side of the door, because when the Maquisards emerged
they'd be going the other way – to their right, towards the
stream and open countryside. André presumably unlocking
the door for them, then going back to finish whatever tasks
he'd reserved for himself – or making a final check on
the positioning of the charges, maybe, and/or re-locking
internal doors. They'd have placed one charge inside each
tube: wouldn't matter how far in, blow a hole in it anywhere
and you'd have converted it to scrap.

That hum was – she realized – traffic. A distant, rumbling
sound: from the main road, presumably, at least a kilometre
and a half from here. Therefore *heavy* traffic. Truck convoy
moving east?

Even be coming *here*?

The turn-off to the bridge was to the northeast from here,
and the distance say two kilometres . . . Flatbeds finally
coming for the casings? Actually *might* be? Guichard had
mentioned it as a possibility, in considering – with Jacques,
in the fire-bomb context – various things that might conceivably go wrong. No one had thought it likely – this late,
and with no preparations made. Jacques had concurred: if

transport had been expected, Wachtel would have had the place open and ready and a team of loaders standing by.

'Half the night, if necessary. Still *could* happen, but—'

'If it did –' Guichard to André – 'it'd be up to you, you'd be on your own. Depending on how far you'd got, eh?'

'Yeah, but – don't worry . . .'

The growling hum was steady: no slowing for that turn-off, or rising note such as you'd get from trucks approaching. There was a happier interpretation therefore – Boches on the run, pulling out through Sens towards Troyes and points east. Thirteen minutes past twelve: she showed Saurrat the green-glowing face of Marilyn's watch. Back then to the point that André hadn't wanted to admit even the possibility of a convoy of the specially adapted trucks looming leviathan-like out of the night to wreck his chances of fame and glory. Which if it *was* his driving force in all this, pretty well guaranteed he wouldn't be trying anything as rash as murdering the chief witness for the prosecution. One shot would rouse the village, and the keys then might not get back to his father, who if interrogated wouldn't hold out for ten minutes – if that. And even if he might fool Guichard with some yarn such as having acted in self-defence, Rosie having tried to kill *him*, André would know he'd never sell it to Jacques, whose record as a *résistant* had already given him – one had come to realize – the right to be taken seriously, and who certainly was not one of André's admirers.

Touch wood, that was a fairly sound assessment. She reached left-handed over the boy's head, to touch the door. Getting as bad as Lise, she thought: Lise's belief in what she called 'Fate' – some malignant influence against which one was powerless. Leaning back against the wall, then: checking the time. Twelve fifteen. As projected, zero-hour. Owls were vocal again, in the woods to the south. Nothing else: no traffic sound now, she realized; a convoy had passed, that was all. Her right hand in the jacket pocket, ball of the thumb caressing the pistol's safety-catch. But André was safe from *her*, too, tonight. First because the successful conclusion of this operation was as important for her as it was for him, and second because the body of André Marchéval, shot either in the street or inside the factory and the door then shut and locked, would lead directly to his father – who'd be talking before they even *asked* him.

But in any case – killing him in cold blood, which as things had turned out now would be closer to plain revenge—

Correction: for 'revenge', read 'justice'.

A tug at her sleeve: 'Listen!'

Key scraping in the lock . . .

They heard it click over, then a squeak of hinges. A man's whisper: 'Go on!' Emerging then – from this angle of sight, initially like a bulging of the wall itself: then for a moment static . . . She raised a hand – with no more than a metre of darkness between them – and he reciprocated, in the same gesture giving the boy's shoulder a comradely squeeze. Padding away then, soft-footed and close to the wall. One out and away: and now a second – swifter than the first, breaking into a trot before the night swallowed him. Two to come, before André. This one she thought might be Duclos – shouldering through, checking round quickly and seeing them – a grunt as he swung away – and from inside a clatter, the fourth man's Sten caught up on the half-open door. He'd pulled back, swearing, then came on through but glancing back, stumbled . . . Recovering, lurching away. Might have been audible right up in the square – if anyone had been there to hear it.

Waiting for André now. She moved another pace out from the wall. Thumb easing the safety off the Llama. Purposes of self-defence only, Marilyn's *extreme caution* . . . And aware that (a) her own analysis might be based at least partly on wishful thinking, (b) he might use a knife rather than a firearm. Although until the boy *did* take off . . .

Positioning himself to do just that – like a competitor in a relay race, ready to snatch the baton and run. And from that moment, with everything working out as planned, to the next – the crash of an explosion – inside – and a fire-coloured flash outlining the doorway, blinding orange, reverberations slamming through the ruined night and – like some super-imposed recording – Charles Saurrat's squawk of alarm overtaken by a man's despairing wail – 'Ah. Jesus *Christ!*' The boy had staggered against her: all part of the same cataclysm, you couldn't have separated any one split second from the next. She was in the doorway but in that moment not seeing anything, flash-effect still blinding her: then a torch-beam wavering around inside another open doorway, one of a pair in the near-end of a Nissen-like shed – inside the factory area now, this was – with a line of identical curved-roof shapes away to the right, only this one open. Reek of burning – scorching – as she dashed in; the torch fell, went out as it hit the tarmac, but she'd seen him as he reeled against the timber door-jamb and she was there, holding him up against it, Saurrat diving past her to pick up the torch – and André sliding steadily downward, despite her effort to hold him up. Saurrat – with the torch working again, its beam poking around in fumes, a smell like shoeing horses, repeating 'The keys – the keys' and then a shout of *'There!'* As surprising as anything else – *she'd* have looked in André's pockets. André on his knees by this time – balancing, she'd let go of him – moaning 'Christ, what's *happening* . . .'

'Try to stand?'

'Stand. Christ . . .'

Torch-beam licking over him. No obvious sign of wounding. But she'd seen the Sten lying further inside, leant to scoop it up, slung it over her left shoulder. Both André's hands rising as if to shield his eyes, the torch stabbing this way – the boy's idea of helping?

'Came to kill me, didn't you?'

'*Kill* you?'

Could have, too. Who'd know, piece it together? Shoot him, and clear out – with *everything* accomplished? Saurrat asked her, as she looked round to see where he was, 'Shall I go with the keys?'

'No. Help me get him up. I think his jacket's burning. Can't leave him here, I can't manage on my own. André—'

'But the keys, he said *so* important—'

'Wouldn't help his father – or any of us – if we left him here. So –' it was dawning on her as she spoke – 'we'll take him *and* the keys to the manor.'

'But – see . . .'

In the torch beam, André's head lolling, face above the beard black-looking. Head falling back then as her own movement tilted him: eyes half open, their whites showing momentarily. *Flesh* burnt? She told the boy, 'Between us we'll manage. He's conscious again – I think . . . Jacket first – it *is* smouldering. André – you've got to help too. Come *on* now!'

'Oh, Jesus . . .'

'Just *try*. Come on – *up* . . . Charles, *help* me. Here. *Now*, André – that's it, that's it—'

'But all that way?' Silly question from Saurrat.

She told him, 'No alternative.' Making it *this* far, anyway: André was up, more or less, sagging between her and the corrugated door, arms round her neck and heavy on her shoulders. The boy was helping now – to some extent. She pushed one of André's arms off her and swung round beside him with his left arm round her shoulders, her own left hand clamped on that wrist. 'Lean on me, André. We'll get you to your father. Your face is – scorched, I know, you've had a bang on the head too, haven't you? Doctor'll fix it anyway. Stay that side, Charles. Edge him forward now. That's it . . . Try to walk, André. Or just *shuffle*. Come *on*!'

'But where, what . . .'

'*Try* . . .'

Thinking of trying a fireman's lift, which in SOE training had been child's play, probably was even in the Girl Guides, but he was about twice her weight and her left shoulder still wasn't up to much hard usage. Doing press-ups for instance, she'd found she could only manage at a slant with nearly all her weight on the right arm, using the left simply as a prop. She had him off the door, anyway: and the smouldering woodsman's jacket off – at last. Next stage, out into the street and *lock* the bloody door, be gone and out of their reckoning before they woke up to—

Should be going on one's own. *Should* be. Over that bridge and—

Thud of a more distant explosion. Not a big one, more like a gunshot. She realized – *Jacques* . . .

Might draw them: divert them. Especially if it did start a good-sized fire. No one jarred out of sleep by the sound of an explosion at some distance could be sure exactly where or what: so now another *and* a fire – second blink, they'd be sure they *did* know. Charles began, 'Monsieur Jacques' bomb—'

'Did you hear it, André?'

'He say Jacques' *bomb*?'

'Bomb *you* made.'

The answer had to be concussion: flung back violently against something particularly solid, she guessed. And the scorching, the facial burns – what she remembered Ben referring to as 'flash', burning caused by shell-bursts. Something like it, anyway: and from the concussion, awareness coming and going – but mainly absent, this far. Except for that startling accusation out of more distant memory.

Blast-damage affecting the nervous system – i.e. brain – she
supposed, including ability to move. Hadn't happened to
her like that, but – different, several ways. She had her left
arm out, in contact with the door to the street. Wondering
whether if this hadn't happened he would have tried to kill
her. With such a positive view of *her* intentions, wouldn't he
have reckoned on pre-empting them? She told him, 'We'll
get you to your father anyway. Don't know what then, but
– *get* you there, that's the thing. Charles – the shed door
inside – nip back in, shut and lock it?'

'*D'accord*—'

'Use the torch but only downward. . . André, we're going
to edge out sideways. Lean against me. If you really tried,
might find you could move quite well. That's it. Door's
behind me, nothing in your way. Come on, come on . . .'

If he'd used a knife: let the boy get away first, then had
the field to himself?

So why bloody *not* be taking off on one's own?

The boy was back, on André's other side. 'It's locked.
Hellish racket up there, vehicles and—'

'Nothing happening inside the factory though?'

Not *yet*, there wasn't. She *hoped* . . . Answering that question now: *for Jacques and Colette's sake, that's why* . . . Because
if the Boches found André – then inevitably nobbled his
father too . . . A flickering light in the sky was the Poste
going up like firewood: you could hear *that* well enough.
Sergeant Hannant would know kids had played in it at
times; and the fact Boche troops had been billeted there
could have made it a target for *résistants*. Easy target, might
be all – a demonstration, no loss to the village either: *might
even be kids at play!*

'André – can you see? See the torch?'

'Hunh?'

Responding to his name but not to questions. Manoeuvring
him through: just about *were* through. '*This* door now,

Charles?' And thinking ahead: one, that from here it was about thirty metres to the bridge: two, into the stream somewhere down there – for cover, which she'd thought about before – and three, say four hundred metres – three-fifty, maybe, but in present conditions a long haul anyway – to the bottom end of the wall that ran down this side of the manor's grounds.

'I've locked it.'

'Fine.' As far as one knew there'd be nothing to tell anyone inside that it had just been used as an exit. The tube in which the charge had blown prematurely was in that locked store-shed, no reason to think they'd find it the minute they got in there. Smell it, maybe, catch on soon enough, but not *that* soon.

Time now – her left wrist up where she could see it – twelve twenty-nine.

'Doing well, André . . .'

He was, too. Groaning and gasping – more gasps than regular breaths – and by no means steady on his feet, but shuffling along, the down-gradient doubtless helping. Having found he *could* stay up: like a child taking its first steps.

'Doing *much* better!'

'What is it with him?'

'Mainly what I think they call *une commotion cérébrale.*' A quick racking of her own brain had come up with that, as a translation of 'concussion' . . . 'André, you're doing well . . .'

As one might talk to a child. His helplessness meanwhile triggering thoughts in the back of her mind of perhaps being able actually to get him out – quick vision of a Hudson pick-up from Parnassus. If one could somehow persuade Jacques . . . First things first though – being committed to this now – to get him under cover. He *was* doing better: halfway to the bridge now, roughly. Not breaking any speed records, but better than it had been and much less weight on her: mostly a matter of just steering him – *not* having to break one's back . . . Returning to her interrupted thinking about using the stream-bed as their line of escape, though – better *not* get out into the manor's trees after passing the end of the first wall. You'd be on the wrong side of the house for access to Monsieur Henri's end of it; and once having left the trees there'd be no cover as good as the stream. Crossing the garden in front of the house in fact there'd be none at all. Stay in the stream to where the wall on the *west* side of the house ran down to the stream, therefore. Out there, and then only – what, sixty or seventy metres, say?

Under the Briards' noses, of course. Have to watch out for the bloody Briards, who'd most likely be awake and taking notice. And Monsieur Henri doubtless sweating blood . . .

Send the boy ahead to give him his keys and warn him she was bringing André?

Better not. Safer, *let* him sweat a little. Might yet need the boy's help here. And his arrival might alert the Briards: one didn't want to find a whole reception committee waiting. The Boches might already have been on to Monsieur Henri: certainly would be once they realized the factory had been the target. They'd want him there, then—

Christ. *Without his keys* . . .

Twelve thirty-six now. Jacques, she guessed, would be back in the *auberge*, having started for home as soon as he'd thrown his bomb in.

'Hear that?'

The boy had asked it: she muttered an affirmative. Sky flickering with light over the Poste end of the village, and 'that' had been a car or truck coming from the direction of the manor, passing the market square at speed. There'd been several before that. Twelve thirty-seven – another eight minutes, there should be about nineteen explosions.

Unless they – Wachtel and Gaspard Legrand, one thought
of – had got in there already.

'André. We're nearly at the stream and we're going to
climb down into it. Think you'll manage?'

'Hunh?'

An automaton, shambling on. Cold water was good
for burns, she remembered. Charles said, 'I've done *that*
before.'

'So where's a good place to get him down?'

'Right at the bridge here. I'll get down first. OK?'

'André – slow up, stop a minute?'

'You said – using the stream . . .'

So he'd caught on. Mulled it over, finally made sense.
Charles had gone ahead, prospecting. She explained, 'To
get to the manor without being seen. Along the stream-bed,
wading.'

The boy's whisper: 'Here. Where I am?'

'Who's that?'

'Charles Saurrat, he's helping us, was to have got the
keys straight back to your father – remember?'

'Why're we doing this?'

'To save all our lives. Yours, your father's, Jacques' and
Colette's, my own too. Charles?'

'Here. *Here* – here's my hand. Monsieur André—'

Groping forward: surprisingly, under his own steam.
'Where?'

'Here.' Rosie was with him: climbing some of the way
down so as to steer him on down to the boy. But he was
managing it pretty well on his own. Physical coordination
returning towards normal maybe. Saurrat was murmuring
to him down there now. She whispered into the dark,
'Help him bathe his face.' Twelve forty-one: four minutes
to go. She let go, slid down the rock-and-earth bank, found
them both crouching, André whining, moaning. With relief,
maybe? She and the boy had to drag him up then, and there

were only about *two* minutes to go by the time they were plodding up the bed of the stream, through water less than knee-deep. There was a dam on the river, Jacques had told her, where this stream branched off from it, to maintain a minimal supply of water to the factory. André was coping surprisingly well, sloshing along in front of her. If she hadn't forced him to start moving, she guessed, he'd still have been lying there inside the factory. Although the time she herself had had concussion – spinal, after a fall from a pony when she'd been nine or ten years old, on holiday from France at her uncle's place in Buckinghamshire, she'd come off and landed on her back across a tree-stump, one end of a make-shift jump – she hadn't lost consciousness until several hours after the fall. Fainted at high-tea, been put to bed, doctor summoned, woken late next day with no memory of those hours at all, beyond having started out for the ride that afternoon. All she knew of it even now was what she'd been told.

You could smell the fire – like rubbish burning. Smoke might be an element in the darkness. Time now – twelve forty-three.

'Your charges should blow soon.'

No response . . .

'André?'

Hoarse whisper, after a moment: '*My* – charges?'

'PE. In the factory, charges *you* placed?'

Obviously no memory of it. But as information, explanation, might add up eventually. There was a new sound now – distant, and nothing explosive about it, more like a landslide or coal thundering down a chute. She guessed – the Poste, roof falling in? André, looking around at her, stumbled but then recovered with an arm out to the bank: instincts and coordination definitely returning to normal. Saurrat called back to her, 'The wall here – see?'

Eastern boundary of the manor's grounds, a wall about

three metres high, buttressed where it ended close to the
stream. They'd already passed it, were now therefore crossing the manor's garden frontage. Hence no trees at all
now: she hadn't seen up there, had been preoccupied
with monitoring André's performance. Couldn't hear the
fire now, she realized: the building's collapse might have
snuffed it out. Certainly still smell it . . . She hitched the
strap of the Sten higher on her shoulder: didn't especially
want it, had been averse to leaving it there, was all.

Twelve forty-six. Visions of failure: charges defused, all
of this for nothing . . . More trees in sight ahead, towering
against stars. Nature impervious, aloof, everlasting, only
humanity chasing itself around like crazed insects intent
on self-destruction.

A charge exploded. One single, distinctive thud – not
all that loud but solid, clearly defined. Then another just
like it: and three more hard on each others' heels. Saurrat
laughing: André crouching, head down, immersing his
face in the stream again. Now a rapid tattoo of the same
explosions. Rosie's feeling was of partial satisfaction in
that at least something had been achieved – minimally
eighteen rockets that would *not* be fired when the time
came for the next bombardment of English towns and
villages. Helping André up again: the three of them in
a close group then, knee-deep in the moving water, listening . . .

To silence, for a moment. Then she could hear men's
voices thinned by distance: could imagine the Boches' fury
– and that there surely *would* be reprisals.

'Charles – can we get up the bank here?'

'Easy.' Splashing a bit further along. 'Here . . .'

'Go on, André. Very, *very* quiet now.' Needing to tell
him more – that his father's door would be unlocked so
they could just slip in as he had on Monday night, but
that the Briards would most likely be awake and looking

out – so not just quietly but silently, as well as invisibly and speedily. Cats being well and truly among the pigeons now, and moonrise not far off. Thinking ahead too, as they filed through the trees towards the manor: having parked André in his father's house, persuade Jacques to assist with transport, call for a Hudson pick-up. Persuade André that after his success tonight Baker Street would surely give him the benefit of any doubts – and that the last thing she'd ever thought of was to kill him.

In his shoes, she asked herself, would *she* buy it?

A door slammed. Could have been Monsieur Henri's. They'd stopped, in the edge of the trees. Open lawn to the right, behind it the Manoir St Valéry a rectangular bulk against black, star-studded sky, and closer, harder-edged, the stable block overlapping this end of it.

Saurrat whispered, 'Might have been Briards.'

Coming out, though, or going back in?

She pointed to their right: 'Best *that* way.'

Between the stable-block and the main building. It would mean passing very close to the Briards' door. But with luck if they were on the lookout it wouldn't be this way, more likely towards the northern entrance to the stable-yard – the front of the house, Boches-occupied part. If so, the risk in passing so close was mainly if at the same moment one of them happened to be entering or leaving – if they'd just gone out, for instance, coming *back* . . . Mentally crossing fingers; crouching with the other two in the darker-than-dark cover of the trees, last pause before a fifteen- or twenty-metre transit to the corner of the stable-block and then about the same distance past the Briards' door to the porch sheltering Monsieur Henri's.

'Charles – we'll be close behind you. André, from here on, not even *whisper*. Your father's door'll be unlocked. As it was for you before – remember?'

He grunted, she gave him a push and he was up trotting

after the boy. She herself close on his heels. And *this* far –
OK . . .

At the corner, then. Drawing a couple of deep breaths.
And hearing—

God, *no* . . .

'Car coming!' Whisper from Saurrat. She'd already recognized it as a petrol-engined vehicle – therefore Boche –
coming up the drive from the road. Now or never, therefore:
she hissed, 'Let's *go!'*

Running. Rosie praying that the Briards – *if* they were
up and about – might hear the car's approach and go to
a window at that end. The car surely going to the *front* of
the house?

Unless it had been sent to fetch Monsieur Henri. Which
in the circumstances was not at all unlikely . . .

Into the porch: Saurrat trying the door – which *was*
unlocked – and should have been, but by this time might
not have, if the old boy had panicked . . . She squeezed in
behind André – Saurrat was already in – Rosie twisting
round to shut the door, feel for the bolt and slide it over –
the car *might* have been coming into the stable-yard, some
Boche leaping out to barge in here . . . Behind her as she
pushed the bolt home she heard Monsieur Henri's urgent
whisper of 'Saurrat? I was told you'd leave my keys and—'

'Why yes, *patron,* and here they are, but—'

Scrape and flare of a match being struck, candle-light
spreading: a croak of '*André?* André – my *God*—'

In one of several small bedrooms, formerly no doubt servants' rooms, André sat on the iron-framed bed while his
father paced nervously around. Rosie was on a hard chair,
Saurrat leaning against the wall. A table-lamp on the floor
glowed dimly, but the curtained window was in shadow.
Monsieur Henri said, 'So you saved his life. Thank you. You
too, Saurrat.'

André's beard had been mostly burnt off right down to the skin, which was lobster-pink with other patchy discolouring and seemed to be sweating blood and mucus. She'd helped him bathe it in an enamel bowl of cold water – not touching it, just dipping his face in – then arranged a clean towel to cover it – over his head, hanging draped over his shoulders; but he'd raised the front part of that now, although she thought it would be better left covered.

There was heavy bruising to the back of his head, as well. Origin of the concussion, obviously.

She answered his father's comment about having saved his life with, 'It's true if we'd left him there for the Boches to find they'd have shot him or strung him up. But they'd also have been here in two shakes interrogating *you*, M'sieur.'

'Why do you say that?'

'Can you imagine they'd believe you weren't in it together? Your own son and you didn't know what he was doing? Where'd he have got the keys from?'

'Perhaps – you're right . . .'

'So you'd know whoever *else* was in it, and they'd want to know that too.' She glanced at André – who was alert enough to have caught the implication. He'd said it himself when they'd been talking in the forest: *a red-hot skewer applied to a man's eyeball . . .*

An admission that he'd never even *hope* to resist interrogation.

She asked his father, 'Will you get the doctor for him?'

'Perhaps I should . . .'

'You could say it was for you. Shock at the news of an attack on your factory. You might have had a stroke, even. But if they haven't yet *told* you—'

'Only Legrand, saying the Poste was alight but he saw no danger to the factory. André – *should* I call Dr Simonot?'

'I'd say not. Safer not to draw attention.' His voice was a cross between a murmur and a husky whisper. 'Best thing might be to lie low here until Guichard brings his men out into the open – a matter of only days, perhaps, and by that time maybe –' a hand moved towards his face but didn't touch it – 'be OK, rejoin them. Jacques Craillot might let Guichard know where I am. Ask him to do that, Justine?'

'I'll suggest it. But – better have the doctor.' She urged his father, 'For the burns. I wouldn't worry much about concussion, but all that could get worse – septic even.'

'As soon as I can, I'll get him.'

'Good.' Rosie got up. 'Tell him about the bruising as well, he might have something for it. Now we must go – moon'll be up soon.' Glancing at her watch: 'My God, it *will* be!'

Quarter past one: fifteen minutes, roughly. Monsieur Henri was stopping her, though: his hands on her shoulders, nervous eyes on hers: 'Come in the morning? To work, ostensibly?'

'Tomorrow.' She thought about it. 'If it's possible to get here – yes. But don't count on it. We don't know how they're going to react, do we?'

'No reason they'd stop you, just because there's been sabotage by Maquisards. Nothing to do with *any* of us. But with André here alone, you see, when I'm at work—'

'The factory'll be closed, surely.'

'Production will be shut down, but there'll be clearing up, and all sorts of decisions to be taken. Heaven knows—'

'I'll come if they let me. Probably early.' A glance at Saurrat: 'Come on, Charles.' Pausing, then: 'That your telephone?'

He'd heard it too – one jangling ring, from downstairs, in the hall. Making for the door, muttering, 'I'll be back, André. This'll be Wachtel, I dare say. Oh, God . . .' It rang again as Rosie and the boy followed him down, and by the time they were crossing the hall towards the front door he had the receiver pressed against his ear, was shouting into the fixture on the wall, 'But that's *terrible!*'

Listening again: also gesturing to her to stop, wait. A palm over the voicepiece, and a whisper, 'Legrand again.' Then loudly: 'I can hardly believe this! How would they have got in? How on earth could—'

She was at the door, easing the bolt back – very carefully, alert to the likely proximity of the Briards. Hearing him again: 'Very well – tell him I'm on my way. I'll come by bicycle. By the time I had the *gazo* warmed up . . . What? Of *course* I've got my keys! What sort of question's *that*?'

Chapter 17

A very *good* question, she'd thought – and one that was liable to provide Monsieur Henri with grave problems. She hadn't seen it so clearly, until this moment: had thought of the keys being returned to him quickly as an adequate covering of tracks.

She *hoped* she was wrong now, but . . . Waiting with the door unbolted but still shut: his braying into the phone would be audible out in the yard when it was open, she wanted to hear him hang up before she moved. Hoping to God meanwhile that she wasn't thinking straight – because if she was, it wouldn't be only *his* bad luck.

Work it out later. Talk to Jacques. Who'd also be in the soup: as *she* would be. And no immediately obvious way out.

He'd hung up, at last. She eased the heavy door back and slipped out, pulling the boy with her and taking care not to catch the Sten against the door.

'Go on, I'll follow.'

Back over the same route, to start with. There'd been a car or truck manoeuvring somewhere at the front, a bark of German and a sound of boots scrunching gravel – distraction for Briard ears, she hoped. She left the cover of the porch, followed the near-invisible and silent Saurrat, loping past the Briards' entrance to the stable-block corner and on again into the shelter of the trees; through them to the wall.

'Charles – hold on . . .' A hand on his arm. 'Not back the way we came. Other side of this wall instead – up to the road *here*.'

'Then over and through the orchards. OK.'

'Would it get *you* home?'

'Sure. Quickest way, for me.'

Down to the bottom, round the buttressed end of the wall on the stream's bridle-path, then up to the road. Pausing there, with the wall a black slab receding into darkness on her right, edging the road towards the village. A flickering, pinkish glow amongst trees along there would be from the smouldering remains of the Poste; those trees were the ones around the start of the timber-yard track. She was only looking that way for a few seconds but in that time a heavy truck passed slowly – going away, in the direction of the church – in bulky silhouette against the glow.

Fire-truck maybe.

'OK?'

Whisper from Saurrat – negotiating roadside thorn hedging and strands of wire. It was the same the other side, she remembered, having noted it *en passant* a couple of times from Jacques' *gazo*. Checking up and down the road again, before crossing. Nothing, though, certainly no traffic on the move. Only – a double-take, as she joined him on that side – a hint of a first show of moonlight leaking up over that end of the village.

Jacques put a brandy in front of her, on the kitchen table. She'd given him the Sten – first extracting the magazine and clearing the breech – and he'd taken it down to the cellar. Telling her now, 'You cut *that* fine enough.' Referring to the fact that the moon *was* up now, silvering the eastern sky and silhouetting the church spire as sharp as a dagger-blade. He was topping-up his own *fine*, and Colette's: in pyjamas with a jacket over them, Colette with a bath-robe over her nightdress, the robe's belt cinched tight, indenting her hour-glass figure. They'd both been practically stunned with relief when she'd stumbled in through the side-door from the alley: since when of course she'd given them a blow-by-blow account of events from the time she and Charles Saurrat had set off around the back of the Poste, to just a few minutes ago when he'd parted from her in the orchard behind the *auberge*. Saurrat lived in the third cottage along from the *gendarmerie*, and his father managed the timber-yard. But he could have got home as easily the other way round, he'd explained, crossing the road between his own house and the bridge.

'Your fire-bomb saved everything, Jacques.' She took a long drag at her cigarette. 'Without it, they'd surely have been in to check the factory.'

'Emile Guichard's notion, that fire-bomb.'

Colette asked her – while Jacques was dispensing brandy – 'Do you think André will be all right?'

'Yes – as long as his father gets the doctor out to him. The burns are the worst of it – at least, I'd *guess*—'

'He's lucky then.'

'Let's hope so. Only thing is—'

'Here's to us.'

Jacques – glass raised: Rosie tossed back about half hers, and shut her eyes for a moment. 'Wow. *That* hit the spot.'

'You said –' Colette's hand on her arm – 'only thing is—?'

'I was going to say that I think Boche suspicions are bound to focus on Monsieur Henri. Then if they search the house—'

'But *why*—'

Jacques said, 'Because of the keys.'

'Exactly.' Rosie nodded. 'It's obvious the other two would never have let theirs out of their possession . . . All right, another set could have been made at some time or other –

ages ago even, might have been a spare set in the factory somewhere, or in the *gendarmerie* even – that was the sort of thing *I* had in mind, vaguely – but the Boches'll grab at the *obvious* answer – won't they?'

'It was André's plan.' Jacques had nodded. 'Based entirely on the use of his father's keys. His and his father's participation – that was the big thing, as he wanted us all to see it. Guichard, I may say, wasn't sold on it, but –' a glance at his wife – 'happened to suit *our* book, didn't it?'

'Because of the alternative.'

'Exactly. And Emile went along with it finally for the same reason – your threat of bombing, Justine.'

'Laid it on thick, didn't I?'

Colette asked her, 'Are you sending a message to London that it's been done?'

'Well – I *will* be . . .'

'The issue of *le patron*'s keys, though.' Jacques had been standing, moving around, but he joined them at the table now. 'I'm afraid you're right, Justine, it's not a good prospect, is it? My guess is they'll want to be done with us here good and quick – matter investigated, action taken, Heil bloody Hitler . . .'

'Investigation and action by Linscheidt and company, d'you think?'

'I'd doubt it. But – only guessing.' His thick, work-hardened hands were flat on the table, one on each side of his own amber-glowing *fine*. Glancing up – about to say something else, evidently deciding against it. Rosie thinking about punitive detachments – SS, typically – and guessing it was what he had on his mind too. She asked them both, 'How would Monsieur Henri stand up to interrogation, d'you think?'

No answers. Jacques looking away – at the clock, its hands standing at twelve minutes past two – and Colette with her elbows on the table, hands covering her face, forehead creased above the fingertips . . . Despite, Rosie thought – wondered – having apparently been quite *unwor-ried*, over a period of years, by *le patron* knowing she and Jacques were *résistants*?

Hadn't thought of him being subjected to torture or threat of torture, she supposed.

She tried, 'You see, if he was the sort of man who could be expected to hold out . . .' Pausing: both of them watch-ing her, Colette peeking between spread fingers, Jacques motionless, expressionless. She went on, 'It's possible they might see it as an operation by Maquisards, who'd only have wanted the loan of his keys. No question of anyone else in the village being involved?'

'You mean he might keep his mouth shut?'

'Well – involving *us* wouldn't get him off the hook, would it?'

Jacques looked down at his glass, shook his head slightly. Colette took her hands away from her face. 'I wonder if there's any way to get André out of the manor.'

'Surely not in present circumstances. Not certain I'll be able to get *into* it, even.'

Jacques glanced up. 'You've agreed to go to work this morning, you said?'

'Yes. Monsieur Henri wants help with André, of course. If he has to go to the factory – or stay there, he's there *now*, probably, they were on the phone to him when Saurrat and I left. But – Colette, about getting André out – at the moment, I'd say not a hope – I'm sure you'd agree, Jacques. But later on – *maybe* – and other circumstances permitting, I could call for a pick-up from England. You mentioned a landing-field you and Joseph Lambert used, Jacques, – a code-name beginning with "P"?'

A nod. Brown eyes on hers, puzzled-looking . . . 'Code-name "Parnasse".'

'Thing is, André having been in Boche hands, SOE rules

say he should be brought back for de-briefing. London would certainly co-operate. So – if *he* agreed, and you'd help with transport—'

'I doubt he'd want it. Just at this time, I'd guess the Forêt d'Othe's as far as he'd want to get. Anyway, Mesdames, the point here and now – if we can stick to it for say two seconds – is that if they do turn the heat on Monsieur Henri—'

'None of us is safe.'

Colette had said it. Or rather, Rosie guessed, brought herself to admit it – to even Jacques' surprise. He'd stared at her for a moment, then tossed back what was left of his brandy – putting the glass down then and moving that hand to enfold one of hers. 'You're right, my darling. None of us is. But then again – in years now, who *has* been?' Gazing at Rosie: '*You* haven't – for more than ten minutes at a time, eh?'

'Well—'

'And there isn't a thing we can do about it, is there?' He lifted his wife's hand to his lips, and kissed it. 'Come on. What we *can* do is get some sleep.'

She could have sent Baker Street a message confirming the destruction of the rocket casings, but (a) it wasn't all that essential – Marilyn's signal had said Jupiter cancelled, not Jupiter postponed – and (b) it was hardly fair to the Craillots to transmit from the *auberge*. Especially as the district might by now be under close radio-detection surveillance. Her earlier transmissions would have been at least approximately charted, now there'd been sabotage action in this same previously quiet area, and there'd surely be detector vans deployable from Sens or Troyes.

With the light out, ready for bed – essential chores completed, clean gear put ready for the morning and cyanide capsules transferred from today's – which God willing she'd launder when she had an hour or two to spare –

she opened her curtains just enough to take a cautious look down the road towards the factory. She'd heard a truck passing, just as she'd got up here, had stood motionless for a few seconds – as so often, half expecting it to stop – but it must have been either a patrol passing through or a truck returning to the manor. The road was empty now in any case: some patches of it moonlit, others shadowed, no movement discernible – in fact not even a *parked* vehicle in sight.

She was down for breakfast at six, finding Colette already there, with porridge on the stove.

'Did you sleep, Justine?'

'Oh, yes. I was tired. How about you?'

'Not much. My own fault – cognac always does me in. And it makes Jacques snore, which doesn't exactly help. Help yourself to coffee?'

'Thank you.' She took it black, despite its peculiar taste. Hadn't slept all *that* well. There'd been dreams too, including the one Ben called the Rouen Nightmare, which she hadn't had in months, had begun to think maybe she'd escaped from, finally . . . She pulled a chair back: 'Jacques down yet?'

'Sweeping, out there. The pavement.'

'Ah.' He'd also be seeing whatever was going on out there.

'May I borrow Yvette's bike again?'

'Of course. They're due back at the weekend, you realize?'

'Yes – you told me. I'm looking forward to meeting them. Obviously that's one reason you wouldn't dream of – well, not being here.'

'We wouldn't consider it in any case. Leaving the place empty?'

'Mightn't it be as well to let them stay where they are for the time being – with their cousins? Until things settle down, or – after all, there are battles being fought, in that direction?'

'I'd sooner have them with me. So would you, if they were yours. But if it did seem safer for them to stay there – when the time comes—'

'Only two days to the weekend, Colette—'

'We're aware of it. Jacques in fact will be speaking to them this evening. At least, I *hope* . . . Here – porridge.' She brought her own to the table as well as Rosie's. 'God knows how long my lord and master'll be.' A querying glance: 'He's a good man, you know?'

'One of the best ever, I'd say.' She dipped her spoon in, raised it and blew on its steaming contents. 'Quick on the uptake, too.'

'Surprised you on occasion, has he?'

'Impressed me, certainly.'

She wasn't going to mention that Victor Dufay had told Michel that Jacques wasn't all that bright – or that her own first impression had seemed to bear it out. 'Colette – a thought I had, in the night – about Charles Saurrat. If Monsieur Henri *were* to be interrogated—'

'Let's pray he isn't.'

'But in case he is – don't you think Saurrat should be warned? Best of all, might clear out now, until it's over? After all, he has a brother-in-law with Guichard, hasn't he? And Monsieur Henri wouldn't have the feeling for him that he must have for you and Jacques?'

'I'm not sure that any such feeling would –' she shrugged – 'be likely to save the day, exactly . . . But – yes, I'll suggest it. And on that subject – if *you* felt inclined to disappear, Justine—'

'No. Thanks, but—'

'We wouldn't have to be involved. You told us who you were, we accepted that in good faith, now you've gone – heaven knows where or why—'

'*I* wouldn't know where or why – or how. And in any case . . .' Shaking her head. Partly because she'd given them her word she'd see it through – one principle in SOE doctrine being to keep one's word, since otherwise the firm itself would be discredited – also because if there was even a glimmer of a chance of getting André out to London—

'Ah. Speak of the devil . . .'

Jacques: sound of the front door shutting: then the bolt banging over. Clatter of a broom tossed into a cupboard then, and a few heavy steps. Clash of the swing door . . . 'Sleep all right, Justine?'

'Not badly, Jacques, thank you. Is anything happening, out there?'

'Practically nothing that I could see. Despite sweeping every square centimetre a dozen times.' He stopped at the stove, where Colette was ladling out more porridge. 'Trucks down by the square – may have come from Sens, in which case they'll have brought troops, presumably, but I didn't see any – although I was privileged to see Wachtel go rushing by. Driving himself – which could mean they're stretched. But otherwise nothing in or out of the manor at all. Thank you, *chérie*.' He took his bowl, and asked Rosie – who'd finished, was about to get up – 'Going to try your luck, are you?'

'Might as well.' On her feet. 'See if they'll let me by is the first thing.'

'Wouldn't think of joining the boys *au vert*, would you? Emile'd make you welcome. Until things blow over?'

Colette said, 'I just tried her on that, Jacques.'

'Oh.' Shrugging. 'And you told me she'd spit in your eye, didn't you?' A wink at Rosie as he put his bowl down. 'I must admit, getting you out *might* be a problem. On the other hand—'

'Why not check that – see if they'll let you deliver charcoal somewhere? I don't mean check on my behalf, necessarily, but since we don't know what's been going on we should act just normally – don't you think?'

'*If* they'll let us.'

'*Chérie*—'

'I didn't mean to say it in that tone. I was thinking of road-blocks and so forth. No, I agree with Justine – one heard explosions – gunfire maybe – one's naturally *concerned*, but—'

'Exactly.'

Jacques' hands were light on her shoulders as he stooped to kiss her. 'Luck, Justine.'

Colette had kissed her too – after Jacques, standing back, had said to her, 'Now *your* turn . . .' Cycling out of the alley now, five minutes later; swinging right, past the butcher's and baker's shops, thinking that this was Thursday – August 10th – and she'd met those two for the first time on Sunday. Less than four days ago, but she felt she knew them better than one might come to know others in as many years.

One of the great things, in this racket. By and large, those who were with you damn well *were* with you.

Some vehicle which hadn't been in sight when she'd started was coming up behind her from the direction of the village, and the entrance to the manor was still about a hundred metres ahead. She pedalled more slowly: if it was going to turn in there, let it do so well before she did, leave her to face the sentry's challenge on her own, *sans* audience or complications. She had a presentiment that she *would* be stopped this time, and required to show her papers, although last time – yesterday – she'd been let by unchallenged, and the day before she'd come with Colette, whom of course the Boche had recognized . . .

Car coming up close on her left now. Pillared entrance

gates about thirty metres ahead. Pedalling normally – slowish – and keeping well over to the right.

Staff car, camouflage-painted, soldier-driver on his own in front, wearing a helmet. Two officers in the back: most noticeable was the tall young lieutenant from the *gendarmerie* – Klebermann, he of the small head – even smaller for the huge cap surmounting it – and protuberant ears. The other man she barely saw. The car was slowing, about to turn in; Rosie free-wheeling by this time, but aware that it might be unwise to be seen as hesitant or dithering: being here because she'd made perfectly legitimate arrangements with Monsieur Henri, there was no damn *reason* to dither.

Glancing back. Nothing else coming. Swinging over . . .

The staff car had slowed to a crawl as it entered, Klebermann with his head in the wound-down window, apparently conversing with the sentry who'd come out of the black-painted guard-hut. Another soldier was emerging from it: turning *her* way and at the same time unslinging his Schmeisser machine-pistol. The other one – Klebermann too – also turning this way, showing interest. The car had stopped.

Rosie dismounted, wheeled the bike towards them.

'Halt!'

She didn't recognize any of them except Klebermann – who was out of the car now, standing with his long, booted legs apart, fists on his hips. It was the soldier he'd been talking to who'd bawled at her: fattish, early twenties, looked as if he spent all his spare time indoors. Schmeisser still slung, but levelled near-enough in her direction, his right hand resting on it and the other one extended now towards her.

'Papers!'

She leant the bike against herself, reached into her jacket's inside pocket. In the same moment – actually as she looked down, to cope with the pocket which was rather narrow for

easy extraction of the folded wad of papers – she saw that
the officer who'd been in the car with Klebermann – and
was now getting out – was SS. An *Oberleutnant* – somehow
roughed-up, savage-looking. Just that quick sight of him –
a glance of a second or two seconds' duration – chilled her.
He looked – well, exhausted – but also the adjective that
had occurred to her first – *savage*.

Exuding malice: a glare of loathing directed personally
at *her*.

Klebermann had said something – to her? – in German.
She stared – let him see her bewilderment . . .

'*Pardon?*'

'*Fräulein –*' he was consulting a notebook – 'Justine
Quérier?'

'*Mais oui, M'sieur!*'

Further bewilderment at being named: letting him see
that, but *not* see the sudden fear of imminent arrest.
Guessing he'd have her name there on an arrest list with
others, probably including *Craillot, Jacques; Craillot, Colette;
Saurrat, Charles* . . . They'd have been at it all night, she
supposed – questioning, analysing: would already have
Monsieur Henri in custody. Klebermann had muttered
something to the guard who was still waiting for her papers:
and his SS friend – she hadn't looked at him again but was
very much aware of him and of his movements – had
just stalked past her, back towards the gates. Klebermann
clearing his throat before trying his French on her now: 'For
what is it that you come here?'

'At the request of Monsieur Marchéval. It's been arranged
I should work for him – as *femme de ménage*.' Pause: searching for signs of comprehension, and not seeing any; maybe
she'd spoken too fast for him. Her hand was still on the
papers inside Thérèse's jacket: nobody had told her they
weren't wanted now, but the soldier who'd demanded them
had been upstaged by Klebermann – who was framing

words in French again: 'You – *domestique*, *chez* Monsieur Marchéval?'

'But *yes*, my captain!'

'*Leutnant – pas capitaine.*'

'Oh—'

The SS lieutenant was returning towards the car: she thought he'd glanced at her as he passed. Klebermann meanwhile gesturing to the soldier, telling him – in German, but the tone of voice made his meaning obvious – 'It's in order, let her pass.'

'*Jawohl* . . .'

Waving her on, into the manor grounds. The SS man was getting back into the car – stooping double as if *crawling* in, then flopping back. Mad dog back into its kennel . . . Relief, the sudden miracle of deliverance, had her actually murmuring thanks to Klebermann – who ignored her, had turned away to address the other soldier – whom she recognized now as having been on guard here the day before. Distracted, she made a hash of mounting to start with but got herself together then, got going – around the car and on down the middle of the drive towards the manor: slight left-hand bend, then similarly to the right – with the house in sight now, framed between banks of rhododendrons. She could hear the car coming up behind: had in her mind an image of the SS *Oberleutnant* – darkly unshaven, slack-mouthed, eyes red-rimmed, and that vicious, beaten look. As if he'd been out on a drunken bender, been picked out of some gutter. The weirdest thing though, and most frightening, was that impression of intense hatred. Even though one's reaction was entirely reciprocal . . . Ahead now was where the drive divided, encircling the central lawn and flagpole, the right-hand branch leading to Monsieur Henri's wing, left one curving round to the front of the house but with an offshoot into a parking area – in which she had a quick sight of another staff car and several small trucks. Klebermann's car sounding uncomfortably close behind as she swung away to the right – wondering at the last moment whether it was going to follow, herd her along . . . But – SS, for Christ's sake. She wished she had a private line to Jacques, to warn them. Just as one swallow didn't make a summer, there'd be others, surely. That one might have had work to do with Klebermann – checking records in the *gendarmerie*, perhaps, or at the factory, or interrogating workers in their houses. Pedalling around the half-circle of drive towards the manor's west wing – *not* allowing herself a second look across at the group of Boches out front, some of whom had been moving up on to the steps, clearing the way for Klebermann's car as it approached. Out of her sight now, anyway, as she rode into the stable-yard, Yvette's bike juddering over the cobbles. She propped her bike against the porch where she'd left it both times before, went in and knocked on the door. A minute passed: she was about to try again – but thinking they might still have him down at the factory – when he opened the door a little way, and peered out.

'Justine . . .'

'It's early, I know, but I *said* I'd—'

'Yes, yes.' Glancing back into the hall: whispering then as he let her in, 'Major Linscheidt's here – in fact about to leave, but—'

'Christ . . .'

Absorbing it, though: and seeing no grounds for panic. Linscheidt, as the Craillots had described him, being distinctly preferable to SS of any size or shape. And she had her own act ready. She pushed the door shut behind her, told *le patron* in a tone for the man inside to hear, 'I've come early, M'sieur, because in the *auberge* they start early, there's always so much to do. But if this is *too* early—'

'No, it's all right. But start in the kitchen, please – it's a mess in there, you'll find, but—'

'Oh, I don't mind, in the *auberge* sometimes you wouldn't *believe*—'

'Your new *domestique*, is this?'

A tall man, in immaculately pressed uniform. Very much as she'd visualized him. Highly polished boots, a patch over his left eye, cropped brown hair greying at the temples. She *thought* greying: the light wasn't good though, where he was standing, having just emerged from the *petit salon*. Boot-heels together, hands behind his back, inclined slightly forward as if for a better view of her. She nodded – 'Monsieur le Commandant –' and attempted a smile which out of shyness didn't quite come off. Glancing instead at Monsieur Henri: 'I'll – start in the kitchen, then.'

'Yes indeed, Major – this is Justine Quérier – whom I've engaged as a replacement for Madame Briard.' A shrugging smile: 'Who it seems has given me up.' He pointed: 'Through there, Justine.'

'But one moment, if you please.'

Looming closer. He had a limp: she remembered Colette mentioning it. Also an Iron Cross. The eye-patch was black. 'I would like your replies to one or two questions. In essence – did you know what was happening last night in the factory?'

'In the factory?'

His accent in French, she'd noticed, wasn't at all bad.

'You must have heard the noise, and so forth. What did you think was happening?'

'The Poste went up in flames, I know *that*. Also there were explosions – I thought guns, they woke me . . .' She asked Monsieur Henri, '*Was* it something in your factory, m'sieur?'

'Look here.' Linscheidt tapped his wristwatch. 'Nearly

seven now. Surely the whole village must be talking about it. That's what I'm after – what they're saying. D'you live alone – not to have anyone to discuss it with?'

'Discuss *what*, M'sieur?'

She was the young girl on whom a house had fallen during an air-raid on Rouen. One moment hardly a care in the world, and the next – lost, dazed, injured, homeless. Safe here, though, and clinging to it – a place to live, companionship, even a job: explosions in the night were *other* people's business.

'Well?'

'I – beg your pardon?'

'I asked, where do you live?'

'Oh. At L'Auberge la Couronne, M'sieur. Madame Craillot and I are distantly related, she's very kindly taken me in and—'

'She and her husband weren't discussing the night's events?'

'About the fire, yes – we were wondering how that could have started.'

'What about the explosions?'

'Well – Monsieur Craillot was saying he'd make enquiries – at the *gendarmerie*, I think. But I wasn't really – following . . . I'm sorry, M'sieur—'

'All right.' Swivelling abruptly to Monsieur Henri. 'Virtual disinterest!'

'A special case, rather.' Glancing at her: 'All right, Justine. Kitchen's through that door.' Back to the German. 'There's an unfortunate background, Madame Craillot was telling me – an air-raid on Rouen in which she was – hurt. She's not . . .' She guessed he'd be tapping his head. 'How she happens to be available for this work, no doubt. But as for what you're trying to establish, Major – I beg you to take my word for it, it would be totally contrary to our people's interests—'

'The fact remains, it was planned with the advantage of inside knowledge. That's quite evident.'

'Well – as I said to Wachtel, perhaps some *former* employee—'

'Whom you can't name – nor can your man Legrand, Wachtel informs me. There's also the business of the keys. I'd have liked to be able to explain *that* to this fellow when he gets here.' The major picked up his cap. 'I must go. If he wants to see you, I'll send word.' Starting towards the door: Monsieur Henri went ahead to open it for him. From the kitchen end of the hallway Rosie heard Linscheidt ask quietly, 'The young woman's simple, that what you were saying?'

'So the doctor hasn't actually seen him?'

She'd asked Monsieur Henri, but André cut in: 'I'd like it if he did. OK, the ointment helps, but—'

Grimacing: which did nothing to improve his looks. Grease of some kind – ointment supplied by the doctor – covered flesh that was now a dark pinkish brown, the skin broken in places and patched with singed stubble. It looked horrible, and he was obviously in pain: on the bed, in pyjamas presumably belonging to his father, propped against pillows which kept the bruised back of his head clear of the bedhead's rails. There was an empty mug and a plate on the bedside chair. His father assuring him, 'I *will* get Simonot out, once this inquiry's done with. You see –' explaining to Rosie – 'I was nearly four hours at the factory – after you left us here – and I had Legrand with me all that time – and Wachtel, some of it. Well, I told them I had a dreadful headache, but being down there what could I do but go along to Simonot's house – got him out of bed, in fact, explained the situation and he gave me the ointment. I had no *excuse* to bring him out here, you see. But as I say—'

'Tell us what's going on?'

She'd cut him short: he'd been gabbling, tongue running away with him – ashamed that he hadn't had the doctor to see his son, she guessed. Although in the circumstances it *would* have been dangerous, he was right: and if the ointment was as effective as apparently the doctor had said it was . . . André asked him, 'You did say SS?'

'Yes. Christ – I need a bath and a shave, a few hours' sleep—'

'SS.' André's half-open, raw-looking eyes on Rosie's. 'We know what *that* means.'

As one SOE agent to another, she thought. She'd noticed that when he spoke his mouth moved strangely – as if he was trying to speak *without* moving it. It had to be fairly agonizing, that frizzled skin and flesh. She told him – and his father – 'I encountered one just now – an SS *Oberleutnant* – at the gates when I rode in. He was with Klebermann. Did Linscheidt tell you anything else of interest?'

'Well.' A hand to his head, as if remembering was an effort. 'Yes. That a *Sturmbannführer* Kroll is coming in over his head to investigate the circumstances of the attack. He hadn't arrived, at that stage – twenty minutes ago, eh, when *you* got here? Some others had, but not Kroll. They're from a battalion that's had a bad time of it, badly cut up in action somewhere or other – remnants being withdrawn eastward. The man you saw –' a nod to Rosie – 'may be one who was at the factory when I was there. I thought half dead – practically asleep on his feet, anyway. He was with Wachtel for a while, then he went to the *gendarmerie* with Klebermann. Wachtel accused me of having provided the keys – Linscheidt took my side, I'm glad to say, pointing out that he has no proof whatsoever!'

André said, 'You feel you've been through it, then.'

'Is that sarcasm?'

'Why, heaven forbid!'

'I *have* been through it! Would you believe it, they'd been rifling my office?'

'And what's the position now?'

'Well – Kroll may be here by now. Or soon. And if he listens to Wachtel . . .'

He'd checked: standing near the window. Spreading his hands, a gesture of helplessness. 'He's bound to, isn't he?'

Rosie suggested, 'Unless he listens to Linscheidt?'

'But *he's* in doubt, now!'

'The vital thing is they shouldn't find André. Find him, they know everything, and—'

'I can't *believe* in this situation.' Appealing to Rosie: she saw tears in his eyes. 'There has to be some way – some *answer*—'

'Not always, Papa.' André's eye-slits on *him* now. 'You take a chance, things go wrong – as in this case I did—'

'They can't be allowed to find you.' There was a shake in his voice. 'In fact, there's no reason they *should* search here. None at all – if there was some way out, about the keys . . .'

'Gaspard Legrand?'

Both looking at her – waiting for more. She shrugged: 'Only a thought. Except that he's something of a collab, I don't know anything about him, not even what he looks like – but if you could pin it on him – *his* keys?'

'Impossible!'

'Suppose his pro-Boche attitude was an act. You've suspected for a long time he was secretly a *résistant*. He could have had a set of keys made on the quiet – could have made them himself, even. You can't *prove* it, but you feel now you should have done something about him long before this – because they definitely weren't *your* keys. Who'd blow up his own factory, for God's sake?'

'Not bad.' André, watching her . . . 'Not at all bad, Papa.

That pose would have been good cover for him, wouldn't it? In your shoes, I'd go for it.'

'Think yourself into the part.' Rosie had been about to put a hand on his narrow shoulder – he'd sat down on the edge of the bed – but he was leaning forward now, head down almost between his knees. Feeling sick, maybe, or dizzy. She told him, 'The part's *you*, really. You've done everything you could to keep your business going, workers and their families employed and safe. That's a fact, you're known for it, the entire village would confirm it – so how would it have made sense to throw it all away now? You *wouldn't*. So who did? Tell them – it could *only* have been Legrand!'

'Once I say this, Legrand will know for certain *I'm* the one.'

'So he'll accuse you, and you'll have to face him down. You're the boss around here – why should they take his word against yours?'

'She's right. It's your best chance, Papa.'

'The other thing is, leave André alone now. Lock the door and forget him. I mean it – don't come near him.'

'Food and drink?'

'I'll bring up whatever there is down there.'

'What about Doctor Simonot?'

'Well – when I can get him . . . No, second thoughts, forget him too. You're not *here*, André!'

'Well, thanks – I wish I *weren't*, but—'

'It might be a two or three-day business – not more. Linscheidt and co won't be staying in St Valéry with the factory out of action – and when *they* pull out, d'you imagine the SS are going to stay here? What for – the fishing? Whatever they do, they'll do it quick and push on. Two days, at most? Then the Maquis'll move in, won't they?'

Eyes like brown cracks in half-cooked meat . . . 'Persuasive, isn't she?' His father sitting upright now, drawing

long, slow breaths, apparently not even listening to what
was being said. Heart racing, she guessed. He'd be scared
of that too. She told André quietly, 'There's an alternative. Suppose before Guichard takes over we find we *can*
move—'

'I'm ahead of you.'

'You are?'

'A flight out to England?'

'Well – why not?'

'Think I'm *stupid*?'

'Far from it. But you'd get the de-briefing over – could
go better than you expect, you did yourself some good last
night, remember—'

'*Good*, did I!'

'And you'd get first-class hospital treatment – which you
may well need, by then. Think about it.' She asked his
father, 'What's in the kitchen that I can bring up for him?'

He'd come down to help, show her what there was. Some
eggs – which she put on to boil – cheese, bread stale
enough to have thrown out, and the remains of a rabbit
stew. There was also the basin to wash out and re-fill: and
chamber-pots to see to. A job for Papa, that one. She found
some jugs for fresh water, and put a kettle on to boil for
coffee-substitute: the last hot drink André would have for
a while.

She took it off again. The chicory mixture had a strong
aroma – hardly likely to be emanating from a locked and
empty bedroom.

Monsieur Henri was back then, and she gave him a
loaded tray to take up.

'Not leaving *you* anything to eat. Come for a meal at the
auberge, maybe.'

'It's – possible.'

'There's coffee anyway. Don't give him any up there,

someone might smell it. Better let him lock himself in and keep the key in there with him – d'you think?'

In case she and/or Monsieur Henri came to grief: at least he'd be able to get out, try to get away. She added, 'After that lot, there'll only be the eggs. Might as well boil them hard.'

He wasn't in good shape at all, she thought – hearing him stumble on the stairs. Remembering that fit of the horrors he'd had, that moan of *has to be some way – some answer* . . . She'd felt a twinge of empathy – recognizing shock and desperation when she heard it, having known it herself a few times; but his son, she thought, probably had very little feeling for him at all. Thoughts jumbled, rushing, treading on each others' heels. Mother's boy: and lover-boy, who if he was going to get out of this alive wasn't going to look half so pretty. And neither he nor his father was likely to hold much back, if the SS went to work on them. Lover-boy having already proved it, *vis-à-vis* the Gestapo – and admitted as much two days ago in the forest, that bit about red-hot skewers, effectively acknowledging that he'd known from the start he couldn't have stood up to torture: alleging that he'd arranged his own Lysander pick-up, to avoid any such ordeal. Total lie – it had been the de-briefing in England he'd ducked out of – but still fair enough, the torture thing. She'd come very close to breaking-point herself – in Rouen, stripped to the waist by a Gestapo torturer wielding a pair of pliers. She'd admitted in her later de-briefing that in another half-minute she'd have been begging to be allowed to tell him everything she knew. So could hardly sneer at these two if *they* broke. Even though one had at least tried, up to that truly frightful point *had* held out. Probably everyone ever born had a certain threshold, she thought. One was *not* entitled to judge, therefore: could admire, certainly, but not condemn.

Except you *would*. When your own life was at stake.

Needn't have been here. Could have flown home, with Marilyn. Home to Ben, for God's sake!

'The eggs done?'

'Oh, yes.' She'd forgotten them. *Le patron* re-entering, putting one empty tray down on the table. It was a table of the old French farmhouse type, with a slide that pulled out from one end for use as a bread-board. Glancing at him as she took the saucepan off the stove: still with fair certainty that he wouldn't even *start* to resist.

Except for the lie about Legrand. Might lay on that act well enough, she guessed – in the hope of saving his own life.

She had a bowl ready for the eggs.

'Thought any more about Legrand?

A moment's blank stare: then a nod.

'Yes. I'll try it. André was saying just now it's the only hope I have.'

'To act it well you've got to believe it – *know* that you're innocent and he's trying to drop you in it. Be indignant – angry – and for *real*!'

'Well. I don't know . . .'

'It's not all that difficult. Just convince *yourself*, to start with. I'll take these up, I'll be quicker.'

'No – I haven't said goodbye to him—'

'Be quick, then. We may not have long.'

Listening to an echo of that 'haven't said goodbye': with a tangential reaction of gladness that she'd asked Marilyn to give Ben the message that she was sorry *she* hadn't said goodbye – if only to have him know it had worried her, that she cared that much . . . Well, he *would* have known it, but—

To have *said* it, was the thing. And – back to earth, to *now* – might as well make some coffee for herself and Monsieur Henri. There was no milk, it would have to be black. Tipping out the kettle, for a start: then re-filling it . . .

A crash from out there in the hall: the first thought in her head was of Papa falling down the stairs, and from that – as she hurried through – *Heart attack, maybe*: and a follow-up reflection that for him it mightn't be a bad way out. For herself or the Craillots either, maybe – take the focus off *him*—

Bursting into the hallway, stopping dead, staring open-mouthed at *Leutnant* Klebermann. Behind him, brushing himself down, a sergeant – not SS – with a Schmeisser.

'Oh—'

Klebermann snapped at her, 'Monsieur Marchéval, if you please!'

Monsieur Marchéval was coming quickly down the stairs – calling down, 'Justine, you all right?'

'Yes, M'sieur, but –' at least *some* warning – 'it's the Lieutenant Klebermann who's asking for you!'

Behind the sergeant, the door leading into the central part of the house stood open. Hence the crash, she realized: if it had been nailed up, and he'd put his shoulder to it. Gazing at it: dumb, astonished – heart hammering, not only from Klebermann's precipitous arrival, but *why* they'd chosen to break through this way. Decision taken, Monsieur Henri found guilty, present usage and division of the manor therefore terminated? That was the instant conclusion: the *only* explanation, in fact – which one was going to have to face and cope with now – while continuing to act simple . . . Monsieur Henri meanwhile negotiating the lower part of the staircase more circumspectly, with his eyes wide on Klebermann: Rosie half expecting a shout from up there of 'What was it, Papa?'

No such thing *yet*, but—

What was the betting Papa had left that bedroom door wide open?

'Monsieur Marchéval.' Klebermann rigid, facing him. 'Major Linscheidt requests you come. Orders also of *Sturmbannführer* Kroll. If you please . . .'

Chapter 18

André had heard all that. Rosie had pushed the forcibly opened connecting door shut – more or less, but it had four-inch nails protruding through it – and waited half a minute before going up: primary objective being to get the bedroom door shut and locked. As they'd left her, stamping away into the main body of the house, she'd quavered – addressing Monsieur Henri but by then seeing only the sergeant's broad back and slung Schmeisser – 'I'll finish cleaning in the kitchen then, M'sieur –' and had no answer. Upstairs now: André wisely not speaking until she'd shut the door: he'd swung his legs off the bed, was sitting bolt upright, mouth opening with straight lips like a ventriloquist's dummy: 'Not going to get away with it, are we?'

'Damn lucky they didn't come up here.' New thought then – to go and open the door of Monsieur's room, so that if they came back to look around they might accept that that was where he'd been. She went out, found the room, and did it. Returning soft-footed to André then: 'I can't stay up here. Obviously. So—'

'He'll go to pieces, you know.'

'Rat on *you*?'

'Well – I'm sure he'd *try* not to—'

'As *you* tried not to?'

'As I told you – tell you again, if we've got time for this

– by the time I woke up to what they were really after, they already knew it all – they were telling *me!*'

'Because you'd already steered them to about a dozen *réseaux*? Thirty or forty agents?' She agreed: 'You're right, we *don't* have time. But one thing in your favour I'll admit, you didn't shop the Craillots. Drew the line when it came to old friends?'

'They didn't come into it. I *was* asked, "Are there any *résistants* in your father's work-force or that village?", but they had no information so I could safely deny it.'

'Personal safety being your watchword. But would you *now*? In half an hour's time, say, if it comes to that?'

'I'd –' a nod – 'I'd try. And pray to God for help. That's the truth, believe me.'

She could see it was. And honest, in its way. But it was 'Hector' she was talking to, not André: 'Hector' who'd helped fill that railway carriage. She *didn't* have time for this, but there were still things she didn't understand and would have liked to. She tried just one: 'What about Joseph Lambert? Hey, wait . . .'

Stepping back further from the window.

'What is it?'

'A truck – three-quarter-tonner – stopping here. Well – nearer the Briards.'

Klebermann – and the SS *Oberleutnant*. And two helmeted troopers, also SS. Klebermann striding to the Briards' door and banging on it: one trooper was staying with the truck. Tilting his head to look up *this* way.

'They've gone into the Briards'. Klebermann and the SS officer I saw before. Briards up against it now?'

'Informing, more likely. Saw something, or heard something.' Eyes shut, and breathing through his mouth – short, panting breaths. 'Tell you, Zoé – if you were in a position to repeat your offer of a flight out to Tempsford – which you're not, of course—'

'Are you serious?'

'I *would* be, but—'

'If by some miracle we can last out without them finding you—'

'Would I get a fair hearing now in England?'

'Fair hearing, certainly, but beyond that I don't know. I doubt you'd face a firing-squad. Even politically, at this late stage—'

'But *you*'d have killed me.'

'The preference has always been to get you back. But you know the rules.' *She* knew she had to move: only needed to see first what was going to happen down there with the Briards . . . 'Baker Street obviously wants answers to certain questions – especially disappearances – and if you'd co-operate, I *suppose*—'

'Why *you* on such a brief, though – in the state you must have been—'

'I met you in Rue des Saussaies – as you remember. And before that, thanks to you, I'd have been trapped on my way from Soucelles to Rennes. *And* I was then on a train to Ravensbrück with other women agents, at least some of whom there's reason to believe must have been caught as a result of your – activities.' She'd shrugged. 'Or you might say, your blunders.' Glancing at him again, but mostly watching the parked truck and the Briards' door. 'I asked you about Lambert – or rather the Lamberts.'

Staring at her: then closing his eyes. A murmur: 'Obviously you know a certain amount already.'

'Tell me what I *don't* know?'

'All right.' A sigh. 'They got Joseph through me. Not betrayal *by* me – they trailed Huguette – his wife – back to the safe-house where she'd arranged to meet him. She'd been with me, yes. Supposed to have been with her sick father in Neuilly – some of the time she *had*. So – they caught him *and* her, then threatened me with what they'd do to her. Oh, also that they'd tell her I'd informed on Joseph.'

'Sure you didn't?'

'I'm telling you the *truth!*'

'Why would they need such leverage when you were already working for them?'

'I was *not*. They were using me, but – I've explained this to you, at least once – only as far as I knew in relation to the escape line in which my sister—'

'Wait.'

Shifting sideways a little . . .

'The *Oberleutnant*'s coming out. Klebermann too – and the trooper. Door's been shut from the inside – Briards staying put, therefore. They're talking at the truck. Going on now – Klebermann and the other – round to the front of the house, I suppose. Yes – rounding the corner. Could have taken a short-cut through here, maybe he doesn't know that.'

'Leaving the two with the truck to watch *us*.'

'Watch this end, and the Briards maybe. *You* don't exist.' She thought: one non-existent, and one brain-damaged: why watch *them*? Moving to the door: 'I'm going. Tell me quickly – the Lamberts – it was *her*, was it, not your sister—'

'The threat to my sister was to keep my father in line – because of the security importance of the new product. But over *my* head—'

'Huguette Lambert.'

A movement of acquiescence. Then: 'Guesswork, or—'

'I think it was Lambert who told Baker Street you'd been turned.'

'Oh, very likely – but purely out of malice, I had *not* been—'

'That's what you told Baker Street, I know. Your mother's friend Bob Hallowell, to be precise.'

'Christ – you *did* come briefed!'

'But *réseaux* with which you'd been in contact were being blown, agents were disappearing – that was the *factual* background to Lambert's report. What happened to your sister?'

'I don't know. Well – sent east, I suppose. Some camp . . .'

'Don't you care?'

'Of *course* I care. Simply was not allowed to know. Whereas Huguette Lambert – they told me where they were holding her, frequently assured me she was all right and being well treated—'

'So eventually you and she would live happily ever after.'

'We were in love. Completely – *lost* . . . I don't know if you've ever been in that – condition—'

'You don't, do you?' The truck was still down there: one man leaning against it, smoking, the other one inside. She looked back at André. 'If we got out of this, would you still come back with me?'

Acquiescence again . . . 'Except if the balloon went up before that, I'd rejoin Guichard.'

'You wouldn't be fit to. We're talking about the next two or three days: and in England you'd go straight into hospital. In any case you've made your mark with Guichard – it was a successful operation and you led it – right?'

Peering: nodding, then. 'Yes. One might *hope* . . .'

'It's fact. Even in London, at least to *some* extent—'

'All right. If as you say, in the next two or three days—'

'This a promise?'

'Well—'

'Because I might arrange the pick-up before I see you again. A Hudson with a doctor, maybe. Could save your life, you know!'

'All right.'

'But in case it *doesn't* work out—'

'Uh?'

'Can't bank on it exactly, can we?' She'd handed him a white handkerchief. He looked up from it questioningly, and she showed him: 'Cyanide – in this corner. Observe the deft needlework?'

Tongue-tip moistening cracked lips: 'Sure the needle-woman won't need it?'

'She's got another one.'

Nodding slowly . . . 'It's for yourself of course that you're concerned.'

'Also for Jacques and Colette. Even young Saurrat. You said you had doubts about withstanding torture – and Christ, who *doesn't*—'

His head more trembling than shaking: 'I'd sooner take my chances.'

'You mean let us take *our* chances.'

'The truth is I'd never use it.' Poking at the capsule's outline. 'I've thought about it, often. I've dropped more than one down storm-drains.' A shrug – faint gleam of humour, even: 'See *your* way of looking at it, of course: heads you win—'

'André –' frowning into eyes like cracks in greasy plaster – 'the odds are we *won't* get out of this. Unless this SS creature's stupid – which unfortunately he can't be—'

'I still don't want it.'

'Then *you're* stupid.' He was also 'Hector', for Christ's sake. Looking back at him from the doorway, reminding herself of that.

Third start at making so-called coffee, and this time she hadn't been interrupted. Fairly foul, but strengthening. Eight forty now – felt more like midday. She'd left a broom and a dust-pan in the hallway as evidence of work in progress, and a duster on the rather ugly side-table on which Linscheidt's cap had been when she'd got here. Sipping the hot, strong-tasting 'coffee': thinking that if nothing had happened by say nine o'clock, Justine Quérier would probably make tracks for the *auberge* – having started here just before seven, the agreement being for two hours' work each day, and having no idea at all what was happening. Although maybe concerned for Monsieur Henri – for instance the question of whether he'd want her to bring him a meal from the *auberge* . . .

She finished the chicory-mixture, rinsed the mug out and left it on the draining-board. The only dishcloths were rags, better ones having been taken upstairs for André's use. If he survived without getting those burns infected, she thought – guessed – he'd be very lucky. Even if in a day or two's time she was able to arrange a Hudson pick-up – with a quack on board and an ambulance standing by at Tempsford.

Not that he'd necessarily keep his promise. Unless he was really scared for himself by then.

Well – he *might* be.

Justine probably wouldn't scrub the kitchen floor now, although it needed it. Take too long. Rosie didn't bloody well *intend* to, was the truth. Push a broom around in the hallway instead maybe: or dust in the *petit salon*. She was standing in its doorway, duster, dust-pan and broom at the ready, gazing critically at the over-abundance of rather ghastly furniture without which the room wouldn't have looked nearly so small, when she heard them coming. Like noises-off in some play: a tramp of boots growing louder, coming from the corridor beyond the connecting door: she was facing it, her line of sight actually just past the foot of the stairs, when the sergeant who'd come with Klebermann barged it open again, came through pointing at the nails, warning those behind him – two SS men half dragging Monsieur Henri, and the *Oberleutnant* behind them, glaring around – at her, briefly, but at the hallway and its furniture generally, before pointing at one heavy-timbered, high-backed chair. For Monsieur Henri: they dumped him on it. Rosie – Justine – struck dumb, turning in alarm and utter confusion from that slumped figure to this new, brisk one, the *Sturmbannführer*: less evidently insane perhaps than the *Oberleutnant* but similarly ruthless, savage-looking. Linscheidt then, and Klebermann. The room seemed full of them. *Le déluge*, she thought. Not *après moi* but *autour de moi* – and with a horrifying sense of inevitability, the remorseless unfolding of what Lise would call Fate. *Because I shouldn't have been here in the first place.* Like being in a pit that was filling up – swastikas, jackboots, belts with *Gott mit Uns* in gilt on their buckles, sound-effects in that brutal-sounding language.

Monsieur Henri slumped unconscious or semi-conscious in the chair with its thick, ornately carved arms: Justine started towards him as if to help in some way but then stopped – frightened, uncertain whether she should still have been here or what was happening or about to happen – and the *Sturmbannführer* suddenly noticing her, pointing at her and asking Linscheidt who or what – despite the duster she had in one hand, dust-pan in the other, which she thought might have given him *some* clue – and others including the *Oberleutnant* turning to look at her while Linscheidt explained – including the bit about her being simple, she hoped. Open-mouthed, glancing nervously from face to face but then back at her employer – still motionless, eyes shut – maybe breathing, maybe not. She couldn't see any broken skin or blood: if they'd beaten him, which she assumed they would have, the blows would have been to his body – ribs, belly, diaphragm, kidneys. He wouldn't have had much resistance to it. She moved quickly out of the *Sturmbannführer*'s way as he strode into the *petit salon*, glanced around it and came out again. His overriding expression, whether natural or assumed, was of contempt more than of anger. Jerking his head towards the other door – the room *le patron* had said he used as an office: the *Oberleutnant* threw that door open and looked in, glared around, came out shouting something like 'No, nobody, nothing . . .'

Linscheidt then – addressing Monsieur Henri in his not-bad French, '*Sturmbannführer* Kroll asks: do you still maintain that you have not had visitors during the hours of darkness?'

No reaction, no reply. He hadn't opened his eyes, mightn't even have heard. Linscheidt repeated the question in the same tone, and the trooper on Monsieur Henri's left punched him behind the ear, knocking him sideways in the chair. Linscheidt tight-faced, looking away – exchanging glances with Klebermann, she noticed: the *Oberleutnant*'s vicious stare was directed at *him*, then. She'd never been exactly fond of any Boches, but there were two distinct varieties in here, she realized. Monsieur Henri's eyes had opened: he was straightening himself slightly, or trying to. Wincing at the effort: they obviously *had* been knocking him about. Stammering weakly, 'There have been no visitors. Please.' Licking his thin lips; there were tear-streaks on his face. Tears welling in his eyes again as he added – lifting a limp hand as if requesting permission to speak in class – 'Madame Briard only tells you what she hopes will make things bad for me.'

Linscheidt put that into German, and Kroll growled something – angry, threatening – which was then interpreted as 'The *Sturmbannführer* says you should remember that the penalty for answering his questions with lies is death!' And in reply to *that*, she saw, another movement of that hand: a *dismissive* gesture. She thought, *Incredible* . . . Then reassessing: it might have been less dismissive than *submissive* – recognition of there being no answer or way out, that his helplessness was absolute. She caught her breath then – startled by a bark of German addressed, it seemed, to *her* – and which Linscheidt then took up in his capacity of interpreter: 'Mam'selle Quérier: the *Sturmbannführer* asks, are *you* aware of persons having visited Monsieur Marchéval during the night?'

She shook her head – mystified . . . 'I'm not here at night, M'sieur. Two hours a day only – and this is my *first* day, as you know.' Gabbling, as Justine would: 'I've been here longer than two hours now, but that's only because I don't know – understand – and I thought Monsieur Marchéval when he came might want me to—'

Tailing off . . . With the thought – sudden flash of hope – *They're looking for evidence of someone having been here, not guessing anyone might be here now. Why should they – why would* anyone *have been so crazy as to hang around?*

Kroll was braying again to Linscheidt, though; who translated, 'You would have noticed in the course of your work whether bedrooms have been used, for instance.'

'No, M'sieur – not bedrooms. Only the kitchen and in here a little.' Nodding towards the *petit salon*: 'And in there, I was *about* to—'

'Raschler.' The *Oberleutnant* jerked to attention: Kroll told him – with the accompanying gesture his meaning was obvious – 'Search the whole place.' Maybe having realized his mistake or slowness in about the same moment she'd begun to *hope*. Monsieur Henri's eyes, she saw, were on her – pleading, the way a dog's eyes plead. But so much for hopes . . . Kroll had shouted at Raschler to hurry: now he was leading Linscheidt into the *petit salon*. He was quite a short man – strongly built, athletic-looking, walked with a springy strut – but Linscheidt towered over him, following him through that doorway. Monsieur Henri's gaze *still* on her. She remembered again his anguished appeal, *There has to be some way, some answer* . . . If there was, she wished to God *she* could see it. Her notion of pinning the guilt on Legrand obviously hadn't got him anywhere.

The *Oberleutnant* having checked the kitchen, pantry and

cloakroom came more or less at the double across the hall to the stairs, jerking his head at one of the troopers to go with him. Rosie bracing herself for disaster now: with only Justine's ignorance and simplicity, total lack of complicity or guile to cling to – and no faith whatsoever in André keeping his mouth shut. Monsieur Henri still watching her – at least, watching this way – through tears and spasms of trembling. She guessed that his endurance this far – the fact he wasn't on his knees begging for mercy, or whatever – would be rooted in desperation to protect his son. His eyes and Rosie's – and others' – shifting to Kroll and Linscheidt emerging from the *petit salon* – having discussed God only knew what, but Linscheidt certainly wasn't looking any happier for it; he'd beckoned to Klebermann, was sending him to the telephone. While upstairs, doors were being wrenched open and slammed shut: now a shouted order from the *Oberleutnant* and a series of crashes: kicking a door open – she knew *which* door. Anyway kicking *at* it; it was a well-built house and the woodwork wasn't flimsy. Meanwhile from behind her Klebermann was having to shout into the telephone: she heard, '*Oui – veux parler avec Captaine Wachtel: Vite, s'il vous plaît!*' From upstairs though, another crash – of a different kind, those two together she guessed putting their shoulders to it. Klebermann was shouting in German now, presumably with Wachtel on the line. Most others were looking upward – as if it were their eyes they used for listening – and at the next heavy thump she heard the door give – splintering, cracking timber, door smashing back and a shout of Germanic triumph. Kroll pushed past Linscheidt, dashed up the stairs: the other SS trooper went up close behind him and the sergeant moved to stand beside Monsieur Henri – whom Linscheidt was asking from that straight-backed but slightly forward-leaning stance of his, in a lower, confidential tone, 'You have known all the time there *was* some person up there?'

Wide, wet eyes staring up – wandering towards Rosie then back to Linscheidt: a deep breath, and a nod.

'My son.'

'Your – *son?*'

Klebermann – back from the telephone – intervening: 'His son *and* daughter were arrested – some months ago. We had the report from Geheime Staatspolizei in Paris – remember, Herr Major? It was by way of—'

'I remember what it was by way of.' Expression of distaste on Linscheidt's gaunt features. Distaste for the Marchéval family, Rosie wondered, or for Gestapo methods of ensuring collaboration? There'd been shouting up there, and now a racket of boots clattering on the stairs. Linscheidt inclining closer to Monsieur Henri: 'You lied to the *Sturmbannführer* – despite his warning. Couldn't you have guessed he'd have the place searched?' *Le patron* mouthing – gasping, almost retching – as if he was trying very hard to speak and couldn't. Linscheidt glanced towards the stairs and then at Rosie: 'Glass of water!' Back to the old man then: 'For God's sake, save your life, from here on answer *truthfully!*' Hearing this as she moved away, hurrying to the kitchen: remembering Colette telling her there was a degree of *rapport* between those two. *Because* of the Gestapo blackmail? Filling a tumbler from the tap, she heard the SS party coming off the stairs – with André, obviously. She *dreaded* whatever was to follow. Hands shaking, heart racing. Kroll's voice out there high, insistent, a longer, quieter utterance from Linscheidt and then Kroll again, that peremptory tone, and Linscheidt's interpretation: 'You collected the keys from your father and returned them to him later in the night – is that correct?'

'Yes.' André's voice was husky. 'It was my scheme, not his. I persuaded him.'

Plain statement of fact. Maybe he *was* going to answer truthfully. In which case . . . She took the glass of water in with her – although it was unlikely Monsieur Henri would get any now. They'd put André in his striped pyjamas in a lower chair turned away from his father's, she saw – so they couldn't easily see each other, especially as each had an SS thug in close attendance. The others were grouped mainly behind Kroll, except for Linscheidt who was beside him. Kroll screaming at André again – apparently straight at him, although it was again for Linscheidt to interpret: '*Sturmbannführer* Kroll demands the names of those who were with you in the sabotage action against the factory!'

'They were Maquisards. I never met them before, don't know their names.'

More German, then: Linscheidt's translation and Kroll's fury. Which was dangerous – as Linscheidt obviously realized, and she could *see*. Pent-up, barely restrained violence visible in both him and the *Oberleutnant* – Raschler. She had a vision of their unit's defeat in battle, military humiliation, the fury and bloodlust stemming from that, maybe. And/or frustration at being diverted to this backwater: maybe that most of all. Waiting with her glass of water in both hands – she'd had to drink some – behind Linscheidt and Klebermann and their sergeant; she could see Monsieur Henri between Klebermann and the sergeant, but not André. Linscheidt interpreting again: 'The *Sturmbannführer* says there must have been participation by individuals in the village. You were caught in the blast of an explosion, it's plain enough that you could not have made your way here without assistance. In any case we have information that at about one o'clock this morning voices were heard outside there. You would be wise to answer truthfully this time: who brought you here?'

'Nobody. I was the last out of the factory and it was up to me to return the keys. I think I was unconscious – for a few minutes. I'd suffered a blow to the back of my head – somehow – but when I came round I was able to – get here.'

There was a moment's silence: Rosie edging sideways, to get a sight of him, but she couldn't: not only for people in the way, but furniture restricting movement. Kroll meanwhile demanding an immediate interpretation, but Linscheidt had been putting some further question and was only getting André's answer now: 'Having spent most of my life here I was able to find my way quite easily in the dark.'

Linscheidt interpreted the previous answer and that one. Shifting feet meanwhile, mutters, Monsieur Henri's short, hard breathing. Kroll, scowling as he listened to the flow of quiet German, was moving forward – hands clasped behind his back, eyes on Linscheidt. He'd stopped now between the prisoners – the troopers stepping back out of his way – and Rosie saw his right hand move to the pistol holstered on his belt.

A Walther 9-millimetre parabellum. Talking again – Linscheidt had finished – he was using it as a pointer, indicating father and son alternately. Hands together swiftly then, in a practised movement racking a round of 9-millimetre into the chamber. Linscheidt meanwhile telling them, 'The *Sturmbannführer* desires to remind you, monsieur –' Monsieur Henri – 'and to advise *you* –' André – 'that the penalty for lying to him is death.'

Waiting then, with his eyes on Kroll, who put a short question in German to Monsieur Henri. Linscheidt's gaze shifted: 'Please answer truthfully. Your son was brought here at about one o'clock – by whom?'

Monsieur Henri was gazing past Klebermann at Rosie. The quick and truthful answer of course: if he'd only lifted one hand, pointed. But then he would have been declaring his son a liar – which would have meant *his* death. She'd put the glass of water down on the edge of a table near her. Holding her breath, almost: guessing that he'd support André's earlier statement, therefore would *not* answer truthfully. Please God . . . Hers and all other eyes

were on Kroll and on Monsieur Henri, whose answer he
was awaiting with the pistol at arm's length now – left eye
closed and the pistol absolutely steady.

'Well?'

Monsieur Henri's lips moved: he croaked, 'He came
alone. As far as I *know*, that is, he—'

Kroll fired, at a range of about one metre. Rosie with
both hands over her eyes, choking back a scream: *le patron*
seemingly half rising from the chair, the bullet stamping
a scarlet flower between his eyes, smashing through the
thin bridge of his nose: blood in a spray, red mist. He'd
fallen back, was sliding downward; there was mess and
shattered mahogany where the bullet had exited through
the back of his skull. Justine, she thought, *would* faint: she
was on her knees, forearms on the cane seat of a chair
which earlier had been kicked aside to make way for
André's when they'd dragged it forward; in an attitude of
prayer – unintentionally and only for seconds, before a hand
clamped on to her arm and jerked her up: the *Oberleutnant* –
in close-up, bawling some explanation to Kroll.

Who'd given him the go-ahead. Gesturing to the SS
soldiers meanwhile – ordering the removal of Monsieur
Henri's body, which was in a heap on the floor now.
Raschler jerking her arm, demanding, 'You work here –
domestique?'

She'd nodded – vaguely. Justine in shock: seeing him
through tears. André was in her field of view now – would
have been if she'd looked that way – through several others
having shifted. The *Oberleutnant* shouted into her face in
guttural, laboured French, 'In the room where he was is
food and water. *You* carry up – uh?'

Blinking at him, shaking her head: 'No food in this house.
I looked when I arrived this morning. It's why I was waiting
– *le patron* when he returned might have required—'

'There *is* food, up there! Eggs, and—'

André said, 'My father cooked the eggs and I took them up.'

'*Silence!*'

Because the prisoner hadn't been invited to make any contribution. But *had* volunteered it, chosen to back her up. From what, she wondered – blind instinct? He had nothing to win now, not a hope in hell: this wasn't speculation, he couldn't surely have any doubt of it. She could breathe again now – for the moment anyway – Kroll had barked something at the *Oberleutnant* – with a silencing gesture to *him*, and something like 'You're wasting time!', and Raschler had let go of her. Justine sagging, using the back of this small chair for support: looking round as if wondering where she was, and catching her first sight of André's mutilated face: hand to her mouth, gasping – and still confronting that reality, that it would be *his* turn now. Which half an hour ago – or fifteen minutes, whatever – he hadn't been able to face up to as the virtual certainty which even then it had been. Rosie glancing round, seeing that the water-glass was in her reach, on that table. She had it: was edging round the sergeant – there was room to, and most attention was on Kroll and Linscheidt and the removal of *le patron*'s body; there'd been a general shifting of positions after the killing. Justine slithering to her knees beside André's chair, murmuring '*Ah, mon pauvre!*' A *stricken* Justine, with in the same hand as the water she was offering him, her handkerchief. He'd got that, curled fingers round it, but not the glass which dropped and smashed as the sergeant grabbed her, pulling her away from the prisoner and lifting his hand to hit her, forestall incipient hysterics, her weepy protest of 'That poor man's *face!*' Linscheidt's intervention saved her from the slap – might have saved her life even – Linscheidt pointing towards the kitchen, shouting 'Sergeant, get her *out!*'

*   *   *

Might have saved her life, if otherwise it had been left to Kroll to deal with her. But her memory of the ensuing period in the kitchen was a blur. She might have passed out – had been on the floor with her back against a table-leg when Klebermann had come through and she'd emerged from never-never land to hear him telling her that the hall floor and that chair would need washing down, but that she'd have to come back to do it later or tomorrow, because everyone was required to assemble now in the market square and there was room for her in a truck with the Briards – it was ready to leave now.

Staring at him, while it sank in. Then: 'But I have my bicycle here . . .'

'Collect it tomorrow when you come to clean up. *Move*, now!'

'Madame Briard can clean up.' On her feet, but groggy, and heart still pounding. *Not* so damn fit . . . Justine, anyway, however slow or simple, would know well she had no job here now. And more immediately to the point – this market square business: a *ratissage*, punishment of the whole village?

André had said – his last words to her – *I still don't want it.* But he'd taken the cyanide capsule. Whereas if he'd rejected it – which he could have done, more or less publicly and with no worsening of his own situation: well, Christ . . . But effectively, by taking it he'd backed her up for the second time – which she'd had no logical reason to expect. Barely knowing how she'd managed it in any case. Without prior thought – only an instinct that with his father out of it, all the weight on him now . . .

'Mam'selle!'

'Oui. Oui.' Inclination of the head to Klebermann as she let go of the kitchen table: 'Pardon . . .'

The hallway was deserted, both connecting and front doors standing open. In the yard – she'd glanced round half expecting to see Monsieur Henri's corpse dumped somewhere out there – were two trucks with their engines running, one with Klebermann's sergeant behind the wheel and the other with its driver just embarking: another Boche pushed her up and slammed up the tail-gate. It was the first time she'd embarked in such a vehicle since departure from Fresnes prison for the Gare d'Est and Ravensbrück. The Briards were on the bench-seat on the left, and there was room for her at this end of it – which was preferable, she thought, to facing them. The man was a nonentity but his wife did resemble a toad – *and* had given evidence against Monsieur Henri this morning.

Would be giving it against André, now?

The front passenger door had slammed, and the truck rolled forward: passing Klebermann's, which then followed. Other vehicles were standing at the front of the house and in that parking area. Neither she nor the Briards spoke. She wondered how they'd fare when the Boches pulled out. Pull out too, maybe: she guessed they'd have to. Although with about five exceptions – seven if you included the Craillots' daughters – the whole village were collaborators at least technically. They'd swear they hadn't been, hadn't known what they'd been manufacturing, et cetera – and probably *would* take it out on the Briards – who'd betrayed their beloved *patron* and his son – who'd been an active *résistant*, planned and led this attack by Maquisards . . .

'Mam'selle?'

Madame Briard. The truck had slowed at the gates, was turning out on to the road and picking up speed again. Rosie was watching out of the back to see Klebermann following, and didn't look round.

'Well?'

'The things people say about us are not true, I'd have you know.'

'For your sake I hope you can prove it.'

'Prove? Why should *we*—'

'I know nothing about you, and I don't want to.'

She'd fiddled her blouse out to hang outside her skirt; had now located the capsule in its hem and begun working it round to the front where she'd be able to get at it if she had to. If, and when. The same problem, though, which she'd remembered after André had refused her offer: basically a matter of judgement and timing, but you might say also of nerve – that as long as there was any hope at all, you wouldn't use it, but if you left it too late you mightn't be in a position to. How it had been in Rouen in fact, a year ago . . . The truck was braking, pulling in to stop with two wheels on the pavement halfway along the front of the market square. She took in the set-up pretty well at a glance: a crowd which must have comprised just about the whole village, Marchéval work-force and their families, had been herded in along the back of the square, beyond the covered market area – which was slightly raised – pavement-level. There were Boche soldiers here and there, in groups of two or three, and at each end, to the right and left of the roofed centre, SS troops with Spandau machine guns on open-topped personnel-carriers. Klebermann's truck was coming up to stop behind this one, and there were others, bigger vehicles, parked off the road on the opposite side, what had been the frontage of the Hôtel Poste but was now an area of blackened devastation, some of it still smoking – that stench like burning rubbish which she'd been aware of during the night. She was waiting to get down into the road as soon as the tail-gate was dropped – being disinclined to arrive apparently in company with the Briards. Most of the soldiers around the covered area and keeping the crowd back were carrying Schmeissers: and that was Wachtel, Linscheidt's engineer – moon-faced, the early sun glinting on his spectacles. She'd seen him only once before, on her first visit to the manor with Colette –

who with Jacques would be somewhere in that crowd . . .
Tail-gate banging down: she was down too, her view of
it all much more limited, and the soldier telling her to
go *that* way – around the covered area to the left, not
through it. She saw Klebermann striding over towards
Wachtel: his sergeant was backing that truck away. She
wondered whether if she made a break for it they'd shoot:
in fact it would be fatal anyway, only draw attention to
oneself: the grim truth was that walking obediently into
this, wooden-soled shoes clattering on the cobbles, one
had no more option than a prisoner in an extermination
camp sent to join others in the gas chamber. Which the SS,
who ran and staffed such camps, would doubtless regard
as right and proper.

She told herself – seeing Klebermann exchanging salutes
with Wachtel a dozen metres to her right as she passed
round that end of the covered area – *Soon be running like
bloody rabbits . . .*

But here and now – what?

Maybe *they* were wondering. Maybe only *Sturmbannführer*
bloody Kroll—

There was a rope – no, a cord, about the thickness of a
washing-line and with a noose in it – dangling from one of
the roof-supporting timbers. Below it, a market-stall table,
and a bench. Klebermann staring as if he too had just seen it:
Wachtel shrugging, explaining. Out of her sight now as she
passed: wondering whether André might have been left on
his own or unobserved for long enough to fiddle the capsule
out of the slot in that handerchief. His alternative would be
to bite on the handkerchief itself – *if* they'd let him keep it
anyway . . .

'Justine!'

Colette, and Jacques: they'd seen her coming, were edging through the crowd towards her. Rosie feeling a surge of
relief in the reunion, her arms out to embrace them, both of

them at once. Colette whispering as she clutched her, 'Are you all right? Is it true *le patron*'s been killed?'

'Shot – by a sod of a *Sturmbannführer* name of Kroll. I *saw* it. How long have you been here?'

Her question and Colette's 'What about André?' had overlapped: Jacques told her, 'Hours. Soon after you went off, they routed us all out.' Nodding towards the dangling cord: 'We'd guessed that was for Monsieur Henri, but – for André now.' Jacques unshaven, hard-eyed, adding, 'It's not set up for a hanging. Not enough drop to break a man's neck. That's strangulation – torture.' Rosie answering Colette then – others listening, pressing close all round – 'They found him in a bedroom at the manor. Kroll was questioning them both – then shot Monsieur Henri – for lying to him, he said—'

'What was M'sieu André doing there anyway?'

A stooped, hollow-chested, heavily moustached individual: Jacques reminded her, 'Guy Fortrun – you met, I'm sure.'

She remembered – when she'd gone into the bar to tell him he was wanted on the telephone, some request for charcoal. A day ago – a *month*? She told him, 'It seems André led the Maquisards last night – and they got in using his father's keys.'

A whistle shrilled. German-French shouts for silence: '*Attention!*' Kroll was in the centre there, with Raschler – and now Linscheidt, head and shoulders taller. Also the two SS men whom she'd last seen preparing to drag Monsieur Henri's body out. And André: they had him between them, lifting him on to the bench and from there forcing him up on the table. A murmur – collective growl – running through the crowd: reaction, she supposed, not only to what was happening now but also to the fact this *was* André Marchéval, *le patron*'s son – and getting their first sight of his burnt face. Fortrun swearing, in a low, repetitious rumble: Colette with a hand pressed to her mouth, eyes brimming. Others weeping too. André had his hands behind his back, Rosie saw suddenly: from the way he stood and those two had handled him it was obvious that they were tied or handcuffed. So if either the handkerchief or the capsule on its own were in the pyjama pocket – on the left breast of the jacket . . .

Maybe he'd got rid of it. As he'd said, *wouldn't* ever use it.

Better than being strangled on that cord, André . . .

Might have it in his mouth – only have to bite on it. Please God . . . Her concern by this stage was as much for André personally as it was to save herself and the Craillots from the consequences of his breaking down. For André, one might say, not 'Hector'. They had the noose over his head and were working it down – he'd tried to twist away – his mouth open, a cry of pain as it scraped down over his face, and the crowd reacting with a growl of anger – and soldiers in turn reacting to *that* – Schmeissers and Spandaus levelled, and the SS menacing on those vehicles. The noose was down round André's neck, one of the guards tightening it. André still open-mouthed – panting, gulping air.

Probably did not have the capsule in his mouth, she thought. An echo in her head again: *truth is I'd never use it*. He'd been telling the truth then: less 'telling' in fact than rather shame-facedly *admitting* it.

Linscheidt's voice now, as surrounding noise fell away. He was using a megaphone, calling for silence.

'I speak on behalf of *Sturmbannführer* Kroll, who has the duty of investigating sabotage action which took place last night and in which the prisoner André Marchéval took part.'

Silence. They'd want to hear this anyway. Distantly, the rattle of a train. Linscheidt was embarking on a résumé of the night's events as background to this – performance.

One, the provision of keys by Henri Marchéval. Two, his son injured by premature triggering of an explosive device, but managing to get from the factory to the manor – primarily to return the keys, although on account of his injuries he'd been obliged to remain there, a logical deduction being that if he had not had help from others, he couldn't have got there in the first place: and this had been borne out by a witness statement to the effect that when he'd reached the manor – at about 0100 – there *had* been others with him.

'He'll pay for his own criminal actions – as his father has already paid for his. But *Sturmbannführer* Kroll has the duty also of identifying those who were with him. So – any of you who can identify such persons – step forward, *now!*'

Silence, again: broken by some German comment – Kroll to Linscheidt, she thought. The SS guards had been adjusting the cord, taking up the slack and securing it so that it was vertical, although André's head was tilted slightly sideways and downwards by his own effort to keep his face clear of it. She could see what Jacques had meant: they could increase the tension or lessen it, have him up on his toes or lift him right up, actually to hang. It *must* have been rigged up for Monsieur Henri, she supposed. Then Kroll had had the surprise gift of André, hadn't then needed the old man, had settled for using him as an example to his son. Something like that: combined perhaps with sadism pure and simple . . . The guards were standing back now. From the crowd, nothing more than murmurs, whispers – and a baby crying. She wondered where the Briards had hidden themselves, but didn't want to risk drawing attention to herself even by as much as turning her head. Conscious that she was still a stranger here and might well be seen by some as a handy scapegoat: if for instance Madame Briard chose to elaborate, add that among the voices she'd heard had been a woman's – which she *might*, if she thought of it . . .

Kroll had been talking to Linscheidt, and now the megaphone came up again.

'*Attention!* The prisoner – André Marchéval – knows he can make it easier for himself by naming the persons concerned. I am instructed to inform you that any of *you* who may be able to name them can do him the same favour – he could ask to die by a bullet instead of – in great discomfort. And *you* could then go home.'

Kroll speaking again. Behind him were Wachtel and *Oberleutnant* Raschler. Linscheidt, she saw suddenly, seemed to be arguing with Kroll: maybe questioning whatever he'd just said. And the others – Klebermann there too now – watching and listening with tense expressions. Kroll's voice high-pitched again, insistent on – whatever . . . Linscheidt staring at him until he'd finished: then still hesitant, but turning back this way.

Hesitating *again*, then, with the megaphone half up and his one eye blinking steadily – as if driven by his doubts. Glancing round at Kroll again: finally shrugging, turning back. He cleared his throat.

'In the event of guilty persons not being identified either by the prisoner or by others, *Sturmbannführer* Kroll warns that hostages may be taken from amongst you and – summarily executed. Now – you have one minute—'

André kicked the table away from under him. Understanding his move in retrospect – the only way, since the moment itself had been virtually explosive, instantaneous, totally unexpected – he'd folded suddenly at the knees, dropping his full weight on to the cord so that it jerked bar-taut and wrenched his head back, while in the same convulsive movement he kicked out with his legs – sending the thing crashing over. A roar from the crowd . . . The thin cord had torn the skin of his neck – she saw blood running – and the body dancing, threshing around on the jerking cord, legs still kicking wildly a few feet above the

cobbles. The crowd's reaction – shock, women's screams –
was cut off by a blare of fire from a Schmeisser: which was
in Raschler's hands, the *Oberleutnant* firing over the people's
heads. Some were on their knees: mothers crouching with
hands over their children's eyes. The body already moving
less though – twitching more than jerking, and turning on
the cord, André bringing his tied wrists into Rosie's view as
if he might have been *showing* them to her. *See, no hands?*

But Linscheidt was prominent suddenly – had his back
to the still slowly turning body, long arms spread horizontally to bar the approach of the SS guards. Who'd have
taken André's weight off the cord, no doubt – maybe so
ordered by Kroll, the programme being slow and perhaps
intermittent strangulation, not the quicker death André had
chosen. Kroll was face to face with Linscheidt now – he had
that Walther out of its holster, brandishing it. Linscheidt
weaponless, fists on his hips – the two guards had backed
off – he was talking down at the smaller man and pushing
his authority even further by gesturing to the *Oberleutnant*
to return that Schmeisser to the trooper from whom he'd
borrowed it. She'd *thought* that was what he'd done, but
people who'd had a clearer view from other angles said later
that he – Linscheidt – had actually grabbed it, presumably
having had reason to feel threatened by it – which was close
enough to the truth but not definitively so, according to
Gaspard Legrand, who it transpired spoke and understood
German and had been able to hear as well as see it all. He
told Jacques later that it had been Kroll screaming an order
to the SS men in respect of André that had sparked it off,
then *Oberleutnant* Raschler's threatening behaviour with the
machine pistol: Linscheidt hadn't 'grabbed' it, only calmly
and authoritatively put his hand on the stubby barrel and
depressed it: rather like telling a child not to point guns.
But Linscheidt hadn't been prepared to stomach either the
prisoner being sadistically kept alive or Kroll's plan for

others to be taken and shot: he'd told Kroll that in his view the investigation and punishment had been completed satisfactorily and that he'd not stand for any further killing. Both Marchévals had clearly been involved and had been dealt with in accordance with the *Sturmbannführer's* brief, but no evidence had emerged of other villagers having taken part; if Madame Briard – who anyway was known to be a liar and to have borne a grudge against Henri Marchéval – if she *had* heard voices in the stable-yard, they could well have been those of Maquisards, who'd still have had half an hour in which to get away before the moon rose. Therefore, further punitive action as proposed would amount to murder – to which he, Linscheidt, would bear witness if necessary. And finally, when Kroll had insisted furiously that such decisions were for him alone to make et cetera, Linscheidt had challenged him with 'In that case you'd better be prepared also to shoot me and my officers.'

Jacques queried, 'But that SS thing backing down – did he think up some way of saving face?'

Legrand nodded. 'That it suited him very well not to be delayed here. If Major Linscheidt was so easily satisfied . . .'

They were sitting, by this time – all of them, several hundred people – and had been for the past hour. André's corpse still dangled – no 'niceties' were being observed as yet – but it was understood, Sergeant Hannant had told Legrand, that once all the SS had pulled out, the people were to be dispersed back to their homes. Holding them here for the time being was for their own safety, on Linscheidt's orders.

Chapter 19

She'd coded her message to Baker Street and was waiting for midnight to send it off – from her bedroom in the *auberge*, Jacques having agreed that there was very little danger in it now. A dangerous assumption maybe, but there were certainly no detector-vans around and it was a happy thought that the technicians in the *Reichssicherheitshauptamt*'s radio-monitoring centre in Paris would very likely be getting ready to draw stumps by now. As to danger, she'd tentatively suggested a *gazo* lift into the woods in the afternoon or early evening to get this signal out, but Jacques had turned her down, seeing a possibility of anti-Maquis patrols from Sens for instance, following the Maquis action here, maybe even SS remnants still in the deep field. For the same reasons he'd decided to wait a day before trying to contact Guichard or Guichard's people: he was impatient to, although another factor was that with any luck he'd have more to tell them tomorrow, the crucial issue being that Linscheidt and company might have pulled out by then. Sergeant Hannant had confided that it was on the cards.

Getting towards the magic hour. Transceiver ready – plugged in, night-time crystal fitted, aerial wire looping from the window. She'd set Yvette's alarm-clock, in case she dropped off, to wake in panic in the dawn. Wouldn't take much doing – snoozing off – after the strains and stresses of the day and very little sleep last night. Eyelids tending to close: and thought processes muzzy. The enciphering was all done and checked anyway – she'd seen to that as soon as she'd got up here, while she still could think straight, the plain-language draft reading *Destruction of all V2 casings and associated machinery at Marchévals carried out successfully night Wednesday August ninth. Operation was planned and led by former SOE agent 'Hector'. 'Hector' hanged and his father shot by SS in reprisal today Thursday. SS unit has since withdrawn eastward and original German garrison unit is expected to depart tomorrow Friday, after which Maquis under Tamerlan plan to occupy St Valéry with headquarters in the manor. Tamerlan's intention being to interdict use by enemy of the Sens–Troyes road and railway. Request pick-up for myself from Parnassus field soonest, confirming either by signal or message personnel previously agreed. Will listen out from noon to 1300 Friday in hope of early confirmation.*

In other words, *Get cracking, Marilyn dear . . .*

They'd cut André down eventually, and by special dispensation from Linscheidt his body was in the custody of Doctor Simonot, Sergeant Hannant and the *curé* – to whom Rosie had been introduced by Colette in the market square this morning. There was to be a funeral Mass for the pair of them, father and son together, within the next few days, subject to the departure before that of the Boches. One could envisage the graveyard black with people – every man, woman and child from the village and surrounding neighbourhood, and doubtless Maquis from the forests – honouring 'Hector', whom she'd come here prepared to kill and whom hundreds had seen die heroically.

Instead of talking – shopping her and the Craillots. Which admittedly wouldn't have saved his life: but for the quick way out, that bullet in the head. You could ask yourself for evermore what he'd been proving to whom – to the village, SOE, even to *her*.

She'd tell them all she knew, in England, and if asked

for her own view would advise that 'F' Section SOE should keep its own counsel, maybe destroy the Marchéval file. Nobody'd be brought back to life by keeping it; and here in France nothing would prevent André Marchéval becoming a Hero of the Resistance. She'd attend the funeral Mass herself if it took place before the Hudson came for her.

Would Edna, Daphne, Maureen object? Or Lise, or Noally?

If so, apologies. And love, and deep, *deep* regret. But there'd be no point in trying to swim against that tide.

Red-headed Daphne's brittle laugh: 'You mean fart against that wind?'

'But you see –' explaining herself to them, as the train rushed on – as in her memory and imagination it always would – never arriving, only for ever rocking, drumming east – explaining, 'You see, what *we* know we'd have to prove – what that crowd know is what they *saw*!'

She didn't know if they'd heard. Anyway was slipping into dream, the train's racket fading and the women's images blurring, seeing instead – as she *would* soon, maybe even at Tempsford if Marilyn brought him with her – well, crikey, a nod as good as a wink – *there*! Large as life and bursting with it, bellowing and waving at her across the airfield in the day's first light, and herself running – *racing* – howling *hello*, my darling, *hello*! No more goodbyes, Ben darling—

Alarm-bell . . .

Bloody thing. Cursing, reaching to shut it off, reaching then for the Mark III's headset and settling the 'phones over her ears. Checking routinely – switches to 'on' and to 'send' – and the message coded into its five-letter groups propped in the raised lid of the carrying-case. All set: a glance at the ammeter as her fingers found their own way to the Morse key. But pausing there – hovering just clear of its plastic knob as a new thought hit her: *Last piano solo ever?*